PRAISE FOR THE BRIDGE KINGDOM SERIES

"Heart-pounding romance and intense action wrapped in a spell-binding world. I was hooked from the first page."
—Elise Kova, *USA Today* bestselling author of
A Deal with the Elf King on *The Bridge Kingdom*

"Exquisite, phenomenal, and sexy, *The Bridge Kingdom* is the epitome of fantasy romance perfection. I adored Jensen's world and characters. Aren and Lara were magnificent individually and together, a couple you'll root for from beginning to end."
—Olivia Wildenstein, *USA Today* bestselling author of
House of Beating Wings

"An epic, action-packed tale of love, revenge, and betrayal."
—Jennifer Estep, *New York Times* bestselling author of
Kill the Queen on *The Traitor Queen*

"The next installment in the Bridge Kingdom series is not to be missed. Do not walk to pick up this book. Run."
—Jennifer L. Armentrout, #1 *New York Times* bestselling author of
From Blood and Ash on *The Inadequate Heir*

BY DANIELLE L. JENSEN

THE MALEDICTION TRILOGY

Stolen Songbird
Hidden Huntress
Warrior Witch
The Broken Ones (Prequel)

THE DARK SHORES SERIES

Dark Shores
Dark Skies
Gilded Serpent
Tarnished Empire (Prequel)

THE BRIDGE KINGDOM SERIES

The Bridge Kingdom
The Traitor Queen
The Inadequate Heir
The Endless War
The Twisted Throne

SAGA OF THE UNFATED

A Fate Inked in Blood
A Curse Carved in Bone

THE
TWISTED
THRONE

THE
TWISTED
THRONE

DANIELLE L.
JENSEN

NEW YORK

For those who still believe in love found in unexpected places, this story is for you. May these pages offer you a glimpse of adventure and the courage to chase it.

THE
TWISTED
THRONE

1

AHNNA

All her life, Ahnna Kertell had held authority in Ithicana. Princess. Commander. Regent. All positions that she'd used in defense of her homeland.

Today, she gave up all her authority, though her goal remained the same: do whatever it took to protect the people of Ithicana.

Ostensibly, her abdication was necessary to fulfill the terms of the Fifteen-Year Treaty—to become a bride of peace for the crown prince of Harendell. An alliance her mother had signed all those long years ago. A vow that Ahnna had reaffirmed to King Edward of Harendell in order to gain his support in the war against the Maridrinians.

And not once in her life had Ahnna Kertell broken her word.

Sitting on a rocky ledge on the highest point of Northwatch, Ahnna surveyed the island holding the mouth of the northern end of Ithicana's famed bridge, watching the traffic in the market below her.

She'd never much liked this island.

Southwatch, the island she'd lived on and protected for nearly a third of her life, was green and lush, the buildings blending into the landscape much as they did throughout the rest of Ithicana, making the whole of it seem alive and nearly sentient at times.

Northwatch looked like nothing more than a huge block of rock that some giant or god had cast into the sea. Three times the size of Southwatch, it was covered with warehouses and silos and feedlots, the mouth of the bridge contained by an enormous fortress, the perimeter of the island bristling with stone fortifications that held Ithicana's famed shipbreakers. Three large piers jutted into the sea, and with several ships in port, the merchant crews were busy unloading cattle that would be run through the bridge and sold in the Southwatch market.

Even from her lofty perch, the smell of the animals filled Ahnna's nose, their calls of distress over the rough passage across the strait loud as they ran through chutes into large pens. Already, a dozen prospective buyers gathered around to inspect the stock. It would be only a matter of minutes before the jarring racket of a Harendellian-style auction took over the island as they bid for the remaining stock that Aren hadn't purchased to feed the people.

That, more than the landscape, was why Ahnna didn't like Northwatch: because it didn't feel like Ithicana at all.

A boot scraped against rock, and Ahnna instinctively reached for the knife at her waist before relaxing at the sight of her twin brother.

Aren lowered himself onto the rock next to her and dangled his legs off the edge. "You're jumpy."

Ahnna shrugged. "No Ithicanian worth his salt makes that much noise climbing a cliff—I assumed you were a Maridrinian rat we'd neglected to exterminate."

Aren's jaw tightened. Rather than calling her out for the comment, he gestured to the ships below. "The Amaridian vessel was full of fortified wine. The captain invited me to sample his wares, and he was generous with his pours."

"Since when can't you hold your drink?" Her tone was more acidic than she'd intended, and Ahnna winced. She and Aren had been flinging jabs at each other since before they'd learned to speak, but though she loved her brother dearly, her jabs no longer held affection. "I'm sorry."

Silence stretched between them, and then Aren shook his head and sighed. "You don't have to go, Ahnna. The Harendellians are practical—they'll be more than willing to accept beneficial trade terms in lieu of you as a bride. I'll negotiate a deal with Edward. You can be back in command of Southwatch within a fortnight."

God help her, but there was a part of her soul that desperately wanted to take the offer. The part that was terrified to leave. But allowing it to make decisions would make her a coward. "No. Not only did I give my word, but I already gave them concessions in order to gain their assistance with Maridrina."

"It's not breaking your word if the Harendellians agree to a change of terms. All they care about is the perception they're coming out ahead in the transaction, and there are things I can offer that don't cost us money. Besides, it's Mother's word, not yours."

Ahnna's eyes fixed on the last cow being prodded off the ship. The handlers poked it in the haunches with sticks to get it to move while the animal lowed, head swaying back and forth, disoriented. It started down the gangway, and Ahnna's heart lurched as it slipped and fell, sliding down the slick surface. It struck out with its feet, the boards on the sides of the gangway pulling loose.

She rose to her feet despite knowing there was nothing to be done if the cow went into the water. It thrashed about, hind legs sliding over open air, and Ahnna sucked in a breath. But then the cow righted itself. Calling loudly, it trotted down the chute to join the rest of its herd, little knowing that it had escaped one death only to be delivered into the hands of another. "My word matters to me," she said. "When I met with Edward to secure his aid in liberating Northwatch, I recommitted to my intention to wed William as part of the deal. I'm not putting Ithicana at risk for the sake of my feelings."

Given Aren had done just that, twice, she might as well have stuck a knife in his back and twisted.

Instantly regretting her words, Ahnna watched her brother rise to pace back and forth along the ledge, his temper fraying. It always did when they were together, and she knew it was her doing. Knew that she needed to stop punishing him. Except her anger, always simmering in her core, refused to concede.

Aren rounded on her. "This is because of Lara, isn't it? You intend to make me choose between my wife and my sister."

It was about Lara. And it wasn't.

Once the traitor queen, but now the queen of legend. Slayer of Ithicana's enemies, liberator of the people, chosen of the kingdom's guardians, and soon-to-be mother of its heir. Many had forgotten that Lara had caused the death of thousands of Ithicanians.

Ahnna had not.

"I'm not asking you to choose anything," she answered. "I'm going to Harendell. End of discussion, *Your Grace*."

She tried to step past him to reach the path leading down the steep incline to the market below, but Aren blocked her way. "This is madness," he snarled. "Harendell is *not* like Ithicana. They'll force you to give up everything you love, make you wear gowns and corsets, and imprison you in parlors to do needlework all day. You'll go from being the commander of Southwatch to being a Harendellian prince's—"

"Wife?" she interrupted, because if he finished the statement the way he no doubt intended, she'd have to hit him. And because she didn't want him to put voice to everything she'd be giving up. "What I'll be is the future queen of Harendell."

"Which, given it means a life of teatime and embroidery, is the last thing you want." Aren lifted his hands to rub his temples, then met her gaze. "I know you don't want to go, Ahnna. Ithicana is everything to you."

She didn't want to go. Yet neither could she bear to stay. "It's because Ithicana is everything to me that I'm going. Ithicana is weak, Aren. More than that, we're *broke*. Maridrina has nothing to export, and Valcotta is funneling everything it can into Maridrina. The only revenue we have is the tolls paid by Harendell and Amarid, and they are half what they were before the invasion. We need gold, and lots of it, to rebuild what was lost and keep our people fed while we do it." She gestured to the cattle. "How many of those cows did you buy to be butchered and distributed to your people?"

"Fifty head," he muttered.

"And how did you pay for them?" When he didn't answer, she added, "How did you pay for the shipment of grain you bought yesterday? The barrels of nails? The lumber? The wool?"

Silence.

"How much do you owe Harendellian and Amaridian merchants, Aren? How in debt are we to the north? How long can you keep buying on credit until they realize our credit is no good?"

More silence.

"As soon as they realize you can't pay, they'll know just how weak Ithicana is. And the weak are always the greatest targets. It will be pirates first, but how long until one of the northern nations takes a page from Silas's book and goes after the bridge itself? Would you like me to remind you how it goes for Ithicana when we lose the bridge?"

"I don't need you to explain the stakes."

"Don't you?" She glared at him. "Even once we've overcome this hurdle, too many people know their way past our defenses for our shores to ever be fully protected again. I can do more to defend Ithicana as queen of Harendell than I ever could as commander of Southwatch."

Aren's tone was bitter as he said, "You're wrong about that. They'll put a crown on your head, but the only decision you'll ever get to make is who sits next to who at the dinner parties. You'll be *nothing* compared to what you are now."

Ahnna's chest tightened to the point that she couldn't breathe, a thousand retorts forming in her head, but her throat strangled every last one of them. "Even if that's the case, it's the right choice. Harendell's trade is worth more than I am. You're coming out ahead."

"You make it sound like I'm selling you," he snapped.

"I'm selling myself. Do me a favor and put the profits to good use."

Tension simmered between them. Sucking in a mouthful of air, Ahnna gestured to the pair of ships approaching from the north, sunlight glinting off royal-blue paint and shining gilt, the flags snapping in the wind. "My buyers are here. So why don't you sober up, order the pier cleared as it should have been an hour ago, and go greet them like a proper king."

Not responding, Aren twisted on his heel and stormed down the path. Jor and Lia rose from where they'd been waiting and followed, the rest of his honor guard notably absent. Likely with Lara, who needed her back watched far more than Aren did, for Ahnna was not the only Ithicanian who hadn't forgiven the queen.

Dragging in breath after breath of air, Ahnna tried to ignore the sweat dripping down her back as she watched the ships draw nearer. One of them held the man she was supposed to marry.

William, Crown Prince of Harendell.

She made a face, the memory of his portrait filling her mind's eye. He looked like his father, King Edward. Slender, with chestnut hair and green eyes, his features were handsome in a beautiful and yet entirely uninteresting way. Her cousin Taryn had taken one look and said, "I'd bet the only fighting he's ever done is in a courtyard duel with dull rapiers."

Ahnna was inclined to agree; nothing about his fancy clothes and trim build suggested a man dedicated to combat, though there was a chance the artist had taken liberties in the likeness.

Perhaps it wasn't such a bad thing to be wed to a man who didn't make violence a daily part of his life. God knew, she brought enough of that to the table. Reaching up, Ahnna touched the scar that bisected her face, still red despite the salve Nana had given her to help it fade.

Would he find it ugly?

The answer to that was abundantly obvious.

Ahnna shook her head sharply. It didn't matter what he thought of her looks or her of his. This was a political arrangement, and she'd been raised not to expect sentiment within it. *You are a princess,* her mother's voice echoed inside her head. *Your hand will bind the most powerful nation in the north to Ithicana, just as your brother's eventual marriage to a Maridrinian princess will bind the south. This treaty offers Ithicana a chance at peace.*

So far, all the treaty had brought to Ithicana was war, but Harendell was *not* Maridrina.

And *she* was not Lara.

One of the Harendellian ships drew away from the other, heading toward the eastern pier despite there being a vessel still moored. She should go down and prepare to meet it, but Ahnna wasn't ready. Wasn't ready to let go of Ithicana, her friends, and her family just yet, and with the pier still full of wine casks, there was time yet to remain up here.

Where she could breathe.

With practiced hands and steady feet, Ahnna circled the peak of the island, pausing only when the market and port were completely out of sight and all of Ithicana stretched out before her. The bridge snaked its way between islands, the mist shifting around the stone, making it seem alive. Gone was the stink of cow, and instead, the wind smelled of salt and jungle, with a hint of sharpness that spoke of coming rainstorms.

Her home.

Abruptly, Ahnna's skin prickled, some sixth sense telling her danger lurked. Jerking her weapon loose, she whirled.

To find herself face-to-face with one reason she needed to leave Ithicana behind.

Lara stood on the rocks, her long honey-colored hair blowing behind her in the wind. She wore a Maridrinian-style dress over her rounded belly, the diaphanous silk rippling with each gust, her feet encased in delicate sandals. Ahnna hadn't the slightest idea how the other woman had climbed in such attire, but then again, Lara wasn't the type to be restricted by something as inconsequential as clothing. Or even something as consequential as pregnancy. "What do you want?"

A grimace formed on Lara's beautiful face, her blue eyes vibrant against her suntanned skin. "You know he didn't mean what he said. Fear makes him say stupid things."

Once a spy, always a spy, Ahnna thought, but she only said, "I don't need you to make apologies for my *twin,* Your Grace. As it is, our conversations are none of your damned business."

"I'm not apologizing for him. I'm here to tell you that he's wrong." Lara picked her way through the rocks, closing the distance between them. Ahnna forced herself to sheathe her weapon, though her instincts still demanded she remain on guard around this woman. It had always been that way, even before Ahnna had known what Lara was. What she was capable of. Ahnna had passed it off as her own uneasiness and inexperience with outsiders, but she should've trusted herself.

How many people would still be alive if she had? How many people would still be breathing if she'd trusted herself and put a knife in Lara's chest the moment she arrived?

Instead, Ahnna had left her brother alone with the most dangerous woman on two continents, and Ithicana had paid the price tenfold. "What part of what he said was wrong? You don't need me here. And I know you don't want me here, Lara."

Lara huffed out an amused breath, ever and always difficult to provoke. "You're wrong about that."

Ahnna's temper flared. She resented the level of control Lara wielded. Resented how she'd been reduced to a pawn on the queen's game board. "It was your damned idea to use me to gain Harendell's support in the war. Why are you backtracking now?"

The other woman opened her mouth to speak; then her brow furrowed, and she gave the slightest shake of her head. "The people trust you, Ahnna. More than they trust Aren, and far more than they'll ever trust me. It would help us if you remained."

That wasn't what Lara had intended to say—Ahnna was certain of it. Even now, after everything, Lara still hid things like the spy she'd been. Like the Maridrinian she still was. "Go for another swim with the sharks, Your Grace. Perhaps that will bolster the sentiment of the people."

Lara tensed ever so slightly then exhaled. "I'll take that as a *no* to remaining in Ithicana."

"I made a vow to King Edward that I'd travel to Harendell once the war was over. You and Aren may have forgotten that vow, but I have not."

Silence.

"I haven't forgotten."

"Then why are you both trying to make me break my word?" Ahnna demanded. "Why are you both working so hard to keep me from going?"

"You're Aren's sister. He wants you to be happy, and you'll be miserable in Harendell."

Ahnna's hands balled into fists. "How is my happiness worth more than filling Ithicanian children's empty bellies and rebuilding their homes? My happiness isn't the reason Aren is digging in his heels. Tell me the truth or fuck off."

Silence stretched between them, and then Lara sighed. "He's worried that your going to Harendell will make the situation worse because you'll damage our relationship with the crown."

Hurt pooled in Ahnna's stomach, because she hadn't realized her brother had so little faith in her. "I got along just fine when I met Edward to negotiate."

"He's not thinking of Edward." Lara looked away, her eyes on the bridge, though Ahnna didn't think she was seeing it. "The women of Harendell are far from powerless. They might not wield weapons or fight in wars, but they influence everything that happens, every decision that is made. None is more powerful than Queen Alexandra. Or more dangerous."

Ahnna suppressed a shiver at the name of the woman who'd soon be her mother-in-law, remembering how Keris had told her that the queen would *toast your name while poisoning your cup.* "You picked up all *that* during your months of drowning yourself in wine in the company of sailors in the seediest port taverns of Harendell? I didn't realize the nobility frequented such establishments."

Spies had reported that was how Lara had spent the weeks after the invasion. Drinking while Ithicana lost battle after battle to the Maridrinians, Ahnna's people forced to flee their homes for Eranahl or hide in the isolated outer islands. *Drinking* and God knew what else while Ithicanians were dying, as Ahnna had spent every waking minute either fighting to keep people alive or digging graves when she failed. It was only after Aren had been captured that Lara had roused herself to action. Why hadn't she assassinated her father immediately? Why hadn't she done something to try to stop the Maridrinians? To stop the war? Why had Aren been the only one who'd mattered?

"Drunk men talk, and I've been trained to listen, even when I'm deep in my own cups. It's the queen of Harendell the people fear crossing, not the king."

Ahnna shrugged. "I've no intention of stabbing them in the back, so I'm not particularly concerned."

The queen of Ithicana's jaw tightened, the first real crack Ahnna had seen in her composure, and though her bravado was feigned, Ahnna relished having landed a blow.

Lara's voice was clipped as she said, "It's that lack of concern that has Aren worried."

"I was trained for this," Ahnna retorted. "But more than that, I understand the stakes. The last thing I'll do is willfully make things worse for the people I've spent my life protecting."

The wind gusted, the only sound to break the silence between them as they stared each other down.

"Here," Lara finally said, holding out one hand, a deeply familiar necklace of gold and gemstones hanging from her fingers. "Take it."

Ahnna's heart skipped, and she curbed the urge to snatch the necklace out of Lara's hand, because it should never have been hers in the first place. "Aren gave it to you."

"And I'm giving it to you."

He'd be furious if she took it, but instead of declining, Ahnna asked, "Why?"

Lara hesitated, cheeks sucking in as though she were biting them while she considered her words. "A reminder of the stakes."

Ahnna stared at the glints of gold and emerald and black diamond, a replica of Ithicana's larger islands. Her father had given it to her mother, who'd almost never taken it off, and Ahnna had a thousand memories of it gleaming around her mother's throat. A dull ache formed in her chest, her feelings about her parents always conflicted. "It's just metal and rocks. Besides, when have you *ever* seen me wear jewelry?"

Lara held her hand over the cliff, the necklace swaying back and forth over empty air. "Then I suppose it doesn't matter what I do with it?"

She opened her fingers, and the necklace dropped.

Gasping, Ahnna lunged, her knees scraping across rock as she snatched the falling necklace from the air and almost toppled over the edge from her momentum.

Her pulse thrummed, for though the necklace was safely clutched in her hand, she still felt the horror of almost losing it. Fury rose in her chest at Lara's carelessness.

Rising to her feet, she started around the peak, needing to get away from the other woman before it came to blows. "You're such a bitch."

Lara followed her. "As are you. In another life, we probably would have been friends."

Ahnna opened her mouth to retort, but then the scene in the harbor caught her attention. She shaded her eyes, her skin prickling. The vessel that had carried the cows had departed, and the naval ship, flying a purple flag to show that royalty was aboard, was approaching to take its place.

Approaching *far* too swiftly, because those who were supposed to be manning the sails were fighting one another on the deck.

"What is going on?" Lara muttered, shading her eyes.

Ahnna had already broken into a run.

Instinct guided her feet as she slid down the rocky trail, her eyes bypassing the Northwatch market for the piers jutting out from the island. The Harendellian vessel was flying toward pier one, no one aboard seeming to notice the waving arms of the port master warning them to slow down. The dockworkers around him were tense, their hands on their weapons.

Ahnna skidded to a stop, squinting at the ship as Lara drew up next to her and demanded, "What will happen if it hits the pier?"

Northwatch's pier was made of bridge stone. The ship would be what suffered.

"Stay here until it's safe!" Ahnna broke into a sprint down the switchbacking path, leaping off ledges where she could, the faint slap of sandals behind her suggesting that the very pregnant queen had ignored her order. Which was no fucking surprise.

Dread filled Ahnna's stomach, flashes of the night she'd lost Southwatch to the Maridrinians filling her vision every time she blinked.

She couldn't let that happen again.

"Sound the alarm!" Ahnna screamed, trying to catch the attention of those manning the nearest watch station. The wind stole the words, sending them flying over the seas. One of the sentinels appeared to be half asleep, the other one picking his fingernails. She was going to have their heads.

A rock whistled past her ear, Lara's aim perfect, for it smashed against the wall next to the nail picker's hand. He whirled, mouth dropping as he caught sight of both his princess and his queen sprinting toward him. "Call the alarm," Ahnna shouted. "The Harendellian prince is in danger!"

The man only gaped at her. Snatching up his signal horn, she sucked in a deep breath and blew a series of notes.

Below, every Ithicanian fell still as they listened to the code. The second the last note faded, they all burst into action, their training taking hold.

"The Harendellian crew has mutinied." Ahnna tossed the sentinel his horn. "Make sure the shipbreakers are manned."

Then she was running again.

Lara was already ahead of her. The skirt of her gown was tucked into the mesh belt above her pregnant belly, revealing muscled legs that moved with shocking speed. Ahnna lengthened her stride, barely managing to catch up to her. "If a Harendellian royal is assassinated on our shores, there will be hell to pay. They'll blame us."

Lara nodded, then reached over her shoulder and withdrew a narrow blade that had been hidden beneath her gown, the metal glistening in the sun. They raced through the market, now close enough to see that the deck of the Harendellian ship was a melee. Harendellian soldiers were fighting the crew of their own ship for control, the decks covered with corpses and blood. Whether the crew had mutinied against the crown or been infiltrated, Ahnna couldn't say, and it didn't much matter given that the soldiers were cutting them down without mercy.

Yet her instincts screamed warning.

What was she missing?

The Harendellians had regained some control, and the sails dropped, the ship slowing.

But it was too little, too late.

The ship slammed against the heavy stone of the pier. Wood crunched, the impact knocking all aboard off their feet, the battle stopped in its tracks.

But only for a heartbeat.

Clambering upright, soldiers and crew threw themselves at each other again, blades and blood glinting in the sun.

What was going on?

Aren stood in the middle of the pier, weapon in hand, as he shouted orders. Behind him sat row after row of wine barrels that the Amaridians had delivered. Slowly, the lid on one of them rose, eyes peering out.

Oh God. This wasn't a mutinied crew. This was an Amaridian attack.

Lara screamed, wild and desperate. "Aren! Behind you!"

Her brother's eyes widened, and he started to turn.

But it was too late.

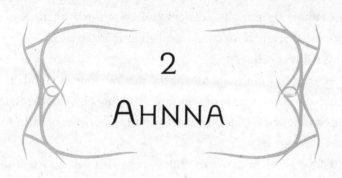

2
AHNNA

THE TOPS OF THE WINE BARRELS LIFTED AS ONE, AND THEN MEN spilled out of them, armed to the teeth.

Amaridian soldiers, but every one of them wore tunics of identical cut and color to what Ithicanians wore.

Aren lifted his weapon, but the Amaridians ignored him. They sprinted toward the Harendellian ship and then leapt onto the deck to join the fray.

To the other Harendellian vessel sailing in fast, it would appear Ithicana was attacking the royal vessel.

"Protect the prince," Ahnna screamed at the Ithicanians in earshot, but it was chaos. Three nations of soldiers fighting in a melee. The Harendellian soldiers were panicking, attacking the Ithicanians trying to help them, Ahnna's people forced to defend themselves.

If she didn't keep the prince alive, it could mean war with Harendell. And that wasn't a war Ithicana could win.

"Stay out of the fight," she shouted at Lara. She threw the necklace at her, then raced toward the ship, eyeing the gap between it and the pier. Gathering herself, Ahnna leapt, flying over the space and rolling across the deck onto her feet.

Everywhere was blood and carnage, Ithicanians and Harendellians and Amaridians dead or dying, but still the battle raged.

"Pull back," Aren shouted, his voice barely audible over the crash of weapons and the screams of the injured. But the Ithicanian soldiers heard their king, withdrawing and dragging the wounded with them.

Ahnna ignored the order.

Snatching up a fallen blade, she flung herself into the battle, cutting through the enemy ranks. "They aren't Ithicanians!" she shouted at a group of Harendellians fighting back-to-back, their uniforms splattered with blood. "They're Amaridians!"

The soldiers gaped at her.

"Amarid is trying to assassinate your prince!" she screamed. "Go to him!"

It took three Ithicanian arrows whistling past her and into the backs of Amaridians before the Harendellians finally sprang into action.

Casting a backward glance, Ahnna saw Lara, Aren, and a dozen others with bows picking off the Amaridian soldiers and mutinied crew members, but the ship had drifted too far away from the pier for them to board.

Swearing, Ahnna raced after the soldiers, leaping over bodies as she searched for any sign of Prince William, praying the portrait she'd seen of him was accurate. She caught sight of a group of Amaridians massed on the rear of the quarterdeck, moving against a tall man in a uniform thick with braids and brass. Sunlight glinted off hair more copper than the portrait, his features more masculine than the artist had depicted, but the uniform left no doubt in Ahnna's mind that this was Prince William.

The man she was supposed to marry.

If both of them lived long enough.

Ahnna cut into the Amaridians, hamstringing men and then dancing out of range as they turned on her, only to lunge back and open their guts. Her focus narrowed, her attention all for the fight, adrenaline fueling her body, leaving only corpses in her wake.

The Amaridians were losing, but she knew they'd never surrender. Knew they'd fight to the last man, because Ithicanians didn't take prisoners.

They took heads and then dumped them on Amarid's beaches.

Which was why when she saw a group of Amaridians on the far side of the deck setting a fuse, the wind carrying the acrid smell of smoke, she knew what they intended.

"Jump!" she screamed at William, but he ignored her, too engaged in the fight. "They're going to blow up the ship!"

"Ahnna, get off!" Lara screamed above the noise.

But she refused to let William die.

Ahnna threw herself through the Amaridians, ducking and striking, nothing mattering but getting to the prince. He lifted his weapon, but she parried his sword hard enough to knock it from his hands.

Then she shoved him overboard.

She prayed that he knew how to swim, then dived in after him, seawater closing over her head. Catching the prince around the waist, she forced him down and down.

Boom!

The impact of the explosion drove the air from her chest, nearly tearing the prince from her grip, but Ahnna held on. He struggled, trying to return to the surface to breathe.

Boom!

A second blast surged through the water, flipping her over, obscuring her vision with a froth of bubbles. The prince fought against her, unable to hold his breath as long as she could, but she knew the surface would be a death trap of burning debris.

And bodies.

Which meant Ithicana's guardians would soon turn the waters red.

Adrenaline giving her strength, Ahnna caught the prince's face and forced him to look at her. She'd expected to find panic in his expression, but instead she found only grim determination. Meeting his gaze, she pointed in the direction of the island, and he nodded once.

Remaining underwater, they swam hard toward the nearly sheer rock of Northwatch. Away from the blood and carnage.

Steady, she ordered herself, keeping her kicks smooth so as not to attract attention.

So as not to appear as prey.

But something caught hold of her ankle, jerking her back.

Bubbles raced past her face as she screamed, slamming her free foot against whatever had hold of her, but the grip was implacable. Pulling a knife from her belt, Ahnna twisted, finding an Amaridian staring up at her.

She kicked him in the face, but he didn't let go, climbing her body in an attempt to reach the surface, pushing her down in his desperation. Slamming her knife into his ribs, Ahnna jerked herself upward, her chest burning like fire.

It was too far.

She wasn't going to make it.

Then hands caught hold of her wrists and yanked upward.

Ahnna's face broke the surface, and she gasped in a mouthful of air only to be splashed in the face by a wave. Coughing and spluttering, she wiped the water from her eyes.

"You all right?" A Harendellian accent filled her ears, the prince treading water in front of her, blood dripping from his temple.

"Yes." The word came out as a croak, and she swallowed to clear her throat. "Don't splash. The sharks will already be lured by your blood."

His jaw tightened, but he didn't panic. Only slowed his motions, mimicking her.

"This attack is Amarid's doing, not Ithicana's," she said. "One of their merchant vessels just delivered those barrels. They're trying to frame us."

"That's not how it looks."

"I know, which is why we need to get on the island so you can signal the other ship not to attack. If they do, Northwatch won't have any choice but to turn the shipbreakers on them. We'll have war on our hands."

Instead of debating her words, he asked, "Where can we climb out?"

Ahnna barely heard the question, her senses warning her. Sucking in a breath, she slipped beneath the water. Sure enough, a dozen feet away, a gray shape circled, familiar streaks on its sides. A large female she'd seen often before. Many of the older sharks were familiar to her, and those in the north were more . . . *reasonable* than those near Southwatch.

Less used to human blood.

The shark headed toward Ahnna. Keeping between it and William, she swam forward, hand outstretched. Just before her fingers brushed the shark's snout, it turned away, though it continued to circle. She surfaced to take a breath and then sank back beneath the surface, moving to keep between the circling animal and William. It moved in again, and though her heart thrummed, Ahnna met it, again pushing the shark away.

Mine, she silently told the female. *Go find something else.*

Seeming to accept Ahnna's supremacy, the female veered away in the direction of the pier.

Surfacing, she managed only a breath before William said, "We've been spotted."

Three figures were swimming hard toward them. "It's the prince," one of them gasped. "Kill him! We have to kill him!"

Amaridians.

"You armed?" William asked.

Her knife blade was stuck in the ribs of the man who'd almost drowned her. "No. You?"

He lifted a knife with a wicked edge. "Fight or flee?"

A wave pushed her against him, and as she turned to look at the Amaridians drawing closer, she could feel his rapid breath against the back of her neck. The surf was pushing everything toward the island, including their attackers. Tearing her eyes from them, Ahnna found the marker on the cliff that no one but an Ithicanian would know the meaning of. They were close to a route of escape.

But not close enough.

"Fight," she said.

His eyes met hers, the color obscured by the light reflecting off the sea. Yet she was struck by his fearless calm despite them being surrounded by death on all sides. The spy reports all said he was a rake and a bacchanal, which might well be true, but their insistence that William was a coward was undeniably false.

"I defer to your expertise," he said. "Tell me what to do."

"Take a deep breath," she answered, watching one of the Amaridians jerk beneath the surface, his companions not noticing he was gone. "And sink deep."

His jaw tightened. "I'm not leaving you to fight alone."

"I'm not alone," she said. "Trust me. Go as deep as you can."

Harendellian men didn't listen to women—that was what all the spies said. That was what Aren said. William only sucked in a deep breath and sank beneath the surface.

Slowly treading water, Ahnna watched the larger Amaridian swim toward her, his eyes murderous as he swung his blade at her head.

Except she was a killer, too.

Diving beneath him, Ahnna rotated and caught hold of his shirt. She clambered onto his back and wrenched her arms up under his sternum, driving the air from his lungs.

Down they sank, the soldier clawing at her, trying to get free, but Ahnna ignored the pain. In her periphery, she saw a surge of crimson bubbles and a flash of gray fins, but she held on even as she prayed it wasn't William the sharks had taken.

The Amaridian fought her, struggling as they sank deeper, the current pushing them ever closer to Northwatch. Yet for all her skill, he was stronger and tore loose from Ahnna's grip. He lifted the hand holding the blade and moved to strike, but then a gray form streaked past, and his arm was . . . *gone.*

Blood clouded the water, but before it obscured her vision, Ahnna saw terror fill the man's eyes. He screamed, bubbles exploding from his mouth as he tried to reach the surface.

But the striped female circled back and shot past Ahnna's shoulder, powerful jaws closing around the man's torso, turning the world red.

It would be a frenzy. Ahnna knew it. Had seen it.

She needed to get William out of the water.

Twisting, Ahnna searched the depths and found him motionless as instructed, watching. At her gesture, he rose to the surface.

"There's an opening to a tunnel about ten feet down," she said with her first breath of air. "Follow it for about another twenty feet, and you'll reach an open chamber. There are stairs leading to the surface."

"Is there any light?"

There was tension in his voice, and Ahnna was tempted to lie. Anything to get him to safety. Except the last thing she needed was him panicking in the unexpected darkness. "No. But the alternative is being eaten. These sharks have been raised on the flesh of men, and there is enough blood in the water that they'll attack anything that moves."

Clouds of smoke from the burning ship drifted past them, and in the distance, a shipbreaker deployed with a loud crack. Then another. "They're firing warning shots at your other ship. We need to hurry."

He gave a tight nod. "I'll follow you."

Ahnna took several rapid breaths, then filled her lungs as full as she could before diving deep.

William did the same, swimming next to her as the sea tugged them back and forth, mercifully calm today, though that could change in an instant.

Ahnna searched the smooth rock of the island for the opening that had been cut generations ago. It had been years since she'd swum this route—Aren had once done it on a dare, and she'd been unwilling to let him go alone—but some things one couldn't forget.

Usually the terrifying things.

Catching sight of a shadow of a deeper shade of black, she grabbed William's sleeve and gestured. He hesitated, then nodded, following her into the cave.

The only darkness she'd ever experienced like this was that inside the bridge.

Except inside the bridge, one could *breathe.*

Terror bit at Ahnna's heels as she pulled herself through the tunnel, the rocks slimy where they weren't sharp, her hands bruising and slicing open as she blindly reached for the next handhold. Logically, she knew the large sharks wouldn't pursue into the tight tunnel, but she kept waiting for teeth to close around her legs, for the sharp pain of her bones being split and her flesh rendered.

They didn't hurt Lara, she reminded herself. *Why would they hurt you?*

Because you failed. Because you didn't protect Ithicana.

Ahnna turned her guilt into strength, clamping her bloodied hands around the rock and climbing. The tunnel bent upward, and she dragged herself along as fast as she could, feeling William's hands bump against her bare feet. *Just get him out,* she told herself. *That's all you need to do.*

But would it be enough? What if the Harendellians believed the attack was Ithicana's doing? What if they'd seen her push William into the water and not understood why? What if the battle had already begun?

Everyone who mattered to her was fighting for their lives on the pier, and she needed William to help her stop it.

The tunnel widened, her hands no longer knocking against rock. Her fear only grew as she lost her perception of up and down in the open space. Breathing out bubbles, she felt them brush against her nose. Then her forehead. She followed them, her head finally breaking the surface. Sucking in a breath, Ahnna braced her hands on the sides of the space and heaved upward.

Only for her skull to smack against something hard.

Hissing in pain, Ahnna closed her fingers over cold metal bars.

No.

There was a surge of motion next to her. William broke the surface, only her grasping his shoulder keeping him from slamming his head against the bars the way she had. He dragged in breath after breath, broad chest pressed against hers in the narrow confines as he asked, "Which way?"

"Back the way we came."

The silence was thick enough to cut, then he said, "Pardon?"

"They've installed bars since last I was here. Likely because we gave up this route to Harendell to use for the retaking of Northwatch from the Maridrinians." Ahnna silently cursed Northwatch's commander, Mara, who had neglected to disseminate the upgrade to the island's defenses.

Or maybe she just didn't bother telling you.

"Back down and then *what?*" There was a hint of anger in his voice, though whether it was at her or the situation, Ahnna didn't know. "There is a battle between my people and yours about to begin, if it hasn't already. You think *anyone* is going to notice us in the water before the sharks eat us?"

There wasn't a chance in hell.

"I've followed your lead because you are Ithicanian," he went on, his tone more aggravated than afraid. "But I'll not follow blindly, so if you've a strategy, tell me what it is. Otherwise, we will do this my way."

His tone annoyed her, but his point was fair.

Taking a deep breath to calm her racing heart, Ahnna considered the options.

They weren't good.

William took hold of the bars and yanked. Over and over, and Ahnna fought the urge to tell him it wasn't going to work and instead kept her mind on the problem.

There were other ways onto Northwatch, though it would require them swimming a fair distance, which was risky given the carnage in the water. And knowing that Mara had barred this tunnel, what were the chances she hadn't done the same to every other route onto the island? The battle would be over and done by the time they made it to shore.

"Well?"

"I'm trying to think of a solution," Ahnna growled. "Perhaps attempt the same rather than making so much noise."

Ignoring her, William shifted in the water, his legs bumping hers as he braced his feet against the sides of the chamber. He grunted with effort, and she felt thick muscles bulge as he heaved against the solid steel.

It was a waste of effort, but Ahnna let him struggle while she thought.

If Mara had wanted the passage totally blocked, she'd have filled it with stone. There had to be a way past these bars.

A way only an Ithicanian would think to use.

Ahnna smiled.

"Would you mind lending your strength?" William snarled, his breath hot against her cheek in the blackness. "Or are you too busy *thinking*?"

"Not every problem is solved with biceps, Your Highness."

As he huffed out an irritated breath, Ahnna reached up and took hold of the bars, finding where they'd been set with mortar. There was no lock, and the steel was thick and strong.

Feeling along the walls of the tunnel, she found a narrow ledge, her fingers brushing against the smooth glass of three bottles Mara had left for any Ithicanian who found themselves in this predicament. Elation filled her. Taking a firm grip on the bottles, she lowered herself, running her thumbs over the markings on the glass to confirm what they contained. "I need you to hold me up. I need both hands to do this."

"To do what?"

"I'm going to blow up the mortar holding the steel in place."

She waited for the cowardice she'd been warned of to rear its head, but William only muttered, "Bloody Ithicanians and your explosives." His hands fumbled at her waist, legs bracing against the rock as he lifted her.

His breath was hot against her breasts through the thin fabric of her shirt, his fingers digging into the muscles of her sides. Yet his arms were steady despite the effort it must have taken to hold her in the awkward position. He was a far cry from the weakling the spy reports had described.

Ahnna reached through the bars, but the angle wasn't good for setting a charge. Given there'd be only one chance at this, she needed to set it up perfectly.

Clutching the bottles against her chest with one hand, Ahnna gripped the bars with her free hand and slung one leg over his shoulder, trying not to think about the fact that his face was now pressed between her legs. Easing around so that she was sitting squarely on his shoulders, she pulled free the wax sealing one of the bottles and set it carefully into position. Unstopping another, she created the longest fuse the space would allow, then set the jar next to the other.

With the last jar in her hand, she hesitated. "We're only going to have maybe ten seconds to get out of range of the explosion. When I give you the word, I need you to drop. We'll push ourselves down as fast as we can to get out of the way of the debris."

"How do you know this won't collapse the whole tunnel?"

She didn't.

But her whole world was at stake above them. She refused to abandon them for fear of her own life. "The explosion won't be that strong. Have a little faith, *Your Highness*. This is what we do. Ready?"

His fingers contracted on her thighs, the sensation reaching deep into her core. Then he said, "Do it."

Ahnna poured a few drops onto the end of the fuse. The chemicals immediately reacted. A bright glow illuminated the darkness and a crackle filled the air.

"Now!" she shouted, then drew in a deep breath as they dropped.

Ten.

Water closed over Ahnna's head, the light fading from view as they used their hands to push themselves down and down into the water-filled tunnel.

Nine.

Eight.

Her elbows collided against the rock, but she couldn't afford to be careful.

Six.

Five.

Ahnna could no longer see the light of the fuse, but that didn't mean they were out of range of debris.

Four.

Three.

If the tunnel collapsed, could she get turned around? Could she get them back to the surface of the ocean without drowning?

Two.

This wasn't going to work. She'd made a mistake.

One.

Nothing happened.

Shit.

There must have been a gap in the fuse line and it had gone out, which meant they'd need to do this all over again. Swearing silently, Ahnna started to swim upward.

Light abruptly flared, bright enough to hurt her eyes.

Boom!

A second later, the water surged, slamming her against the walls of the tunnel. Her head hit a rock, stunning her, bubbles rushing past her face.

But hands gripped her thighs, shoving her upward. *Swim!*

Clawing at the walls of the tunnel, Ahnna swam upward until her head broke the surface. Acrid smoke burned her eyes, and she fought the urge to breathe. Bracing her legs and back against the tunnel, she scaled it, finding that the bars had blown vertically. It would be tight, but they could get through.

Below her, the prince gasped and coughed on the smoke. She needed to get to the top and open the hatch to let in fresh air, then she could come back for him.

Climb!

The hot metal of the bars seared through her shirt, but Ahnna ignored the pain, forcing herself past them. Higher and higher she climbed, until she had no choice but to inhale.

Smoke burned her lungs, coughs racking her body, but she pressed onward. The tunnel turned horizontal, and ahead, she could make out a rim of light around the door.

Stumbling, she collided with the heavy wood, fumbled for the latch, and then was out into the open air.

Falling to her knees, she gasped in several mouthfuls of clean air, still coughing hard.

She needed to get William out. Needed to keep him alive so that he could stop the battle. Twisting, she hurled herself back into the cave opening.

Only to collide with William's solid chest.

He fell backward, and she landed on top of him, both of them coughing, eyes streaming tears.

"You . . . need . . . to stop . . . the . . . attack." She could barely get the words out.

To his credit, William nodded and rolled out from under her, on his feet in an instant. "Which way?"

They'd come up inside the market, and she raced toward the nearest shipbreaker, seeing its crew taking aim at the Harendellian ship.

"Stop!" Ahnna screamed, throat burning from the smoke as she shoved the two soldiers manning the breaker away from the mechanism. "Send the message down the line to stop shooting at them!"

"But they'll get inside our range! They could take the pier!"

"Stand down!" she barked, and because he looked like he might argue further, she added, "That's an order."

You have no authority to give orders any longer, a voice whispered in her head, but it was easy to ignore as the soldier lowered his hand from the release mechanism. The other man picked up a signal horn and blew a series of notes relaying her order to stand down.

William had shouldered his way through the mass of Ithicanian soldiers and was sprinting down the debris-strewn pier. Sliding to a stop, he waved his arms, attempting to catch the attention of the attacking ship.

The scene fell silent. Ahnna clenched her teeth as she strode down to the pier, searching for signs of Aren or Lara while she waited to see what the Harendellian ship would do. Whether they had seen their prince. Whether it was enough to stop the attack.

Then the ship ran up a white flag.

Lowering his arms, William turned. His eyes locked with Ahnna's, and her stomach flipped at the intensity of his gaze.

Whoever had painted the portrait she'd been given truly hadn't done him justice, for he was remarkably handsome. Barefoot and clad only in breeches and a shirt, his fancy coat discarded in the water, there was no mistaking the thick muscle that spoke to a life spent wielding weapons for more than just sport. Sunlight glinted off copper-colored hair clipped short, as was common in the Harendellian military, but long enough that it curled down over his forehead. His cheekbones were high and his jaw strong, his clean-shaven chin sporting a dimple that softened his tense expression. Not the princeling everyone said he was. Not even close.

"Is it safe for them to approach?" he called.

Ahnna nodded, even though she didn't have the authority to allow it. William inclined his head, then turned back to his ship to wave them closer.

It was only then she realized that the eyes that had met hers hadn't been green.

They'd been as amber as a setting sun.

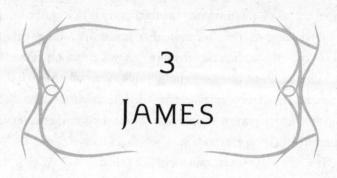

3
JAMES

WHAT A BLOODY, BLINDING MESS OF A SITUATION.

Holding his position, James watched the *Victoria* approach, coming up on the opposite side of the great stone pier from where his own vessel had sunk, still-burning debris littering the gentle swells.

So many lives lost, many of them his friends.

But he couldn't focus on that right now.

The moment the gap between ship and pier narrowed, dozens of his soldiers jumped over the rail, led by George, his lieutenant and friend. They encircled him, their weapons held at the ready as they stared down the watching Ithicanians, including the woman who'd saved his life.

He didn't know her name. Yet God help him, the vision of her suspended in the water, hand outstretched toward a shark three times her size, would be burned into his mind until the end of his days. Entirely fearless, a woman whose equal he'd never met in his life.

"Come, Major General! We need to get you to safety." Georgie tugged at his sleeve, trying to get him aboard the ship.

James only waved away his friend with irritation. "Stand down. This was Amarid's doing. They had men disguised as sailors on our ship who took control for long enough to bring us up against the pier, where more Amaridians were hidden in wine barrels."

"Ithicana may have conspired with Amarid," Georgie insisted, gripping his arm this time. "This could be a trap."

Pulling out of his friend's hold, James again locked eyes with the Ithicanian woman. She'd knocked him overboard before the explosion, nearly getting herself killed in order to save his life. "It's no trap. Ithicana is innocent, and blame for events rests on Amarid. Stand down and sheathe your weapons. My father is expecting me to return home with a princess bride, and I can't imagine the Ithicanians will be keen to give her over after this display of ineptitude on our part."

Georgie's eyebrows rose. "I'd hardly say that being attacked by your own crew qualifies as ineptitude. Amarid must have been working on this for months, and it's the spymasters who failed to discover the plot. It's not your fault."

"Everything is my fault, Georgie," James replied. "You should know that by now. Take stock of the situation while I speak to the Ithicanians."

Ignoring his friend's protests, James started down the pier, two of his soldiers rushing to flank him on Georgie's orders. The woman approached as well, picking her way over the smoldering debris of his ship, the pace giving him ample time to finally take a good look at her.

And then to look again.

Tall and lean, her long dark hair clung to the side of her face, which was beautiful enough to make a blind man look twice. A long scar stretched down from her forehead, crossing her brow and onto her cheek, but rather than detracting from her appearance, it only accentuated the fierceness of her hazel gaze. Having shed much of her clothing in the water, she wore only snug trousers and a thin undergarment that did little to hide the pert breasts underneath. A woman so fierce that even sharks gave way to her, and apparently a soldier of some degree of importance, judging by how the Ithicanians did the same.

"God," one of his soldiers muttered. "If I'd known *that* was what the Ithicanians were hiding underneath those masks they wore, I'd have worked harder to get them off."

"Show some respect," James growled. "She saved my life."

Both men straightened in surprise, but he barely noticed, his eyes all for the woman before him.

"Have you come to declare war, or are we still friends?" she asked, her voice light despite the fact that blood dripped from a small cut at her temple. There were other marks of violence on her body. Faded scars on her suntanned arms, the knuckles on her right hand looking like they'd been broken more than once. Nothing like the ladies at court, for while they dueled with words, this was a woman who left blood in her wake.

Realizing he was staring at her, James said, "I've made it clear this was the Amaridians' doing." His cheeks warmed as she crossed her arms beneath her breasts, the darker hue of her nipples visible through the wet fabric, though she seemed to either not notice or not care. "Once King Edward learns of today's events, Harendell will retaliate. It would be in Ithicana's best interest to reconsider allowing Amaridian merchants to trade at Northwatch, given that this act of violence was as much against Ithicana as Harendell."

She only lifted one shoulder and then let it drop, seemingly unconcerned by the carnage around her. "If Ithicana refused trade with everyone it crossed swords with, the bridge would be empty."

Irritation bit at James's guts. His father argued that it was this sort of pragmatism that made Ithicana ideal for managing trade through the bridge, but her lack of concern for Amarid's actions today rubbed James the wrong way. "I expect that's not your decision to make."

Her jaw tightened, and she opened her mouth with the obvious intent to retort, but he was spared an argument by the arrival of two Ithicanian men.

The tallest, a man near in age to James, stepped to the fore and said, "Rather an exciting morning, wouldn't you say, Your Highness? I was expecting to drink the contents of those barrels, not fight them."

God, but these people were blasé. And informal. "Indeed. I'd like to speak with the individual in command to make my apologies for Harendell's failure to prevent this situation."

The tall man looked over the edge of the pier at the sunken ship and frowned. "Apologies aren't going to move that mess. That's weeks' worth of work."

Grinding his teeth, James said, "I'll discuss recompense with the commander of Northwatch." That was who he'd been told would deliver the princess into his care.

"Commander Mara's occupied, so you'll have to content yourself with me."

The last thing James had any intention of doing was bargaining with a midlevel officer with grand opinions of himself. "That's unacceptable, I'm afraid. This conversation requires an individual possessing a certain degree of authority."

The older Ithicanian man who'd been silent abruptly laughed, slapping a hand against his thigh. "A certain degree of authority. Someone should write it down for posterity."

James's escort stiffened, not at all happy about the mockery, but it wasn't the older man's disrespect that made James's spine prickle. It was the pregnant woman who approached. Her honey-blond hair was a mess of tangles, her face smeared with dirt and blood, but her ruined gown was of the finest silk. Even that he might have disregarded, but the eyes glaring at the tall Ithicanian were a *very* distinct shade of blue.

Shit.

Understanding of exactly whom he was speaking to struck James right as the pregnant woman said, "Aren, this was a blow to Harendell. Do not make light of it." She turned her glower on the older man. "That goes for you as well, Jor."

This was Ithicana's goddamned king.

James had insulted Aren *fucking* Kertell.

Bowing low, James spent a heartbeat silently cursing the Ithicanian penchant for avoiding any markers of rank in their attire, then straightened. "My apologies, Your Majesty. I . . ."

"Thought I'd be taller?"

The older Ithicanian burst into laughter, and the king joined in before clutching at his side.

"Bloody hell, that hurts. I think I broke a rib when your ship blew up next to me."

Casting her eyes skyward, the blond woman—the queen of Ithicana—rounded on James and extended her hand. "It is the greatest of pleasures to meet you, Your Highness. I only wish it could have been under better circumstances."

"Likewise, Your Grace." He took her hand and carefully kissed her scarred knuckles, painfully aware of his bare feet and ruined clothing. However, unlike the Ithicanians, Maridrinians were something he had experience with. "We'd intended for somewhat more pomp and infinitely less violence."

"Fortunately for you, Ithicana is more comfortable with violence than pomp," King Aren interjected, and James did not fail to note the way he took his queen's hand, pulling her close. Theirs was a match much discussed at court, and it would appear that the rumors that the Ithicanian king was deeply in love with his Maridrinian wife were true.

But James was *not* here for fodder for the court's rumor mill. "I must ask, is Your Grace's sister, the Princess Ahnna, safe and unharmed?"

God help him if she wasn't. Circumstances couldn't get much worse.

A faint smile formed on the king's face. Then he turned to look at the Ithicanian woman who'd rescued James, who now appeared as though she'd rather be anywhere but on this pier. "You might have introduced yourself, Ahnna."

Things could *always* get worse.

Bowing low, he said, "Apologies, Your Highness. Allow me to introduce myself. I'm—"

"We know who you are, William," Aren interrupted. "Given you've been betrothed to my sister for most of her life."

Things could always get much, *much* worse.

Lara gave a soft cough that sounded a great deal like "*wrong prince*," and Aren rocked on his heels, eyes narrowed as he looked James up and down. "You're not William."

"I'm afraid not."

Princess Ahnna's suntanned cheeks were blushed pink with discomfort. "William has green eyes, whereas yours are . . ." She trailed off, her hazel gaze meeting James's for a brief moment before she looked away, her disappointment palpable.

James might have flinched, but he was long used to such a reaction.

"Amber eyes of *fucking* Cardiff," Aren said with a scowl. "Edward sent his goddamned bastard."

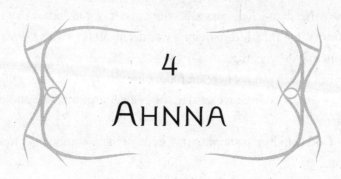

4

AHNNA

As soon as she'd seen his eye color, Ahnna had known who James was, but there'd been no chance to tell Aren, and she certainly hadn't expected her brother to make such an ass of himself.

"Aren." Lara's voice was reproving, but he only said, "William couldn't be bothered to come himself?"

James inclined his head. "No insult was intended, Your Grace. As we've just witnessed, the seas are fraught with danger, and tension between Harendell and Amarid is high. Her Grace, Queen Alexandra, was loath to risk the heir to the throne when so many would be glad to see him dead."

So the opinions of William's character had not been off the mark, after all. The missive had said it would be him coming to retrieve her, but even so, Ahnna felt like an idiot for having mistaken James for William.

"If the seas are so dangerous, perhaps I should not be risking my sister," Aren said. "Ahnna is, for the time being, the heir to Ithicana's throne."

Ahnna bit the insides of her cheeks, because it had been Ithi-cana who'd requested that steps be taken toward a wedding, not Harendell. Yet instead of pointing that out, James only said, "I defer to your judgment, Your Grace. If you deem the risk too great, Harendell would gladly defer the princess's arrival to a later—"

"I will leave for Harendell now," Ahnna interrupted. "Amarid spent a great deal of resources on this attack, and I doubt they'll make another attempt with our guard up. Travel now is as safe as it will ever be, and"—she glanced over her shoulder at clouds growing in the east—"it looks as though a storm is brewing, so we should not linger."

Aren glanced east, started to scoff at what was clearly only a small squall, then fell silent as their eyes locked.

I need you to trust me, she silently willed her brother. *Ithicana needs this.*

I need this.

His jaw tightened, and he appeared ready to argue, but Lara rested a hand on his arm. As always, he conceded to her influence. Silence stretched, then Aren said, "There is no safe time. The seas are always dangerous, and delaying will only give Amarid the time to organize another attack." He turned to the soldiers lining the pier. "Get this mess cleared up and their ship tied off. Move!"

The Northwatch guard rushed to obey, and James said, "I will need time to collect the bodies of the fallen, Your Grace. They were good men, and they deserve to have their remains returned to their families."

Jor looked over the side of the pier, and he gave a shake of his head.

Aren sighed. "There will be little to retrieve, I'm afraid. The sharks move quickly and without mercy when there is blood in our waters."

James's expression didn't change, but as he said, "Understood," Ahnna saw the flash of grief in his eyes. Pain over the loss of soldiers and crew that she rarely witnessed in experienced commanders. Which, given what she knew from her research on the royal family, he most certainly was.

"I'm sorry," she said. "For the loss of your men. We should have been better prepared."

Amber eyes locked on hers. They were the color of expensive whiskey, the sun illuminating flecks of gold in them, the very outer rim an inky black. Cardiffian eyes, if she'd ever seen them, and Ahnna shivered, because the people of the northern kingdom were said to cast spells, many of their women known to be witches.

"My thanks, Your Highness." His voice was different than it had been before he'd known her identity. Bland and nearly inflectionless. She didn't like it. "However, we brought the conflict with Amarid to your shores, so the fault in security lies with us."

"We can spend all day arguing over who is at fault, but the results are the same," Aren snapped, showing no signs of coming to terms with William's absence, though Ahnna wasn't entirely certain why it mattered. "Good soldiers dead and a pier rendered half unusable with debris that will take days to clear. Better to press forward than look back. If you'll excuse me, I intend to do just that." He strode off, shouting orders.

"Ithicana still bears fresh scars from war," Lara said, hand curving over her stomach as she spoke, the exertion so late in pregnancy showing its toll in the pallor of her face. "To have violence rear on our shores so soon is not what we hoped for with this alliance, Your Highness. Or do you prefer Major General?"

Ahnna hadn't focused her recent research on James, though she knew he was the illegitimate son of Edward and a Cardiffian woman, and that Edward had formally acknowledged him as his son and prince. Knew that he was a fighter of some renown who was often sent where conflict was thickest due to his prowess on the field. She'd not dug much deeper because James had felt less important. Her interest had been in the king and queen and, most of all, the prince she was supposed to marry. But *major general* was very nearly at the top of Harendell's incredibly complicated military hierarchy. Higher than William, who held only the rank of captain, his title primarily honorific.

"Whatever your preference, Your Grace. I serve the crown in both capacities." James gave Lara a small smile, obviously as enraptured with her as every other man who ever saw her given the way the tension on his face faded. Ahnna struggled not to roll her eyes as he said, "I am deeply sorry for this distressing turn of events."

A flicker of emotion that Ahnna didn't care to name filled her chest, but she bit down on it, because she knew that when it came to the queen, nothing she felt was ever considered reasonable.

Lara stepped in front of her, forcing Ahnna to take a half step back. "The men who infiltrated your crew, were they unfamiliar to you? Or did Amarid buy off men who'd long been in service?"

"The latter, I'm afraid," James answered. "All handpicked. I won't offend Ithicana's spy network by suggesting that it is not an ongoing problem, though we have the same leverage in Amarid."

A spy network that Lara now ran.

Lara made a humming noise of agreement. "We should vet the sailors of the other ship before you depart. Check them for weapons they should not have so as to be sure Ahnna is safe on her journey. Our spies may have information you don't, so we'll check your crew before Ahnna boards."

Lara was speaking as though Ahnna weren't standing right behind her. As though she couldn't defend herself, if needed. As though she were a child who needed to be coddled and protected rather than the woman who'd led Ithicana through most of the war in Aren's absence.

Anger swelled in her chest, and Ahnna snapped, "It's his goddamned ship, Lara. If he wants your assistance, he'll ask."

James's eyes flicked between them, but he said nothing as Lara stiffened, then stepped to one side. "I'm only trying to ensure your safety, Ahnna. You're important to us."

The words were genuine—Ahnna knew that—but as she looked into Lara's impossibly beautiful face, all she saw was the wolf in sheep's clothing from whom she'd failed to protect Ithicana. The ingénue who'd swanned her way into everyone's hearts with her charm, wit, and strategically deployed bravery, then left the door open for Silas Veliant to do his worst. Ahnna knew that Lara had turned on her father by the time the invasion had occurred. That she hadn't wanted it to happen. But intentions didn't bring back the thousands of Ithicanians who had died as a result of the invasion, and it certainly didn't erase the nightmares of dead families and dead children that walked through Ahnna's mind every night.

You were supposed to protect them! her conscience screamed. *You were supposed to keep them safe!*

"I assume the princess will have an Ithicanian escort, Your Grace?" James asked. "Hand-selected to ensure her safety?"

"Of course," Lara replied. "Our finest—"

At that moment, singing echoed down the pier.

Ahnna's cousin Taryn, along with Lara's half sister Bronwyn, were staggering, arm in arm, toward them, singing a bawdy song about a sailor marooned on an island with a goat. Both women were clearly drunk out of their wits. Which was perhaps no shock, for they were long overdue at Northwatch after an excursion to one of the other islands. They stumbled to a stop, looking around, and Bronwyn shouted, "Holy shit, Aren! I thought you said that Harendellian ceremonies were dull!"

Aren broke off what he was doing to stare at both women, then scrubbed an irritated hand through his hair and went back to barking orders.

"Our finest warriors," Lara murmured. "The most loyal men and women Ithicana has to offer."

Lies.

Taryn was coming with Ahnna because she needed to get away from Ithicana as much as Ahnna did, and Bronwyn . . . Well, Bronwyn was coming because she felt like it. Which was fine with Ahnna, because Bronwyn was the first Maridrinian she'd met whom she actually liked. Bronwyn could lie through her teeth but never *ever* did. Most found her honesty a fault, but Ahnna relished it. "My cousin Taryn Kertell, as well as Princess Bronwyn Veliant, will be accompanying me."

James inclined his head to Bronwyn and Taryn, the picture of Harendellian courtesy, and as she stared at his chiseled profile, Ahnna was struck with the memory of that face between her legs as she'd set explosives not half an hour ago. Her cheeks warmed, and she silently prayed that he'd never mention it to his brother.

"You're not William," Bronwyn said, peering up at James. "You don't build muscles like those dueling with a rapier for the entertainment of the court. Which means you are James."

"Sorry to disappoint."

"Who said I was disappointed?" Bronwyn said with a wink, then gestured to the ship. "That our boat?"

"The *Victoria*, my lady. The servants will be working to make up appropriate quarters, as I'm afraid the ship that—"

"I'm sure it's a great story. Let's save it for when we're at sea," Bronwyn interrupted. "You coming, Ahnna?"

Ahnna looked to her brother, who was standing at the edge of the pier, gesturing angrily at the sunken ship. She waited, hoping he'd look up. That he'd look back. That she, for once, would be his priority. Aren only carried on down the pier, gesturing at the merchant vessels on the horizon waiting to make port.

"Aren will wish to say goodbye to you before you board," Lara said. "He's only—"

"We already said our goodbyes."

"You two need to resolve your differences," Lara said under her breath, then she shook her head. "I'll see that your things are brought aboard. Bronwyn, sober up. This isn't a holiday."

Bronwyn gave a jaunty salute, but Taryn muttered, "Fuck off, Lara," before striding toward the ship. Bronwyn winced, then said, "Will be good for her to get away to somewhere with no Maridrinians."

Ahnna wasn't entirely certain whether Bronwyn was speaking about her or Taryn. Possibly both, and Ahnna didn't disagree. If she never saw another Maridrinian again, it would be too soon.

Lara's face was tight with frustration. "You're Maridrinian, Bron."

Bronwyn only lifted one shoulder. "Yes. But I didn't lie to her face for months. Not everyone is going to love you, sister mine. That's just a fact you must learn to accept." She bent down and kissed Lara's stomach before whispering, "But everyone loves you, little one." Then Bronwyn linked her arm through James's. "You have anything to drink on your boat, Your Highness?"

"Ship." He cast a backward glance at Ahnna, amber eyes flicking between her and Lara before he said, "At your leisure, Your Highness. We sail when you are ready."

Ahnna watched Bronwyn lead him away, wanting to chase after them but knowing that she had to say something to Lara, who was staring at bits of rubble lying on the pier between them. "I hope it goes well, Lara." Blue eyes lifted to meet hers. "Truly. I look forward to learning the name of my niece or nephew. Take care of Aren, because we both know he won't take care of himself." Hesitating, she added, "I'll do what needs doing. Ithicana will have Harendell's support, but more important, it will have its trade and gold so that you can rebuild Ithicana and make it strong again. I swear it."

Not giving Ithicana's queen a chance to respond, Ahnna started toward the ship. The gangplank was in place, and she made her way up it to find a hand reaching out to her. Her eyes shot up to find James waiting for her, arm outstretched. This sort of courtesy was unfamiliar to her: Ithicanians offered each other aid when needed, not out of courtesy, and she stood frozen for a heartbeat before taking it.

His hand was warm, his palm callused. No surprise, given he could clearly fight, though what did shock her was how much larger his hand was than her own. At over six feet in height, little about Ahnna was small other than her breasts, a sore spot in her vanity, and few men other than her brother made Ahnna feel short.

But James did.

"You might have mentioned your identity," he said. "I would have behaved differently, had I known. Apologies for my conduct."

"If you'd behaved differently, we'd probably be dead," she said. "But next time, I'll be sure to inform the sharks to give us time for proper introductions."

It was meant to be a joke, but James didn't laugh. "I've never seen anyone do what you did with that shark. Thrice your size, yet it gave way to you. Why?"

Ahnna hesitated, then said, "By making her believe I'm not prey."

Silence stretched.

"What did it . . . did *she* think you were?"

The air felt suddenly charged, the question deeper than the words suggested, and Ahnna's heart whispered, *I don't know anymore.* Aloud, she said, "Jump overboard and ask."

Again, he didn't laugh, only looked down at her with an expression that made Ahnna feel like more than she was.

Her heart was thundering, the humid air suddenly too thick to breathe, but Ahnna didn't know how to cut the tension. Well, she knew how connections were built when people fought side by side, cheating death, but he was a stranger. More than that, James was an *outsider*. Which meant keeping her walls up.

Realizing she was still holding his hand, Ahnna dropped it and took a step back, suddenly aware that she was sodden and barefoot, her undershirt clinging to her breasts, which probably explained why all the sailors were staring at her. "I should find dry clothes. I'm sure you wish to do the same."

He drew in a sharp breath, then shook his head. "Of course. Apologies."

He gestured to a young woman who stood with a lowered head, her light-brown hair twisted into a tidy knot at the back of her head. "Hazel has served my family's household for many years, and I will leave you in her capable hands while I see to getting the ship under way. If there is any comfort you find lacking, please give it voice. We serve at your pleasure." He bowed slightly. "If it pleases you, I would offer you, and your ladies, my company for dinner."

"Uh . . ." She hunted for words, for while her mother had foisted endless lessons in Harendellian etiquette upon Ahnna, that had been a lifetime ago. "It would be our pleasure to join you. Thank you."

"I look forward to it." James bowed again, then disappeared down the corridor.

"This way, my lady," Hazel said, curtsying. "We must get you out of those wet clothes before you catch a chill."

Ahnna bit down on a snort of amusement, because remaining dry in Ithicana was borderline impossible. *The Harendellians are different*, she reminded herself. *They aren't like you. They haven't had to fight to survive every goddamned day of their lives.*

Following the maid into the stateroom, she glanced around the small room, which showed signs of having been recently vacated by its prior occupant. There was a sock in one corner and a small portrait of a woman nailed to the wall, both of which Hazel discreetly tucked into the pockets of her skirts. "I'll see after your trunks, my lady, as well as bring you warm wash water." She bobbed another curtsy. "This was not how we wished to welcome you, Princess. Your rooms in the other ship were beautifully appointed, and . . ." Tears welled in the young woman's gray eyes, and she broke off, her slender body shaking.

"I'm sorry for your loss," Ahnna said, suspecting that Hazel had known many of the servants on the other vessel and that it had been some twist of luck that had her serving on this ship. No doubt the maid who'd been intended to serve Ahnna was dead.

"Thank you, Your Highness." Hazel blinked her tears away. "We are so delighted to have you come to Harendell, and I hope you'll not judge us harshly on your accommodations, for they are not what was intended. The *Victoria* is a naval vessel."

Ahnna had spent most of her life in accommodations far more uncomfortable than these, for above all else, she was a soldier, but instinct told her that saying as much would not make Hazel feel better. So instead, she said, "I understand. Thank you."

Hazel curtsied, then departed, leaving Ahnna alone in the

stateroom. Toying with the empty sheath of the knife she'd lost, Ahnna went to the window to look out, but her view was away from the pier, so all she could see were merchant vessels waiting for Northwatch's signal to make port. Every minute that these piers stood empty was costing Ithicana gold it could not afford, and part of her wanted to go onto the deck and start urging the Harendellians to depart even as part of her hoped that they'd never set sail. That this ship, a small taste of the changes she was about to face, would be the farthest she ever got from her home.

She struggled to contain the homesickness that rose in her chest. Ahnna had spent a large portion of her life being prepared for this moment. Endless lessons from spies who'd spent time in Edward's court, teaching her their customs, manners, and practices. However, that had been under her mother's reign. Once Aren had become king and made Ahnna commander of Southwatch, there'd been no time in her schedule for dancing lessons or to practice her needlework, because she'd been consumed with protecting the most dangerous location in all of Ithicana. Then the invasion had happened. Then the collision of Maridrina and Valcotta. And keeping up with Harendell's politics and gossip had felt like such a distant concern. Much of the knowledge remained instilled in her, but the emotional preparation she'd undergone seemed to have disappeared entirely.

Or perhaps she'd only ever fooled herself that it was there at all.

A knock sounded on the door, and Hazel entered. "Your trunk, my lady," she said. "I'll go in search of the others. They only had the one."

"There is only one," Ahnna said as a sailor carried in her small trunk, setting it down and departing. "I only have . . ." She trailed off, about to have said that she only had a few belongings. Except that would imply that Ithicana was without means, and kingdoms without means were seen as weak, which was the last thing Aren needed Harendell to believe. "I prefer to travel light and acquire what I need when I arrive."

Hazel looked up from inspecting the contents of Ahnna's small trunk, which was mostly weapons, a few items of sentimental value, and tunics and trousers she'd worn all her life. "We shall have a seamstress brought straightaway, my lady. Day dresses and evening dresses, six of each to start, though you'll need ball gowns once we reach Verwyrd, for you are certain to be the toast of the season in the Sky Palace. An Ithicanian princess . . . Truly, your dance card will always be full."

Ahnna's stomach twisted as she considered the cost of such dresses. Aren had accounts in her name with the Harendellian banks that she could draw upon, but she was loath to spend the funds on dresses given that most of Lara's jewelry had been sold to pay for food for Ithicanian civilians. Never mind the prospect of having to wear them while executing complicated dance steps that she hadn't practiced in years, all under the eye of the most judgmental people in the known world.

"It will be quiet dinners during your journey," Hazel said, holding up one of the tunics. "There are no other ladies aboard besides your own, who are family, and His Highness is soon to be family as well, which suggests less formal attire is . . . is . . . appropriate."

Hazel's tone suggested anything but.

Ahnna plucked the tunic out of the woman's hands, turning her back before removing her damp undershirt and donning the dry garment. Trousers followed, her spare boots forming to her feet as she peered into the tiny mirror on the wall, inspecting the scabbed-over cut on her temple. Warm water arrived, and she allowed Hazel to wipe away the blood smeared on her face, then apply a bit of salve to the cut.

Ahnna expected a knock to sound on the door. For a servant to call through the wood that Aren was on decks. That he'd come to find her. That he wouldn't let her go without saying goodbye.

But the only noises were of the crew making ready to leave, familiar shouts and orders, for ships were much the same no matter the nation they hailed from.

He'll come, she told herself. *He'll come say goodbye. Or at least, come to give you orders.*

Hazel departed to dispose of the dirty wash water, and Ahnna sat on the bunk.

Waiting.

A knock sounded on the door, too rough to be Hazel. Ahnna leapt to her feet, a smile growing on her face because she'd been wrong to doubt him. Flinging open the door, she said, "Figure out how you're going to—"

She broke off because it wasn't Aren standing in the opening.

It was Jor.

"I'm coming with you," the old soldier said, resting his scarred hands on the doorframe. "You need someone you can trust. Someone who knows what's what about these northern vipers. They're all smiles to your face and knives to the back, the Harendellians. Can't stand the fuckers. Also, your cousin is a drunk, and Bronwyn is going to be busy keeping her from falling off the side of the ship."

Ahnna stared at him as the ship bobbed beneath them, moving away from the pier.

He isn't coming.

The realization must have shown in her eyes, because Jor's weathered face softened. "I know he's left you behind a thousand times, Ahnna, but this is the first time you've left him. Aren's more rattled about you leaving than he cares to admit, which means he's being a right prick about it. You know how he is when he's upset."

Ahnna was already moving.

Why hadn't she made the effort to say goodbye? Why hadn't she sought him out? She cursed her stubbornness because this wasn't how she wanted to leave things with her twin.

Out on the deck, she dodged sailors, making her way to the side of the ship.

Please be there.

Her hands closed on the railing, eyes searching the Ithicanians watching the ship move back, the distance between the vessel and Northwatch growing.

Aren wasn't there.

Only Lara stood on the end of the pier, the wind catching at her silken skirts, long blond hair drifting out behind her. Ithicana's queen lifted her hand, their eyes locked as the ship slowly rotated, the sails rising. Watching each other as Ithicana slowly disappeared in the Harendellian ship's wake.

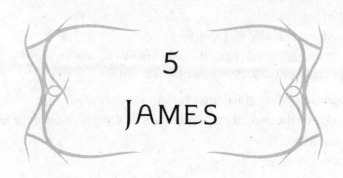

5
JAMES

ABANDONING AHNNA TO HAZEL, JAMES WENT IN SEARCH OF Georgie's quarters. There was little time, the Ithicanians eager to have their pier cleared so that they could return to the business of trade, which meant he needed to get this vessel under way.

"Make ready," he said to Drake as the captain fell in alongside him. "I'll be back on decks shortly."

Opening the door to Georgie's cabin, James slammed it shut behind him, letting out the string of curses he'd been holding in check, half of which were directed at Aren *fucking* Kertell.

"I see Ithicana's king made an impression," Georgie said. "The men told me what he said. Did he truly believe the queen would allow Will to venture into Ithicana's waters?"

Instead of answering, James wrenched off one of the boots he'd taken from Georgie when he'd boarded. "Why are your feet so goddamned small?" He threw it at Georgie, who was lounging barefoot on his bunk.

His best friend caught the boot, laughing. "Not all of us are graced with flippers for feet, Jamie. Though I suppose we should all be grateful, given that they allowed you to outswim Ithicana's man-eaters."

"My survival had nothing to do with luck." He leaned against the door. "And everything to do with Ithicana's princess."

"Is she what you expected?"

They'd known little about her beyond Ahnna's age, that she was the king's twin sister, and that she'd held the rank of commander of Southwatch Island. The first contact they'd ever had with her was when she'd appealed to his father for support against the Maridrinians, but she'd worn a mask to the brief meeting she'd had with him. No spies had ever seen her face. No portrait had ever been painted. No one but his father had so much as spoken to her.

Ahnna Kertell was an enigma.

"I hadn't considered what she might be like," James finally said. The image of her in the water with her hand outstretched to the shark again filled his mind's eye, no less vivid than it had been in the moment. Dangerous, but also . . . His mind hunted for a word, but nothing quite suited Ahnna Kertell's wild beauty.

Georgie was silent for a long moment, then he said, "I never really thought of the Ithicanians as human, always wearing those masks and refusing to speak beyond what needed to be said. I half thought, and I don't think I'm alone in this, that they would be monstrous beneath the masks. To see that they are flesh and blood, same as us, was almost a shock."

James blinked, trying to clear away the image of Ahnna, but all he could see was her. A woman who would fight until the bitter end, screaming defiance until her last breath.

"Almost would have been better if she was monstrous," Georgie said, tugging at his long hair. "Then there'd be novelty to her.

Bloody damn, Jamie, Will's going to hate everything about that woman, not the least of which that she's *huge*. Taller than me, which means she'll be taller than him, and while she was a beauty at one point, that scar . . ." His friend shook his head. "Will's going to be an unrepentant ass about having to marry her. He likes a certain type, and Ahnna Kertell could not be further from it."

James frowned, disagreeing almost viscerally with his friend's criticism, but Georgie's prediction of Will's reaction was spot-on. William liked girls who made him feel better about himself, and Ahnna would only bring into stark relief his brother's inadequacies, real and imagined. "Will's tastes are irrelevant. This treaty was signed by our father, and he always holds to his word. If he has to drag Will down the aisle and pin him to the ground before the priest to make the wedding happen, he'll do it."

James knew this was the case, because it was his father who'd made him set sail to retrieve Ahnna despite James's every protest that the betrothal should be broken.

"I wouldn't bet against you on that," Georgie said. "And in the end, it's of no matter. Will can wed her, get her with child, then send her to stay with your aunt at Hemsford, where she'll be out of sight and out of mind until he needs her to produce a spare. She'll likely be happier for it. Did you see she was wearing trousers? Trousers! My God, Jamie, she's going to be eaten alive at court."

Instinctively, James snapped, "She's a soldier, not some vapid courtier, and she saved my ass from being blown up and from being eaten alive, so show her some respect."

Georgie sat up straight, setting his boot on the floor as he eyed James. "I don't disrespect her, Jamie. Truly. I just feel bad for the woman. Sending her to marry Will is a cruelty. Like capturing a wild animal and demanding she play at being a pet. Either she'll lash out or her spirit will die, but never will she be tamed. Might be better for all involved if she begs her brother to renegotiate with your father. For better trade terms for the use of Ithicana's bridge, I'm sure all of Harendell will be happy to forgo an Ithicanian bride."

Except better trade terms would mean more goods flowing south, and everything James had worked for demanded that they flow north to Cardiff. He rubbed at his temple, feeling a headache coming on. "None of this is within our power to influence, and we've more pressing matters."

"Such as your own attire?"

"It's disrespectful to engage in diplomatic relations in bare feet." Aren Kertell clearly had little enough respect for him, and looking like a drowned rat hadn't improved the situation. "I need something to wear to dinner."

"I think I've found a solution." Georgie rose from his bunk, retrieving a pair of well-worn boots from beneath. "No amount of polish is going to make these shine, but they should fit. Clothes were more of a challenge. For one, you are obnoxiously tall, and two, most of our men rarely avail themselves of laundresses. Sodden trousers are better than ill-fitting or malodorous garments, though I've set Hazel the task of sewing you some replacements. Here." He held out a starched shirt. "Best I could manage, given the circumstances."

"It will do." James took the shirt, well aware that they were skirting the true pressing matters at hand, namely, the list of casualties sitting next to the washstand. An entire ship beneath the sea, dozens of men lost, and all as a result of an act of visible aggression by Amarid. And a surprising act in that James had been the apparent target. His name was much cursed in Amarid, given his service in the border wars, but other than vengeance, there was little to be gained in killing him. He was the king's bastard, heir to nothing, all of his power predicated on his family's goodwill. And this had been a strike that would have taken months of planning and endless resources.

He was not worth it. Not by any stretch of the imagination. Yet worth it or not, there was no denying that Amarid had tried not only to kill him, but to pin his death on Ithicana, which meant their motivations required deeper scrutiny than he currently had time to give.

Pulling off his shirt, James winced at the already purpling bruises on his torso, then put on the clean garment, eyes running down the list as he fastened the buttons.

Most of the names were familiar to him, some close enough to be called friends, but he could not allow himself time to grieve. That would come later, when he notified their families of their deaths. He'd made the choice to put nearly all his officers and soldiers on the *Victoria* so that his first meeting with the Ithicanians would not have all of them looking over his shoulder, and James wasn't certain whether that had saved lives or cost them. Because the men he'd brought with him were all capable fighters, and with them, he might have done better against the mutinying crew.

"You think war is on the horizon?" Georgie asked, straightening his own attire. "This attack can't go unanswered."

"War has been on the horizon for two decades." James folded the page, shoving it into a pocket of his still-damp trousers. "We've flirted with it as much as Amarid, but this . . . This was *bold*. And on the surface, foolish, given that we have an army double the size of Katarina's, and her navy has not recovered from the losses it took when Silas attacked Eranahl. Yet Katarina is no fool, which makes me think there is more at play here than can be seen on the surface."

There were few alive as clever as Queen Katarina of Amarid.

"Will Ithicana deny them access to the bridge?"

"Not according to Ahnna." James tucked in the shirt and refastened his belt. He glared at his image in the mirror. "This is a mess."

"Just as well. You hate speeches, but you like to fight." Georgie clapped him on the shoulder. "Let's go get the farewells over with. Be careful not to lift anything heavy, or you're going to burst the shoulder seams on your shirt."

James would give a thousand speeches if it would bring back the men who'd died, but he only nodded. "I need your sword. Mine is at the bottom of the Tempest Seas."

Georgie sighed, then extracted his own and handed it over, hilt-first. "I want it back."

Hefting the blade, which was a Cavendish family heirloom, James grinned at his friend. "We'll see. I've always liked the weight of it."

Together, they strode back on decks, which were thick with activity as the crew loaded trunks belonging to the passengers, along with supplies to make up for what had been lost on the other vessel. Ahnna was nowhere in sight, but James marked Hazel escorting one of the crew, who was carrying a small trunk, in the direction of the princess's stateroom.

Descending the gangway, James approached Ithicana's monarchs, who stood waiting, a group of hardened soldiers behind them.

"Your Majesties," he said, bowing low. "By your leave, we will depart."

Aren's hazel eyes skipped past James, searching the decks, then he huffed out an irritated breath that sounded a great deal like, *Have it your way, Ahnna,* then added in a tone devoid of emotion, "Deliver my sister safely to Verwyrd."

"Her comfort and well-being are my utmost priorities, Your Grace," James said. "The princess will be shown every courtesy."

"Good. Safe travels." Aren turned on his heel and strode up the pier, half the guard following him and the rest remaining with their queen.

Lara watched her husband with an unreadable expression, then turned her distinct Veliant eyes on James. Though she was head and shoulders shorter than him, slender, and very pregnant, there was something about Ithicana's queen that screamed danger, and the desire to rest a hand on the hilt of his borrowed sword tested his willpower.

"Ahnna kept Ithicana alive despite everything my father threw at her," she said. "No one in the kingdom is more beloved, but our loss is Harendell's gain. I hope the ties of marriage will bring our nations close, and that both our peoples will reap the benefits of our alliance."

James inclined his head, lying through his teeth as he said, "I hope for this as well, Your Grace." He hesitated, then added, "Amarid is up to something. If your spies discover anything, we'd appreciate it if you shared what you've learned."

All the queen said in answer was, "Safe travels."

Taking three steps back, James then turned and walked up the gangplank, joining the captain on the quarterdeck as the man gave the order to depart, Georgie remaining on the main deck to give orders to the soldiers on watch.

The ship was well away from the pier when Ahnna appeared. Weaving around the crew and soldiers, she went to the rail, staring back at Northwatch. Queen Lara lifted a hand in goodbye, but Ahnna did not so much as twitch in response. Bad blood between them, though clearly it was one-sided, which was understandable. Gathering information from Ithicana was always a test of Harendell's spies, but *all* knew Lara Veliant's role in the Maridrinian invasion. Just as all knew her part in ending it. Yet ending it had not brought the thousands killed by the Maridrinians back to life, and while Aren had forgiven his wife's sins, it appeared that Ahnna had not. Though at the cost of her relationship with her own twin brother.

Being not of a forgiving nature himself, James respected Ahnna's defiance even as he cursed it, because in the face of that sort of stubbornness, what hope did he have in convincing her to go back?

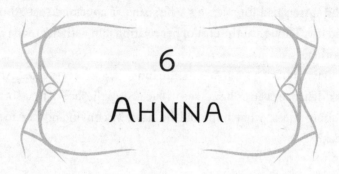

6
AHNNA

AHNNA REMAINED AT THE RAIL OF THE SHIP AS THE SUN SLIPPED low in the sky, pulling her spirits with her as they left Ithicana's waters.

As she left her home forever.

The roughest storm wouldn't make her seasick, but the anxiety building in her stomach had her ready to spill her guts overboard.

A cough broke her reverie, and Jor came up next to her, resting his elbows on the railing. "The captain is hosting dinner in his quarters," he said. "They're waiting on you."

A dinner that was sure to include every officer on the ship, as well as James, which meant it would be the first step she'd take in securing their favor, but all Ahnna wanted to do was watch the waves.

"Did you have a look around?" she asked Jor. "Thoughts?"

"Good ship. Solid crew. Experienced soldiers." Jor pulled the toothpick he'd been chewing out of his mouth. "Though they're all rattled. Harendell and Amarid normally gnash teeth with political posturing, embargoes, and discreet assassinations. This is an unexpected escalation, and it has them all worried that worse is to come. If there are infiltrators aboard, I couldn't pick them out at first blush. Even so, you'll want to be on your guard. You armed?"

"Always."

"Thatta girl."

Setting aside her emotions, she asked, "Why would Amarid put so much effort into killing James?"

"He's apparently got quite the body count," Jor answered. "Until recently, he's spent most of his time on the Amaridian border. They hate him."

"I don't debate that. Except why not just assassinate him? Why go through all this cost and effort to frame Ithicana?"

"To ruin the alliance?"

Ahnna made a face. "Maybe."

Jor hesitated, then said, "Rumor has it that Edward favors him over William. Might be that Amarid hoped to avoid Edward's retaliation by framing Ithicana. Two birds, one stone."

It made sense. Yet there was something about it that didn't smell right to her. Namely, what possible reason did Ithicana have for murdering James and destroying its relationship with Harendell?

Silence stretched between them, but it felt tense rather than comfortable. Jor didn't want to be here, she knew that. His place was at Aren's side, especially now, and regret pooled in her stomach that she hadn't refused to allow him to come with her.

"We'll need to organize a schedule for watch," she said to break the tension. "Discreet, so they don't take offense. Among the four of us, we should be fine."

Drunken laughter abruptly spilled across the deck, and Ahnna winced as she recognized Taryn's voice.

"Three of us," Jor said. "Two, really, because Bronwyn will have her hands full, so it's just you and me, girlie." He shook his head. "I love Taryn like a daughter, Ahnna, but she was a shitty choice to bring for your guard. If she's not half in the bottle, she's barely able to drag herself out of bed, and while Bronwyn keeps her spirits up, Taryn doesn't see too far beyond her own storm clouds."

"Then it's a good thing I didn't bring her to watch my back."

Jor tossed his toothpick into the waves. "Then why is she here? Other than to make a fool out of Ithicana? Bronwyn's a Veliant, so not only is she not our problem but the Magpie's training will ensure she doesn't say or do anything without thought. But Taryn will pour Prince James's fancy wine down her throat until she's passed out on the deck, all while spewing information that we'd rather the Harendellians not be aware of." He lowered his voice even further. "The *last* thing Ithicana needs is our largest ally finding out just how weak we are. And how badly we need them. Allies can become enemies right quick if there is something as valuable as the bridge to be gained."

Ahnna's stomach tightened, the reminder not something she needed. "Because she's my cousin, and she's not well. I need to take care of her."

"There are other ways. Better ways. Certainly ways that wouldn't put her antics in front of King Eddie's bastard!"

"I need to keep watch over her."

"Why? Because she validates the venom that spews from your lips about Lara?"

Ahnna flinched, it striking her that Jor's jabs hurt as much now as they had when she'd been a girl. More so because he was taking the side of the outsider. "No," she said reluctantly. "It's because Taryn was planning to kill her."

Silence.

"After Aren declared Lara would remain queen, Taryn got drunk. I was dragging her back to her room, and she said that if she'd known Aren would forgive Lara, she'd have killed her on Gamire. I think she's been waiting for the baby to be born before she tries." Her eyes burned. "I know I should've told Aren, all right? But I also know what he would've done. I've lost enough people without losing my cousin."

"Ahnna . . ."

"It's not her fault." She leveled a finger at him. "Did you even bother to ask her what the Maridrinians did to her during the year she was their prisoner? Do you even care how badly they hurt her?" Not waiting for him to answer, she added, "Not only does Taryn have to carry that hurt in her heart, but she also has to carry the guilt of knowing that she was the one who was supposed to be watching over Lara. That she was the one who was duped, which means that she believes what happened is her fault."

"We all had the wool pulled over our eyes."

"Yes, but she thought that Lara and she were close. Friends, even. She trusted her. Liked her." Digging her nails into her palms to feel the pain, Ahnna added, "More than just liked, I think. To discover her relationship with Lara was all lies and manipulation destroyed Taryn worse than what the Maridrinians did, so I can understand why she wants Lara dead. But I'm also not going to allow it to happen, so that's why she's with me. That's why she's on my watch. Because only I, and now you, know the danger."

Jor exhaled a long breath. "I'm too old for this shit. But fine. Fine. We just need to find a way to keep her clear of the courtiers when we arrive."

"I already have a plan for that," Ahnna said. "However, if you'll excuse me, I'm late for dinner."

She crossed the main deck, then climbed the stairs to where the

captain's quarters were located. Above, clouds were thickening.
The brisk wind, smelling of rain, caught at her hair. The storm she
had noted before their departure was rising, but it seemed they'd
skirt up the western edge of it, so she carried onward. The pair of
soldiers flanking the doors bowed at her approach, then one of
them opened the doors, stepping inside to announce at top volume, "Her Royal Highness, Princess Ahnna of Ithicana."

All the men at the table rose to their feet, and she stared awk-
wardly at them until a servant hurried forward to pull out a chair
directly across from James. Taryn and Bronwyn had remained
seated, but Ahnna noted that while Taryn's garments were plain
Ithicanian garb, Bronwyn wore a Maridrinian gown, her brown
hair twisted up into elaborate braids, ruby earrings dangling from
her earlobes, and her face bearing subtle cosmetics. Looking every
bit the princess she was.

For a moment, Ahnna regretted not putting more effort into
her appearance but immediately shoved away the thought. She intended to be forthright and honest to the Harendellians in every
way she could, and that meant portraying herself as she was, not
disguising herself in a costume so that they would believe her
something she was not. Besides, James wore a shirt that was obviously borrowed, the cuffs leaving his wrists bare and the seams
looking ready to burst if he lifted anything heavier than a cup. Not
a prince consumed with vanity but a soldier who wouldn't allow
vanity to interfere with duty.

Approaching the table, she allowed the servant to push the seat
beneath her, none of the men sitting until she was settled.

"We are honored by your presence, Lady Ahnna," James said.
"Allow me to make introductions." He gestured to the portly man
at the far end. "Our captain, Sir John Drake." His hand moved to a
handsome man with long brown hair tied with a ribbon, the med-

als on his uniform gleaming brightly. "Lieutenant George Caven-dish, lord heir to the earldom of Elgin."

The lieutenant gave her a rakish smile. "A pleasure, Your High-ness."

"Ahnna is fine," she replied, because no one in Ithicana ever called her by her title.

"Of course, my lady. Please call me Georgie, everyone does."

"Only if you call me Ahnna."

His smile grew. "It would be my honor, Lady Ahnna."

Titles clearly weren't a battle she was going to win, but the loss was softened by Georgie's wink.

James carried on around the table, introducing the men, who were all high-ranking officers and lords, their coats heavily deco-rated with medals, ribbons, and tassels. Many were names she'd heard mentioned in spy reports, and she focused on each of their faces so as to commit them to memory. Important men with power, wealth, and influence, and she'd be wise to earn their favor.

Finishing his introductions, he said, "Lady Taryn was just regal-ing us with the tribulations of transporting Harendell's cattle through the bridge to be sold at Southwatch."

Lady Taryn hiccuped, then exclaimed, "Remember when Aren cracked three ribs and broke his arm during one of the runs, Ahnna? He's hated cows ever since, though I'm not sure whether it's because he remembers the pain or because he fell face-first into a pile of shit." She hiccuped again, trying to cover the sound by taking another mouthful of wine.

The men all chuckled, and Ahnna bit the inside of her cheeks, confident that the amusement was more for her cousin's drunken-ness than for the anecdote. A servant moved to refill Taryn's glass, but Ahnna reached over to cover the top. "Water."

Taryn gave her a murderous glare. "No one dictates what I

drink, especially you, Ahnna. I'm shocked you're not on your third bottle by now."

In truth, Ahnna had not drunk to excess since the night South-watch had fallen to the Maridrinians and hadn't been able to stom-ach the taste of white wine at all, for it brought back too many memories. Of waking in a half-drunk haze to the sound of alarm bells and screams, the fight upon her the moment she'd opened her bedroom door. The jolt of adrenaline that had come from her face being sliced open was the only reason she was still alive.

"Ahnna used to be fun," Taryn said. "She used to have a sense of humor. Now all she cares about is duty." She hiccuped. "Though perhaps that will help her fit into Harendell, as you're all a stiff lot."

Nothing Taryn said was a lie, but this behavior couldn't stand. "Taryn"—she stared into her cousin's eyes, silently trying to con-vey the importance of the moment—"*please.*"

Her cousin met her gaze for a long time, then her eyes welled with tears. "Apologies. I've had too much to drink." She looked down, unable to hold Ahnna's eyes any longer. "Excuse me."

Rising to her feet, Taryn hurried from the room.

"I'll check on her," Bronwyn said. "Don't wait on me."

The room was silent, and Ahnna stared at the table, uncertain of what to say to remedy the situation. The last thing she wanted to do was reveal Taryn's trauma to strangers, but the alternative was to allow the poor opinion these men likely had of her to stand.

James spared her by saying, "We were discussing the cattle runs, which are, of course, quite relevant to us. Lady Taryn seemed knowledgeable on the subject."

She lifted her gaze to meet his amber eyes, which reflected the candlelight, making them glow. Ahnna's interactions with Cardif-fians were limited, and none had eyes quite the vibrant hue of his. For a heartbeat, she felt transfixed. It was said that those from Cardiff had magic, and looking into James's eyes, she believed it. "Very knowledgeable. Taryn is a respected warrior in Ithicana and served as the king's personal bodyguard for many years, but what she is famous for is her singing voice."

Picking up her glass, she took a small sip. "The cattle are always terrified when we first drive them into the bridge. It's dark and noisy and confined, and they are prone to stampeding, which causes injuries and deaths. We do what we can to keep them calm with animals like goats and donkeys, which are used to the bridge, but I've never seen anything work quite so well as when my cousin sang. Her voice would echo up and down the bridge, and by some trick of the acoustics, it drowned out the howling of the wind. The clatter of hooves. Like magic. The cows followed her through the bridge, mild as milk, arriving at Southwatch without a single injury."

"Walking calmly to slaughter!" Georgie lifted his cup. "To cattle! On whose simple minds Harendell makes its fortune!"

"To cattle." Ahnna lifted her glass. "And to Harendell running even more of them through the bridge in the coming season."

All the other men echoed her words, drinking deeply, but to her surprise, James's brow furrowed, and he did not drink. Setting her glass down, Ahnna asked, "Are you invested in something other than cattle, Your Highness? Steel, perhaps?"

"I'm as invested in cattle as any here," he replied. "However, to increase trade in cattle, steel, and other goods through the bridge risks saturating the market and driving down prices. It may not be in our merchants' best interest to flood the Southwatch market, given the Maridrinians can barely afford to buy the cattle we run through the bridge already. And they've certainly little need for our steel now that the war with Valcotta has ended. Better to sell in other markets."

There was no argument she could give for the steel, but cattle were a different matter. Ithicana's taxes were per head. The more animals the Harendellians ran through the bridge to Southwatch, the more gold went into Aren's coffers. Gold that he could subsequently use to buy cattle to butcher for Ithicanian civilians, and he could buy more cattle if the price was low due to oversupply. But she could hardly admit that the Harendellians' financial losses were a benefit to Ithicana. "The Maridrinians are suffering a famine, and you think of profit?"

James didn't so much as flinch. "Harendell is sympathetic to Maridrina's plight, but we must also protect our own. Tolls to use the bridge are high, but more than that, they are fixed per head, which means that if the price of cattle falls any further, our merchants will lose money selling at Southwatch. It is not Harendell's duty to feed all of Maridrina while they rebuild; that falls upon Valcotta's empress and her consort, for all know the part they played in Vencia's destruction."

Your countrywoman ensured Vencia's destruction, Ahnna thought. She'd heard the tale of Lestara's betrayal of Maridrina before Silas's Cardiffian wife was transported through the bridge, her banishment to Harendell being Keris's punishment for her treason. Except given that research into the royal family had revealed no connection between James and Cardiff beyond blood, Ahnna suspected the jab would not land as intended.

James continued to meet her gaze, and it felt like everyone else in the room disappeared as he stared her down. "Of course," he added, "if Ithicana chooses to buy directly from us and take the loss between markets, it would have our support and admiration."

Every ounce of goodwill and respect that Ahnna had felt for him disappeared in a rush of anger, but she bit down on the retort that he was a money-grubbing Harendellian. "Under the Fifteen-

Year Treaty, Harendell is allied with Maridrina. Don't you think it shortsighted to abandon them during their time of need when tension is clearly rising between Harendell and Amarid?"

James tilted his head, silent for a long moment before he said, "Ithicana could reduce its bridge tolls, which would allow goods to be sold at a reduced rate to the Maridrinians. We could share the burden of supporting our ally during these troubled times."

It was an obnoxiously reasonable solution, and there was no way to counter other than the truth. Only that was not the cause of the unease blooming in her chest. For living memory, Harendell had aggressively exported through the bridge, and those exports accounted for almost half of Ithicana's revenue. Yet the way James spoke suggested that other markets had become available to them. If that were true, then Ahnna's goals of increasing trade might well turn to preventing the loss of it. Her heart rate escalated because Ithicana was depending on her, and it felt like she'd already failed.

Don't jump to conclusions, she told herself even as her instincts whispered that James would be no ally in achieving her goals. That if anything, he was very much her adversary.

"With the utmost respect, Your Highnesses," Georgie said, picking up his glass, "we are going to need to open another few bottles if the conversation topic remains this dull. Tolls and taxes? Treaties and alliances? Doom and gloom? It's not fit conversation for our first night aboard together." Taking a mouthful, he set his glass down on the table.

Only for it to slide sideways as the ship was broadsided by a wave.

The Harendellians all cursed, grabbing their glasses before they toppled, but Ahnna rose to her feet. "Quiet!"

The men fell silent as she listened to the groan of the vessel, feeling the way it rolled over the waves, her heart breaking into a gallop as she marked the storm's shift.

Discarding her glass, she bolted outside as the ship's bells began ringing, nearly colliding with Jor. "The storm shifted," they both said at the same time, and as the captain appeared, she added, "We need to head west."

He didn't even seem to hear her, and Ahnna marked how all those on deck weren't watching the storm to the east but rather staring west.

James brushed past her, stopping next to the second mate, who was frantically gesturing out to sea as he explained something to the captain.

Ahnna squinted, her chest tightening as she spotted the lights of ship lanterns. "Merchant ships trying to outrun the storm?"

James shook his head. "Lookouts have counted three Amaridian naval vessels shadowing us," he said. "But they're not making any move to come closer, so we may make it to the mainland."

"They don't need to come closer," Ahnna said. "That storm is going to push us into them."

The ship's captain heard her words. "It's just a squall!"

Ahnna lifted her gaze to the swirling clouds, bolts of lightning illuminating the blackness, not understanding how they didn't see what she saw. "That's a ship killer if I've ever seen one."

Jor added, "Not because she's more violent but because you won't know her weight until she's swung her first punch. We need to get out of her way."

"If we head west, they'll board us," the captain argued. "Especially if we enter Amaridian waters!"

"The seas are too rough to board," Jor snapped. "If we stay just west of the storm, their fleet won't be able to stay together. We wait until they're blown in different directions and then make a run for it in the dark."

Walking to the railing, Ahnna rested her hands on the polished wood and stared at the distant lights. Every ship captain with a brain between their ears would be flying away from the storm, but these vessels pressed closer.

James had come up next to her as she spoke, and his elbow brushed hers, the conflict that had risen over the dinner table set aside in the face of a mutual adversary.

"Why are they taking these risks?" she demanded. "Why is your death worth so much to them?"

He didn't answer, and knowing it was a question to be asked if they got through this alive, Ahnna shifted her thoughts to how they might escape. Turning to face the captain, she said, "We cut east in front of the storm."

The captain blanched. "Are you mad?"

"Ahnna, there's not enough time," Jor shouted. "The storm is nearly on us."

"Exactly. They're far enough off that if they try to pursue, they'll get caught in it for sure."

"I say we hold the course," the captain said. "Skirt the edge of the storm."

"The storm is pressing southwest." Ahnna held a hand up to the rising wind. "She'll push us straight into Amaridian waters, and when she blows herself out, we won't be able to outrun them. Not on this tug."

"The *Victoria* is the prized jewel of the king's fleet!" The captain's face purpled. "There is nothing like her on the seas."

"Your *Victoria* is slow!" Ahnna jabbed a finger toward the Amaridians, the wind tearing her hair loose from its tie. "Whereas they build for speed. This is our only chance, and we're wasting it on arguments!"

"Ahnna, it's too risky!" Jor shook his head. "You're going to get us all killed."

"If it were Aren standing before you with this plan, you wouldn't hesitate," Ahnna shouted. "Tell me I'm wrong."

His jaw tightened, but it was Taryn's voice that said, "If it were Aren, we'd already be sailing east. But unlike him, Ahnna's *never* led us astray."

Ahnna met her cousin's red-rimmed eyes, and then rounded on James, who was the only one present with the power to over-rule the captain. "I've spent my life on the Tempest Seas. Storms are what I know best."

James was watching her with a strange, distant expression, like he was caught in a memory, but then he nodded. "They say the tempests defend Ithicana, so let us pray they will defend its princess tonight," he said, then shouted at the crew. "Follow her orders! I'll personally toss anyone who argues into the sea, and he can try his luck with the Amaridians!"

Ahnna was already running. "Give her to me!" she shouted at the helmsman, then grabbed the wheel and spun it, the ship rotating east. "I need every sail you have!"

For a heartbeat, no one moved, and then the crew leapt into action.

"They're putting on pursuit," someone shouted.

Good, Ahnna thought, remembering all too well the sight of the Amaridian fleet besieging Eranahl on Silas's orders. *I hope the storm claims every last one of you.*

James joined her at the helm, the rising winds ruffling his hair, his eyes on the flashing lightning to the north.

"We need to keep as close to the front as we dare," she said, straining to hold the wheel in place, the ship already beginning to lean at a deadly angle. "They'll keep farther south on the belief we'll lose our nerve, and they'll be able to run us down when the storm loses power. Which means we can't lose our nerve. Hold the course, then swing around the eastern side of the storm and head north. We should have enough of a head start to get to the mainland before they catch us."

"How close do we dare?"

"Close." She braced her boot against the deck, seeing him do the same. "Everything needs to be tied down, and everyone who doesn't need to be on deck should go below. This will be rough."

No sooner had she spoken the words than the rain began.

Vicious cold droplets stung her cheeks, and Ahnna squinted to protect her eyes, gaze fixed on the churning mass of clouds to her left. The wind was howling now, screaming its fury like an angry beast, the seas writhing beneath the onslaught. The ship rose and fell with violence that increased with every swell, waves washing over the main deck and forcing the sailors to catch hold of whatever they could to keep from being swept overboard.

Ahnna tuned out their shouts, her ears all for the groans of the ship, the rigging straining against the ferocity of the wind. "You're all right," she whispered to the ship. "You can do this."

"Two are moving south and east, but the other is on our tail," a lookout cried, though how he could see much of anything in the growing darkness and driving rain, Ahnna didn't know.

"Ahnna," Jor roared from where he clung to a rail. "Back off! You're going to tear the ship apart!"

She ignored him, her attention all for the wind and the ship, the vessel moaning in agony as it crashed through the towering waves. The *Victoria* might not be fast, but she was *strong*, and she'd outlast the Amaridian ship in this violence.

The main deck disappeared beneath a wave, and Ahnna clenched her teeth when the water cleared and several sailors were gone. *You can't help them,* she told herself. *They are already lost. Save who you can.*

"Get below!" she shouted at James, her arms shuddering from the strain of holding the wheel in place. "It's not safe!"

He ignored her, instead grabbing a rope and looping it around the quarterdeck's railing and then around himself. Lifting the remaining length, he shouted, "Let me tie you to the rail!"

Before she could answer, a wave exploded over the deck.

It smashed into Ahnna, knocking her away from the helm and sending her flying backward.

Her head slammed into the deck, water choking her, the world spinning. Ahnna clawed at the wood, trying to stop her body from rolling, but she couldn't get a breath of air. The ship leveled, and she scrambled to her hands and knees, cursing as she saw the wheel spinning, the ship rotating south. "No!"

Stumbling back to the helm, she caught hold of the wheel. Except given the chance to race away from the storm, the *Victoria* was taking it. "Come on!" Ahnna heaved as hard as she could, but she wasn't strong enough. Couldn't get the leverage on the wet deck.

You've killed them all, her conscience screamed.

Then hands closed over the wheel, a solid chest pressing against her back. "Together!" James shouted. "Heave!"

Hurling all of her strength into the task, Ahnna eased the wheel back to position, inch by painful inch, the *Victoria* groaning in protest. *Please don't break,* she prayed of the rudder. *Please be as strong as I need you to be.*

The ship rotated perpendicular to the storm, the angle of the deck terrifying, only the press of James's body and her grip on the wheel keeping Ahnna from sliding off the side of the ship into the murderous sea. Wave after wave rolled over the ship, choking her with seawater and obscuring her vision, forcing her to rely on sound and feel to guide the vessel.

James didn't fight her when she adjusted course. The strong

muscles of his body strained to keep the ship from fleeing the on-slaught, his ragged breath hot against her temple. Thunder roared overhead, lightning illuminating the whitecapped seas all around them.

Boom!

"The Amaridian ship on our tail was hit!" someone shouted. "It's sinking!"

One down.

Ahnna clenched her teeth, debating whether to hold the course. Her instincts screamed to stand strong, but below, she could see that the crew was floundering with the incessant deluge of rain and sea. With the other ships having sailed farther south, she could chance giving the crew some respite. "We'll ease southeast!" she shouted. "Then tack north when we reach the edge of the storm."

The stubble on James's chin brushed her temple as he nodded, and inch by painful inch, Ahnna eased the wheel around, scream-ing orders to the crew to adjust the sails. Mouths moved as her orders were relayed, sailors struggling across the decks to obey.

Crack!

Ahnna's eyes snapped up to the rigging in time to see a piece of sail go flying into the darkness, lines swinging and pieces of rig-ging falling.

"Get down!" James let go of the wheel to pull on her shoulders, but Ahnna held on, knowing that if she lost control of the ship, it would break apart when she tried to force it back on course.

A line swung toward her, a piece of broken timber twisted around it. Ahnna leaned sideways, feeling it pass her ear—

Right as a wave swamped the deck, taking her feet out from under her.

Ahnna slid down the tilted deck, clawing at the wood for purchase. She screamed as she hit the railing, her body toppling over-board.

Only for her fingers to close around the rail.

Terror flooded her veins as her eyes fixed on the sea below her feet, for if she fell in, there would be no surviving.

"Ahnna!"

James's voice reached over the wind.

"Hold the course!" she screamed. "Hold it!"

Because if he didn't, they'd all be lost.

The ship steadied, groaning as though it felt the pain of the damage the storm had inflicted, but it did not swing farther south.

A wave rolled over the deck, slamming into her, but Ahnna clung fast to the railing. Choking on seawater, she slung a leg over the edge, hooking her booted ankle against the wood even as she was struck again and again.

She was desperate for air, but the sea gave her no respite, seem-ingly intent on drowning everyone aboard if it could not sink them.

Hold on! she silently screamed. *Get over the rail!*

As she tried to pull herself over, the ship jerked, and her ankle slipped. Another shriek tore from her lips as she fell, dangling from one hand, the waves kissing the bottoms of her boots. Beg-ging her to let go and allow the Tempest Seas to claim her.

Not yet, she told the sea even as her fingers slipped. *I'm not ready.*

A callused hand closed around her wrist.

"I got you," Jor shouted. "Pull!"

Ahnna heaved, toppling over the railing to land in a heap. Coughing, she fought to get air in her lungs as another wave struck.

But the storm's ferocity was easing.

As she blinked salt from her eyes, it was to find James still at the helm, Taryn guiding him on the course.

Toward a horizon that gleamed with stars.

"We're through the worst of it," Jor said. "North, Taryn, north!"

Her cousin nodded, gesturing as she explained to James how to tack against the stiff wind, shouting orders to the crew as she did. Jor rose to his feet, and then leaned over the rail to look back in their wake. "Not a glimmer of light," he said. "I'm sure the pricks are out there, but they won't be catching us this time."

Ahnna finally managed a breath that filled her lungs, and she nodded. "Good. As soon as the wind eases, we need to get men in the rigging to see about repairs. I can't tell what was broken in the dark."

Jor knelt before her. "I'm sorry, Ahnna. I should have trusted you."

All her life, she'd sought validation from Jor. For him to care for her the same way he did Aren—like a father, for her own had had little time for her. Yet now that she was faced with it, all Ahnna felt was a wave of discomfort, and she looked away. "It could have gone either way."

Climbing to her feet, she hissed as pain knifed through her body and pressed a hand to her ribs.

"You all right?"

"Yes." Mastering the pain so it wouldn't show on her face, she crossed the deck where James was handing off the ship to one of the crew. "Keep heading north," she said to the man. "No lights. With luck, we should be in sight of the mainland by morning."

Then she started walking away.

"Your Highness," James called out, but she pretended not to hear him because her composure was cracking, and she didn't want him to see.

"Ahnna!"

She kept walking.

Only for his hand to close on her arm, pulling her to a stop. "I'm sorry," he said, face lost to shadows as the lights were extinguished. "Going to your aid meant abandoning the helm, and—"

"It was the right choice," she interrupted, pain and nausea twisting in her core. "Risking the lives of everyone aboard this ship for the sake of mine would have been a fool's move."

"Your life is worth more."

"It's not." Ahnna hated that sentiment. Hated the idea that a title and a name made her life worth more than anyone else's. "Though apparently yours is, and I'd like to understand why Katarina was willing to lose so many men to see you dead. And why she wanted to pin it on Ithicana."

James let go of her arm like he'd been burned. "I don't know why they are doing this."

"Figure it out. Or more people are likely to die."

Ahnna walked away from him, picking her way through the tangled lines and broken pieces of wood, hardly able to see anything in the darkness. Someone lifted the hatch to allow her to go below, and Ahnna clenched her teeth in pain with each step down, pressing one hand against the wall as she walked the corridor in the darkness until she found the door that belonged to her room.

It was dark inside, and wet, the porthole glass having been smashed in the storm. Feeling around in the dark, she found her chest overturned but sealed tightly. With a grunt of effort, Ahnna righted it, then replaced the soaked mattress on the frame, her ribs screaming.

Climbing onto the bed, she rested her cheek against the sodden fabric. Each breath sent spikes of pain through her as she stared blankly, afraid to close her eyes. Afraid to invite in the parade of the dead who haunted her, who she knew would be joined by those who'd died today at Northwatch. Those who'd drowned tonight in the storm. However, with only the blackness of night before her, the visions didn't wait for sleep before they came.

Grabbing a fistful of the blanket, Ahnna shoved it into her mouth, and then she screamed.

Screamed until exhaustion took her, and then, in her dreams, she screamed louder still as she knelt before those who'd died because she'd lowered her guard. Those who'd suffered because she'd ignored her instincts. Those who would still live if only she'd *just kept watch.*

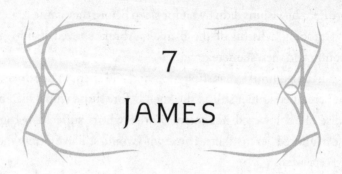

7
JAMES

JAMES STARED BLEARY-EYED AT THE CHIP IN HIS TEACUP, ONE OF
the few pieces not to have smashed during the storm. Beneath the
last drops of reddish-brown liquid, the leaves stirred, and he
looked away to avoid reading the signs. Too late, for his eyes had
already picked out the pattern.

Strife.

As if he didn't know that.

He tossed the dregs overboard, and not for the first time,
James regretted learning the customs of the Cardiffian side of
his family. His mother's family. When he was a boy, his father
had sent him in secret to live for weeks on end with his mother's
brothers, Ronan and Cormac. His uncle Cormac had taught him
to see the stories of his ancestors in the stars. To read the future
in leaves in a cup. To believe God an amusing fabrication of
southerners.

It was the last that formed the wedge between Cardiff and Harendell, the wedge between his father's people and his mother's.

For while Cardiff cared little for whom or what Harendell chose to worship, the opposite was not the case, and Harendell had tried to force religion on Cardiff's people countless times.

It always ended in violence. War.

Strife.

Which is why James had proposed to both his father and his uncle a different way of achieving peace: appealing to something that both nations worshiped in equal measure.

Wealth.

And they'd been well on their way to achieving it until the message had arrived from Ithicana requesting fulfillment of the terms of the Fifteen-Year Treaty. Now everything that James had fought to achieve was at risk of falling apart.

James stared into the waves, but instead of seeing the whitecaps, all he saw was Ahnna suspended in the water, hand reaching out to the shark. He silently cursed his father for not breaking off William's engagement to her. *Our relationship with Ithicana is old and secure, whereas our relationship with Cardiff is new and delicate,* his father's voice repeated in his thoughts. *I won't risk jeopardizing one for the sake of the other. Not when we can have both.*

Both seemed less and less a possibility after having spoken to Ahnna, for there was no doubt in James's mind that she intended to capitalize on her position to keep trade flowing south through the bridge, the religion of wealth as much shared by Ithicana as by Harendell and Cardiff.

"Fuck," he muttered, scowling at the surf.

"My thoughts exactly," Georgie said from behind him. "I just spoke with our dear Captain Drake."

James glanced to the quarterdeck where the man in question stood. Drake had hidden below while Ahnna and the crew had sailed the *Victoria* through the storm.

"The captain wishes to make port in Sableton and avail himself of the shipyards there rather than pressing on in a damaged ship to make port in Elmsworth." Georgie rested his elbows on the rail and looked out at the coastline. "Seems he doesn't have the nerve for Ithicanian sailing."

"Do any of us?"

"That we do not, my friend. Once in a lifetime was enough for me. I was murderously seasick but too terrified to vomit. Misery, I tell you. Misery of the purest form."

"Could've been worse."

"Debatable. A good melee with the Amaridians would have been far more honorable than clinging for dear life to my wash-stand, which was the only thing in the room bolted down. On that note, we're taking inventory, but many of our supplies were ruined with seawater, so expect lean pickings until we make port."

"Perhaps not entirely lean." James jerked his chin to the old Ithicanian man who'd accompanied Ahnna. Jor was currently leaning against the rail of the ship with a rod, a bucket containing three large fish next to his feet.

"Good God, they are feral, aren't they?" Georgie muttered. "I swear if we cast the lot of them into the sea, they'd harness a whale to ride to shore ahead of us."

James snorted softly, then sipped at the fresh cup of tea one of the servants had poured. "I think *pragmatic* is the word. Ithicana is harsh, and I suspect those who sit on their asses fare poorly."

"Ithicana is as rich as sin, Jamie. The biggest market makers in the known world. They don't need to live wild. They choose to. They aren't like us. *She* isn't like us."

There was no denying that, yet James said, "Show some respect for the woman who saved your neck."

Rather than being even remotely chastised, Georgie eyed him with interest. "Firstly, my good man, you always seem to think I speak my own views when in fact I speak the views of those whose opinions actually matter. Secondly, what do said views on the princess matter to you? You're not the one who has to marry her."

"Courtesy." James scowled. "What sort of gentleman can I claim to be if I allow slanderous words to be spoken of the princess who is not only in my care but who has saved my life? Twice."

"Three times," Georgie corrected with a smile. "Since you're keeping count."

Three times. Whereas he had stayed at the wheel when she'd nearly gone overboard, leaving Ahnna to save herself. Shame burned in James's stomach, and he reverted his gaze to his cup. That it had been the right move was not in question, and Ahnna herself had absolved him, but he was still haunted by his lack of action while she dangled over the seas, fighting for her life.

"While I know you ape at being a gentleman better than most," Georgie said with a chuckle, "we both know you've little claim to the word. And you've not historically put on the pretense around me. You're a soldier, first, and a courtier only under duress, so don't think to fool me with talk of *courtesy*." His friend then slapped his thigh sharply and exclaimed, "Don't tell me you admire her?"

"Certainly not." James handed off his teacup to a passing servant lest he look at the dregs again, feeling his cheeks heat with embarrassment. "However, I do respect her, soldier-to-soldier."

He chafed under Georgie's scrutiny, but his friend only shrugged. "That I believe, though I am disappointed. It would've been amusing for you to be the one involved in a scandal for once."

"I was born a scandal," James replied sourly. "No need to make things worse."

"You know I feel differently, but I've reconciled that particular matter to be a point of contention within our friendship," Georgie said. "What's more, the lady in question approaches, so time for you to ape the gentleman once more."

Several appropriate retorts rose to James's lips, but he didn't have time to deploy them before Ahnna was in earshot. She was moving stiffly, to which, given that every part of him ached from the strain of holding the wheel against the storm, James was sympathetic. "Good morning, Lady Ahnna." He inclined his head, and out of the corner of his eye, he saw Georgie bow low, murmuring, "Your Highness."

"Good morning, my lords." She accepted a cup of steaming tea, balancing the saucer with ease despite the motion of the ship. "No sign of the Amaridians?"

"They'd not dare sail so close to Harendell's coastline, my lady," Georgie said.

"I think we may need to reconsider our opinions of what they will and will not do." Ahnna pushed her long hair, which was woven into a thick braid, back over her shoulder. Her hands were marked with scrapes and scabs, her cheek with a purple bruise— further injuries to add to the old scars already marking her body. "Have you put more thought as to why Queen Katarina is willing to risk so much to see you dead? Or why she believes she can pin your death on my brother?"

"To start a war between Ithicana and Harendell," he said reflexively. "If my father believed Ithicana's king had me killed, he'd come for blood. Which would mean pulling resources from the Lowlands, which would allow Amarid the opportunity to attempt to reclaim them. We've been warring with them over that territory for decades, so the chance to win it back is well worth the cost of a few ships."

"Except what possible reason could Ithicana have for killing you?" she demanded. "Not to hurt your feelings, Your Highness, but you're rarely more than a footnote in our spies' reports because your role has always been focused on said conflict in the Lowlands, which is no concern of ours. We gain absolutely nothing from killing you, but we'd lose our most powerful ally in the north. It doesn't make sense, and Queen Katarina would know such a ruse wouldn't work on your father because there is no logical reason for Ithicana to want to harm you."

Except that there was, but only if James's ambitions were not as secret as he'd believed.

James's heart lurched. If Ithicana learned that he was attempting to divert trade from the bridge to Cardiff, they would have grounds to want him dead. If Amarid intended to use that as grounds to frame Ithicana, it meant that Katarina knew about his role as mediator between his father and his uncle, and that . . . that was impossible. No one knew.

No one.

Ahnna's eyes narrowed, and though he'd not allowed anything to show on his face, James knew his silence had spoken volumes. "What aren't you saying?" she asked.

Georgie coughed. "It's a delicate matter, my lady. Not fit for your ears."

Ahnna's brow furrowed in annoyance even as James looked to his friend in confusion, because he had no idea what Georgie was talking about.

"I'm a soldier, my lord," Ahnna snapped. "I do not put much weight on propriety when lives are at stake."

"Of course." George gave a soft cough. "It concerns a recent fight that took place between His Highness and the Beast of Amarid. Prince Carlo Serrano."

Oh, bloody hell.

"I know who the Beast is," Ahnna said. "What happened?"

"A border skirmish." James glared at Georgie. "Not justification for any of this."

"Jamie, with respect, the man lost half of his capacity to father children because of your well-placed boot. I doubt there is anyone the Beast hates more than *you.*"

"You kicked the Beast of Amarid in the balls?" Ahnna demanded. "And he lost a testicle?"

"This is not fit conversation," James growled even as Georgie said, "That's the sum of it. I was there, so I'm happy to reenact the fight if someone wishes to volunteer to play the Beast."

Ahnna's face filled with incredulity. "You think Katarina sent three ships and hundreds of men to kill you for revenge over her son's testicle?"

Why did she insist on using that word? "No, I don't—" James broke off, because while he didn't believe that was the motivation, it was better than Ahnna digging deeper down a hole he wanted left unexplored. "Who can say? The Amaridians are proud people."

"Yes, they are," she replied, but James could see she was not convinced. "Which is why I'm surprised Carlo didn't demand to have personal vengeance over his lost testicle."

James squeezed the bridge of his nose, desperate to be away from this conversation even as Georgie declared, "Because he's now possessed of only half his courage!"

Ahnna's lips parted, but she was cut off by a shout from overhead, "Sableton on the horizon!" and instead looked toward the sea.

Within moments, the haze that was Harendell's coastline appeared, and James heard Ahnna's breath catch.

"I've seen it on maps," she said. "But I'm not sure I ever appreciated how large it was until this moment. I've never traveled farther north than Emesmere Island, where I met with your father."

They'd passed Emesmere just before dawn, the island being the southernmost landmass controlled by Harendell, most often used as a harbor of last resort, for there was nothing there but rock. Ahnna's meeting with his father had been brief, and she'd worn a mask the entire time, which had delighted his father to no end. "You've never been to the continent?"

"I've never left Ithicana," she answered. "Never needed to. Never wanted to."

What changed? James wondered, because it had been Ithicana who'd abruptly pushed for a wedding date to be set. Ahnna had been of marriageable age for over a decade, yet Ithicana had seemed content to keep her. Why now?

The port city of Sableton grew, smoke rising from countless chimneys, the piers bustling with ships beyond counting. Yet even from here, James felt the shift from the wilds of Ithicana and the Tempest Seas to the pretense of civility that reigned over his homeland. And next to him, gooseflesh rose on Ahnna's arm as though she felt it, too.

"How long will it take to journey to Verwyrd?"

"Two days by coach," he answered, watching how the wind caught at the tendrils of hair that had come loose from her braid. "Longer if it rains and the highway turns to muck."

"Is the Sky Palace as tall as they say?" There was a wistfulness in her voice that he'd not heard before, and he wondered if that was how she'd sounded before Silas and his daughter had brought war to Ithicana. When, according to Taryn, Ahnna had lost her humor.

"Touches the clouds," James said.

The corner of her mouth turned up. "Of all the places in Harendell that I've read about, the Sky Palace of Verwyrd is the place I've desired to see the most."

It was the first genuine smile he'd seen touch her face, and it had been elicited by the place that he hated most. The place of his birth. The place of his mother's murder. Home to the Twisted Throne and to the people of equally twisted morals who fought for a piece of it. A place that would devour a woman like Ahnna Kertell. Yet all James said was, "Welcome to Harendell."

8
AHNNA

SABLETON WAS THE LARGEST PORT CITY IN HARENDELL AND, much like Vencia, was the nexus for merchants intending to ship their goods through the bridge. The air smelled of fish and tar, the docks bustling with sailors and workers loading and unloading vessels of every size and shape, crates of goods moving to and from the vast warehouses lining the wharf. The large shipyard boasted several vessels in different stages of completion, and as the wind blew over her, Ahnna inhaled the scent of cattle from the lots beyond.

She had never seen anything like it.

Resting her elbows on the rail, she eyed a pair of Amaridian merchant vessels that sailed past. For all they spat and snarled at each other, the two nations conducted an impressive amount of trade with each other, much as Valcotta and Maridrina had always traded despite being continually at war. Yet as James joined her at the rail, she turned to him and said, "Will Harendellian ports start refusing Amaridian vessels after this attack?"

"No."

His hands gripped the rail, and her eyes were drawn to them. Large, with long fingers marked with fresh scrapes from the fights, but also a multitude of old scars. Strong hands. Unbidden, the memory of him gripping her thighs as he lifted her filled her mind's eye. Ahnna forced her gaze back to Sableton. "Then why make demands that Ithicana do so?"

"I am in no position to make demands of Ithicana," he said. "It was a suggestion."

A *strongly worded suggestion,* she thought, but only said, "Seems hypocritical. It might have happened on Ithicana's shores, but it was Harendell they attacked. Trade sanctions from Harendell seem more appropriate."

"Such a decision would come at great cost to Harendell's merchants and is not to be made lightly."

"Yet you'd have Ithicana make similarly costly decisions before the blood on Northwatch pier had even dried."

He exhaled a slow breath, then turned his head to look at her, sun reflecting in the amber of his eyes. "As pertains to trade with Amarid, my opinions matter little and yours, arguably, even less. This is a speculative conversation with no tangible worth, given that neither of us has the ability to influence the trade policies between Amarid and Harendell. Silence is preferable to a fruitless argument."

He wasn't wrong, but irritation flared in Ahnna's veins, and she said, "If you spoke out of turn or above your station, then just say so, Your Highness. As a courtesy, I'll allow you to retract the statement."

"I retract nothing." His eyes narrowed. "The Amaridian merchants haven't dared to bring violence to our ports, but they dared to bring it to Ithicana's. Which suggests that they are of the opinion that they can get away with it. It behooves Ithicana to remedy that opinion lest Amarid begin to question what else they can get away with in Ithicana's waters. But again, my opinion is of no relevance." He turned his glower on the port. "This conversation is over."

Ahnna scoffed. "Are you seriously ordering me to be silent?"

"I'd never be so presumptuous as to order you to do anything," he retorted. "But I am most certainly suggesting it."

The captain and Georgie chose that moment to join them, and Ahnna stewed in silence as the port master quickly made room for the *Victoria*'s impressive bulk, dockworkers tying off the vessel and pushing the most ornate gangplank she'd ever seen in place next to it. With its polished wooden rails and gilt, she felt almost compelled to remove her boots lest she soil the crimson carpet. On the dock waited several dozen uniformed soldiers standing in neat rows, and as James offered his arm to her, six of the soldiers lifted trumpets and blew a series of notes.

All around, the bustle paused, and Ahnna's skin crawled as she felt the scrutiny of hundreds of eyes. Though she was still irritated by his comments, Ahnna took James's arm, and her fingers tightened reflexively at how exposed they were. All it would take was an Amaridian in the crowd skilled with a bow, and they were both dead.

"This is an unexpected arrival, and few will suspect your identity, much less be prepared for it," he said softly. "We'd intended to make port at Elmsworth and take a riverboat to Verwyrd, so that is where any potential attack would have been planned."

"They'll recognize you," she said between her teeth. "Or at least that cursed purple banner flying from the mast. It's your life that hangs in the balance, Your Highness."

"The local garrison is prepared."

"You just said they weren't prepared!"

"Prepared for proper ceremony," he hissed, pulling on her arm. "Now walk. The longer you stand there, the longer you invite an assassin to take advantage of the opportunity our position gives."

Ahnna bit down on a curse of irritation and allowed him to lead her down the gangplank, her eyes taking in everything as she hunted for threats, though the soldiers kept sailors and civilians well back.

If this was a *lack* of preparation, Ahnna couldn't help but wonder what had been intended in Elmsworth. The soldiers formed ranks around their small group, marching in lockstep to the beat of the drummer at the fore. More soldiers waited at the end of a dock, as did a carriage decorated in gilt pulled by a team of six black horses, their trappings plated in polished silver, purple feathers fastened above their ears.

The coachman opened the door, James taking Ahnna's hand to help her inside. She sat on the velvet-cushioned bench as Bronwyn and Taryn climbed in, sitting across from her, which necessitated James sitting next to her. As he did, the shoulder seam on his borrowed shirt split, and he exhaled an aggrieved breath.

"Perhaps we ought to take the time to commission you a new wardrobe before we travel," Ahnna said. "At the rate you ruin clothing, you'll be naked by the halfway point."

"We'll have time aplenty, given your own wardrobe needs to be remedied," he muttered. "You look as though you stumbled out of the jungle."

"He's not wrong," Bronwyn said. "And I have to admit, that awful grayish green you Ithicanians insist on wearing is not your best color."

Ahnna shot her friend a glare. "My choice of attire has proven to be good foresight on my part, given that we keep being at-

tacked. I'd be dead thrice over if I was wearing a gown and corset."

"A valid point." Bronwyn rested a boot on her own trousered
knee. "It's much harder to fight in skirts."

The carriage began to move, rocking from side to side as the
horses increased their pace, causing Ahnna's body to press up
against James's. Having spent her life in the tight quarters of Ithicana's small vessels, she was used to contact, but Ahnna found
herself intimately aware of the heat of him. Of each part of her
body that was touching him.

"There will be no more attacks, no more fighting," James said,
shifting restlessly. "You will be under guard at all times until we
reach Verwyrd, so your attire should befit a lady, not a soldier."

Ahnna gave a soft snort. "If there is anyone who should be
under guard at all times, it is you. You're the one the Amaridians
are trying to kill. With a proper bodyguard, you won't have to
worry about ruining any more of your princely clothes."

He cast his eyes skyward. "I can take care of myself."

"Given the number of times I've had to save your life, I beg to dif-
fer," Ahnna countered. "Indeed, I think it prudent that I continue
to attire myself in such a way that I'll be able to provide you with
the protection you clearly need."

Bronwyn and Taryn were both smirking, and it struck Ahnna
that this was the first time since before the war that she'd seen her
cousin both sober and happy. It made baiting James, which was
probably not a wise choice, seem very much worthwhile.

"You are insufferable." He glared out the window, seeming to
be trying to compress his broad shoulders to create more space
between them. "Do as you will. But don't come weeping to me
when you stumble into the consequences of your lack of deco-
rum."

"Oh, you have my word on that." Ahnna rested her elbow against the side of the carriage, admiring the buildings they passed as they bounced over the cobbles. She wanted to get out and walk so that she might better see the purpose of all these structures, which did not seem to be homes. Inns, perhaps? Or taverns? Seeing a pair of women with dresses cut so low that their breasts almost spilled out, she suspected more than a few were brothels. Ahnna was struck with the sudden urge to see inside one, for Ithicana had no such establishments, prostitution being illegal.

"What is going on in those buildings?" Bronwyn asked, pointing to large structures from which emanated smoke and steam.

"Foundries," James answered curtly. "Several of the commercial foundries, Cartwright being the largest, built up production in Sableton after Ithicana began allowing the shipment of weapons through the bridge to be purchased by the Maridrinians. The market has collapsed, for obvious reasons, so they converted much of production to farm equipment. Hammers, spades, horseshoes, and the like. Less profitable."

"But much more peaceful," Ahnna said, not forgetting how Silas had cleverly used Harendellian weapons in his invasion. "I've never had anyone attack me with a horseshoe."

"Indeed," James said, scowling out the window.

They passed into a large square lined with market stalls overflowing with food and goods, the plenty that Harendell enjoyed on display. At the center of the square was a large statue of King Edward, whom she recognized easily from her brief meeting with him. Though the piece was from his younger years, he was not much changed, and Ahnna was struck by how much James resembled his father, the only notable trait that he'd received from his mother being his amber eyes.

She knew as much as anyone about the indiscretion that had

led to James's birth, which was to say not much at all. His mother had been a servant of Cardiffian heritage, and Edward had had an affair with her while betrothed to Alexandra. Had kept up the affair even *after* he was wed, even when Alexandra herself fell pregnant with William, for apparently, he'd been deeply in love with his mistress. The affair only ended when James's mother was murdered, and it was said that she'd cursed her murderer with her dying breath. The infamous words, *My son's fate will be revenge upon her.* The speculation was that Alexandra was the *her* in question. While that made a certain amount of sense, it had always struck Ahnna as odd that if the rumor were true, Edward hadn't hanged Alexandra for killing the woman he loved. For it meant that he either knew a different truth or had spent the last twenty-six years with a woman he loathed.

She risked a sideways glance at James, who was staring broodily out the window. He undoubtedly knew the truth, but there were limits to how far she'd push him, and asking him whether the queen murdered his mother was far outside those boundaries. The spies said that Alexandra hated him, but they made no mention of whether the feeling was mutual. Yet the thought drew to the forefront of her mind the conversation she'd had with Keris just before he set sail to Devil's Island, his voice filling her head. *Alexandra is Harendellian to her core. She'll kiss both your cheeks and pour you a cup of tea, then smile prettily with her ankles crossed as you choke to death on the poison she put in your cup. She'll then blame Amaridian assassins so that your brother doesn't come sailing in to avenge your death.*

Words that now felt prophetic, and goosebumps rose on Ahnna's skin despite the heat of the day. Had Alexandra thought to kill two birds with one stone, then frame Ithicana for throwing the rock? Perhaps those hadn't been Amaridian soldiers but privateers hired by Harendell's queen?

No, she decided, shoving away the thought. Alexandra was a threat, but hers was a poison-in-the-cup variety, not coordinated military strikes. Katarina avenging her son's balls was more believable than that.

"Fernleigh House," James abruptly said, and Ahnna jerked from her thoughts to notice they were passing through a gate in a high stone wall. They headed up the lane, to either side of which was a short-clipped lawn with no discernible purpose. The lane curved around a large statue, and Ahnna caught a glimpse of the manor house itself. Constructed of a honey-colored stone, it was perfectly symmetrical, with a grand portico supported by twin columns. A row of men and women waited on the steps, large doors flung open behind them.

The other carriages transporting their party pulled up next, and Ahnna heard Jor's distinct laugh, along with Georgie's voice. The coachman opened the door, and James stepped down, holding out his hand to her. Ignoring it, Ahnna stepped onto the gravel, inhaling air that smelled of roses as she took in Fernleigh. Ivy climbed the sides of the large manor, birds flitting among the leaves.

"It is my pleasure to introduce Her Most Royal Highness, Princess Ahnna of Ithicana, as well as her companions, Princess Bronwyn of Maridrina and Lady Taryn of Ithicana," James said, then rattled off the names of the staff members standing on the steps. "If you'll excuse me, I have matters to attend to. Georgie, with me."

Then he disappeared inside.

As Georgie followed, he said, "Fernleigh has a lovely orangery. I suggest you take your tea there today."

"A wonderful suggestion, my lord," the older woman James had identified as the head housekeeper said, eyes jumping between Ahnna and her friends. "We will have baths drawn so that the ladies might wash and dress for tea while the orangery is prepared. We were not expecting noble visitors, so please forgive our disarray."

"I don't think she likes your clothes either," Bronwyn said under her breath. "You sure trousers are a hill you wish to die on, Ahnna?"

"Yes," Ahnna growled, then smiled at the woman who was looking down her nose at Ahnna's attire despite being a full head shorter. "A bath would be lovely. I thank you for your gracious hospitality."

They were led inside, the large entrance hall illuminated by a chandelier, the crystal sending a rainbow of color dancing across the marble tile of the floor. A circular table sat at the center, holding a large vase of white roses. The grand staircase rose and then split into two directions, an oil portrait of King Edward on a rearing horse gracing the wall at the top of the landing. Ahnna struggled not to smirk at the thought of her brother decorating Eranahl with a giant oil painting of himself captaining a ship.

They were brought into the west wing, the hallways covered with more portraits of past monarchs, their unsmiling faces watching Ahnna as she walked, the feeling more than a little oppressive.

"Your rooms, my lady." The housekeeper opened a door, revealing a large room decorated with birchwood furniture and damask upholstery. The open window had a view of the rear of the property, which was dominated by a hedge cut into what looked like a maze. Ahnna walked to the window and took in the scope of the grounds, which were surrounded by the city. So much space, and until they'd arrived, it had held only the serving staff, while the rest of the city's populace was crammed into small stone houses with barely enough room to breathe.

A footman came in bearing her trunk, and as he departed,

Hazel said, "By your leave, my lady, I would make arrangements for you to see one of the city's modistes for a dress suitable for dinner tonight." She coughed delicately. "They often have gowns that were never paid for, and I can alter it to fit you as well as anything made for your measurements."

"Thank you, but I've no need of dresses."

Hazel's jaw tightened, and she smoothed her already impeccably tidy hair. "My lady, I'd ask you to reconsider. There are expectations for a lady's appearance, especially once you join the king's court."

"Then I'll cross that bridge when we reach Verwyrd." Ahnna gestured to the door. "However, I would like a bath before tea."

Hazel bobbed a curtsy. "Yes, my lady."

Once she was gone, Ahnna rounded on her friends. "In my discussion with James about trade—"

"That was an argument," Bronwyn interrupted. "You two seem incapable of discussions."

Ahnna's cheeks warmed. "In our *argument*, he implied an alternative market for trade that doesn't require using the bridge. I want you two to see what you can learn about new markets or expanding markets, because our spies haven't reported anything of the sort. We need their business, so if we have competition, Aren needs to know. Be discreet, and have Jor do some digging with the footmen."

"We're supposed to be watching your back, not spying," Taryn said. "I know that it seems as though all these attacks were directed at James, but that doesn't mean that there aren't people who want you dead. Even when he assumed disguises, Aren always kept his guards close when he traveled onto the continents. There are a thousand threats in this kingdom, Ahnna, and while I know you can hold your own, you also have no experience outside of Ithicana. No amount of research, no amount of reading spy reports, is really going to prepare you."

"There are soldiers guarding Fernleigh," Ahnna said. "I'll be fine."

Taryn shrugged. "I'll go find Jor and then see what I can learn in the kitchen."

"You've been betrothed to William for . . . what? Around eighteen years?" Bronwyn asked, watching the door close behind Taryn. "Didn't it occur to you to get the lay of the land by visiting before you arrived to marry the crown prince?"

It had, but Ahnna had convinced herself that she didn't have to. That Aren wouldn't go through with marrying a Maridrinian princess and that she'd be released from her own obligations as a result. When that hadn't manifested, she'd been busy with Southwatch. Then busy fighting for her life.

And because you didn't want to, her heart whispered. *A choice for which you will now bear the consequences.*

When Ahnna didn't answer, Bronwyn said, "You're not that much taller than me that Hazel can't let out the hem of one of my dresses for you to wear."

Part of her bristled, tired of the reminder that nothing about her was good enough, but Ahnna only shook her head. "Your gowns are Maridrinian, Bron. Friends as we are, I'd rather go to tea naked than wear a dress from a Veliant court. I want the Harendellians to see me as I am. To never forget the nation I represent, and that means dressing like an Ithicanian. If they take offense to that, it's on them."

Silence stretched.

"I know how you feel about my sister," Bronwyn finally said. "Except keep in mind that Lara also came to Ithicana with the goal of helping her people. And I'd bet my last coin that Lara used far more cream than vinegar to get everyone to trust her. To do what she wanted. You might consider learning from her example."

Anger bloomed in Ahnna's chest. "I am not Lara. I am nothing like her. And I refuse to stoop to her level to achieve my goals."

Bronwyn opened her mouth as though to say something, then looked away. "I respect your desire to be honest and forthright, Ahnna. I truly do. But I can't help but think that you care more about doing everything differently from Lara than you do about succeeding in your goals. The Harendellians won't respect you if you walk in wearing the same clothes you do to hike through the jungle. They'll think you're a joke. They'll smile to your face and laugh while your back is turned. Play the fucking game, Ahnna, or you're going to lose."

Not giving her a chance to respond, Bronwyn departed, slamming the door behind her.

Play the game play the game play the game.

Ahnna rested her head in her hands, skull throbbing as the words repeated. It wasn't that she didn't understand the need to play politics, it was that she wanted to do it on her terms. In a way that she could feel proud of.

Except was that only another way of putting herself first?

Opening her chest, Ahnna surveyed her clothes. All drab colors, leather and cotton and linen suitable for trekking through the jungle. New and clean but nothing like the gowns the Harendellians wore. Imagined laughter echoed through the room.

They'll think you're a joke.

Lurching to her feet, Ahnna started to the door, intent on taking Bronwyn up on her offer. Except as her fingers rested on the handle, she paused, memory filling her mind's eye. Lara, dressed in Ithicanian garb, perfectly mimicking Ahnna's people. Their delighted voices filled her ears, telling her about their admiration for how Lara had adapted. How she'd abandoned her Maridrinian ways. How she was the true queen of Ithicana. All of it fading to screams and hollow eyes as they realized they'd been deceived. That it had been an act. That the queen they'd fallen so hopelessly in love with was responsible for the dead children they held in their arms.

"I will not be her," Ahnna hissed.

She paced the room, bending her mind to a solution. Valcottan women wore trousers—Zarrah herself wore them exclusively, and she was the empress. No one laughed at her. Ahnna drew into her mind an image of what the Valcottans wore, the lush silks and decorative embroidery, and when Hazel entered, she said, "I am hoping for a compromise."

The young maid nodded slowly as Ahnna explained, then said, "I will arrange for the purchase of fabrics, my lady."

As she departed, Ahnna went to the window and looked out over the gardens. She'd do what it took to earn the Harendellians' respect, but she would never, ever let them forget she was Ithicanian.

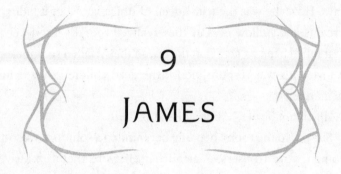

9

JAMES

"Your Highness!" the butler exclaimed as he pursued James and Georgie through the manor. "What has happened? Your attire!"

"At the bottom of the Tempest Seas, my good man," Georgie announced. "We lost the *Defiant* to Amaridian treachery. James has been forced to borrow from those under his command, which has resulted in several split seams."

His friend poked at his ripped shirt. "What *was* going on in that carriage, Jamie?"

"Nothing of note." Other than Ahnna being the most infuriating woman he'd ever met.

Entering his father's study, James went to the desk and drew writing supplies in front of him. He swiftly drafted a letter to his father explaining what had occurred, folded and sealed it, then handed it to Georgie. "I need you to ride to Verwyrd with all haste. Explain everything. Amarid is up to something, and unless the spies have discovered information in our absence, we are not prepared."

Georgie sighed. "You're making *me* deliver the news that we sank the queen's ship?"

"Better you than me."

"I can't argue that." Georgie tucked the letter inside his coat, then rounded on the butler. "Supplies and the best horse you have. And after that, please do track down something suitable for His Highness to wear."

"Yes, my lord." The butler turned on his heel and strode out.

"When will you leave?" Georgie asked as James began writing another letter, this one to the Ithicanians, namely, Queen Lara. "Hazel mentioned a visit to the modiste?"

"You'd have better luck stuffing me in a dress than you would Ahnna Kertell," James muttered. "We'll leave tomorrow."

"Why the hurry?"

"Because I do not care to belabor this particular responsibility." When Georgie didn't respond, he added, "I have other matters requiring my attention. We're behind schedule."

"Behind schedule," his friend murmured. "Well, that certainly will not do."

His friend's tone suggested something other than agreement, and James set down his pen. "What are you trying to imply?"

"Only that all involved might be happier if you took your time." Georgie walked backward toward the door. "Safe travels, Jamie. I'll look for you at Verwyrd."

"Safe travels."

James turned his focus to finishing the letter to Lara, setting it aside to be put on the next ship to Northwatch. The rest of his officers had been given instructions prior to disembarking the *Victoria,* and they'd be on their way to ensuring that Harendell was well positioned should Amarid attempt to make a move.

"Sir, a letter has arrived for you." The butler crossed the room, setting a silver tray with a folded note on the desk. There was a small drawing of a foxglove flower on the corner, and his stomach clenched. *How? How does he know I'm here?*

There were times when James truly believed that his uncle could see the future, though logically, he knew that it was because his uncle Ronan had spies everywhere.

"Sir?"

James realized the butler had asked him a question. "Pardon?"

"Lady Ahnna will take tea in the orangery today. Do you intend to join her, my lord?"

James stared at the tiny flower, knowing that his uncle would be asking him to account for Ahnna's presence. To explain why the betrothal had not been canceled. Why James had not dealt with the situation as he'd promised. Overtures of peace between Harendell and Cardiff did not erase generations of bad blood. What trust his uncles had for his father was tenuous at best, and James was the link that held it all together.

"No," he said. "Give her my regrets."

"Dinner, sir?"

He shook his head. "I've business in the city. Ensure she is well cared for in my absence."

"Yes, sir."

As the man left the room, James unfolded the page.

Ninth hour. Don't be late.

10
AHNNA

"HAVE YOU LEARNED ANYTHING?" AHNNA ASKED WHEN HER friends met in her room after dinner, having not been willing to bring up the topic with so many servants listening.

"Not about new markets, no," Taryn said, and then met Bronwyn's gaze for a moment, the pair silently communicating. "There's more resentment toward Ithicana than I realized. I'm not sure if the spies are missing it, or if this shift is recent. Either way, there is a sourness toward Aren and the bridge." Her jaw worked side-to-side. "And you."

Not at all the news Ahnna had hoped for.

Bronwyn sighed. "The grievances are much the same flavor as what the Magpie used to convince us Ithicana was the villain. That you exercise near-total control over trade between the northern and southern continents and use that control to extort punitive taxes and tolls. There's a lot of resentment among the staff, especially given they are unaware of the true state of Ithicana. They think Aren sits on his throne of gold and feasts while he abuses his power, and I think the only reason they said as much is because they believe a Maridrinian is sure to be like-minded." Bronwyn made a face. "Which is honestly a possibility. The Maridrinians pay even higher tolls."

Ahnna rubbed at her temple. "I'd thought the rumors of Ithicanian wealth had been put to bed by the Maridrinians when they discovered we don't actually have hidden stockpiles of gold."

"Times are tough, and that always fosters strife." Bronwyn thought for a moment. "There may be more to learn, but servants will say only so much to a lady." Her friend rolled her eyes, and it occurred to Ahnna that this was probably the first time Bronwyn had been treated like the princess she was, for surely that had not been the case on the compound in the desert, and it definitely hadn't been the case in Ithicana. Her words suggested that she found it all an inconvenience, and yet she slipped into the gowns and jewels of rank with the ease of someone who'd worn them all her life.

Ahnna went to the window and looked out into the darkness. "We're leaving in the morning, so there might be more to learn as we travel."

The butler had told her that James was in the city making arrangements, and that was why he'd missed dinner. She'd seen him through the glass walls of the orangery, dressed in black trousers and coat, throat concealed by a perfectly knotted cravat, and boots polished to a shine. He wore one of the strange flat-top hats that wealthy Harendellians wore, yet rather than foolish, he looked . . . Well, Ahnna wasn't willing to put words to what she thought of James's appearance, only that *foolish* was not at all the word she'd use.

Attractive, the rebellious part of her soul whispered. *And formidable.*

Annoyed at herself, she responded, *How about arrogant, condescending, and uptight?*

"Pardon?" Taryn asked, and Ahnna realized she'd said the words aloud. "Nothing. We should all get some rest. From the sound of it, we have a full day in a carriage tomorrow, with another to follow."

"Not the luxurious riverboat that was promised," Bronwyn said, then linked arms with Taryn, giving her a slow grin. "Come sing me a song so that I sleep like a babe."

Taryn's cheeks turned pink, and Ahnna hid a smile at her cousin's reaction. "See you in the morning."

As they left, Hazel came inside with folded white fabric in her hands. "Are you ready to undress, my lady?"

It felt as though she was being treated like a child who could not manage her own buttons, but Ahnna understood that this was how things were done in Harendell. And she was not quite stubborn enough to die on every hill. "Thank you."

Hazel unfolded one of the white garments, revealing a nightgown that laced high on the neck and would reach down to Ahnna's ankles. "Your maid neglected to pack sleeping garments, my lady, so I secured something appropriate."

Given how hot Ithicana always was, Ahnna preferred to sleep nude, but she kept that to herself as she kicked off her boots and unfastened her belt. Her tunic and trousers followed, but as she lifted her undershirt, Hazel's face blanched. "My lady! Why didn't you mention you were injured?"

Ahnna glanced down at her side, her ribs marked with virulent purple bruises from where she'd hit the ship's rail. "Just bruises, nothing broken."

"How are you moving about?" Hazel clutched Ahnna's clothes to her chest, eyes wide. "You should be in bed!"

"That would make it worse." Ahnna picked up the nightgown and pulled it over her head, feeling rather silly in all the frills and lace. "I know from experience."

"It's horrible that you've been made to fight all your life." Hazel shook her head. "It should be the responsibility of the men. It's terrible that you've had to endure so much violence."

Ahnna started to laugh at the idiocy of that statement, then reconsidered. "Do you have family, Hazel?"

"In Verwyrd, my lady. My parents and two elder sisters, who have eight children between them."

"Imagine, if you would, that every single day, Verwyrd risked attack from those who would gladly kill everyone they found." When Hazel stiffened, Ahnna added, "That is what it is like in Ithicana, with the only freedom found during the typhoons, which bring their own variety of pain."

"It sounds horrible."

"Sometimes." Ahnna fastened the laces at her throat, then sat as Hazel retrieved a comb. "But it's far worse if you don't know how to take care of yourself. Imagine being in such a situation and relying on the men in your family as your only form of protection. Imagine being caught by enemies while you are without those men, and you cannot protect your nieces and nephews because women are not taught to wield a blade. Imagine watching them die because you cared more about propriety and a man's vision of femininity than the skills it took to face reality. Would you thank them for protecting you then, or would you curse them for limiting you?"

Hazel drew in a shaky breath. "I would curse them, my lady."

"I know you think poorly of me for not wearing beautiful gowns," Ahnna said. "Except all my life, I've been fighting to protect those I care about, and I can't do that if I'm trussed in yards of silk and satin. I have no wish to be disrespectful, but I need to be able to move, which means compromises must be made." And to herself, Ahnna added, *I need to remember who I am and why I'm here.*

"I understand, my lady." Hazel drew the comb through Ahnna's loose curls, gently teasing free the knots that had formed. "I am sorry for pressing you on the matter, it is only that I know how the ladies of Harendell are." She was quiet for a long moment. "They don't cut with blades but with words, and I think you will never meet women as cruel as those in Verwyrd. They despise anyone who is not like them, and they will not respect your reasons as those of the common classes will."

"If I am to be their queen, they will learn to respect me as I am."

"As you say, my lady." Hazel set aside the comb, then swiftly plaited Ahnna's hair. "Is there anything else you require before bed?"

"No."

Hazel stood, waiting with her arms politely crossed. Understanding that she wouldn't leave until she'd tucked Ahnna into bed, Ahnna climbed onto the towering piece of furniture. Then Hazel pulled the blankets up around her chin as though she were a child. It was a struggle not to laugh, especially given the maid was nearly a foot shorter than Ahnna. Yet as the blankets were tucked around her, Ahnna found herself asking, "Has His Highness returned?"

"Not last I heard, my lady." Hazel patted the blankets. "Business in the city, and he's known to keep late hours."

That piqued Ahnna's attention, because James had struck her as an individual who was always to bed at a reasonable hour, not out and about when illicit behavior was likely to occur. "I see."

"Good night, my lady." Hazel snuffed the candles so only the single lamp remained, flame turned low. Drawing the curtains on the bed, she left the room.

Ahnna stared up at the canopy of velvet, considering what Taryn and Bronwyn had told her. Though she was not prone to tears, her eyes stung at the knowledge that so many souls resented her people just for trying to survive. That they believed Ithicanians lived in the lap of luxury when every single Ithicanian toiled daily against adversity to provide for their family. To care for their friends and village. A struggle made so much more difficult with all that had been lost and with no means to rebuild other than toil.

It felt as though each step Ahnna took deeper into Harendell revealed another obstacle, and breathless panic began its slow rise in her chest, her head throbbing and her hands like ice as a future where she could do nothing to help Ithicana played out before her. The lace of her nightgown made her neck and wrists itch, her ribs ached, and something in her snapped.

Flinging herself out of bed, Ahnna tore off the nightgown and left it in a heap, pacing naked back and forth across the floor. The oppressive sense of being caged only grew.

Going to the wardrobe, she pulled on clothes and boots, fastening a knife to her belt. Opening the heavy drapes, Ahnna unlatched the window and looked out. The peculiar maze of hedges was illuminated, and lamps burned all around the property, rendering it nearly as bright as day. She could make out the figures of soldiers patrolling, but they had the look of men who were only going through the motions.

Testing the strength of the trellis, Ahnna found it secure, and she climbed down until the ground was near enough for her to jump. Her boots hit the soft turf and she rolled, coming to her feet and swiftly darting to the shadow of a statue. Then to the next.

And then she was in the maze.

It was darker inside, the leafy greenery rising higher than her head, but the skies were clear enough for her to keep her sense of direction as she unpuzzled it, the focus it required easing the panic in her heart. Solving the maze had been all she'd originally intended to do, but then she found herself on the far side of it, the wall at the rear of the property only a short distance away.

Didn't it occur to you to get the lay of the land by visiting before you arrived to marry the crown prince? Bronwyn's voice filled her head, and Ahnna grimaced, more than understanding what a mistake that had been.

Crouching at the exit of the maze, Ahnna considered how that mistake was best rectified. In all her brother's adventures on both continents, she knew Aren had pretended to be a commoner, and those were the people he fraternized with under his many aliases. "I know everything there is to know about the nobility and the wealthy merchants," he always said. "That's who we spy on. I want to know about everything else. Every*one* else."

And given that her own knowledge was driven by spy reports, it meant what she knew about Harendell was equally biased toward those who ruled. Yet those who ruled served the people, so it was important that she understood them just as well.

Watching a soldier pass on patrol, Ahnna waited for him to be out of earshot, and then she broke into a run. Her long strides ate up the ground, and with a soft grunt of effort, she jumped, catching hold of the edge of the wall. She hooked her ankle over the edge, then swiftly rolled over the top, landing in a crouch on the cobbles on the far side.

To find herself face-to-face with a young boy, his cheeks streaked with dirt. "You robbing them?" he asked.

Ahnna considered her answer. "Yes."

He grinned. "Good. The bastards deserve it." Then he scampered into an alley.

Rising from her crouch, Ahnna walked down the lane, heading

in the direction of the wharf, where there were certain to be sailors and merchants drinking and gossiping. The cobbled streets were worn smooth by the passage of countless feet and carriage wheels, the gutters piled high with a shocking amount of horse shit. Lamps flickered at each intersection, illuminating the faces of people trudging home after a day's toil, none of them paying her any attention.

This area seemed to be mostly homes, long buildings with doors at equal intervals, shapes visible through curtains on every level, which suggested to her that a different family lived on each floor. Over the smell of manure, she picked out the scents of woodsmoke and cooking food and human urine, the stench so oppressive Ahnna fought the urge to cover her mouth and nose.

She was used to the smell of the sea. The scent of a storm. The wildness of the jungle. The press of humanity felt like being buried alive, and for a few moments, Ahnna debated fleeing back to the relative peace of Fernleigh House. Only to see a familiar tall figure cross in front of her and head down a side street.

James.

She hadn't come into the city to spy on his *business*, yet Ahnna found herself breaking away from her trajectory to follow him. She stayed well back and kept her head down. There was still enough traffic of people and horses that he took no notice of her footfalls.

James walked with purpose, those he passed giving way, though she noticed how he nodded at the women, ever courteous. That he did so even outside the view of peers who might judge him made her smile, because she'd never met anyone whose politeness seemed so ingrained in his soul.

James paused beneath a streetlamp to consult a piece of paper, then headed up to the door of one of the buildings, knocking sharply.

Ahnna headed into the shadows of the neighboring staircase, watching as a woman holding a baby opened the door. The moment she saw him, the woman's face crumpled, and a wail tore from her throat. Ahnna instantly knew what James was doing, because she'd had to do it many times herself.

Delivering news of the fallen.

An older woman appeared, taking the baby, listening to whatever words of comfort James gave as he handed her coins. He inclined his head, said a few more words, then descended the steps and continued down the street.

Ahnna didn't follow. This was miserable work, though she respected him for doing it himself rather than delegating it to an officer, because it did mean something to hear the news from the one under whom your loved one had served. Perhaps not in the moment, but later.

Or so she'd been told.

Watching until his long strides took him out of sight, Ahnna sighed, then retreated to the main street, and then followed it down toward the sea. It wasn't long until the street grew more crowded and raucous, drunk men and women spilling in and out of brightly lit buildings loud with music and laughter. It smelled of ale, vomit, and humanity, and Ahnna scanned the names of the various establishments, trying to decide which one to enter.

The Fabled Flask seemed a good mix of sailors and merchants, so Ahnna went inside. It was full of circular tables surrounded by mostly men dressed in stained shirts and baggy trousers, the floppy hats the sailors favored on the tables next to them. They were either conversing or playing cards or dice. None paid her any mind. A hearth burned low against one wall, though the added heat was hardly necessary, for the room was so thick with the scent of sweat that Ahnna nearly walked back out again.

She wove between the tables, heading in the direction of the bar, where she saw some empty space. Only to draw up short as a man stuck a thick leg out in front of her. He was heavyset with a bushy mustache, the front of his shirt stained with grease, his piggy eyes looking her up and down. "Why don't you have a seat, lass," he said, patting his lap. His hand bore a long scar down the center of it, though it was hard to see through the grime.

His friend laughed, the sound nasal as a result of a nose that had been broken and poorly set. His other companion only shook his head and said, "You never learn, do you, Jasper? Keep your hands for the barmaids."

Jasper belched, then slapped his knee again. "Have a seat, girl. I don't mind that scar of yours none. Let's have a visit."

Lifting one eyebrow, Ahnna looked Jasper up and down, then said, "I'll pass," and stepped over his outstretched leg.

Only for his hand to crack hard against her backside.

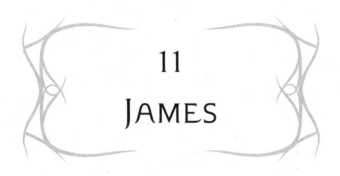

11

JAMES

HE'D NOTIFIED THE FAMILIES OF THE EIGHT MEN FROM SABLETON who'd lost their lives to the Amaridians, the process having drained James worse than the battles themselves. What were words and coins compared with a lost husband or son? *Nothing* was the answer, but words and coins were all he could give.

The clock tower at the center of the city began to toll the ninth hour. The note hadn't given a location, but James knew that it wasn't about him finding the agent. It was about the agent finding him.

James reached the end of the street, his skin prickling with the sensation of being watched, and then a soft whistle caught his attention. He turned his head to see a shadow standing between two buildings, and his stomach clenched at the familiar height and breadth.

His uncle Cormac.

Cutting into the gap between buildings, he followed his uncle until they reached a side door, which Cormac opened, revealing a dirty kitchen lit by a single candle. Taking a seat at the table, his uncle gestured for James to sit.

He did so. "What are you doing in Sableton, Uncle?"

"I'd ask you the same, except I've heard." His uncle rested his elbows on the table, face faintly illuminated by the candle as he said, "Scrapping with the Amaridians, the *Defiant* sunk, dozens of men lost." Cormac tsked with dismay. "Yet in the midst of all that, you didn't find a way for the Ithicanian woman to fall over the side so that we might be rid of the problem she causes?"

James realized he was standing, though he had no memory of rising. "I'm not murdering a woman in cold blood."

His uncle shrugged. "Which is why you should have let the Amaridians do it."

"Standing by and watching a woman be murdered is no better than doing it myself," James snapped. "Besides, it wasn't Ahnna they were trying to kill. It was me."

That made Cormac sit up straight. "Now, why would they be wanting to do that?"

"You tell me. Because I can think of only one reason they'd try to kill me and frame the Ithicanians, which is that Katarina has discovered our alliance. That she knows we plan to redirect trade north to Cardiff rather than south through the bridge. That she knows I'm at the center of the negotiations, which means she knows that my connections to Cardiff didn't die with my mother. If Ithicana knew the same, it's feasible that they'd ally with Amarid to stop it."

"Do you believe Ithicana suspects? Do you believe they planned the attack together?" His uncle's voice was toneless, and James's skin crawled.

"No." He hesitated, then added, "Ahnna saved my life. If she knew our plans, she'd have let the sharks feast."

Cormac made a noncommittal noise, then said, "Perhaps. However, the fact remains that promises have been broken, nephew. Your father, through you, indicated that this betrothal would never be seen to fruition. Spoke with such confidence that the Ithicanians would never send their princess, giving him a viable reason to look north to Cardiff as a consequence of the slight. But they have sent her, and if an Ithicanian woman becomes queen of Harendell, everything your mother dreamed of will be dust on the wind."

James's mother had died when he was only four years old, but while his memory of her face had faded, how much he'd loved her, and she him, remained as vivid as though it were yesterday. The idea of failing her in any way never ceased to fill James with a desperate panic, as though doing so would erase that love entirely.

"Get rid of Ahnna Kertell," his uncle said, "or I'll be forced to report to Ronan that your loyalty to your blood, and to the people of Cardiff, is nothing but empty words. He will not take that news well."

"My loyalty is as strong as it has always been," James growled. "But it does not come at the cost of my morals. I will not see any harm come to Ahnna Kertell. There are other ways to break betrothals than murder, none the least that she is a poor match for William."

"I agree with that. It seems the Ithicanians breed them as fierce and fine as we do in the north." His uncle whistled between his teeth. "That princess has legs that any real man would dream to have wrapped around him, but William has no taste for a woman he has to look up to."

James blinked as he remembered the feel of those long legs wrapped around him in the cave under Northwatch. Then his uncle's words registered. "How do you know what she looks like?"

Cormac shrugged. "Got a good look at the princess as she climbed over the wall of Fernleigh House. She followed you for a time, but then headed in the direction of the harbor. Maybe we got lucky and the princess is boarding a ship to Ithicana, solving our problem for us."

James was already on his feet, because knowing Ahnna as he was coming to, *luck* was not in the stars tonight.

"Is there anything else you require from me tonight, Uncle?" he demanded. "Or may we adjourn?"

Cormac spread his hands wide. "I think you have larger problems to manage than mine."

James was already out the door.

12
AHNNA

AHNNA TILTED HER HEAD, SHOCK GIVING WAY TO RAGE THAT this gutter pig of a man would dare to lay hands on her. Her hand balled into a fist, and she turned, already swinging.

Only to find empty space where Jasper had once been, because the man was already sailing through the air to land with a crash on the neighboring table. Men cursed and barmaids screamed, glassware shattering every which way as a black-clad figure picked up Jasper by his shirt and slammed him back down on the table. "You dare to lay hands on a lady?"

James.

"I didn't know!" Jasper squealed, trying to pull free from James's grasp. "She ain't dressed like a lady!"

James only slammed him down again. Ahnna moved to intervene, because she could bloody well handle her own fistfights, but the broken-nose man had picked up a chair.

"I don't think so," she snarled, grabbing him by his greasy hair and bouncing his head off a table. Only to see the third man swing at her from her periphery.

Ahnna ducked, hearing a growl of fury, and then James's fist connected with the third man's head. He dropped, out cold, but now more men were throwing themselves into the fray.

A red-haired woman with breasts the size of wine casks shrieked a string of curses and tried to slap Ahnna, but she sidestepped the drunken swipe and punched the woman in the throat. Only for a chair to slam against her back.

Hissing in pain, Ahnna picked up a broken piece of the chair and cracked the man who'd hit her across the head, then hit another man who tried to punch her with a blow to the stomach.

"Stop, you fools!" The barkeep was standing on his bar, screaming at the top of his lungs. "It's Prince James! Stop, you cursed idiots—you're fighting with the king's son!"

At first, Ahnna was convinced that veins were running too thick with ale and anger to hear, but a handful of level heads seemed to register his pleas, calming their fellows. The bartender pointed a finger at James, who stood half a head taller than any man in the room. "It's Prince James!"

"King's bastard," she heard more than a few mutter, which was either brave or stupid, in her opinion, because James had come out of the melee uninjured while groaning figures lay on the ground all around him.

The barkeep's finger moved to her. "And that ass you slapped, Jasper? It belongs to the goddamned princess of Ithicana. Be glad it was our good prince who knocked you flat, for if Ithicana's king caught word his sister was so abused, he would cut off the offending hand and mail it to your mother!"

Aren would do no such thing, but it was a well-worded threat, so Ahnna let it stand. Her gaze moved to James, who looked so furious that he might start another brawl just to spend the emotion. Instead, he pulled some coins from his pocket and slapped them on the bar. "For the damages." Then his amber eyes fixed on Ahnna. "We're leaving. Now."

There was only one man alive she took orders from, and her brother wasn't here. Yet as she looked around at the mess of tables, broken glasses, and spilled drinks, Ahnna allowed reason to hold sway over her pride. Shrugging, she picked her way through the mess, taking up a bottle of whiskey as she passed the bar, then headed out the door of the Fabled Flask.

James's boots made heavy thuds down the steps after her. "Have you lost your bloody mind? You have no business being out on your own at this hour, much less in an establishment like this!"

Pride once again took over, because she was Ahnna Kertell, and she went where she fucking wanted to go. Scowling, she crossed the street toward another alehouse.

"Where are you going?" James demanded.

"I never got my drink." She tried stepping around mounds of horse shit, but it was everywhere, so she gave up. "Nor my conversation."

"You are to return to Fernleigh immediately, Your Highness."

Ahnna snorted softly, watching him stomp angrily through the shit out of the corner of her eye. "You are neither my king nor my father, which means you don't have any authority over me, *Your Highness*."

She could feel frustration seething from him, but Ahnna didn't care. He had no grounds for ordering her about, especially given she'd have been reasonable if he hadn't spoken to her as though she were a child. He didn't have to agree with her choices, but he did need to treat her like a grown woman when criticizing them.

"You are a lady, Ahnna," James hissed, stepping into her path. "There are certain standards of behavior expected from you, and this is not it. You will return with me to Fernleigh this minute!"

"I'm not a lady." She sidestepped him, taking a mouthful from the neck of the bottle. "And if you want me to return, either ask me nicely or make me. Because ordering me about will get you nowhere."

"Fine."

Instead of asking her nicely, as Ahnna had expected, James's hand closed around her arm. Before she could say a word, he flung her over his shoulder. A squawk of protest tore from her lips, but he ignored it. His shoulder pressed against her hips as he draped one arm around the back of her thighs and started up the street.

"By all means, wiggle," he said. "I'll be sure to drop you in the largest pile of horse sh—" He shook his head. "The largest pile of manure I can find."

"Asshole," she growled, debating whether the indignity of being dumped into a pile of shit would be worth kneeing him in the ribs.

"You aren't the first to say so."

"Put me down!"

"No." His arm tightened around the back of her thighs. Shockingly close to the ass he'd just violently defended, and Ahnna wondered if he realized it as he added, "If you're going to act like a child, I'm going to treat you like one."

"Does that mean I'm to be spanked twice tonight?"

She'd thought that the suggestion would so deeply offend his sense of propriety that he'd put her down, but instead James said, "Don't tempt me."

Ahnna's entire core tightened, but she managed to say, "You'd make quite the scene."

James scoffed. "It's going to take more than this to gain attention in Sableton's tenderloin. Which is exactly why you shouldn't be here."

It was a hard point to argue. Everyone spilling in and out of the taverns, inns, and brothels looked drunk, or well on their way to becoming so, the noise of music and laughter deafening. Prostitutes propositioned potential customers from windows and balconies, but in the alleys, she saw those who worked the streets engaged in various acts that made her cheeks color. A man shouting "Thief" chased a young boy up the street, and no fewer than four fistfights broke out by the time they'd reached the edge of the district and James set her down.

"What were you doing in the tenderloin?" he asked. In the light of the streetlamp, she saw that the sleeve of his coat was torn from the brawl.

"I wanted to speak with the people without them knowing who I was," she said. "I wanted to hear their concerns. At least, that was my plan until you picked a fight with them."

"He laid hands on you. He's lucky I let him live." James's eyes narrowed. "What concerns?"

She debated telling the truth, then thought better of it and said, "About anything. A good ruler listens to her people."

"I don't disagree, but rulers don't venture out alone."

"I didn't think you would agree to me venturing out at all, in your company or otherwise, so I did not bother asking."

James exhaled. "It's not appropriate for us to be alone together, much less in the tenderloin at night."

Yet they were alone now. Ahnna knew the rules unwed noblewomen were held to in Harendell. Safeguards so that their purity would never be called into question, but to hold her to those rules seemed asinine. Her claim to *purity* had set sail when she was fifteen in a fumbling encounter with Aren's friend Gorrick, who'd afterward begged her not to tell her brother.

That was always how it was. Wine and desire would trump good sense, but afterward, the men would always beg her discretion, terrified of what Aren would do if he learned they'd been fucking his sister in the bunkhouse. They'd either ignore her or refuse to meet her eye afterward, which had made her heart ache so badly that she'd stopped having encounters years ago, what desires she felt satisfied only by her own hand.

Absolutely none of which she intended to admit to James, so she only shrugged.

"How did you get past the guards?"

"It wasn't hard," she said. "If they were under my command, they'd be disciplined because if I could leave so easily, then anyone with half a mind to enter would have no difficulty."

"And I *would* discipline them if not for the fact that it would necessitate admitting that you'd left unattended."

"I assume they'll figure that out when we walk in the front gate."

"For the sake of your reputation, we'll go back in the same way you came out." He hesitated, then added, "I understand that you are not used to these limitations, Your Highness. That they seem foolish and biased against your sex. However, railing against me will get you nowhere, because they're not my rules, and while I am sympathetic, the queen will be nothing of the sort. You already have the odds of gaining her favor stacked against you by virtue of you being Ithicanian, and everything you do that reminds her of that fact will be a reason for her to make your life miserable."

He gestured for her to start walking in the direction of Fernleigh, and Ahnna did so without argument, because it struck her then that he spoke not just of her situation but also of his own. "I've heard of her reputation," she said, not certain whether this was a conversation she should start.

"Every bit of it is deserved." His tone shut down any further questions she might have had.

They walked in silence, it not taking long for them to reach the portion of the wall she'd climbed over. "Here," she said. "Then through the maze and up the trellis to my window." She knew she should apologize, but instead, Ahnna said, "I'm fine from here. You don't need to lower yourself to climbing in the back window."

"A good attempt," he muttered. "But I'm not that easily duped. I'll see you inside your room, and then I'll post a guard beneath it."

Any desire to apologize evaporated. "It's not a trick. I just don't need to be tucked in a second time tonight."

"No, but I might need to tie you to the bed to keep you from further foolish pursuits."

Ahnna's cheeks flushed at the sudden vision of how that might go, and as if realizing what he'd said, James pressed fingers to his temple. "Your single greatest skill seems to be driving me to madness. No more discussion. I'm taking you back to the house, and that's the end of it."

Ahnna only nodded, words escaping her.

James jumped and took hold of the top of the wall, lifting himself until he was looking over. He remained in that position, watching, then heaved himself up so that he was sitting atop the wall. Reaching down, he offered her his hand, barely visible in the darkness. "Leave the whiskey."

Gripping the bottle tightly, she jumped and caught his hand, allowing him to pull her atop the wall. Though his size spoke to considerable strength, it still shocked her how easily he lifted her. As though she weighed no more than tiny Hazel. It was no wonder he'd knocked those men in the bar unconscious with one blow. Realizing she was staring at him, she said, "You should really learn to say *please*," took a mouthful of the whiskey, then dropped to the soft turf below. Without waiting for a response, she bolted to the entrance of the maze, hearing James's curse of annoyance as he followed her.

The maze remained as brightly lit as it had been when she'd traversed it before. Retracing her route, Ahnna lifted the bottle of whiskey to take a small mouthful, intending to discard the rest, for she could feel the faint buzzing of the alcohol in her veins. As she did, Ahnna saw smears of blood on the bottle and her fingers.

Frowning, she examined her hands. Except for a small scrape on her right knuckles, which hadn't bled, she had no injuries.

"Are you hurt?" she demanded, rounding on James, who strode a few paces behind her. "You're bleeding, because this blood isn't mine."

"It's nothing."

Hissing between her teeth at the stubbornness of men, for she knew well how they'd let *nothing* turn to rot and rot to a cold corpse in a grave. "Let me see."

"It's fine," he protested, but she'd already caught hold of the hand he'd used to pull her atop the wall, blood glistening crimson on his pale skin. "James," she growled, "you have glass stuck in your knuckles."

"I'll pull it out before I retire to bed."

Huffing out an aggrieved breath, Ahnna tugged him to the center of the maze, then pushed him down on the bench next to the fountain. Water sprayed from the top, then poured down a series of tiered basins, the noise loud enough to drown out her curse as she held the injury up to the lamplight. Sloshing some of the whiskey on her hands, she then poured some on the sharp shard of glass embedded between his first and second knuckles. "This is going to bleed a lot. Will need stitches."

"I'll have one of the servants look at it."

"I'll do it," she grumbled. "It's my fault."

Retrieving her kit from where it was stored in a pouch attached to her belt, she extracted a needle and length of gut thread. "Old habit," she said before he could ask the question of why she had such supplies on her person. "I was raised primarily by my grand-mother, my father's mother, who is Ithicana's most accomplished healer. She made me learn the arts while I lived with her. If you ever find yourself in need, I'm quite accomplished at delivering babies."

"Seems unlikely, but if I find myself with child, I'll keep the offer in mind."

Smiling, she pinched the edge of the glass and eased it loose, then used more of the whiskey to rinse away the blood until she was certain no more shards remained.

"What of your mother?"

"What of her?" Ahnna's jaw tightened by reflex, and she bent closer to the injury to hide her reaction.

"You didn't reside with her?"

Ahnna laughed softly. "Hardly. All her time was for Ithicana and the bridge. Having children was a duty she had to fulfill as queen, and once she'd done so, she wanted little enough to do with us. With me, most especially, because she preferred my brother's way of thinking. My value came from how I served Aren and as a bargaining chip in her dreams for Ithicana."

"Dreams?"

Nightmares, in Ahnna's opinion, but she said, "She hated how isolated we were. Desired to open our borders so that our people could live more like those in Harendell and Maridrina. Aren was, and is, like-minded."

"Is that why your people stopped wearing masks at North-watch?"

"In part, I suppose." She hesitated, then said, "I never asked him. Only obeyed the directive."

Ahnna waited for James to ask whether she supported the change, but he said, "Were you close with your father?"

"No. He loved my mother so much, there was nothing left over for anyone else," she answered, threading the needle. "And he died for it."

"I'm sorry."

"Don't be. It was a long time ago." Ahnna turned his hand into the light, holding the wound closed as she carefully began to stitch. His palms were callused from soldiering, but his nails were trimmed and clean, the two things feeling at odds with each other. They well represented the dichotomy that was James, the exterior he presented not quite concealing the man she suspected lurked beneath. "They weren't cruel by any stretch of the imagination, and I was given every privilege. It's just . . ." Ahnna sighed. "She did her duty because she had to, not because she wanted to."

"A ruler needs an heir." His breath was warm against her cheek as she worked. "It's the way of it."

"I know." She knotted the last stitch, cutting the thread with her knife. "But knowing your mother bore you because she had to is a burden I wouldn't wish upon any child. All children deserve to be wanted, and I'll never—" Ahnna broke off, shaking her head. "Whiskey makes me say foolish things."

"It's not foolish," he murmured, and Ahnna lifted her face to meet his gaze, the lamplight illuminating his amber eyes. Making them look like they burned from within. "You're not like I expected you to be, Ahnna Kertell."

"Much less ladylike, I assume." She broke their shared gaze, then unknotted the cravat tied at his throat, slowly pulling loose the fabric, abruptly aware of the distance between them.

Or the lack thereof.

"No, I expected that," he answered as she fastened the fabric around his hand, knotting it. "Expected you to be willful and obstinate. Violent and wild. What I did not expect was compassion."

There was something in his voice that made her chest clench, and Ahnna said, "You don't seem happy with the discovery."

James lifted his bandaged hand, catching hold of her cheek and lifting her face so that she was looking at him. "I'm not," he said, and she leaned closer so as not to miss any of his words. "Because it makes everything so much harder."

And then he lowered his face and kissed her.

Ahnna should have been shocked. Horrified at the transgression. But she wasn't.

Something in her, deep and primal, had felt this coming. The culmination of the tension that had sung between them from the moment she'd knocked him off the side of the ship. And that part had Ahnna wrapping her arms around James's neck, not resisting as he pulled her onto his lap.

His bandaged hand pressed against the small of her back, tongue in her mouth, the taste of him making her ache for so much more. For everything.

And then he jerked away.

"Shit!" He rose, lifting her as he did, only to set her down on her feet with such force that Ahnna stumbled backward. "Fucking hell!"

She pressed her fingers to her lips, still feeling the sensation of his kiss, watching as he paced up and down the small clearing at the center of the maze. James had kissed her. James, who only ever made proper choices, had kissed her. And God help her, but that kiss had burned into her soul in a way she hadn't dreamed possible.

Then reality reared its head.

Ahnna twisted to look toward the distant manor, searching for any lights. Any sign that anyone had been watching.

That they'd been seen.

Was that a curtain moving? Or a trick of shadows?

"This was a mistake."

Ahnna pivoted back around to find James no longer pacing, his eyes fixed on her. "I know," she said. "I—"

"Why are you here, Ahnna?" he interrupted. "Do not lie and say that any part of life in Harendell appeals to you. You can't follow the rules for one night, and they will soon be forced upon you like manacles, but you mean to tell me you are ready for a lifetime of this? Go home. Go back to Ithicana, where you belong. Because not only are you not wanted in Harendell, but this kingdom is going to eat you alive if you stay."

Hurt flooded her chest, only for anger to rise in her heart's defense. "I am here because my mother gave her word. Because I gave my word. And your father had every opportunity to negotiate for something other than me, and he chose not to. So perhaps ask yourself whether this is a matter of me not being wanted, or of you wanting something well beyond your reach."

Shoving past him, Ahnna wove through the maze. Only some vestige of self-preservation stopped her at the edge of it to allow a yawning guard to walk past. When he was gone, she moved between the shadows of the statues, then scaled the trellis and climbed into the open window of her room.

Latching the pane shut, she closed the drapes and donned the nightgown, carefully replacing her clothing in the wardrobe. Climbing into bed, Ahnna pulled the blankets up to her chin. Only then did she lose control of the floodgates holding her panic in check.

What have you done? her conscience screamed. *You fucking fool!*

Ahnna shoved her fist into her mouth and tried to silence her gasping breaths, the sobs that kept threatening to tear loose.

She'd come here to save Ithicana, and in one moment of lust, she'd jeopardized everything. All it would take was one word of her transgression from James to his father, and she'd be sent home in disgrace. In her mind's eye, Ahnna saw herself walking onto the pier at Northwatch, forced to admit that every bit of suffering that would come during storm season would be her fault. Because she'd kissed the wrong prince. Wanted the wrong prince.

Felt something for the wrong prince.

Ahnna drowned in her terror, in the wild hammer of her heart and the roar of her pulse, breathing so rapidly the room spun around her. Then, bit by bit, she pulled herself back from the edge.

"He might not tell," she whispered. "It was his mistake, too."

Not only are you not wanted in Harendell, but this kingdom is going to eat you alive if you stay. James's voice echoed in her thoughts, but this time, the sentiment didn't fill her with hurt. It filled her with defiance.

Because she fully intended to prove him wrong.

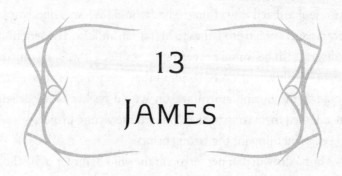

13
JAMES

He hadn't slept. Hadn't even bothered trying, for James had known his mind would give him not an ounce of peace after what he'd done.

His father's voice filled his head: *Your brother gets to make mistakes, but not you. William is Alexandra's son, heir to the throne, and that means the only individual who will ever question him, ever judge him, is me. Whereas you were born out of wedlock to a Cardiffian woman whom half the kingdom believed to be a witch, so everyone questions you. Everyone judges you. If you are perfect, they will see only my son. But the moment you err, all they will see is your mother's eyes staring out of your face, and they will turn on you, sure and true. If that happens, everything your mother dreamed and fought and died for will be lost.*

Last night had been one error piled on the next, culminating with his mad decision to kiss Ahnna *fucking* Kertell.

In the light of day, James did not understand why he had done it or what he'd been thinking, only that the compulsion to make Ahnna *his* had overwhelmed every drop of common sense in his body.

Ask yourself whether this is a matter of me not being wanted, or of you wanting something well beyond your reach, Ahnna's voice whispered, and James turned his face to the misting sky, the words striking truer than she'd known because the answer was *both*.

"Good morning, Your Highness."

James jerked, finding Ahnna descending the steps of Fernleigh toward the waiting carriage. Her hair was woven into a tight coronet of braids that emphasized the hard lines of her face. Regal. Fierce.

Beautiful.

But not his. Never his.

"Good morning," he said, opening the door of the coach. "We'll need to travel all through the day to reach the inn at Willowford, where we will stay the night."

"I look forward to seeing the country," she said, then climbed into the coach. It rocked again as her guardsman, Jor, climbed onto the buckboard, the old man pressing his sleeve to his mouth as he coughed violently.

"Flux?" the coachman asked.

"Your shitty weather," Jor responded, then broke into another bout of coughing.

Bronwyn and Taryn appeared, and James watched their faces closely for any sign that Ahnna had told them what had happened the prior night, but their expressions showed nothing as they greeted him and climbed in next to Ahnna. Hazel was the last member of the party to join them, the young maid carrying a picnic basket, which she set on the floor of the coach before climbing inside.

Taking the reins of a horse from a footman, James mounted and pulled the hood of his cloak forward, nodding at the coachman to proceed, the twelve soldiers accompanying them forming up ahead and behind.

They rode through the dawn streets of Sableton, but as they reached the edge of the city, James saw a familiar figure standing on a street corner, soldiers passing him by without a second glance. His uncle Cormac wore Harendellian clothes, but how anyone could mistake him as anything but Cardiffian—with his height and breadth and *wildness*—James didn't know. His uncle's eyes locked on his, and James heard the message as surely as if his uncle had screamed the words.

Get rid of her.

14
AHNNA

THE JOURNEY PASSED WITHOUT INCIDENT, WHICH, UNFORTU-
nately, meant endless hours with little respite from her own
thoughts. It became swiftly apparent that James's solution to what
had happened between them was avoidance, for he rode through
the ceaseless drizzle with his hood up, and he took dinner at the
inn in Willowford in his room while she ate with Bronwyn and
Taryn in the one they shared.

Which was perhaps for the best. To pretend that it had never
happened. And to keep their distance from each other lest it happen again. Not that she wanted it to happen again after he'd been
such a prick about it.

Her companions continued to hunt for more information on
the *new market* that James had alluded to that could compete with
the bridge, but beyond confirming that the rise of negativity
toward Ithicana was not limited to Sableton, they discovered
nothing. Debating the possibilities was impossible, for Hazel rode
in the carriage with them, which meant that Ahnna was left to
stew over the puzzle.

It couldn't be Amarid, given recent aggressions. Nor Cardiff, for that border was closed to travel. There were many other nations farther north, but they were all tiny, and even combined, they were nothing compared with accessing Maridrina and Valcotta. Picking at a scab on her bruised knuckles, Ahnna considered the possibility James hadn't meant a new market, but rather a *new way* of accessing existing markets. Which meant transport using ships rather than the bridge.

Shipping had always been the bridge's greatest competition, but while the Amaridians, and occasionally the Cardiffians, risked the Tempest Seas to avoid the tolls, Harendell had historically only done so during the calm season. They could afford to pay, so there was no need to lose lives and vessels to the storms. Except what if that had changed? What if the Harendellians were investing in a fleet capable of weathering high seas? What if they saw the inevitable losses as acceptable in the face of the bridge's tolls?

Questions Ahnna couldn't hope to answer in a coach trundling down a muddy road, unless she went to the source himself. Leaning her head against the window, Ahnna watched James riding his horse, his eyes on the trees surrounding them. Unbidden, the feel of his lips against hers came rushing back, along with the hard press of his fingers against her back, nothing about him hesitant.

Nothing about him afraid.

An ache formed low in her belly, and more to punish herself than out of any interest, she asked, "Hazel, how would you describe Prince William?"

Her maid looked up with a start from the garment she'd been mending. "Oh, he's very handsome, my lady. The muse of many artists, or so I've heard. Once you are wed, it will be a blessing to sit across the breakfast table from him every morning."

Bronwyn started coughing, and Taryn barely suppressed her laughter behind her hand.

"I've no doubt." Ahnna shot both of her friends a glare. "But I am more curious as to his character."

"Oh!" Hazel looked down at the needle and thread in her hands. "Well, of course he's very princely."

"Of course," Bronwyn murmured, and Taryn elbowed her in the ribs.

"Everyone speaks of his great wit," Hazel continued. "A tremendous conversationalist. Very popular with his fellows, for he is always surrounded by others."

"So just like his brother?" Bronwyn said with a straight face.

"Oh, they are nothing alike at all, my lady," Hazel answered, then made a face, finally hearing Bronwyn's sarcasm. "Do not hold Prince James's taciturnity against him. He spends most of his time with soldiers, whereas William is at court, and therefore more comfortable in the company of ladies. It's an unfair comparison."

"So I'm coming to understand." Bronwyn glanced out the window, then her eyes met Ahnna's. "You might need to pick another argument if we are ever to hear a word out of him again."

Ahnna's cheeks warmed. "I'll pass. Silence is preferable."

Bronwyn grinned and said, "I don't foresee that as an option."

A rap sounded against the glass, and Ahnna nearly started out of her skin. James had reined his horse close to the coach without her noticing. She slid open the window. "Is there trouble?"

"No, we're here. As we round the bend, you will get your first glimpse of Verwyrd and the Sky Palace," James said, his eyes forward. "You mentioned an interest in seeing it, and this is perhaps the best view now that the clouds are clearing."

Here. Already.

Ahnna swallowed hard, her heart racing. Not in anticipation of seeing the Sky Palace for the first time, but because very soon, she'd be meeting the prince she was to marry.

A sudden surge of empathy for her brother filled her for how he must have felt on Southwatch the day Lara had arrived, knowing nothing about the woman he was supposed to spend the rest of his life with. Yet as that long-ago moment rose in her mind's eye, Ahnna was again struck with the anticipation her brother had radiated as Lara's ship had docked. As though every unknown about the Maridrinian princess made her more, not less, desirable.

Ahnna wished anticipation filled her stomach, but the feeling was all-too-familiar dread. Not because William was an unknown to her, but because she was an unknown to him. Beyond her name, no one in Harendell knew anything about her, and in her heart, Ahnna knew that she would not elicit the reaction Lara had when Aren had first set sights on his new wife.

Ahnna was too old, too tall, too scarred, and she couldn't help but remember what Keris had told her about Queen Alexandra. *She didn't choose you, which means no matter what you do, you will never be good enough for William in her eyes.*

And then Verwyrd appeared.

All Ahnna's thoughts of her own inadequacies fled as she stared out the window. Next to her, Bronwyn whispered, "Fuck me, that's something."

The road had curved to run along a ridgeline, which offered them an unobstructed view of the river valley below. The vast Eldermoor River split into two, creating a large island that contained the city of Verwyrd, which was surrounded by towering walls that provided additional protection on top of the swiftly flowing waters. Twin bridges joined the island to the mainland, both heavily fortified, with towns sprawling on both the east and west banks. All of which would have been impressive if not for the structure dominating the center of the island. It rose like a massive tower, perfectly symmetrical, and yet even from here, Ahnna could tell that it had not been made by the hands of men. Nor was it a natural formation created by the earth.

No, much like the bridge that had dominated her life, the Sky Palace had surely been created by God or some higher power, the massive column of smooth rock seeming to touch the clouds. Carved in its side was a spiraling path that led to the top, on which a palace made of gleaming white stone was perched, the stained-glass windows of its spires sending rainbows of color dancing across the sky as the sun struck it. Colored banners hung from the sides of the tower, all royal purple to indicate that the monarchs were currently in residence.

"How do you get to the top?" Taryn asked, pressing her hand to the coach window.

"I usually walk," James replied. "However, there are small carriages pulled by mules accustomed to the heights that transport those who don't wish to subject themselves to the exertion. It takes about half an hour to climb."

"Not particularly convenient," Bronwyn muttered. "Imagine all that effort to get up and down every day."

Ahnna barely heard, her eyes all for the reach of the tower and the view one must have from the top. She'd always gravitated to the peaks of the mountains in Ithicana, or even to the bridge top, for seeing the vastness of the world around her had always put her at ease. Reminded her that she was of little consequence to the earth and sea and sky, just a speck of creation. "It's beautiful."

Sensing eyes on her, she turned her head to find James regarding her. He looked away as their eyes met, gaze fixing on the Sky Palace. "You don't agree that your home is beautiful?"

"The Sky Palace is one of the great wonders of the north," he answered, though it was no answer at all.

Ahnna returned to her examination of the tower and the palace atop it, though curiosity burned through her at James's response. His face was impassive, but the slight tightening of his grip on the reins suggested his thoughts were less than calm.

Which was perhaps fair. The journey to retrieve her had been disastrous, a ship lost and dozens of soldiers killed, as well as the *Victoria* taking significant damage. As the most senior officer, he'd be held accountable for the losses, and though there was nothing James could have reasonably done to predict or prevent any of what had happened, a reprimand might be in his future. And of course, there was *that* which she prayed would remain unspoken.

"Has anyone ever fallen off the top?" Bronwyn asked, breaking Ahnna from her thoughts.

"Generations ago, throwing criminals off the top was a method of formal execution," James answered. "Though the practice ceased when the city was built up beneath, for obvious reasons."

"So, no one falls off anymore?"

"I didn't say that," James replied.

There was a coolness to his tone that stifled conversation. Ahnna and her friends watched out the window as the carriage began its descent into the river valley. Their escort formed up to either side, the caparisons on the horses fluttering and the soldiers' armor gleaming in the sun, and it wasn't long until the sides of the road were filled with civilians. They cheered and threw flower petals as the coach passed, with endless choruses of "God bless Ithicana" and "God bless the good princess" filling Ahnna's ears. Their words reminded her that Harendell held to religion in a much more performative manner than did Ithicana, where God and the Great Thereafter were accepted truths, with little time spent belaboring the details. Yet she couldn't help but question if the sentiments were genuine, given the resentment toward Ithicana she'd seen in Sableton and Willowford.

The crowds grew as they entered the town, the coach wheels bumping over the cobbled streets, which were lined with buildings made of timber and river stone, the walls thick with ivy and their roofs made of neat thatch. The people were shaded by drooping trees that Taryn, who'd been to Harendell many times with Aren, told her were called willows, and many wooden boxes filled with flowers of every color did a fair job of covering the scent of humanity.

They reached the bridge, which had heavy fortifications manned with uniformed soldiers, and while the gates were open, Ahnna didn't miss the murder holes in the stone above as they trundled beneath. The Eldermoor ran deep and swift, several boats visible upon it, and then they were in the city of Verwyrd itself. The capital of Harendell.

The buildings in the city were larger and taller than those in the towns, though made the same way, and Ahnna marked the finer clothes on those watching and calling their well-wishes. It was picturesque, but the charm was much reduced by the stink of shit, animal and human. The press of humanity in Verwyrd was still repulsive to her, though Taryn and Bronwyn, both used to cities, seemed unmoved by it.

The procession paraded her through the city streets, rising toward the base of the tower, which was encircled by a low wall. They passed between the gates, and Ahnna's eyes jumped over the many buildings made of stone and wood, the scent of horse strong.

"The royal stables are here," James said as they drew to a halt. "We'll abandon this carriage for one designed for the climb. Horses do poorly with heights."

He dismounted and handed off the reins before opening the coach door. Ahnna's heart hammered, her mouth dry and throat tight as she took James's hand. She stepped down, not failing to notice how swiftly he let go of her once she stood on the ground.

Dozens of soldiers in uniform waited in neat rows, as well as grooms with their heads lowered in deference, all of them bowing as she straightened her tunic, though she saw the curiosity in their eyes as they took her in.

"This way, Your Highness," James said, then offered her his arm, his reluctance to do so made apparent in the tightening of his jaw. As though having her hand on him was the very worst thing he could imagine.

Ahnna understood, because she felt the same way. But she did it anyway, hoping that her sweating palm wouldn't be noticeable through his coat. She allowed him to lead her to a smaller but significantly more ornate carriage pulled by a pair of bored-looking mules with peculiar rubber coverings fitted over their hooves.

"We use mules in the bridge," she said because the silence only made the tension between them worse. "Donkeys, too."

"Those two are named Buck and Brayer." James gestured at the animals. "My sister, Virginia, always names the new teams. Buck, he's the one with the darker nose, bites, so mind yourself around him."

The mule in question chose that moment to bray loudly, revealing yellowed teeth. Ahnna smiled, though the animal provided only a heartbeat of levity before her anxiety returned in full force. Climbing into the small carriage, she settled on the thick velvet cushion, James sitting across from her. Bronwyn and Taryn climbed in, and out the window, she watched Jor clamber up with the driver. He looked exhausted, dark shadows marring his eyes, and she'd not failed to notice his endless coughing. He needed rest, but he wouldn't get it unless she ordered him to bed. Which she fully intended to do.

The carriage began moving, soldiers opening wooden gates to allow them into the spiral path leading upward. An elaborately patterned iron fence with gilded leaves was bolted to the side, but it was low enough not to disrupt the view as they began to circle higher and higher. It gave her an incredible vantage of the city, and Ahnna picked out the enormous cathedral at the southern end of the island, then the river, then the entire valley, which was forested except where land had been cleared for farms.

The wind gusted, rattling the windows of the carriage, and Ahnna stiffened as the spiral made a strange moaning sound, eerily similar to the wind within the bridge. Taryn met her gaze, acknowledging that she heard it, too.

Around and around they circled, taking Ahnna higher than she'd ever been in her life, the countryside spread all around. Forests broken up with checkerboards of crops, all of it lush green.

The carriage shook as the wind blew harder, and then the mules turned into the tower so that they were enclosed on all sides in a tunnel. Sliding open the glass, Ahnna reached out and touched the stone, which was smooth. "Bridge stone." She shook her head. "Aren said that Devil's Island was made of the same. I wonder how many such monuments to higher powers exist in the world."

And how many had been lost to time.

The carriage navigated the last spiral, then exited into a courtyard formed of polished white rock fitted together so perfectly, the walls appeared nearly seamless. It stopped before a low set of stairs that were at least two dozen feet wide, at the top of which stood an older man in a uniform similar to that which James had worn the day he'd arrived in Northwatch, but with more medals and a crown upon his head. A man familiar to Ahnna not only from their single brief meeting, but also from all the statues and portraits she'd seen of him since arriving in Harendell.

King Edward.

At his left stood a striking woman in a royal-blue gown trimmed with ermine, a glittering tiara woven into her light-brown curls. She was of average height but so painfully thin she appeared gaunt, her green eyes sharp as tacks. Alexandra. And it struck Ahnna then that she'd seen nary a portrait of the queen since arriving in Harendell. Which . . . felt strange. Ahnna set aside the thought for later consideration, eyes skipping over the retinue of men in uniforms and women in lavish gowns, searching for a face to match the portrait she'd received of William.

The carriage door opened, and James stepped out, someone shouting at an incredible volume, "His Royal Highness, Prince James, Major General of His Majesty's Royal Army, Sixth Division, and Protector of the Realm."

"Fancy." Bronwyn accepted James's hand to step out, Taryn following, the same loudmouth shouting, "Her Royal Highness, Princess Bronwyn of Maridrina, and Lady Taryn of Ithicana."

Trumpets abruptly blared, accompanied by vigorous drums, and when they trailed off, the man shouted, "Her Most Royal Highness, Princess Ahnna of Ithicana, beloved sister to His Royal Majesty, King Aren of Ithicana, the Master of the Bridge."

Never in her life had she been announced in such a fashion, but there was no time to consider the Harendellians' choices as her eyes fixed on James's gloved hand.

You can do this, she told herself. *Ithicana needs you to do this.*

She closed her hand over his fingers, allowing him to draw her out of the carriage, everyone silent as her boots hit the smooth white stones of the sprawling courtyard. Ahnna bowed, keeping her eyes on Edward's polished boots once she'd straightened.

Everyone was silent, and her heart skittered as she realized that there were at least a hundred courtiers in the space, all dressed in uniforms or finery, the jewels glittering in the sun a jaw-dropping display of wealth. All staring at her with undisguised interest.

And judgment.

King Edward cleared his throat. "Long has Ithicana been a strong and true ally of Harendell, and we welcome Princess Ahnna and her escort with all our heart. We invite you to treat our home as your own, and to celebrate your arrival, we will dine tonight with our dear friends and family in a private banquet to honor both Ahnna and the great nation of her birth."

Ahnna inclined her head, repeating words she'd memorized a lifetime ago. "I thank you for your hospitality and gracious welcome, Your Grace."

Edward gave her a grave nod, then turned, Queen Alexandra taking his arm as they walked inside the palace, trumpets blaring in triumph that echoed between the walls surrounding them, then up to the minarets that touched the clouds. A pretty young woman with light-brown hair the same color as the queen's followed at their heels, the cane in her hand tapping lightly along the floor, the diamonds in her tiara glittering as she walked alone—undoubtedly Princess Virginia.

Is William not here?

"Your Highness," James said, offering his arm.

Ahnna took it, her fingers pressing against the hard muscle of his forearm as she discreetly scoured the faces of those she passed, searching for one that might belong to the man she was supposed to wed.

"He's not here. Look straight forward and smile," James said softly. "The sharks are circling."

Ahnna jerked her face forward, plastering on a smile even as her mind raced. Why wasn't William here? What did that mean?

Had he learned what she and James had done?

No. No, if they'd been seen, she wouldn't be here now.

They walked up the steps and into the palace, only a lifetime of training pulling Ahnna away from her thoughts enough to notice the thickness of the oak doors they walked through, the murder holes they walked beneath, and the watchfulness of the heavily armed guards who flanked it. Even having a palace in the sky was clearly not enough to render it safe.

White stone gave way to thick carpet, their boots making soft thuds as they walked down a high-ceilinged hall, the stone walls decorated with countless portraits of unsmiling Harendellians in elaborate attire, their eyes all seeming to watch her. To judge her.

They reached a set of open twin doors framed by grim guards holding spears, and James steered her inside, Bronwyn and Taryn following. A servant shut the doors behind them, and Ahnna took in the space, which she suspected was what the Harendellians referred to as a drawing room.

The room was as high-ceilinged as the hallway. The wall opposite the door held floor-to-ceiling windows with an incredible view of the southern end of the valley, the blue drapes that framed them made of velvet so thick it would obscure even the brightest of the sun's rays. To her left was a fireplace big enough for her to walk inside, the mantel made of carved marble with blue veins that matched the curtains, a low fire burning against the faint chill in the air. None of the furniture matched, all made of different polished woods and rich brocades, but rather than making the room appear haphazard, it made Ahnna feel as though she'd stepped into the space of a collector with exquisite taste.

And even more gold.

Edward and Alexandra, as well as Virginia, waited for them in the room, along with several guards and even more servants, all standing dour-faced with their backs against the walls. Alexandra's tiara caught the light, the enormous diamonds glittering like stars, but it was the symbol of the faithful hanging from her neck that stole Ahnna's attention. A circle with a spiral weaving inward to surround a yellow diamond the size of a pigeon egg. The icon was familiar to Ahnna, for it represented the path through life to the Great Thereafter, all goodness drawn to the glow of divinity. She'd never seen it worn as jewelry, though that might be because Ithicanians wore little jewelry at all. It did confirm what she'd been told, which was that the queen was deeply committed to the faith.

The doors shut behind Ahnna, and the bland expression on Edward's face was immediately replaced with a grin. Reaching up, he pulled off his crown and tossed it on one of the plush chairs. "Ahnna," he said, approaching and taking her hands. "It is my pleasure to finally reunite with my co-conspirator against Silas!" He laughed and squeezed her hands. "We were more than a little disgruntled not to find the Maridrinians in full force at Northwatch. Led the attack myself. Most fun I've had in years, though it was over far too swiftly."

"We did not know you were there yourself, Your Grace." She wasn't certain whether to bow, given that he had her firmly by the hands, his gray eyes locked on hers. Though he was in his sixties, there was no denying that he'd been an incredibly handsome man in his prime, his mid-brown hair now laced with gray, and his eyes framed with wrinkles. Again, she was struck by how much James resembled him, though Edward was not nearly as tall or broad.

"I was incognito during the battle," Edward said, letting go of one of her hands to touch the side of his nose. "It's the only way I get to do anything fun."

Despite her anxiety, it was impossible not to be infected by his grin, and she smiled. "Ithicana thanks you for your allyship, Your Grace. It will never be forgotten."

"You will call me Eddie when we are among family," he said. "For we are family now, yes? Or close enough to it, assuming Will doesn't get lost in a wine hall on the way to the wedding. The little shit will miss his own funeral, a corpse puppet hauled about by the fools he calls friends so that they might drink on his credit."

Ahnna blinked, even as the queen snapped, "Edward!"

"What?" he demanded, looking over his shoulder at Alexandra. "He is willfully embarrassing us with his behavior, and Ahnna deserves to know the sort of man she's about to be saddled with. Thank God Ithicana has delivered us a woman with strength and character, else Harendell would be destined for a string of useless kings who spend the people's gold on wine and whores."

The queen's mouth drew into such a tight line that it all but disappeared. "If you would show him but a little kindness—"

"Kindness?" Edward's grip on Ahnna's hand tightened almost painfully. "Alex, it is your excess of kindness that has turned our son into the drunken barnacle that he is. Five years of hard duty on the border fighting Amaridians where no one cares about his blood, only about his rank and skill with a blade, would do his character a world of good. Turn him into a man rather than a boy who suckles the golden tit of privilege every goddamned day of his life."

Ahnna bit the insides of her cheeks, barely able to process the information that had just been poured into her ears, much less think of anything appropriate to say, silence seeming the most prudent course of action.

"He is the heir." Alexandra hissed, clutching at the pendant resting against her chest as though it gave her strength. "The heir is to be protected!"

"So you keep telling me, and so has he been," Edward replied. "However, that does not excuse him from his duties to the crown. Find him. Remind him."

"Father, I can find—" James started to say, but he fell silent as the king's eyes shot to him.

"You have your own actions to answer for, my son," Edward said. "Alex, find William."

The queen inclined her head. "As you say, Your Grace." Then she strode from the room in a swirl of skirts, guards scrambling to open the doors ahead of her.

The moment the door shut, the mood of the room shifted, and Virginia said, "Well, I daresay, you couldn't get a more honest introduction to the family, Ahnna. And truly, Father, was that necessary? *The golden tit of privilege?* Really?"

"It's the truth!" Edward answered.

"Perhaps, but it sounds like something you thought up during a sleepless night and have been waiting for just the right moment to deploy. I can tell when it's off the cuff as opposed to something you composed while sitting on the privy throne, you know."

Edward snorted. "Ahnna, this is my daughter, Virginia. Mind yourself around her, for her wit cuts like a knife."

The Harendellian princess approached, and it was then that Ahnna realized that the young woman's eyes were not entirely focused on her. Blind. Or, she amended as Virginia pushed her father out of her way and gripped Ahnna's arms, near to it. She pulled Ahnna into an embrace, either not noticing or not caring that Ahnna was stiff as a board. "Welcome, Ahnna of Ithicana. I look forward to glorious stories of your adventures, which are surely far more exciting than anything I've ever experienced. You shall be the sister I always wanted, because brothers are wildly irritating."

Ahnna felt her whole body twitch, remembering how she'd said something similar to Lara when she had arrived. Did Virginia suspect her intentions, as Ahnna had of Lara? Was this all an act to gain her trust? To cause her to lower her guard?

She was spared responding as Virginia launched herself at James, arms going around his neck. "Irritating, but I am so happy you are alive, brother. I hope you slaughtered a dozen of those Amaridian fuckers."

"Ginny, language," the king murmured, though he seemed amused by her response. "From George's explanation and Jamie's report"—he pulled a crumpled piece of paper from his pocket to examine—"we have Ahnna to thank that your brother still breathes." He scanned the page. "Knocked him forcibly off the ship before it exploded, then guided him to safety through shark-infested waters, and then . . . sailed with skill and bravery through a storm to escape the Amaridian fleet." He shoved the page back in his pocket. "Look at you playing the damsel in distress, my boy!"

James's cheeks turned a brilliant red. "Merely giving credit where it was due, Father."

"Ha ha! I jest—I'm sure you acquitted yourself as you always do!" Edward pulled his son into a tight embrace, pounding James's back vigorously. "On my word, they'll bleed for this. Katarina has bitten off far more than she can chew with this outrage. If she wants war, we'll bring it to them, sure and true!"

"Oh, we're hunting down our foe as the sun begins to gleam," Virginia sang out, her father joining in at top volume. "With a boom and a crash, and a whack and a scream, we'll cut down the 'Ridians 'til the blood begins to stream!"

The king broke off laughing, then turned his attention to Taryn. "Lady Taryn, we are so delighted that you are here to attend your cousin. I've heard a rumor that you've a lovely voice. I'll make arrangements for you to hear the university's choir perform, for you are sure to appreciate it." Then he took Bronwyn's hands. "Princess Bronwyn. Those Veliant eyes are unmistakable. We've several members of your family of various generations married into our noble houses, though from what I've heard of your unusual upbringing, you aren't close with them. I should say, your brother Keris writes the most delightfully entertaining letters. Truly a gift for words, that man, and I hope to keep up a frequent correspondence with him if for no other reason than the joy it brings to my days."

"That should please him," Bronwyn replied. "The only thing Keris likes better than hearing himself speak is writing everything that he's said down so that it can be repeated."

"Ha ha!" Edward grinned. "Good to see you share his wit. Can't say the same for many of your relations, though I've heard only great things of Queen Sarhina."

"Always a few bad apples on every tree, Your Grace," Bronwyn said. "Sarhina is not one of them."

"It is my most fervent wish that she brings peace and prosperity to Maridrina."

Ahnna opened her mouth to suggest that his wish would be achieved if Harendell increased its exports through the bridge, but Edward turned to her and said, "Your journey has been long, Ahnna, and you are no doubt in need of rest so that you might prepare yourself for the banquet in your honor tonight. Virginia, would you escort the princess and her companions to their rooms?"

"Of course." The princess accepted her cane from a servant, then said, "If you would follow me, ladies."

The younger woman led them out into the corridor, cane making no noise as she tapped it against the thick carpet. They walked to a large staircase that split into two, rising to the second level. Virginia headed upward, mouth moving slightly. Counting, Ahnna determined, the princess obviously having memorized the number of steps, along with a host of other cues to allow her to move about the palace.

Seeming to sense her thoughts, Virginia said, "I was not born blind. My eyes began to fail when I was ten, and I resolved to learn to navigate the world before I went blind, so I am quite comfortable in all of our family homes. I do see shadows and the outlines of figures if the lighting is good, though it is only a matter of time until it will be only darkness."

Ahnna considered giving her condolences, but instead said, "You seem prepared for that eventuality."

"Seeing nothing provides a certain degree of clarity." Virginia stopped before a door and opened it to a room filled with sunshine. "Lady Bronwyn, these are your rooms. Your trunks have already been placed inside, and a servant waits to attend to your needs. If there is any comfort you lack, please do let her know."

Bronwyn murmured her thanks, then went inside. They carried on down the hall to the next door, and Virginia said to Taryn, "Lady Taryn, you'll find that your rooms include a door that leads to your princess's chambers, for I've been led to believe that you serve the role of not only her lady-in-waiting but also her bodyguard. Is that correct?"

"Yeah," Taryn answered, then winced. "I mean, *yes*, Your Highness."

"Wonderful. Do let the maid know if there is anything you require."

They carried on up the corridor, Virginia stopping without hesitation in front of a twin set of doors. Slipping a key from her pocket, she unlocked it and went inside. Ahnna's eyes flicked back down the hall to where Jor silently trailed her, and he gave a nod.

Entering, Ahnna watched the other princess cross the room to sit on a green velvet sofa. Hazel, who'd obviously been waiting, exited, shutting the doors behind her.

"I have but one question," Virginia said as Ahnna perched on the chair across from her. "Why have you come to Harendell?"

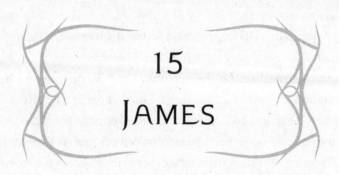

15

JAMES

AFTER THE WOMEN DEPARTED, HIS FATHER MOTIONED TO SER-
vants and guards alike to leave the room, saying nothing until the
door shut behind them. "Drink? You look as though you could use
one."

"Please."

Unbuttoning his coat, James tossed it on a chair before slump-
ing on a sofa, watching as his father made some sort of concoction
out of various alcohols, knowing that whatever it was would kick
like a horse hoof to the head.

"Ahnna is lovely," his father said, stirring a drink and then adding in a liquid that was an alarming shade of green. "I suspected
that I would like her from our brief meeting while we coordinated
our forces against Silas, and I was correct."

"You've spent five minutes in her presence."

"That's all I need." His father approached, setting the strange-
colored drink in front of James. "I'm an excellent judge of character.
Plus, you seem to like her, which is telling. You don't like anyone."

For an instant, panic flooded James's veins that his father had discovered his indiscretion with Ahnna, but the amused smile on Edward's face chased the panic away. His father wouldn't be laughing if he knew that James had kissed Ahnna in the middle of the night in Fernleigh's maze, which was in full view of every window of the house.

"Inaccurate on both counts," James countered because his father would question *why* if he didn't. "There are a good many people I like, just very few of them are at court. As for the princess, we do not see eye-to-eye on much."

"Precisely." His father sipped his drink. "You have a strong preference for individuals who argue with you at every turn. You've always liked difficult things, James, and that includes people."

There was some validity to that statement, but he needed to stomp on any of the positive sentiment he felt toward Ahnna. His goals were counter to hers in every way, and he could not allow himself to be swayed from them in order to appease her. "Sentiment is irrelevant, particularly mine."

His father made a tutting noise but then said, "Your report had notable holes in it, which is fair, given that secrecy is of the essence. What have you learned?"

"Ithicana is understandably weaker militarily than it has ever been, but I believe that also extends to their finances," James said. "Ahnna made overtures about increasing exports on our part through her brother's bridge, under the guise of supporting the Maridrinians, but she resisted suggestions of concessions on tariffs. I believe they seek to rebuild Ithicana using Harendell's wealth. They aren't the allies they once were. Indeed, despite the violent attack that sank our ship on their own pier, Aren showed no interest in blocking Amarid's access to Southwatch, his only concern the practical challenge of removing the wreckage so that trade at the market could continue without delay. I believe they are desperate for gold."

His father took another sip of his drink, expression thoughtful rather than angered. "Ithicana has lost a great deal, but never has it had greater influence in the south. Lara's sister Sarhina, whom she is rumored to be very close with, is on the throne of Maridrina, and her brother Keris is wed to the Empress of Valcotta. Those are no small things, especially given the amount of trade we've historically done with both nations."

"Maridrina is nearly bankrupt." Then, knowing his father took great offense to anyone who didn't drink his concoctions, James took a sip of the green liquor, which burned with such ferocity that he coughed. "The Maridrinians can't afford to buy more, and our goods would sit at Southwatch's market while our merchants were charged daily for warehousing and cattle feed. We'd lose gold hand over fist while Ithicana pockets endless profit."

He coughed again, his eyes watering because the drink continued to burn. "While it is commendable that Valcotta and Maridrina have ceased in their warring, it does mean the Maridrinians have alternatives for trade, and that is not to our favor. For better or worse, the Endless War was good for business and even better for profit."

"War always is." His father swirled his drink. "You have thoughts you are holding back."

James stared at the contents of his glass, uncertain how many of those thoughts he wished to share. Finally, he said, "Cormac was in Sableton. He reiterated Ronan's demand that you break this betrothal."

"I signed a treaty with Ithicana," his father said, expression unreadable. "Gave my word that this marriage would occur. I do not break my word lightly, nor do I have any desire to destroy goodwill with the Bridge Kingdom, so I need more justification than Ronan wanting it to be so."

"Because allowing Will to wed her would be disingenuous." James set his glass on the table. "They sent Ahnna believing this marriage would give them what they need to rebuild their nation, and we both know that isn't the case. Unlike Maridrina and its endless princesses, Ithicana has only one card to play. They have played it believing Ahnna will have influence here. They believe she will secure more trade. They believe that we will support them with our navy. Yet you and I know that those beliefs are misguided."

"So, you would protect Ithicana from their own misstep? You would spare Ahnna the pain of learning she's married your brother for nothing?" his father asked, then smiled over his glass. "I thought sentiment was irrelevant?"

James's cheeks warmed slightly. "It's a matter of honor. If Ahnna understands that she cannot achieve what she wishes by marrying Will, then she may ask Aren to renegotiate. She can wed a Veliant prince or some Valcottan nobleman, or better yet, remain in Ithicana, for that is where she truly wishes to be."

"Unfortunately, honor and wisdom rarely walk hand in hand," his father said. "If Ithicana's circumstances are as dire as you believe and we tell them that marriage will not secure them the trade they desire, that we will free them of their obligation to wed their princess to your brother, what is to stop them from attempting to play their card with Amarid? Katarina does, after all, have a son."

James stiffened. "They would not marry Ahnna to the Beast."

"Are you so certain about that?" Rising, James's father began to slowly pace the room, sipping his drink. "Ithicana has nothing to gain in wedding Ahnna to any of the southern nations that they don't already have, and keeping her gives them even less. Whereas

Amarid is a contentious political relationship, so they'd have much to gain in the smoothing of it, and what better path to peace than a bride? In your quest to spare Ahnna irrelevancy, you would not only be delivering her to a marriage with a monster of a man, but you would also be handing our greatest adversary an alliance with the Bridge Kingdom. The kingdom that currently influences all the power of the south."

James hadn't considered that. Hadn't considered that Aren would stoop so low as to wed his sister to Carlo, whose dark reputation was known north and south. Would Ithicana's king sentence his sister to a life of abject misery for the sake of gaining a powerful ally? His gut told him no, but he'd also seen how Aren had walked down the Northwatch pier without even a goodbye for the sister he was sending away. Witnessed the obvious conflict between Ahnna and Lara. "There was tension between her and Aren that clearly centered on his wife. Ahnna has not forgiven Lara's trespasses against Ithicana."

"Even more reason for her to remain. In Harendell, Ahnna may be irrelevant, but at least she'll be treated with the courtesy she deserves." His father finished his drink and set the glass aside. "Ithicana might well grow bitter when they realize we've no intention of giving them what they want, but what can they say? We held to our word, which included no promises of increasing our trade through their bridge, so while they might be surly over their misplayed card, they will not have any grounds, nor the ability, to take action against us. Most especially once our own plans to the north come to fruition and they understand that we don't need them at all."

"And Ronan?"

"Your uncle won't ruin a once-in-a-lifetime opportunity to open the border over whom your brother marries. He's just seeing how far he can push me."

James wasn't entirely certain that was the case, given Cormac's vehemence over Ahnna, but that wasn't what was troubling him. Picking up the green drink, James downed it despite the awful burn, because though his father was right, every part of him rebelled against using Ahnna this way. She deserved better, but better was at odds with what was right for Harendell and Cardiff.

"It might not be the life Ahnna envisions, but we'll protect her," his father said, coming around the table to rest his hand on James's shoulder.

Ahnna doesn't need to be protected.

"William will get her with child, and then we'll put her up in an estate that she can rule as she sees fit."

A sudden surge of jealousy filled James. Not the first time he'd been jealous of his brother, but the first time in many years. The first time since he'd come to terms with the role that he played in the royal family, and James shoved the emotion behind as high a wall as he could, angry that he was feeling it now.

"She'll want for nothing," his father continued. "She'll never need to lift a finger or worry about anything for the rest of her days. Which I think is far better than the alternative, don't you?"

That wasn't at all the life Ahnna wanted, James knew that. However, he'd also been face-to-face with Carlo, who would be a far worse fate than boredom in a country estate. "Yes."

"Good." His father lifted his hand from James's shoulder, then carried on around the room. "Nothing is imminent, for royal weddings take time. And for all she's against this marriage, Alex will want a spectacle for her son. Ronan will recognize that these coming months are the most critical to negotiate a reopening of the border and terms of trade, and you will continue meeting with Cormac as the liaison between us."

James gave a tight nod.

"In the meantime, let us treat Ahnna to what it is like to be a princess in Harendell, yes?" His father grinned. "Banquets and balls, diamonds and dresses."

That was the last way to impress a woman like Ahnna, but James remained silent as he rose, walking to the door.

"Oh, and I am sure this goes without saying," his father said as James's hand fell on the handle, "but *you* will keep Ahnna Kertell entertained and as far out of your brother's way as can be reasonably managed, else we risk his behavior sending her fleeing whether we want her to or not."

The last thing James wished to do was spend more time in Ahnna's presence, but his father was king.

And kings were to be obeyed.

16

Ahnna

Ahnna blinked. "Pardon?"

"Why have you come?" Virginia repeated. "To Harendell."

Ahnna opened her mouth, then closed it again, confused by the question, given the answer was obvious. "To marry your brother."

Virginia crossed her arms, clearly unsatisfied with the answer, so Ahnna added, "To fulfill the treaty formed between my mother and your father, which included the promise of marriage between myself and William to forge a lasting and secure alliance between Ithicana and Harendell."

The princess's eyes narrowed. "So you are here because you must be here. You are marrying my brother because you *must* marry him."

Ahnna considered the other woman's tone, hearing the edge of protectiveness in it and suspecting the motivations behind the line of questioning. "I am here because I want to be here."

Virginia's face softened ever so slightly. "You were given the choice?"

"Yes," Ahnna answered, because though there had been no choice in her mind, Aren had certainly given her one. "I chose to come to Harendell."

"Why?"

A more difficult question. "Because I hope it will give me the opportunity to do some good." She hesitated. "A union with Prince William will allow us to achieve good things together."

Virginia was silent for a time, and then she said, "I am very protective of my family, Ahnna, but most especially of my brothers. James has the fortitude of an ox, but William is sensitive. Easily hurt, and as you have seen, my father is not always kind to him. If you wish to be on my good side, then you will serve as a shield between William and my father, for you are possessed of qualities my father admires. Make my brother's life better, and I will support you. Harm him, and you will find yourself with a very dangerous enemy."

Though she didn't care for the threat, Ahnna admired Virginia's forthrightness, so she only inclined her head as the other woman rose.

"A word of warning," Virginia said. "If you think I am overprotective, know my mother is thrice so. There is nothing she won't do to protect Will from harm, and she has been more than clear that she does not see you as a suitable wife for him. Don't give her a reason to get rid of you, as my mother has a fondness for permanent solutions to anything she sees as a problem."

The princess left the room without another word.

Crossing the space, Ahnna latched the door, then walked on silent feet through the sumptuous suite, which was all pale-blue velvets and polished wood, until she reached the door adjoining her rooms to Taryn's. Twisting the knob, she pulled it open to find both her cousin and Bronwyn holding water glasses to their ears, clearly having been eavesdropping.

"You're a terrible influence on her," she said to Bronwyn. "At least tell me if you heard everything and spare me the dry throat I'll get from explaining it all."

"We heard," Taryn said, pushing into the room, where she immediately began to examine everything from top to bottom. Her cousin had served as one of Aren's bodyguards for years, so she knew her business.

Bronwyn went to the sideboard holding decanters of water, wine, and a darker spirit. She sniffed the contents of all three. Then, before Ahnna could stop her, she took a large mouthful of the wine.

"No!" Ahnna yanked the decanter from the woman's hand, splashing wine over her wrist. "Are you mad? They could be full of poison!"

"My sisters often question my sanity." Bronwyn shrugged. "Truthfully, I doubt anyone would be so obvious as to poison the wine in your room. It's more likely to be in your gloves, on the hilt of a weapon, or on something you'll touch in passing. Harendell's poison craft is rivaled only by Amarid, and Serin made us study their delivery methods at length. That's the real art, you know. Not the toxin itself, but methods of deploying it that don't fall back on the poisoner. That's the reason my father made such a fortress out of the inner sanctum in the Vencia palace—to control everything that went on around him, which we cannot do. If anyone in the Sky Palace wants you dead, there isn't much we can do to prevent it other than to leave."

"I'm not leaving."

"I know." Bronwyn flung herself down on a chair, tucking her long legs beneath her. "What did you make of Princess Virginia warning you about her mother?"

Ahnna sat on the same chair as she had before, but this time, she leaned back, staring up at the ceiling. "Keris warned me that Alexandra was against my betrothal to William when he was in Eranahl, so it wasn't a shock."

"You never told me that," Taryn grumbled, straightening from where she'd been looking under the bed.

She hadn't told anyone. Hadn't wanted to give Aren or Lara more leverage in trying to dissuade her from coming to Harendell, but now she wondered how much they'd known and hadn't told *her*.

Bronwyn exhaled slowly. "Well, that's concerning. Keris certainly knows all the gossip, but he's not one to trade in anything he doesn't believe is factual. If the information came from him, it's good."

"We should leave," Taryn said. "Aren wouldn't want you here if he knew your life was at risk from Alexandra."

"I'm not leaving." Ahnna sat upright, resting her elbows on her knees. "You know as well as I do how dire the situation is in Ithicana. We're *broke*, Taryn. The people are hungry and homeless, and the only nation with the power to make an immediate difference is Harendell. We need their trade. Need their navy. Need their alliance, and if I run home with my tail between my legs, we'll have none of those things. Especially if they do have plans that will reduce their dependence on the bridge."

"At least you'll be alive."

Alive, but the thought of returning to Ithicana having failed her people yet again made it a worse proposition than dying in the attempt to make a difference. "I'm not leaving."

"At least write to Aren and explain the situation," Taryn finally said. "Put it in code, and Jor or I will track down one of our own spies to deliver it. Aren should know everything we've learned."

Part of Ahnna worried that Aren would bodily drag her back to Ithicana if he knew the risks, but keeping the information from him was reckless, so Ahnna shrugged. "Fine. You write it and I'll sign it. But if you'd both excuse me, I need to get ready for this banquet."

Taryn gave her a long look that said, *You're an idiot*, but abandoned the room for her own, Bronwyn following on her heels. A moment later, Hazel entered with an armload of folded fabric. Beyond, Ahnna could hear Jor coughing in the hallway, the ferocity of it making her frown. Stepping through the door, she looked at the old man. "You all right?"

"Fine," he growled. "It's their terrible weather. I'll be right in a day or two once I adjust."

He shouldn't be here, Ahnna thought, but this wasn't the time to argue with him. "Can you hear anything through the door? Taryn checked the rest of the room."

"Nah, you're good," he said, leaning against the wall. "Place is solid stone and oak, but still, take care in other rooms. They drill holes behind artwork and that sort of nonsense."

Of course they did.

Giving him a tight nod, Ahnna retreated into the room, only for three young men carrying steaming buckets to come up the hallway and enter behind her. They all bowed, murmuring, "My lady," then proceeded into an antechamber. Water splashed, and then the trio exited, shutting the door behind them.

Curious, Ahnna entered the room to find Hazel arranging soaps and sponges next to a large copper tub before a blazing fire. Ahnna allowed Hazel to undress her, then stepped into the bath, wincing at the temperature as she lowered herself into the water. "Do they need to heat water for every bath in the palace?"

"Yes, my lady. We have vast kettles in the kitchens dedicated to the heating of bathing water brought up from the river."

Ithicana was rife with natural hot springs, so the thought of going through so much effort for a warm bath was entirely unfamiliar to her. "The price of living in the sky, I suppose."

"Yes, my lady. In Harendell, inconvenience is a marker of privilege."

Out of the corner of her eye, Ahnna saw Hazel bite her lip, obviously regretting her words, and she gave the girl a wink. "If they had to draw their own water for a day, they might make better choices of where they build their palaces."

A ghost of a smile appeared on the young woman's lips. "Even so, my lady."

Hazel unraveled Ahnna's braids, then poured warm water over the curls and set to scrubbing.

"What should I expect tonight?" Ahnna asked. "The king mentioned that this was a dinner for close friends and family."

"Yes, my lady," Hazel answered. "Though the count I heard in the kitchen was some two hundred guests."

Ahnna choked. "Two hundred?"

"Yes, it is not an event to be missed. The nobility has been arriving in Verwyrd throughout the past week, and everyone is eager to meet Your Highness." She hesitated, then said, "Ithicana's mysteries have long been a matter of intense speculation, and the unveiling of its secrets is a once-in-a-lifetime opportunity."

It was hard not to stiffen, for those secrets were what protected Ithicana. "Unless they've an interest in snakes and sharks, there isn't much to tell."

Hazel made a soft humming noise. "Would you like me to explain the order of a Harendellian banquet?"

She'd learned the protocols in her youth, but a refresher seemed prudent. If she was to embarrass herself, she'd rather it be on purpose. "Please."

Hazel poured information into Ahnna's ears until her head

spun and the water began to cool. Stepping out of the bath, she toweled herself off and donned the velvet dressing gown Hazel held out for her before following the woman into the other room.

"I've been working on garments that matched your instructions, my lady," the young woman said. "Garments in the style of Ithicana but with Harendellian fabrics. I hope they are as you envisioned."

"May I see them?" Ahnna plucked the garments from Hazel's hands, the fabric incredibly smooth. The trousers were the same cut she usually wore, but of the finest dove-gray silk with delicate silver embroidery running up the sides. The tunic was of a darker gray that verged on blue with embroidery to match, the cuffs bearing silver buttons. "These are beautiful. So much better than I imagined."

"Thank you, my lady."

Swiftly donning the undergarments that Hazel handed her, Ahnna then put on the clothing, which fit like a glove, the silk rich and cool against her skin. New black boots polished so that she could see her reflection in the leather came next, then a belt made of silver-wrapped leather, on which was sheathed one of her longer knives. Ahnna sat while Hazel wove her hair into elaborate braids and then applied a hint of cosmetics before giving a nod of approval. "You are beautiful, my lady."

Moving in front of the mirror, Ahnna's breath caught, for not in all her life had she looked like this. Like a princess in truth, not just in name, and she did not see how the Harendellians could laugh at her now. Even James would have to bite his tongue. "Thank you, Hazel."

A rare smile formed on the young woman's face, and she said, "If you will not join them, then you shall beat them, yes?"

"Yes."

A knock sounded at the door, and when Hazel opened it, Jor and Taryn stood outside, her cousin dressed in her usual clothes but armed to the teeth. Bronwyn was nowhere to be seen. "They say it's time. His Highness is waiting for you at the grand staircase," Jor said, looking her up and down. "Delia would be proud, girl. She fought hard for this moment."

Ahnna's cheeks flushed, warmth filling her chest at the idea of making her mother proud, only for the sentiment to fade. That pride would have nothing to do with Ahnna herself and everything to do with achieving the dream her mother had of opening Ithicana to the world. A dream Aren had shared, the pair of them spending hours discussing how it might come to pass while Ahnna had stood on the outskirts, praying to every higher power that the day would never come to pass.

But it was here.

You have what you wanted, Mother. I hope it is all you dreamed of.

Striding down the corridor, Ahnna squared her shoulders and lifted her chin. Let the Harendellians do their worst. She was Princess Ahnna Kertell of Ithicana, and she'd faced down warriors from every kingdom north and south and come out victorious. If they thought to break her with laughter and snide comments, they had another thing coming.

Yet for all her brave words, her palms felt like ice, because Jor had said that it was *His Highness* who was waiting for her. Which meant that finally, she was going to meet the man she was supposed to marry. Dread pooled in her stomach, any anticipation she might have felt in meeting William long since burned away by what she'd been told about him.

It doesn't matter if you like him, she reminded herself. *It doesn't matter if he likes you. This is a political alliance, nothing more.*

Yet the words meant little, for unlike every other political alliance she'd made, this one would begin and end in a bed-chamber.

The artwork on the walls to either side was a blur, her heels making soft thumps against the thick carpets as she strode. The end of the curved hallway appeared ahead, the top of the grand staircase visible. Just before she reached it, Ahnna sucked in a deep breath, praying that Hazel's efforts would pay off.

Then she stepped out into the open, her gaze going down the grand staircase to where a uniformed figure stood with his back to her, tall and broad of shoulder. He slowly turned, and Ahnna's breath caught as her eyes fixed on his face.

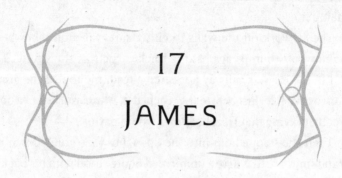

17
JAMES

JAMES'S FIRST THOUGHT AS HIS GAZE LANDED ON HER FACE WAS that no woman ever born was as beautiful as Ahnna Kertell. The second was that constantly being in her presence was going to be very much a problem.

They stared each other down, and then she said, "You again."

"I'm afraid so."

Ahnna sighed. "Let me guess. Your brother couldn't be bothered to find his way out of his wine long enough to greet me properly?"

"He's likely been apprised of the nature of your acid tongue and needs more fortitude."

"How many drinks did *you* need to bolster the courage to escort me?"

Three. All of which he regretted, because they encouraged thoughts he had no business thinking. "None," he replied, "but then again, I'm not the one who has to marry you." He held out his hand. "You coming, *Your Highness,* or shall I request your dinner be brought to the top of the stairs so that we might continue this delightful exchange without interruption?"

Ahnna's hazel eyes narrowed, but she gave no commentary as she descended. Most ladies clutched the railing or the hand of an escort, but Ahnna did not so much as glance down at the steps, moving with the grace of a dancer and the confidence of a lioness. Her hand closed on his arm, grip firm as he turned her down the corridor.

"I confess," she said, lengthening her stride. "I'm surprised to see you will be attending dinner."

"And why is that?" He increased his own stride to match hers.

"Didn't your father keep you behind for a tongue-lashing over the loss of his ship?"

"Hardly. We had a drink."

"So much for not needing liquid fortitude."

"We were discussing more important matters than *you*," he said stiffly, annoyed over being caught in a lie.

Ahnna only made a humming sound, increasing her pace again and forcing him to match or fall behind.

"Slow down," he growled. "This is not dignified."

"Walk faster," she replied. "I'm hungry."

Any faster and he'd have to break into a run, and James did not fail to notice that all the servants were staring at them with concern over the urgency of their pace. "We're late," he said to one, his irritation flaring as Ahnna gave a soft laugh.

"You are behaving like a child, Your Highness," he said, giving another servant a reassuring nod. "A child raised in a barn rather than a palace."

"A boat, if you wish to be accurate, *Your Highness*." She cast a sideways smirk at him, a glimmer of gold cosmetics accentuating her hazel gaze. "You should worry less about what people think of you."

"And you should worry more."

Her gaze snapped forward, and he knew that he'd struck a nerve. Yet rather than enjoying the moment of getting the upper hand in their endless arguments, James felt like an ass. "My compliments to Hazel. She has outdone herself tonight."

The corner of her mouth turned up. "And here I thought to suffer your criticism over my lack of skirts. *Unladylike* and *undignified* and *unbecoming* were words that came to mind."

As though words were even possible with those long legs stretching out with each stride she took, the silk clinging to the muscles beneath, his only thought what it would be like to have those legs wrapped around him again. "The style does not negate Hazel's skill."

"I'll tell her." Her eyes flicked up, catching him watching her. "I see you've availed yourself of your own tailor. Shame. I enjoyed your too-small shirts, for they had about as much give as your sense of propriety."

James's cheek flushed, and seeing they'd reached the doors to the ballroom, he hauled her bodily to a halt, be damned what the gaping guards said. "Never have I met a lady like you."

"Thank you, James," she said with a wink, but there was an odd hollowness to it. "You always make me feel so special. Usually right before you tell me to go back to where I came from."

His lips parted but no retort came forth, and the doors were already opening, the herald announcing them. Yet as their titles poured from the man's lips, he watched Ahnna's behavior *shift*. The smirk fell away, along with the amusement and the nerves he suspected the repartee had hidden, and in its place rose the princess of the wildest kingdom in the known world.

Chin up, shoulders back, and eyes cool, she surveyed the watching nobility with an air that he'd have described as haughty on any other woman. But for Ahnna, it was nothing but the purest form of confidence. Wild and untamed, and every goddamned part of him wanted her.

She's not for you. Never for you.

She tightened her grip on his arm, and instinctively, he stepped forward. Not leading her but matching her as she strode down the long path leading to the head table. The nobility all bowed and curtsied as they passed, the idiots among them tittering about her trousers and scars, but James marked how the real players among them watched Ahnna with interest, reevaluating what they'd believed they were getting with the Ithicanian princess even as they recalculated how they might use her in their own endeavors.

Ahnna's eyes roved over them with dispassionate interest, and James heard one of his sister's ladies-in-waiting whisper, "Did you see how she looked at me? I thought she might leap forward and cut my throat!"

James waited until they'd walked another few paces, then murmured, "Don't let it go to your head, Highness. I've heard Elizabeth say the same thing about the queen's lapdogs."

"You do God's work in keeping my ego in check, *Highness*."

It was a struggle not to smile.

That struggle vanished as his eyes flicked to the head table, the degree to which she'd distracted him rendered apparent as he abruptly realized his brother was not seated to Alexandra's left. Not in the room at all.

Shit.

Stopping before the table, James locked eyes briefly with his father before bowing low. Ahnna did the same, titters that she'd not curtsied filling the air behind them. His father's expression was bland, but James felt the irritation over William's absence seething from him. Alexandra's tight-pressed lips suggested that she'd borne the brunt of his ire.

His father rose to his feet, Alexandra silently rising next to him. "We welcome you, Princess Ahnna, and hope that you will come to regard our home as your own."

"I hope for this as well, Your Grace," Ahnna responded. "Thank you for your gracious hospitality."

His father inclined his head and then sat, James's cue to escort Ahnna to her seat. As he pushed the chair beneath her, he inhaled, struck by the scent of her. Sea salt and jungle, petrichor and lightning, as if the scents of Ithicana were part of her. He stood frozen for a heartbeat, eyes fixed on the woven braids of her hair, the light from the chandeliers above turning strands of it amber and walnut and gold. Like the forests of Cardiff in the fall.

Remembering himself, he moved to her right, jostling the table as he sat, wine and water nearly sloshing over the rims of their respective glasses. Though he kept his eyes forward, James could feel Alexandra's irritation at his error, could sense the nobility watching every facial expression. He prayed they'd blame his endless conflict with the queen for the tension and not suspect anything untoward in his feelings for the princess next to him.

His father recovered the moment, turning to Ahnna, his elbow resting on the table and yet another of his strange mixed drinks in his free hand. "Lady Ahnna. Might I say, you are positively radiant this evening. A true beauty."

A faint blush colored Ahnna's cheeks, her lips parting to speak, but his father added, "It pleases me that you've chosen to wear traditional Ithicanian attire. Most of the ass-kissers who come into my court dress in the latest Harendellian fashions, not seeming to understand how tremendously dull that makes them. Like being stuck in a world cast in a thousand shades of gray when all I dream of is color."

"Your Grace's metaphor would be more apt if I were not wearing gray myself," Ahnna responded, and his father grinned, his infamous charm out in full force as he said, "And yet my point stands, for you are the only one in this room not leaping to claim me the greatest poet of my generation. You are a breath of fresh air, Ahnna. Truly, Ithicana's loss is our gain."

"You should not disparage guests who wear our fashion, husband," Alexandra murmured, sipping from her glass. "They do it as a sign of respect for the culture and morals of our great nation, and while that may not be of any great entertainment, we must acknowledge the courtesy."

He'd warned Ahnna this would come, but James still found himself holding his breath to see how Ahnna would respond. Waiting for the same irreverence she always delivered upon him. However, Ahnna said, "It is not my intention to show a lack of courtesy or to disrespect Harendell, Your Grace. Quite the opposite. You invited me to Harendell as part of a greater alliance with Ithicana, and my intention is to represent with total honesty what both I and my homeland bring to this alliance. To present myself in any other way would be misrepresentation, and I do not wish to begin my life in Harendell with dishonesty."

It was impossible not to respect her words even as James felt his guilt surge about his own dishonesty.

"If these are your goals, I applaud you in your success in achieving them," Alexandra said, then took a small mouthful of her wine.

Ahnna gave the slightest nod, and James winced internally, for the queen's words were no compliment. Ahnna was out of her depth, every one of his warnings having fallen on deaf ears, and he wanted to scream, *Go home before they destroy you!*

Instead, he took a mouthful of wine.

God help him, he hated being at court. Hated how attributes were weaknesses to be exploited, every person in this room grasping and reaching for *more more more* with no care for what was right. Not an ounce of real morality in the lot of them, himself included, for no one was more at odds with Ahnna than he was.

"Your sentiments are admirable, Ahnna," his father said. "And appreciated, for the actions of the Veliants left a sour taste in my mouth. It is good to see that you have risen above rather than been drawn down to their level."

Don't bite, James silently screamed, but a genuine smile warmed Ahnna's face. "Exactly this, Your Grace. I wish to represent Ithicana's intentions without deception."

"I assume those intentions are not to invade?" When Ahnna went still, his father laughed and gave her a wink. "I jest. Which is likely in poor taste, for I know the wounds Maridrina inflicted on Ithicana are far from healed. War takes such a toll, especially on the people who can least afford it."

Ahnna's voice caught as though she'd been about to confirm, but instead, she reached for her water glass, sipping at it before she said, "My people are strong and resilient, and war is no stranger to Ithicana, for every nation, north and south, has brought violence to our shores."

His father's eyes gleamed; he was clearly pleased to discover that Ahnna was not entirely oblivious to the game he played. "Crossing blades in battle one hour only to exchange coins in trade in the next?"

Ahnna lifted one shoulder. "If we did not trade with nations who have attacked us, the bridge would be empty."

"Of course." His father took a mouthful of his drink. "Though I can't imagine how it must have felt to invite the Maridrinians back to Southwatch after everything they'd done. To do business with those who'd slaughtered Ithicanian children, rather than seek revenge against them."

His father was playing on Ahnna's emotions to dig and dig and dig, and though James knew this was the way of politics, he still hated watching it happen.

Ahnna was quiet, then she said, "Silas Veliant was the villain, not the Maridrinian people."

"Silas, yes. But also his daughter." Another sip of the drink. Another smile. "Lara. We were led to believe that Silas's invasion plans were delivered to him by Ithicana's own queen." Not giving Ahnna a chance to respond, his father added, "I can't imagine how it must feel to have to bend the knee to the woman who stabbed you in the back. You invited her into your home, treated her like family, and the entire time, she conspired against you. That is a great deal to be asked to forgive."

His father's real interest was in whether the act of forgiveness was unforgivable. Whether in forgiving his wife, Aren had created a divide with his sister that could be deepened and widened for Harendell's benefit.

The muscles in Ahnna's jaw tensed, and then she said, "Lara killed Silas in the battle for Eranahl, a death I witnessed with my own eyes. She is loyal to my brother and to Ithicana. Carries the heir to Ithicana—my future niece or nephew."

"That you've forgiven Lara speaks to your character," his father responded, deliberately interpreting what she'd said as absolution. "I would not have been able to do so."

Ahnna leaned fractionally closer to his father, seeming to drink in the words, little knowing that he was only validating what James had told him about her strained relationship with Lara.

His father mirrored the motion, co-conspirator in a confession. "I would not be able to sleep at night, tormented by the faces of those who died under Maridrinian blades, all while she lived and laughed. I would be consumed." He waved the hand holding the drink, the contents nearly going over the rim. "You're a better woman than I am, Ahnna."

"That's not much of an accomplishment," she said without hesitation. "For you are no woman."

His father barked out a laugh. "Oh, you are a delight. A balm to my boredom. But let us turn to lighter topics. How do you feel about adulterated spirits?"

Ahnna went stiff as a board, the color draining from her face, and James knew the only word she'd heard was *adultery*. To spare her, he swiftly said, "He refers to mixed drinks. Concoctions of various sorts of liquors and the occasional syrup. It is my father's newest hobby, but show care, my lady, for the sweetest drinks tend to pack the hardest punch."

"A hobby." Ahnna said the word as though it were a foreign concept.

"Father gains a new hobby every year," came Virginia's voice from down the table, his sister leaning forward. "And we must all participate. We are, all of us, very talented at croquet, taxidermy, and rose gardening, to say nothing of horse racing, hunting, tennis, and lawn bowling."

"You make me sound inconstant in my pursuits, darling," his father complained. "Jamie, be a good lad and offer some support."

James shrugged. "You are well rounded in your interests, Father."

"Bullies, all of you." His father motioned at the servants to begin bringing out the food. "All I do is try to expand your minds, and in exchange, I must suffer your abuse. Ahnna, the mixing of spirits is as much an art as it is a science, and our culinary schools are creating whole books on the topic. I would like to take you to visit them, for I think that you might—"

He cut off as the herald abruptly announced, "His Most Royal Highness, Crown Prince William."

18

AHNNA

AHNNA'S FOCUS SNAPPED TO THE FAR END OF THE GRAND HALL with such force that her neck clicked. Her gaze latched upon the man ambling up the aisle between the tables, two other men of a similar age flanking him, all three bearing the grins of those deep in their cups.

"Sorry I'm late," William said. "The races went long, and I had a horse in the final. Took the prize, so it was worth the wait."

Next to her, Edward said nothing, and Ahnna kept her face blank as she took in the man she was supposed to marry. Her mistaking James for him was something to be forgiven, for they were very similar in appearance. High cheekbones, square jaws, straight noses, and mouths possessed of decidedly full bottom lips. But whereas James was ruggedly handsome, his beauty wholly masculine, William was more delicate and finer-boned, almost fragile. Like glassworks that are to be admired but never ever touched. His brown hair did not hold the copper hue of his brother's, and it was longer, nearly down to his shoulders, his eyes green, not amber.

William's attention was fixed on his father as he walked, almost as though he were daring Edward to say something about his tardiness. About his drunkenness. About his impertinence. Yet for all his angry words in private, in front of all these people, the king of Harendell held his tongue.

Just before the head table, the three men stopped, all bowing low. William's two companions moved to the side, devil-may-care grins on their faces, leaving the crown prince standing alone. Only then did William's attention shift to her. A lazy drifting of his gaze, and the utter fury in his eyes made her stomach clench. He hadn't needed to see her to dislike her—he'd come to this dinner already hating her.

"Your Highness," he said. "I'd heard that the Maridrinians had had their way with you, but I did not expect to see it written across your face."

Next to her, James shifted restlessly, but Edward was entirely silent. Ahnna wanted to be angry with him for not putting his son in his place for his rudeness, but expecting that was foolish. Ignoring the sting to her pride, Ahnna stared William in the eye, questioning the right path forward—whether it was better to silently take the insult or defend herself. And it took her only a heartbeat to decide that it didn't matter what she did. This wasn't a battle between her and William; it was a battle between father and son, and she needed only to choose whose side she was on.

An easy choice given that Edward ruled, and so Ahnna said, "It is true that it was a Maridrinian who wounded my face, but that was the only blow he struck. The next was mine, and it left his innards on the outside and him dying a slow death while I cut down his companions." She ignored the shocked gasps from the watching nobles. "I've been cut a hundred times or more by those who desired my death and worse, yet I am the one who still draws breath, whereas they are naught but shit expelled from the asses of Ithicana's sharks."

She could not see Edward's face, but Ahnna did not miss his soft chuckle, little more than an amused exhale of breath that none of the nobility would have heard. But William did, and his eyes narrowed.

"I thought Ithicana was sending me a wife, not a bodyguard."

"Why not both?" Ahnna asked.

"Indeed," Edward murmured. "I've always thought it wise to choose a wife whose strengths compensate for a man's weaknesses."

William's jaw tightened, the blow striking in the way only old and painful grievances can, and though she'd not intended for her words to be taken that way, Ahnna knew where the blame would fall.

"Enough," Alexandra snapped. "William, join us. The food grows cold."

The room was entirely silent as everyone waited to see how the crown prince would respond, and for her part, Ahnna thought he'd turn on his heel and leave the room. Instead, he lifted his shoulder in a shrug, then stepped onto the dais and took his place next to his mother.

The servants moved as though on cue, bringing plates of artfully sculpted greens, setting them before everyone at the head table. Ahnna's heart throbbed, her pulse a roar in her ears as she stared at the artful masterpiece of lettuce and cucumber, which was no outlet for her adrenaline.

So she turned to James, who was staring pensively at his own salad, and said softly, "Thank you."

"For what?" He jabbed at the salad with his fork as though he might murder the lettuce.

"Preparing me. If I hadn't known this was coming, I might already be running."

James's fork hesitated, then stabbed a piece of cucumber. "The night is young."

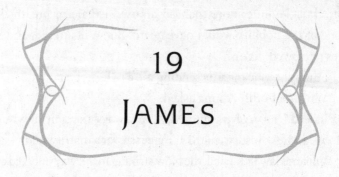

19

JAMES

THE REST OF DINNER WAS A STILTED AFFAIR, HIS FATHER MAKING small talk with Ahnna while Virginia attempted to cajole William into conversation. James had said little, his mind all for the conversation that would come later.

Except later was now, and as he closed the drawing room doors behind him, Virginia tasked with returning Ahnna to her rooms, he silently prepared himself for the battle to come.

"You are a goddamned embarrassment to this family!"

Clenching his teeth, James turned to see his father leveling a finger at Will, skin flushed with anger and too much drink.

"Edward, control yourself," Alexandra snarled, stepping in front of Will. "You will not speak to your son this way."

"Someone needs to!" his father shouted. "Missing the princess's arrival, only to show up drunk and then insult her to her face? She's the twin sister of the king of *fucking* Ithicana, William. Yet you spoke to her like she was an alehouse barmaid who whores for extra coin. Do you think Aren won't hear about how you conducted yourself tonight? Do you think there won't be consequences to the insult you leveled at Ithicana with your behavior?"

Will paled but lifted his chin in defiance. "What consequences would those be, Father? Just what is Ithicana going to do when they hear about my *behavior*? Deny us use of the bridge?" He barked out a laugh. "That's a lark. They need us, not the other way around. We could put her to work in an alehouse if it suited our pleasure, and Ithicana would just close their eyes and think of all the gold flowing into their coffers."

That Will wasn't wrong would only irritate their father more. They brought out the worst in each other, and always had.

"A gentleman behaves as a gentleman not only when it serves his own ends but at all times in good company," his father growled. "She is a princess. A lady of the highest rank. And you spoke to her like a brute!"

"Because she's not a *fucking* lady!" Will shouted. "From her own lips, she is a killer and a savage. You would wed me to a beast for the sake of a promise you made almost eighteen years ago!"

Anger prickled James's skin, and his lips parted to call Will to task, for Ahnna had no more part in writing that treaty than he had. Only for his jaw to snap shut as Alexandra shot him a glare that screamed *Shut up*, a lifetime of suffering her abuse demanding that James obey.

"Yes, a promise," his father hissed. "And lest you forget, I am king. My word is law, and you will obey."

"Already escalated to shouting, have we?" Virginia murmured, having entered in near silence, her elbow bumping against James's.

"I am abundantly aware that I must obey you, Your Grace." Will's slender fingers balled into fists. "Yet for Harendell's sake, I must point out that your stubborn commitment to your word will result in calamity. If I wed her, she will become queen one day. That woman. As. Harendell's. Queen."

"He makes a point, Edward," Alexandra said. "Our son's behavior may have been unfitting of his rank, but who can blame him? The woman arrived at a royal banquet in trousers. She uses foul language and threats of violence like a soldier. She's practically feral, which no one will forget with that ugly scar across her face. And it's not the only one. The servants have told me that she's covered with scars. I recognize that is no fault of hers, for that is clearly the life she was forced to live, but it speaks to her upbringing and to her nature. The princess is inappropriate in every possible way for the crown of Harendell. I told you that committing to a marriage alliance was a mistake. I told you that it was better to choose someone whose character we knew, a lady whose character complemented your heir's and the needs of the nation. But you did not listen, and instead of admitting your mistake and coming to terms with Ithicana's king for a mutually agreeable solution, you stuck your head in the sand and demanded that we obey."

"*I told you, I told you,*" his father mimicked, then snatched up another of his drinks and downed it in one gulp. "There is not enough paper in the world to contain all the things you've *told me to do,* Alex. Yet none of your complaints outweigh the very concrete fact that if we don't keep her, Aren might well use her to secure an alliance with Amarid."

Alexandra lifted her chin. "You wish a concrete complaint? Fine. I was loath to say it out of respect for another lady, but the Ithicanian princess is *too old.* William needs a woman who will give him heirs, and at twenty-eight years of age, Ahnna is past her best years. Which I know you are aware of. And the fact that you didn't request her when she was young, when we might have influenced her character and made a proper lady out of her, suggests to me that you are not as wholly committed to such a close union with Ithicana as you claim."

Silence stretched, and James clenched his teeth even as he felt his sister's fingers dig into his arm, both of them knowing what was about to come. As did Will, because he took a nervous step back.

"Or maybe," their father said softly, "this is exactly what I want. Maybe it is a gift to Harendell that William's blood dies with him, for it will spare the people a long line of incipient useless brats on the throne."

Alexandra sucked in a breath. "You don't mean that."

"Oh yes I do." His father rounded on Will. "Would that I might live long enough to spare Harendell your careless, selfish, and impulsive nature. I forgave your behavior when you were young, but you are nearly thirty years of age and worse now than you were at seventeen. Concerned only for entertaining the fools you call friends, gambling with gold you didn't earn, and drinking until you can barely stand. You call the Ithicanian woman a beast, but better that beast rule Harendell than the half-witted lapdog standing before me."

James cringed, hating how cruel his father could be when deep in his cups. When all the rage that burned in his father's heart poured out upon whoever stood before him.

Tears rolled down William's face. "If you hate me so much, why don't you just pay someone to shove me off the Sky Palace walls? Then you'll have what you really want."

"James," Virginia whispered. "Stop this. Stop them."

"In my darker moments," Edward said, "I've considered it."

"I wish you had. Better the long fall than the long torture that is being your heir."

Alexandra pressed a hand to her mouth, and Virginia sobbed, "James, make them stop speaking like this."

He was already moving. Stepping between them, he said,

"These are words fueled by too much drink, and neither of you mean them."

"Whereas you are sober and stalwart as always, brother. The perfect son. The perfect soldier." William's tone was harsh as he glared at his father. "Why don't you just admit that you wish Jamie was your heir, not me, Father? That you'd rather put your bastard on the throne than your legitimate royal son."

"Stop," James snarled, then pressed one hand against his father's chest and the other on his brother's. Will's chest shook with his sobs. "You will both regret this conversation."

His father ignored him, eyes fixed on Will as he answered the accusation. "I didn't realize I needed to say it. I thought it was as obvious to you as it is to everyone else. Your brother is twice the man you'll ever be, and every hour for the last three decades, I've cursed God for the law that puts you first."

"Stop!" James let go of Will to grab his father by the shoulders, pushing him backward.

He heard the footfalls of Will abandoning the room, Ginny calling his name as she pursued, but he did not let go of his father. "When I was eight, you made me swear that I'd always protect Will. That I'd stand between him and those who meant him harm. Whether you intended so or not, that includes protecting him from *you*."

His father's eyes narrowed. "You don't mean to tell me that you take his side in this? That you defend his behavior?"

"I don't condone his behavior. Nor do I agree with his assessment of Ahnna's character." For which James fully intended to have a separate conversation with Will, once he was sober. "But I am always on my brother's side. I always have his back."

Except when you kiss the woman he's meant to marry. James shoved the thought away.

Silence stretched, and then the rage vanished from his father's eyes, replaced with a grief that was so much worse. "You're just like her," Edward muttered. "Loyal to a fault. Loyal until death."

He only brought up James's mother around Alexandra when he was beyond reason, but now that he had, James knew that his father would rage no more. Would only find a bottle and drink until sleep stole him away from the memory of the woman he said he loved more than life itself.

He shrugged James's hands off his shoulders, pressing fingers to his temples. "I'll speak to your brother. Apologize for my harsh words."

"Now?"

"No. In the morning."

James grimaced. "Now would be better, Father."

"The morning. When my head is clear." Hands still pressed to temples, his father left the room, and James knew that the apology would never come. That tonight, the only person his father would think of was Siobhan Crehan.

Alexandra knew the same.

Taking a breath, he turned to face the queen. His stepmother, though she'd been no mother to him.

"Always the hero, aren't you, Jamie?" Her voice was soft yet cruel. "Leaping into the fray to protect your brother, never mind that all that he suffers is because of *you*. You and your whore of a mother."

He'd long since lost count of the number of times she'd said these words to him over the years. Words made worse because there was much truth to them.

"William is innocent," she hissed. "He has done nothing, and yet Edward hates him for no fault other than that the law names him heir and not you. The Cardiffian witch who birthed you has been dead longer than she lived, yet he remains under her spell, and all know that it is because of you. You have her fell magic in your blood and hold Edward's heart with it as surely as your mother. You are no hero, James. You are the villain who will be William's doom no matter how much you protest otherwise."

Normally, he silently endured her hateful words, but the limits of his patience had been tested tonight, so James said, "What would you have me do, Alexandra? Tell me what to do to make this situation better, because whether you believe it or not, there is nothing I wouldn't do for my brother."

"Half brother," she spat.

James shook his head. "No. We might only share a father, but there are ties that bind more tightly than blood. So tell me what will help. Tell me what I can do. What I can say."

Alexandra was silent for a long time, her green eyes seething with hate, and then she said, "When Edward brought you to me, your tiny hand clutched in his, I could not understand why everyone thought you a curse. I thought you so young. So innocent. So desperately in need of protection." Her lip curled into a snarl. "I should have cast you from the Sky Palace right then and there, for you have been the damnation of all that I hold dear."

When he'd been a child, these words had scared him. Hurt him. Now, knowing that Alexandra would never risk killing him for fear of his father's wrath, her words only made him feel numb. "Is that your answer, Your Grace? That I take the long fall? Is that the solution?"

Silence.

"No," she finally said. "Not even in death will her curse be broken."

Then she twisted on her heel and strode from the room.

20
AHNNA

"I'D RATHER SWIM IN CHUMMED WATERS THAN REPEAT TONIGHT."
Ahnna collapsed on her bed, having dismissed Hazel after again
thanking her for the clothing she'd made. "That was awful."

"Which part?" Taryn asked, flopping down on Ahnna's right,
then kicking off her boots. "The part where you had to make nice
with the dozens of courtiers who told you how delighted they
were to make your acquaintance after spending the whole of dinner mocking you? Or the part where the man you are here to
marry implied that you'd been had by the Maridrinians and were
therefore worth nothing?"

Her cousin's voice turned bitter on the last, and concern caused
Ahnna to turn her head sideways to regard her. The last thing that
Taryn would want was platitudes, so instead she said, "Do you
have any useful advice?"

Taryn lifted her shoulder. "The king seems to like you, and
that's what is important. Edward is hale and healthy, so barring
assassination, he'll be the one determining trade agreements with

Aren for a long time. If my advice were not that we should cut our losses and leave this place, it would be to stay on Eddie's good side. He seemed to enjoy your speech about the hundred cuts, so it was probably worth making William hate you even more."

"I don't want William to hate me."

"Don't you hate him?" There was incredulity in Taryn's voice. "After what he said about Maridrina?"

"He said it to get a rise."

"I'd have stabbed him for saying it."

"Stabbed who?" Bronwyn appeared next to the bed, making Ahnna jump and reach for the blade sheathed at her belt before she realized who it was. The Veliant princess only smirked. "Feeling a bit high-strung, are we?"

"Ahnna's betrothed hates her," Taryn said. "He's also a little pissant who's clearly been indulged his whole life. James might have a stick up his ass, but at least he doesn't snivel."

"Ah." Bronwyn flopped on the bed to Ahnna's left. "So dinner went well."

Ahnna snorted. "Where have you been?"

"Spying."

Another glance revealed that Bronwyn was wearing a slightly dowdy dress cut in Harendellian style, her hair drawn back in a tight bun, a scarf pinned in place. "What did you learn? Anything about the new market?"

"Not a whisper. But I saw plenty." Bronwyn grinned at Ahnna. "This palace has dozens of little curtained alcoves. I thought they must be places for secret conversations, so I hid in one behind the curtain to see if I could learn anything interesting. However, it turns out they are just locations for drunk nobility to have sex with those who are not their spouses, so the only thing I learned was who is having an affair with who, along with a few interesting techniques I'd never seen before."

It was a deflection. Bronwyn told jokes to change subjects, which meant that she hadn't been hunting for answers to Ahnna's mystery at all. And some sixth sense told her exactly what Bronwyn's real mission had been. "I haven't seen her, in case you wondered. Could be that they aren't keeping her at court."

"Who?" Taryn lifted up on one elbow, and Ahnna didn't miss the intensity in her cousin's voice. Nor the scent of wine on her breath. Shit.

"My aunt," said Bronwyn.

"Lestara," Ahnna clarified, though Taryn knew about the harem wife. The Cardiffian princess that Keris had exiled from Maridrina. He'd called in a favor with the Harendellians to take her, and Aren had arranged an armed escort to bring her through the bridge to deliver her to Edward's keeping. She'd been here for long weeks now, but Ahnna had heard little about how the ex–harem wife who'd betrayed Maridrina fared. "You can't kill her."

Bronwyn didn't answer.

"I'm serious." Ahnna sat up, abruptly concerned that she'd misjudged Bronwyn's reasons for coming with her to Verwyrd. "If Lestara dies right after we arrive, we'll be blamed. She's the daughter of King Ronan of Cardiff, and there is enough bad blood between Harendell and Cardiff without us adding to the mix."

"I'm not going to kill her," Bronwyn grumbled. "I just want to make sure that she's suffering as much as Keris thought she would."

"And if she's not?"

Bronwyn didn't answer.

"You can't hurt her." Ahnna rolled onto her hands so that she was looming over the other woman. "Promise."

Azure eyes glared up at her, the color nearly identical to Lara's, though Bronwyn's eyelashes were dark. "How," Bronwyn said softly, "is it fair that you get to be an absolute bitch to my sister for accidentally causing the death of your people, but I don't get to be an absolute bitch to the woman who purposefully caused the death of *my* people?"

Taryn started to rise, but Ahnna caught hold of the back of her cousin's shirt and yanked her back down. "It's not fair," she replied. "Which is why I give you permission to be as nasty to her face as you so wish. But under no circumstances do you cause her physical harm. Like it or not, we aren't alehouse barmaids whose fists only damage the faces we strike. Our actions impact entire kingdoms, and unless you want to potentially cause even *more* innocent people harm, you'll curb your baser instincts."

Bronwyn's glower deepened. "Fuck you and your logic, Ahnna."

"That's a *yes*?"

"I won't hurt her. Physically."

"I hate how forgiving you are," Taryn abruptly snapped. Jerking out of Ahnna's grip, she disappeared into her own room with a slam of the door.

Bronwyn sighed, eyes on the closed door. "Sometimes, she's fine. She sings to herself and laughs at my jokes, and being with her is like being in the presence of a shining sun. And other times, she burns so hot with rage I fear she'll destroy herself and everyone around her."

"It's hard to see her like this," Ahnna admitted. "She always saw the best in everyone. That's why Jor made her Lara's close guard—because she was the only one who didn't cling to their prejudices against Maridrinians." Ahnna inhaled a steadying breath. "Which makes it all the worse."

Bronwyn was quiet for a long moment, then she said, "When I first arrived in Ithicana and saw how Taryn treated Lara, I knew she was a threat. Knew that if she had the chance to kill my sister, she'd take it, and I resolved to kill her first. Had all my plans ready to make it look like an accident, but Lara guessed what I was up to and stopped me. She told me about how when they made their move to take back Gamire, they came across Maridrinian soldiers trying to force Taryn to help them use the shipbreakers. She refused. After all those long months of suffering the worst my father's soldiers could level upon her, Taryn was willing to suffer more to protect her people. Was willing to die before allowing herself to be used to take Ithicanian lives."

"Sounds about right." Her cousin had never wanted to be a soldier, but Taryn was one of the bravest people Ahnna had ever met.

"People always talk a big game about being willing to endure anything and everything for their cause. To die for it. But do you know how rare that capacity really is?"

Bronwyn sat up, pushing Ahnna out of the way as she did and then resting her face in her hands. "Those of us in the compound were pitted against one another, a competition to be the one who'd go to Ithicana to destroy the great oppressor of our people. None of us realized that our father intended to sacrifice the rejects in the name of secrecy, so we were all motivated for different reasons. Honor. Pride. Justice. Loyalty. But me . . . I was motivated by fear. Not fear of losing, but of *winning*. Because there was no worse fate that I could possibly imagine than having to wed a man."

Ahnna remained silent, listening to her friend's confession, because it struck her that she might well be the first to ever hear it.

"We had to sit through these lessons with Mistress Mezat, who taught us the art of the bedroom." Though her head was still in her hands, Bronwyn shook it. "Let me tell you, she held nothing back. All of us were maids, but we learned everything there was to know about pleasing a man in the bedroom by the time she was through with us. What she told us kept me up at night. Haunted my dreams, sleeping and awake, and I went from wanting to win to being desperate to lose so that I could avoid enduring *that*. I had no thought for my people. No thought for politics. No thought for all the good I might do if I took down the great oppressor. All I cared about was protecting myself from the worst horror I could imagine."

It was tempting to offer Bronwyn absolution, but Ahnna couldn't help but wonder if her words would be driven by the fact that, in refusing to win, Bronwyn had refused to attack Ithicana. Which wasn't the absolution the other woman was looking for.

"At the time, I was too lost in fear to hate my own weakness, but since . . ." Bronwyn trailed off. "Hearing what Taryn did, how she stood strong . . . I admire her fortitude. Taryn has a strength that so few people possess, and to allow her to be consumed by anger after she stood strong for so long would be the greatest of trage-dies. I would like to prevent that."

"You cannot hang your own self-worth on whether Taryn chooses to burn herself up or not," Ahnna said.

"No, I can't." Bronwyn rose to her feet. "However, I can hang it on how hard I try for someone I have come to call my friend."

Ahnna silently watched Bronwyn depart into Taryn's adjoin-ing room, then stared at the ceiling for a long time, her thoughts a twisting mess that seemed to make less and less sense with each passing second.

You need to sleep, she told herself. *You can't think when you're this exhausted.*

Which was true. Except someone needed to be alert. She'd sent Jor to bed on her way in because his cough was growing worse by the moment. Taryn had been drinking and was slipping into one of her moods. And Bronwyn was obviously in Harendell on a mis-sion of her own.

You're in a palace in the sky full of Harendellian soldiers, her exhaus-tion murmured. *You don't need to be on guard here.*

Except she'd said much the same the night the Maridrinians had attacked Southwatch. An impenetrable island protected by soldiers and storms, what was one night of letting down the guard to celebrate? Ahnna trailed her fingertip down the scar that marked her face, the permanent reminder of what it meant to lower her guard, then rose to her feet and left the room.

Well past the midnight hour, the halls were quiet and softly lit, the only signs of life the occasional servant answering a bell rung in one of the rooms and the soldiers standing at regular intervals in the hallway, all of them offering her bows or curtsies but no interference as she prowled the hallways. Out of respect, Ahnna did not enter any of the rooms. Though in truth, what she sought was fresh air, the palace oppressive, given she was used to spending her days in open spaces.

Discovering a door that led out into the courtyard, she found herself face-to-face with a soldier bearing medals and ribbons declaring him a captain. "Your Highness," he said, bowing low, "if you wish to venture down to the city, I'll need time to organize an appropriate guard."

"I only wanted air," she said. "May I walk on the exterior wall?"

"I'll arrange—"

"Alone," she interrupted. "I'm quite capable of taking care of myself, which I'm sure you've already heard."

He looked ready to argue, but rather than giving him the opportunity, Ahnna smiled, then started up the stairs leading to the top of the wall that encircled the palace. Where she stopped, her hands pressed against the stone as a slight sense of vertigo took over, a gasp escaping her lips.

For she was surrounded by stars.

This was what she imagined it was like to fly at night. Below, all that was visible were bits of gold from lanterns and torches in the city, and because of the sheer height at which she stood, the starry sky stretched over her like a light-specked dome. It was also cold, the wind biting at her skin.

"You shouldn't be up here alone."

Ahnna whirled, knife in her hand—

Only to find James standing behind her. His face wasn't visible in the darkness, but the height and breadth told her that it was him as much as his voice. The adrenaline surging through her veins moved from fear to something she refused to put a name to.

"I thought I was only forbidden from being alone in the company of a man, not being alone entirely."

James ignored her jab. "It's not safe."

"How fortunate that you're here now to protect me," she said, then silently cursed how breathy her voice had turned. Prayed he wouldn't be able to tell over the noise of the wind.

Instead of retorting, James moved to rest his hands against the balustrade, looking out into the darkness. "I'm sorry," he finally said. "For how my brother spoke to you tonight. It was uncalled for."

His whole body sang with tension that made her think that more had happened than what she'd witnessed. "You might have used more cultured words, but the sentiment was the same. *Leave.* However, you are both destined for disappointment, because your father, the king of Harendell, seems very much to want me to stay."

James made a soft noise, meaning unclear, and then he said, "You aren't a good match for my brother, Ahnna."

That was obvious, but his words still stung. "Why is that? Not pretty enough? Not ladylike enough? Not *Harendellian* enough?"

He huffed out a breath that was pure annoyance. "Because William needs a woman who will make him feel good about himself.

A woman who will elevate him even when it comes at a sacrifice to herself. A woman like . . . like Alexandra."

He wants to be mothered? were the words that rose in her throat, but Ahnna bit down on them and instead asked, "Why is it that you believe I won't?"

"Can you stand here and, in all honesty, claim that you'll hide your skills or knowledge to make him look good?" James asked, twisting toward her. "That you'll let him take credit for your ideas? That you'll let him lead when you goddamned know you'd do a better job of it?"

"This is serious indeed if you've lowered yourself to using profanity in the presence of a lady."

"Fucking hell, Ahnna, take this seriously."

She flinched, not at his words but at the desperation behind them, because something more had happened tonight. Something she hadn't witnessed, and dread pooled in her gut. "I am taking it seriously."

"Then answer the question. Are you willing to do those things? Are you willing to change everything about yourself in order to fit the mold of Harendell's future queen?"

She stared at the shadow that was James's face, the conversation she'd had with Bronwyn rearing in her heart. How far would she go for the sake of Ithicana? How great a sacrifice would she make for the sake of her people? Could she become a woman like Alexandra? Could she mother her own husband? Ahnna's mouth tried to form the word *yes,* but her lips felt frozen, the air stuck in her lungs.

"Go back to Ithicana," James said softly. "You can do more good for your homeland there than you ever will here."

Panic rose in Ahnna's chest, her breath rapid and the world spinning. "I can't go back."

"Why not?" He stepped closer to her.

Because I can't fail my people again. I can't.

"My father and your brother can come to another agreement," James said. "Things that can be offered in lieu of your hand in marriage."

Words meant to be a consolation and yet were damnation, because she was here to improve Ithicana's situation, not make it worse by making her people pay for her freedom.

James lifted an arm, his hand catching the side of her face, thumb beneath her jaw, forcing her to look up at his shadowed eyes. "What are you afraid of, Ahnna? What will happen if you go back?"

"Nothing." Her voice was breathy, but she couldn't seem to steady it.

"Then why are you shaking?" James's voice grew hard. "Are you afraid of your brother? Has he threatened you? Is that why you're doing this?"

"No." Her tongue felt thick, numb, because she didn't want Aren painted as a villain, but neither could she admit the truth. That her homeland was in ruins and her people hungry. That they were destitute and depended on her to save them. That she'd failed before and would rather die than do so again. "The treaty . . ."

"Fuck the treaty." He pulled her closer. "If you've been threatened into doing this, I'll—"

He abruptly jerked backward, hauling her with him, his sharp intake of breath making her instincts flare. Twisting in his arms, she saw the silver flash of a blade. Right where she'd been standing.

"Guards!" she screamed, pulling the knife from her belt and slashing at the black-clad figure. But he danced out of range before lunging again, knife longer than hers and wicked sharp.

Ahnna deflected the attack with her knife, then stepped side-ways, swinging her fist at the assassin's head, but he ducked before rising sharply, fist catching her in the gut. The air was driven from her lungs, but Ahnna slashed at him, knife carving a deep slice across his shoulder.

Behind her came the clash of metal against metal, then a grunt of pain. Ahnna silently cursed as she realized the assassin wasn't alone. That James was fighting another assassin. But alarm bells were sounding, guards running up the stairs, which meant help was coming.

Only that also meant that the assassin needed to kill her now. Or that he needed to run. Even in the darkness, she felt his resolve, and a second later, the assassin threw himself at her with several savage cuts that she barely managed to block.

She kicked him in the knee, risking a glance over her shoulder to find James grappling on the ground with the other assassin, but she couldn't help him. Not with her opponent launching another series of attacks that made her arm shudder each time she blocked.

"You should have stayed in Ithicana, bitch," the assassin hissed. "You might have lived."

"I've never been good at doing what I'm told," she replied even as she threw herself into a roll, coming up between his legs.

He squealed in pain as her shoulder caught him in the balls, knife cutting her back in a downward slice as Ahnna lifted. Her body strained beneath the man's weight, but she was nothing if not strong.

"No!" she heard James shout. "Don't kill him!"

But she'd already heaved the assassin over the wall, his screams splitting the night air. Once. Twice. Three times. And then there was silence.

Catching her balance against the parapet, she turned to find

James with his arms outstretched toward her, a still figure behind him on the ground.

The guards exploded onto the scene, torchlight illuminating the blood splattered against the white stone. It was a mess of voices, made worse by the incessant alarm bells. Then James's hands were gripping her sides, his face inches from hers, breath hot and rapid. "Are you hurt?"

"I'm fine," she answered. "He spoke to me, but his accent was unfamiliar—"

"She's injured!" the captain she'd spoken to earlier blurted out. "The princess. Her back!"

James cursed and rotated her in his grip as easily as if Ahnna were a doll, a stream of profanity rolling from his lips. "Get a bloody doctor!" he shouted at the captain. "Go!"

Then James lifted her into his arms.

For a heartbeat, Ahnna was too stunned to speak, because no one had picked her up, much less carried her, in her adult life, and now James had done it twice. "Put me down!"

He ignored her.

"James, there is nothing wrong with my legs! It's just a scratch!"

"The back of your shirt is soaked in blood," he growled, holding her steady as he descended the stairs. "And if you don't quit squirming, I'm going to drop you."

Given the strength of his grip, it would take more than squirming to cause him to drop her, but Ahnna still ceased trying to extricate herself. "This is ridiculous."

"The doctor will meet you in her rooms, sir," someone said from below. "And we've begun a search for intruders. The entire palace has been locked down."

"Small mercy," she muttered. "Fewer people to witness you carrying me about like an overgrown child."

"No one with eyes is going to mistake you for a child," he retorted, and Ahnna became profoundly aware of the hard chest she was pressed against, his arms beneath her knees and behind her lower back, her cheek resting against his shoulder. If her weight was a burden, James didn't show it as he entered the palace, walking with long strides down the hallways, which, despite the *lockdown*, were full of gaping nobility, every last one of them speculating in dramatic fashion. By the time they reached her rooms, Ahnna was confident that the gossip had escalated to the point that she was on the verge of death, having been attacked by a dozen assassins.

"Where is she?" Taryn's shout echoed out of Ahnna's room. "You will let me go to my cousin, or I will gut you like a pig!"

James entered her room, and Ahnna watched her cousin's face pale at the sight of her, Jor bodily shoving a guard out of the way as he attempted to reach her. Bronwyn had somehow managed to get around all the guards, her blue eyes wide as she asked, "How bad is it?"

"It's nothing," Ahnna growled, then kicked her legs to try to get James to let go of them, but he only tightened his grip until he was able to carefully lower her onto the bed. Taryn was on her in an instant, cutting away Ahnna's shirt.

"Oh, for God's sake," her cousin said, making a face. "It's just a little cut. A few stitches and you'll be fine. You certainly didn't need to be carried."

"I know." Ahnna didn't bother trying to keep the sourness from her voice. "Blame James."

No sooner had the words passed her lips than a wave of dizziness washed over her. Wincing, she tried to focus on the conversation the doctor was having with James and Bronwyn, but the sound of her pulse was drowning them out. Bronwyn's face was blanched, James's jaw tight, and as the doctor extracted several glass vials from a case, she asked, "What's wrong?"

Bronwyn knelt next to the bed. "James says Amaridian assassins poison their blades, most commonly with wraithroot. The doctor can test the wound for traces and then treat you, but you must stay calm."

She'd heard the name before. An expensive poison and not one used by the Harendellians. "Antidote?"

"Of a fashion." Bronwyn smoothed Ahnna's hair back, peeling sweat-soaked strands off her forehead. "If it is indeed wraithroot, it is absolutely critical that you keep your heart beating as slowly as possible, that's why James carried you. If it starts to race, the poison will drive your heart to beat faster and faster until—"

"It stops," Ahnna whispered, remembering her poison lore.

Bronwyn hummed an affirmative. "It's most effective if the victim is exerting themselves, but also if they panic. So just breathe."

The grim-faced doctor pressed a piece of gauze to the wound, then poured a substance from one of the vials onto the blood-soaked cotton. It fizzed, and he grimaced. "Wraithroot, there is no doubt. We will sedate you to keep you calm, Your Highness. If you would drink this—"

"No!" Ahnna jerked away from the proffered vial. "No sedation!"

"It will not harm you," the doctor said in a voice that was probably intended to be soothing but was instead entirely condescending. "It only puts you to sleep until the poison passes from your system."

Put her asleep and *keep* her asleep, no matter what went on around her. Everyone she cared about could be put to sword by assassins, and there would be nothing Ahnna could do to help them. "No! I don't need it. I'm fine."

"Your Highness, you are emotional," the doctor said. "Allow more stalwart minds to aid you through this trial."

"Go fuck yourself!" Ahnna screamed at him.

The doctor scowled. "I do not know how things are done in Ithicana, but in Harendell—"

James plucked the vial from the doctor's hand. "Please wait outside."

"I'm fine," she said as the doctor slammed the door behind him. "I don't need it. I'll calm down."

Yet she could hear the roar of her pulse, her heart racing as though she'd spent hours running up and down flights of stairs carrying a heavy load.

Bronwyn caught hold of her wrist, fingers pressing tight. "It's got her. We don't have much time."

"Ahnna, listen to me," James said. "I've seen men die from wraithroot. Strong men, their hearts tearing themselves apart in their chests because they refused to stand down."

"I'm stronger." The words came out between gasped breaths, her chest spasming. "I'm fine. Don't drug me."

Jor coughed, then said, "We're going to have to pin her. Force it down her throat."

"No!" Her shoulders hit the window, though she didn't remember getting off the bed. "Please don't. Please." Her face was wet, the pain in her chest incredible. "I just need a minute to breathe."

"Ahnna, you're acting a fool!" Jor shouted. "Take the bloody tonic!"

"Ahnna, please," Taryn sobbed. "I can't lose you!"

"Ahnna, you've got minutes to live if we don't do this," Bronwyn pleaded. "It will be okay!"

"I can't." Her eyes skipped among the three, their faces started to blur. "I can't risk it."

James shoved the vial into Taryn's hands, then took a step toward Ahnna. "Why can't you? What do you think will happen?"

"I don't know." Her knees were shaking, the roar deafening. "I need to be alert."

His head tilted, brow furrowing. "No one here will hurt you. I swear it."

"You don't . . . understand." Her chest was in agony. "I need to . . . keep watch. Need to . . . protect . . . them."

Her legs buckled, and James lunged, catching her. His fingers tangled in her hair, holding her head upright. Amber eyes burned into hers as he said, "I'll stay. I'll keep guard."

Her eyes burned, tears leaking down her cheeks.

"I promise, Ahnna," he said. "I will be your eyes until you wake. Please trust me to do this."

He was practically a stranger. An outsider. No part of her should trust him, but Ahnna whispered, "I trust you . . ."

The tonic Taryn pressed to her lips was sickly sweet, making her choke as she swallowed and then burning as it raced down her throat. Her body was in agony, her heart starting to skip, but then the world split into two. Then three.

She slumped, falling against James's chest, his arms around her as everything darkened. The last thing she heard was his voice as he whispered, "I'll keep watch for you."

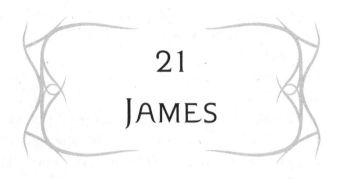

21

JAMES

A BEAD OF SWEAT TRICKLED DOWN HIS FACE AS JAMES LEANED against the cold glass, his own heart racing at a wicked speed. Ahnna was slumped against his chest, deadweight in his arms, but her chest still rose and fell.

Bronwyn had her by the wrist, eyes distant as she monitored Ahnna's pulse, then she gave a slight nod. "Her heart is slowing." Shaking her head, she added, "Such a simple cure."

"And yet I've seen wraithroot claim countless lives," he muttered. "Men who refuse to step away from a fight, then die for their bravery." He looked past Bronwyn to the Ithicanians. "What happened to her? Why is she so afraid to let down her guard?"

"War happened," Jor answered, his eyes shadowed with darkness and illness. "Ahnna led Ithicana through the nastiest war I've witnessed in my life, and she holds the weight of all that happened during her rule on her shoulders. You couldn't begin to comprehend what she endured."

"Is that why she doesn't want to go back?"

Their faces went still, as unreadable as when the Ithicanians used to wear masks. And then Jor shrugged. "Didn't think going back was an option. Promise is a promise, and all that. Ithicana keeps its word."

What are they hiding? Ahnna's secrets? Or Ithicana's?

"As does Harendell."

James twitched, having not noticed his father enter the room. Sword buckled at his waist, shirtsleeves pushed up, his father moved past the Ithicanians to kneel next to James. He pressed his fingers to Ahnna's throat, then made a face. "Coward's weapon, wraithroot. I had a look at the corpse. No identifying features, clothing, or weapons, and his companion is naught but pulp at the bottom of the tower. However, the poison tells us all we need to know."

Amarid.

There should be no question in his mind that it had been the other nation, and yet . . . James had spent more than a decade fighting their western neighbor, and the fighting style of those two assassins had felt . . . different. While at the same time, painfully familiar.

"That's three times the Amaridians have tried to kill you," his father muttered. "And still, we don't know why."

Except James hadn't been their target. This time, they'd gone after Ahnna, which only added to the sickness in his belly.

"Do we know how they got in?"

"Not yet," his father replied. "Though with so many coming for the banquet, it would not have been such a great task to get past our security. She'd have been safe enough if she'd stayed in her rooms. What was she doing wandering without a guard?"

Being who she is.

"*Getting some air* is what she told those on duty," James answered. "I was convincing her to go back inside when they at-tacked." Not the entire truth, but he wasn't about to admit that he'd been trying to get Ahnna to leave Harendell of her own ac-cord. Given that his father seemed intent on seeing this marriage through, regardless of Ronan's wishes, he would not take kindly to James countering him.

"A hard-learned lesson, though she'll no doubt be fully recov-ered in a few days," his father said. "Put her to bed. The doctor will see to her well-being, and I want you to focus on hunting down the way they got in. Someone will be missing a groom or a manser-vant, and I want to know who brought them into our midst."

"I can't leave her."

His father's eyes shot to his, then narrowed. "Why not? Her personal guards are here to watch her, and I've need of your thor-oughness."

"I told her I'd stay."

"She'll be unconscious for hours. Leave and then return, if need be."

"I promised." And because he disliked the depth of his father's scrutiny, he added, "She was attacked in our home. It's the least I can do."

Silence stretched, and James suspected his father was seeing further past the excuse than he might have liked, but all he said was, "As you like. Though you need to learn to be more judicious in your promises, Jamie. You have other commitments."

"Yes, Father."

Straightening, his father surveyed the Ithicanians. "This is not Ithicana, where your royals are protected by the elements and free to do as they please. Show more care."

Jor covered his mouth, coughing, then nodded. "We will keep a closer eye on her, Your Grace."

As his father departed, the doctor entered again, mouth pursed in a tight line as he said, "I see you mastered her emotions, my lord. Well done. I'll stitch her wound, and then all she will need is rest."

"You'll fuck right off is what you'll do," Bronwyn said. "I'll cut off your hands and feed them to you before I'll let you touch her in her sleep. I can stitch her up. Give me that bag."

"You will do no such thing, you crass woman!"

A tug-of-war over the bag ensued, Bronwyn easily overpowering the old man, who looked to James for support.

James exhaled, not in disagreement but in frustration with the Veliant princess's aggressive methods. "It's fine, Doctor. I'll see your things returned to you when she's finished."

"Awful creature," the old man muttered, hurrying to the door. "Veliants are all insane. Every last one of them."

"At least we're not inbred!" Bronwyn shouted after him, then rotated on her heel and dropped to her knees next to James and Ahnna. "Taryn, can you put that kettle back on the fire for some boiled water? Jor, make sure the doors are secure so that fopdoodle doesn't find his way back in here to piss me off again."

Jor coughed again into his sleeve, then shook his head and went to secure the doors, Taryn already stoking the fire.

"*Fopdoodle?*" James asked, shifting Ahnna's weight so that the angle of her neck was better, the scent of her hair filling his nose, though it was tinged with blood.

"Overheard that one earlier, and I've been dying to use it," the Veliant princess said with a grin. "Was it an apt moment?"

"Quite."

She laughed, her distinct Veliant eyes glittering in the light that reflected off the window glass behind them, then her expression grew more serious. "You need to do something about your security. Your soldiers are lazy and distracted, half of them slightly drunk. I have something of an expertise in these matters, and thus far, I'm not impressed. I fully intend to write a strongly worded letter to my sister the queen." She gave him a feral smile. "Of Ithicana, for clarity. Two of my sisters are queens."

"There will be changes made." He was angry as he was unsurprised at her appraisal of the Sky Palace's security. The traffic of nobles and their servants in and out of the palace was extensive and not subject to half as much scrutiny as it should be, and Ahnna had nearly died because of it. "Do you want me to put her on the bed?"

"No, this is a better angle." Digging inside the doctor's case, she examined the labels on the various packages of herbs, then gave an approving nod before murmuring, "Taryn, when that water boils, make a tea of this for Jor. It will help that cough, but it tastes awful. Don't warn him or he won't drink it."

"You're dreadful, Bron," Taryn muttered, setting down a steaming bowl of water and then taking the packet and placing a pinch of it in an empty cup. "Is there anything else you need?"

"The sedative we gave her is a strange one," Bronwyn said, dipping a piece of clean cotton in the water and then allowing it to cool. "Pieces of reality will reach into her dreams. Things she hears. Things she feels. I think it might be wise to sing to her until true sleep sinks in."

"I . . ." Taryn's cheeks flushed, her eyes flicking to James, obviously uncomfortable in his presence. "I don't know what would be the right—"

"The one you sang to soothe the cattle," James interrupted her. "She liked that one."

The young woman stared at him, likely wondering how he knew that piece of information, but then she nodded. Handing the cup to Jor, she said, "This will help your cough, but you need to drink it all."

The old man sniffed at it suspiciously, then said, "I'll keep watch outside." Taking a mouthful, he made a face. "This is disgusting."

"So is your cough," Bronwyn retorted. "Drink it, old man. We need you tonight."

"Too old for this," Jor said, but he left with the cup in hand.

Silence stretched after the door shut, but as Bronwyn lowered the cloth to clean the still-bleeding wound, Taryn began to sing.

James immediately understood why the cattle had followed her through the bridge without complaint: Ahnna's praise was no exaggeration. At first, her voice was as soft as a whisper. Yet it held the power of a spell, the words like a sigh of the wind as it echoed between the stone walls of the bedchamber. A lament if he'd ever heard one. A song that cut to the soul. Knowing his scrutiny would not be welcome, James lowered his gaze to Ahnna, his stomach tightening as Bronwyn pulled back the ruined silk of her tunic and cleaned the blood and remains of the poison from the deep slice next to her shoulder blade, the knife having reached into the muscle.

"Squeamish?"

"No," he muttered, trying to rein in the fury building in him that she'd been hurt so badly with him right there. That the assassins had caught him so unaware. But when he was in Ahnna's presence, it was as though he saw no one but her.

Bronwyn lifted another cloth that was soaking in a tincture she'd made, and as she pressed it against the injury, Ahnna whimpered and stirred. The Veliant princess winced, catching hold of Ahnna's wrist to check her pulse, shaking her head. "Keep her calm."

Fear rose in his chest that the poison would yet claim her and there was nothing he could do about it. So James did the only thing he could think of and ran his fingers over her hair. Smoothed it back and tucked it behind her ear, the gesture rising from a barely remembered memory from his childhood. Of his mother singing to him after a nightmare, soft hands stroking his hair. A sort of comfort that had died with her.

Ahnna steadied under his touch, and he would have stopped, because touching her in such a fashion was not appropriate, but Bronwyn murmured, "Do what you need to. I have to make sure I get all the poison out."

Then she poured the tincture into the wound, flushing it clean. Ahnna tensed, and he again smoothed her hair, the texture like silk beneath his fingers, the braids pulling loose. As Bronwyn worked, he unraveled the lengths, pulling them to the side to keep them out of the blood, his fingers brushing the skin of her back. A faint line ran along the base of her long neck, the skin above sun-kissed bronze, the skin below pale as milk, and he traced it, knowing that it meant endless hours outdoors.

Her back and shoulders were corded with muscle, slender but taut, and those muscles flexed as Bronwyn pressed the needle into her flesh. "Steady," he murmured, watching as the princess's deft fingers bound the severed flesh together, past caring that Ahnna's legs were sprawled across his or that she was nearly naked from the waist up. Only caring that she would wake from this to piss him off with her endless jabs at his propriety and manners. That she would turn that smirk on him again, leaving him grasping for a worthy retort to some clever barb that she'd deliver with no hesitation.

Bronwyn pressed a clean cloth to the wound, and he lifted Ahnna slightly so that she could wrap a length of bandage around her, securing it in place. "We should put her in bed to rest now."

Carefully, James rotated Ahnna's still form, keeping his eyes on the ceiling as the tattered remains of her tunic fell away. Getting his own legs beneath him, he rose, then walked by memory to the bed, still staring at the ceiling.

"Set her down."

With Taryn's song still filling the room, he lowered Ahnna onto the bed, not looking down until he heard Bronwyn cover her with the blankets. Ahnna's face was pale against the blue silk of the pillows, hair spread out around her in loose curls of walnut and amber and bronze, long lashes pressed against her cheeks. So painfully beautiful that James's breath caught in his chest, his heart not allowing him to look away even as propriety demanded he do just that.

Bronwyn's sigh drove his eyes upward, fear making him believe that Ahnna's prognosis was worse than he'd hoped. Except the Veliant princess wasn't looking at him or Ahnna. Her eyes were fixed on Taryn, enraptured by her song.

As Taryn finished, Bronwyn wiped a sleeve across her eyes, then rounded on James, chin up. "Well, thank you for your assistance. You can go now."

"I told her I'd stay."

"It's fine. Ahnna won't care."

Yes, she will.

Pulling a chair next to the bed, he settled into it, then said, "I've been accused of a lack of judiciousness in my promises, my lady. But never of not keeping them."

22

AHNNA

WAKING FELT LIKE DRAGGING HER THOUGHTS OUT OF A QUAG-mire, the events that had transpired rolling across her mind, so when Ahnna finally opened her eyes, she was already cringing with embarrassment.

The first thing she saw was Taryn asleep on a chair against the wall, her cousin's head lolling at an angle that was destined to result in a neck ache, drool dribbling down her chin, though her blade was clutched firmly in one hand. If she was woken, she'd wake swinging.

Ahnna shifted, her eyes landing on a leg clad in black trousers, on which rested a large hand marked with familiar scars. Her gaze traveled up an arm wearing a military uniform, over ribbons and medals to the gold-tasseled epaulets on the shoulders, until it came to rest on James's face.

Unlike Taryn, he was awake. James's eyes were fixed across the room, the skin beneath shadowed with exhaustion, splatters of what she assumed was her blood dried among the freckles on a cheek that showed far more stubble than it had the last time she'd laid eyes on him.

I'll keep watch for you. His voice echoed up from memory, and Ahnna's chest tightened, because he'd kept his word. She could not remember the last time someone had given her their word and kept it.

Then his head turned, and James said, "It's good to see you awake, Your Highness. Everyone will be relieved."

Not for the first time, she was struck by the hue of his gaze. The golden amber almost seemed to glow. A color she'd only seen looking back at her from the faces of the large cats found in Ithicana, and yet somehow it wholly suited him.

"How long was I asleep?" Her words sounded dragged over sandpaper.

Before he answered, James filled a glass from a pitcher of water. "Eighteen hours."

And he'd stayed the entire time. She knew with absolute certainty that he had, because the exact same attributes of his character that drove her to madness also ensured that he'd never break his word to her.

Ahnna drew in an unsteady breath, then pushed herself up on her elbow, wincing as pain lanced down her back.

"Careful!" He set the glass down on the side table so hard, water splashed over the edge, then reached for her. One hand caught the blanket before it slid down to reveal her naked breasts, the other slipping beneath her, lifting her upright. His hand was cool against her skin, the sensation of his touch teasing at a memory that she couldn't quite latch on to no matter how hard she tried, it being somehow tied together with a song she'd heard only once before.

Then James removed his hand, stuffing pillows behind her

back. "Bronwyn seems the sort to get testy if you damage her stitching."

"She did the stitching?" Ahnna drank greedily from the glass he handed her.

"Yes. She appears to have a great deal of training in such things."

"All of Silas's daughters of a certain age do," Ahnna muttered, though she was relieved it had been Bronwyn, not the Harendellian doctor, who'd handled her while she was unconscious. "Have you learned who those assassins were?"

"The use of wraithroot suggests they were Amaridian." James rose to his feet. "And it is a logical conclusion, given recent events."

Ahnna bit the insides of her cheeks, for while the previous attack had been aimed at him, there was no doubt in her mind that she'd been the target of this assassination attempt. Even with her focus taken by the one man she'd been fighting, it hadn't been lost on her how the other assassin had seemed more intent on trying to get past James than on killing him. Which meant that either Katarina had changed her goals, or the assassins hadn't been sent by Amarid's queen at all. Given that she'd been combatting Amaridian pirates most of her adult life, she knew how they fought. And how those men fought wasn't Amaridian at all. But if not Katarina, then who?

Keris's warning, confirmed by Virginia, filled her head, and Ahnna swallowed hard.

"Your guardsman is unwell, and the other two are taxed," James said. "I did not wish to make changes to your security without your knowledge, but it is my intention to select individuals from Harendell's ranks to fill in the gaps."

A wave of concern for Jor crossed over her, but Ahnna said, "That's not necessary. I've lived my whole life—"

"Lady Bronwyn noted several gaps in the Sky Palace's own defenses. Until those are remedied, and until you are wholly well, my men will ensure your protection. I will hear no argument otherwise."

She glanced at Taryn, who was so tired she'd slept through the entire conversation. "Temporarily."

James inclined his head. "As you say, my lady. I recommend you stay in bed and avoid exertion until we can be certain you are free of the poison, but I suspect you will disregard my recommendation. Good day to you."

He turned to walk away, and without thinking, Ahnna reached and caught hold of his wrist. His skin was cool and smooth beneath her overheated fingers, the contact sending sparks through her core as James turned back to her, amber eyes darkening to bronze. "Thank you. For . . ." She trailed off, then shook her head and repeated, "Thank you."

He stood entirely still for a long moment, her hand on his wrist; then he pulled free. "It should not have happened." He walked to the door. "And it will not happen again."

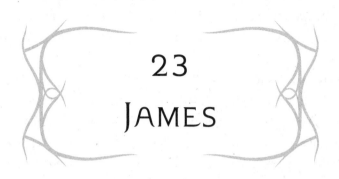

23

JAMES

JAMES DREW IN A RAGGED BREATH AS HE CLOSED THE DOOR BE-hind him, trying to find some measure of calm despite the lingering sensation of her fingers on his wrist burning like a brand. No delicate touch, but strong and demanding, and he couldn't help but wonder what it would feel like to have those hands on other parts of his body.

A cough jerked him back into the moment, and he lifted his head to see Georgie and Bronwyn leaning against the walls opposite each other, seemingly in some sort of standoff.

"She's awake," he said to Bronwyn, then coughed to clear both his throat and his head. "We will select eight of our best to aid you in the princess's protection." As her lips parted to argue, he added, "Of those eight, you may choose which four you prefer."

Bronwyn's teeth clicked shut. "Fine." Then she leveled a finger at Georgie. "But not this pretentious prick."

Georgie chuckled as Bronwyn disappeared into Ahnna's room. "I like her."

"Banish the thought," James muttered. "Else you're likely to end up with your cock shoved down your own throat."

"You're testy." Georgie straightened his coat. "Lack of sleep or something else?"

"Both. Why are you here?"

"Because you were attacked, too, Jamie. You might have been killed. Your father is concerned for your welfare, as well as how personally you're taking this incident."

"I take everything personally." And he'd also spent the entire night thinking about how hard the assassin had tried *not* to kill him.

"True, but you've been sitting in the princess's room for eighteen hours. You must need to piss like a goddamned racehorse."

James started down the hall, Georgie hurrying to keep up with his long strides. "Half of those on guard last night were apparently drunk, the other half not paying attention. I want a list of everyone on duty, for there are to be consequences for this failure. But prior to that, I want you to choose eight of our most reliable men. Ensure they are individuals who will keep their commentary, and their hands, to themselves."

"Understood."

"And where are the assassins' corpses? I need to have a look at them."

"The one you stabbed is in the kitchen cold room. The other..." Georgie gave a half shrug. "I assume they scraped him off the rocks with a shovel, so likely in a bucket somewhere. What do you need to see? There was nothing on them."

"I want to see if I recognize them," James muttered. "Get those guardsmen to Bronwyn to inspect."

Leaving Georgie in his wake, he went down the servant stairs, taking them two at a time. Servants bowed and curtsied as he passed, but other than tight nods, James paid them no mind. The kitchens were as busy as always, the cooks pausing in their shouts as he strode through their ranks, reaching the cold room where meat was stored. A guard stood outside, saluting him and then stepping aside as James plucked up a lamp and opened the door.

A large naked man was laid out on the butcher-block table, his clothing and weapons next to him. James crossed the room, taking in the knife wound at the base of the assassin's throat, then scanning his face. Perhaps forty years of age, the man was bald and clean-shaven, his skin marred by scars that suggested a run-in with the pox in his youth. But he was unfamiliar. Picking up the clothes and weapons, James examined them closely for anything that spoke to identity, including nationality, and when he found nothing, he moved on to the corpse. He checked the body from head to toe for tattoos or distinctive scars, the man's limbs stiff with rigor.

Nothing.

Which was as he expected. Moving to the assassin's head, James drew in a steadying breath, then peeled the man's eyelids back to look at the color.

Brown.

Exhaling the breath he'd been holding, James left the room. "Arrange for burial," he told the guard, then exited the kitchen and headed to his own rooms.

Where his manservant, Thomas, waited with a steaming bath before a roaring fire. "His lordship informed me that the princess awoke and that you were in need of a wash."

"I'm not—" James broke off, seeing his reflection in a mirror. His face was splattered with blood, his coat and the cuffs of his shirt marked with the same. "Fine."

"Will you be desiring a shave, sir?"

"No."

"Very good, sir." Thomas, well aware of James's habits, abandoned the room.

Flipping the latch on the door, James pulled off his boots and clothing, then stepped into the bath, only to hiss at the heat as he lowered himself down. Glasses of both water and wine waited on a table next to the bath, and he downed the first and then the second before sinking beneath the water.

All sound went muted, the world falling away, leaving James alone with himself.

Except he could still feel Ahnna's fingers on his wrist.

Visions of her filled his mind's eye. That brazen grin she always gave him when she was about to say something she shouldn't. Those muscled legs that went on for ages, scandalous in silken trousers, the fabric clinging to the hard curve of her ass. The way she walked like a cat stalking through the jungle. The softness of her lips beneath his, the feel of her tongue in his mouth. His cock stiffened even as his lungs demanded air, and James broke the surface of the bathwater, gasping for breath and sanity.

"Stop it," he growled at himself, snatching up a bar of soap. "She's not for you for more reasons than you can count."

Not the least of which was that Ahnna would hate him if she learned why he was trying so hard to convince her to go home. Or that if he failed in his attempts, she would be his brother's wife.

William might hate her, but he'd still do his duty. So would Ahnna. And the thought of them together made his fingers curl into fists, vicious jealousy turning his blood molten. Not the first time he'd felt that way because of his brother, but never in his life had he felt the feeling so intensely.

"She is not yours," James repeated. "She never was yours and never will be yours."

Yet as James scrubbed away blood and sweat with the soap, he could not banish visions of Ahnna from his mind.

William can't handle a woman like her, envy whispered in his thoughts. *He'll destroy everything that makes her perfect. She deserves better.*

Like you? The half-Cardiffian bastard who has social standing only on the whim of his father? You are worth nothing, whereas she is the jewel of Ithicana.

James threw the soap at the far end of the tub, resting his elbows on his knees as he tried to will the blood out of his cock and back into his brain so that he might think clearly.

But he wanted her. Wanted that wild, irreverent woman to be his, not to tame, but because she ignited the parts of him that he worked so hard to suppress.

"She is an obstacle," he said under his breath. "A problem with the capacity to ruin everything you've worked for. Think about that instead of her tits, you piece of shit."

Ahnna was a problem.

Yet instead of her face vanishing from his mind, his thoughts showed her with naked fear in her eyes at the thought of returning to Ithicana. Fear she refused to confess the source of, and James could not help but remember the obvious conflict between Ahnna and her brother. And his father's suggestion that if Harendell did not keep her, Ahnna's fate would be very dark indeed. Whatever she feared had to be horrible, because he'd seen her face down man-eaters, assassins, and storms, but the thought of going back to Ithicana seemed to almost break her.

And here he was, trying to push her toward it.

Needing to push her toward it, because Ahnna choosing to remain in Harendell wouldn't ruin her. It would be the death of her.

James's eyes went to the clock, the hour late afternoon. The next meeting was not for another week, but that didn't much matter.

Because if his suspicions were true, he and his uncle needed to have a very difficult conversation.

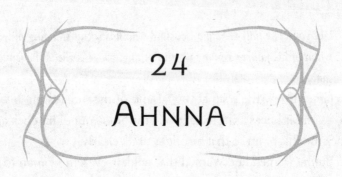

24
AHNNA

"They weren't Amaridian."

Jor, Bronwyn, and Taryn exchanged looks among one another, and then Jor said, "The Harendellians seem convinced otherwise. Clothing and weapons and poison all speak to Queen Katarina. And given they've made two previous attempts to kill James, it makes a lot of sense."

"They weren't trying to kill him, they were trying to kill me." When Jor didn't look convinced, she added, "I've fought my share of Amaridians, Jor. These men fought differently."

"You've fought pirates and common soldiers," he said. "Katarina's dark guild is different, and not something you've ever faced."

"They weren't Amaridian." She crossed her arms and glared, knowing that being tucked into bed like an invalid ruined the effect. "Would you trust me on something for once, Jor?"

He coughed into his sleeve, but then shrugged. "Then who?"

Ahnna met Bronwyn's gaze, and her friend made a face before she said, "I don't know, Ahnna . . ."

"You think Alexandra was behind this?" Taryn asked, looking between them. "That's ... well, that's damned bold, given that Edward has made it clear he favors you."

"Everyone says she ordered the assassination of James's mother, Edward's mistress, out of jealousy," Ahnna said. "So I don't think we should put this past her. She clearly dotes on William, and mothers have done madder things for the sake of their sons."

"For argument's sake, let's say it's her," Bronwyn said. "What do you want to do about it? We can't prove it, because I struggle to believe Alexandra would leave any tracks tying her to those men, and we can't prevent another attempt."

"More guards—" Jor started.

But Bronwyn interrupted him. "That will serve against armed attack, but if it's the queen, poison could come from literally anywhere. Ahnna, you and I have discussed this: You cannot protect yourself from poison unless you control every variable like my father did in his inner sanctum. That's not possible here. Alexandra will have access to poisons of the highest quality. Odorless and flavorless. Poisons that kill in minutes or in days. Dozens and dozens of options, very few of which you can train your body to tolerate, and trust me when I say it's not a pleasant process. If she wants you dead, you will die."

"Then we kill her!" Taryn blurted out. "I'll do it!"

Ahnna sat up straight. "You will do no such thing! Have you lost your head, Taryn? Do you have any idea the consequences that would fall upon Ithicana if you were caught assassinating Harendell's queen? It would make what the Maridrinians did seem like child's play."

The moment the words exited her lips, she regretted them, because Taryn's face crumpled. Sitting on the edge of the bed, her cousin whispered, "I can't do this. I can't live on the edge like this, fearing attack from every corner. I can't sleep. Can't get my heart to stop racing." She pressed her hands to her face. "I wish I'd died on Gamire, because I don't know how to be myself anymore."

"Don't say that, Taryn." Bronwyn wrapped an arm around her, but Taryn only pushed it away and rose.

"I'm going to get some rest," she said. "I'm no good to any of you."

"I'll—"

"Stay," Taryn interrupted. "God knows you have the skill set Ahnna needs."

As her cousin left the room, she picked up one of the bottles of liquor on the sideboard. Given that her own room would have been stocked, Ahnna suspected her cousin had been drowning her anxiety the entire time.

"Where were you when Ahnna was attacked?" Jor abruptly asked, his eyes fixed on Bronwyn. "Because you told me you'd keep an ear on her, yet I heard she was strolling the Sky Palace for hours before that attack, with no sign of you."

"I thought she was asleep." Bronwyn looked away. "Hazel said she'd put her to bed."

"Answer the question, girl."

Ahnna's jaw tightened, not upset that Bronwyn hadn't been outside her door but furious at what she suspected the other woman had been doing.

Bronwyn's jaw tightened, her hand drifting to the weapon at her belt. "Mind your words, Jor. You forget who I am."

"Nah, I haven't." Jor coughed into his sleeve. "There's only one Veliant I take orders from, and that's Ithicana's queen. Now where the fuck were you while Taryn was passed out drunk?"

"Hunting Lestara," Ahnna said, unable to keep the sourness from her tone. "Bronwyn, you promised."

"I wasn't going to kill her! Only . . ." She gave her head a violent shake. "It seems like you don't care about the hurt that creature caused, Ahnna. Athena wrote me. Told me that there were so many civilians dead, they had to bury them in mass graves outside the city. I hate that Keris didn't kill her. I hate that he let that monster live, and I'll never forgive my brother for it."

"So you'll take justice into your own hands, no matter the cost?"

"Wouldn't you?"

"No," Ahnna answered. "Which you know, because Lara still lives." She pointed at Taryn's door. "Stay with her. Perhaps you two can manage to keep each other from destroying everything."

Bronwyn swayed on her feet, like she was debating what to do. Then she said, "I'm a trained killer, not a bodyguard. James has Georgie gathering a selection of guards for me to choose from. I think they'll serve you better than I ever will." Then she left the room.

Jor chose that moment to have a fit of coughing, the sound wet and thick, and Nana's training told Ahnna that his illness wouldn't get better without far more rest.

"Maybe it's best you go back to Ithicana," he said after the fit subsided. "Aren isn't going to hold it against you. I don't see how *Edward* can hold it against you, given all that has happened."

I'll hold it against me.

"The Harendellians have capable men among them," she said. "If what I need is more bodyguards, I'll accept that. But I'm not leaving, Jor."

The same could not be said for her companions, who all needed to be places that were not Verwyrd. Whether they wanted to be or not.

The door to the room opened, and Hazel stepped inside. "The king is here to see you, my lady. He asked me to ensure you were decent."

"Am I ever decent, Hazel?" Ahnna asked, then gave her maid a wink because the girl looked ready to cry, as she had all morning. "It's fine. Jor, wait outside."

Edward exploded into the room a moment later. Footmen followed at his heels carrying large vases of flowers, which they deposited on various tables throughout her room before bowing and departing. When Ahnna moved to get up, Edward waved a hand at her. "My dearest girl, please don't move a muscle. I once had an encounter with wraithroot, and it takes days for the noxious plant to clear the system. You must rest."

Nodding, she leaned back against the pillows, wishing the first opportunity that she had to speak to him alone wasn't with her prone on her back like an invalid.

Edward sat in the chair where James had been sitting when she awoke. To her shock, he reached over to take her hand, patting the back of it. His hands were callused, which she hadn't expected despite knowing he was a fighter of some skill.

"I am so sorry this has happened, Ahnna," he said. "I know it is some small consolation, but we are taking steps to increase the security of the Sky Palace, none the least evicting all the hangers-on who had no business being here in the first place. James is handling the situation, and given how personally he appears to be taking the attack, I anticipate we'll all be locked up tight as a prison before the day is done." Edward laughed. "He's something of a perfectionist, my son. Likes things to be a certain way, and the Sky Palace's security is not to his standards. My fault, but he'll put us to rights."

"I'm sure he will," she said, struck by the obvious favoritism that he held for his elder son. It reminded her of how her mother had treated her and Aren, and given what Virginia had told her, it filled her with sudden sympathy for William.

"That said, I would understand if you desired to return home," Edward said, and Ahnna's heart lurched. "We failed to protect you, and it is not fair to ask you to live in fear."

"I am used to fear," Ahnna replied, wary because she knew she was outmatched by this man when it came to twisted words and politics.

Edward turned her hand over in his, examining the scars. "Yes, I believe you are," he said softly. "William is not capable of rule, Ahnna. He needs a queen who will do it for him. Someone clever and strong who will sit on the throne while he plays with his toys. Someone who brings strength to the table in every possible way. Who will put her strength into my bloodline, which I fear has been watered down by too many individuals who have never known toil. Or loss."

His words seemed to confirm his desire for her to be here, a desire for her to marry William, no matter his son's protests. Still, Ahnna asked, "Do you desire for me to remain in Verwyrd . . . Eddie?"

The corner of his mouth turned up, as though her using his name pleased him greatly. "I do, Ahnna. Very much so. You will be the sort of queen Harendell needs."

Feeling emboldened, she said, "If you wish for me to rule Harendell as you have, I need to learn from you. Obviously, I understand the business between Ithicana and Harendell very well, but I must learn about the other markets in which your merchants trade. Understand the relationships you have with other kingdoms."

He was silent, and for a moment, Ahnna believed that she'd overstepped. Then his eyes locked on hers, and he patted her hand. "Your knowledge of how our two nations work together to reach the southern markets is invaluable, Ahnna. I think it will be I who is picking your brain once you are well."

It was no answer, which all but confirmed in her mind that there were opportunities for Harendell that did not involve the bridge. Opportunities that Edward did not want her knowing about, which meant she was going to need to discover them another way.

Edward rose. "I'll let you rest."

"Your Grace." When he leveled a teasing finger at her, she amended with, "Eddie. Might I ask a favor of you?"

"For you, Ahnna? Anything. Name it."

Glancing toward Taryn's closed door, she said, "It pertains to my cousin. In Ithicana, she was forced to live a martial life, but it is not the path to which she is best suited. She has a voice without equal, and I desire for her to pursue her passion for music rather than to serve me. Would it be possible for those who dictate admissions at the conservatory to listen to her sing?"

Edward grinned. "This is easily done. I'll make the arrangements immediately." Giving her a jaunty salute, he said, "Good day to you, Princess," then left the room.

Hazel appeared, moving to Ahnna's side and immediately fluffing the pillows. "You should sleep, my lady. You have given the entire palace quite a scare. Even the queen has spent the whole of the day in the chapel praying for your health."

Ahnna highly doubted *that* was what Alexandra was praying for.

Lara's voice filled her head. *The women of Harendell are far from powerless. They might not wield weapons or fight in wars, but they influence everything that happens, every decision that is made. None is more powerful than Queen Alexandra. Or more dangerous.*

If it had indeed been Alexandra who'd tried to kill her, then Lara's words had been proved in abundance. As much as Ahnna was loath to take advice from Lara, ignoring her seemed a good way to get herself killed. And her death would have far-ranging consequences.

Taking a breath, she said, "I need you to find me a dress. And then I wish to request an audience with the queen."

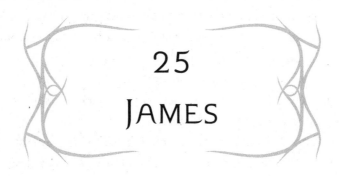

25

JAMES

JAMES HEELED MAVEN INTO A SWIFT CANTER, TRUSTING HIS TALL mare to keep her footing as he wove down the narrow road, the late-afternoon sun doing little to cut through the canopy of trees overhead.

He'd had a look at the second body before he'd left Verwyrd. Not in a bucket, but near to it, for every bone was broken. The skull was caved in, though the man's face had been broadly intact, gray eyes staring up at James before he'd covered the corpse with a tarp and ordered it buried.

It was the Amaridians, he told himself for the hundredth time. *Katarina growing desperate, that's all.*

Except that wasn't what his instincts were telling him.

The scent of woodfire and cooking food tickled his nose, and he drove Maven for more speed. The hamlet of Thistleford appeared as he rounded a bend. It was formed of only a dozen buildings, mostly businesses that served the surrounding farms, and it was quiet but for the inn with the adjoining alehouse. Lute music and the raucous singing of drunks drifted over the creek. Crossing the narrow bridge, James slowed his horse to a trot and stopped in front of the inn. As he dismounted, the stable boy scurried around from the back, taking the reins.

"Want me to put her in a stall, my lord?"

"Just take her for a walk and let her graze, Jack." He slipped the boy a copper coin. "I won't be long."

Jack nodded, but James didn't miss the smirk the boy cast him as he led the black mare away. Taking the steps two at a time, he opened the door. The smell of beef stew and freshly baked bread hit him in the face, along with the stink of years of ale splashed over floorboards.

The regulars all recognized him and pulled off their caps, nodding at James respectfully—he'd long ago trained them not to rise. Elsie set down tankards on a table, her brow furrowing at the sight of him, though she swiftly recovered with a smile. Setting down her tray on the bar, she muttered to the innkeeper, Charlie, to cover for her, then sauntered across the room toward James. "Well, this is a welcome surprise, Your Highness. We'd all heard that you had quite a spell of adventure retrieving the Ithicanian princess. Decided you needed some respite from her graces?"

Her accent was a flawless replica of those common to these hamlets and the surrounding farms, as was Charlie's when he deigned to speak a few words. "Something like that," James answered, allowing Elsie to slip her arms around his waist. "But I cannot linger."

Her pink lips pouted, the lashes surrounding her golden-brown eyes fluttering. "Then we'll have to make the most of the time you have, my lord."

He made a noncommittal noise, ignoring the grins of the regulars as she led him toward the stairs. They were too narrow to walk up side by side, and Elsie slipped behind him, fingers toying with his belt as they climbed. As they reached the top, she slid around him and then pushed him against the wall, full breasts pressing against his chest. "Miss me, Jamie?"

She stretched up on her tiptoes to kiss him, and James turned his head so that her lips landed on his jaw. "Is he back?"

She was silent for a long moment. "You're not to meet for another week."

"Can't wait."

"And here I thought you'd come to your senses and abandoned all that nonsense about not mixing business and pleasure."

"It was never just pleasure for you, Elsie," he said. "It's always been business."

She'd been his lover for almost a year before he'd learned she was also an agent of his uncle, and he'd never forgiven the deception despite understanding the necessity.

Sighing, Elsie said, "True. But I miss your fingers almost as much as I miss your cock, Jamie. Not yet found anyone who quite measures up."

"My condolences. Now, is he here or not?"

She huffed out a breath. "Yeah."

Twisting away, Elsie led him down the hallway, and then used the key in her skirt pocket to unlock the usual door. Closing and locking it behind them, she edged past the bed to a door that led to the neighboring room, knocking her knuckles against it. "He's a week early, Cormac."

A lock flipped on the far side, the door swinging open. Elsie flopped backward onto the bed, glaring at James as he walked through the door, shutting it behind himself.

Only to find a knife blade pressed against his throat. "It's me, Uncle."

Amber eyes framed by deep crow's-feet bored into his for a long moment before his uncle lowered the blade. "We make plans for a reason, boy. There are a good number of people in this kingdom who'd be happy to see me dead."

"I think you know why it couldn't wait."

His uncle grunted, moving across the room to the pair of chairs where he held court with his network of agents and spies. He was as big as James was himself, though age had stooped his shoulders and grayed his hair.

"It's about the woman, I assume."

"Was it you?"

Cormac sat in his chair, legs stretched out in front of him. "Yes."

Fury raged through him, his suspicions confirmed, and James balled his hands into fists as he struggled to keep from lashing out. "I said I'd take care of it."

"Aye." His uncle toyed with an amulet of the family constellation around his neck, the only nod to astromancy that he kept on his person while in Harendell. Even wearing *one* was bold. Cardiffians had been burned at the stake for less, albeit usually women. "But you haven't, have you? You got complacent in the years when it seemed Ithicana wouldn't give their princess up. All words of certainty that your father wanted this alliance as much as we do, that good King Eddie would break the betrothal if it came to it, but you were wrong. Quick like a fox, he sent you to retrieve the princess, and it was all, *Uncle, I'll deal with it. The marriage won't happen.* Yet lo and behold, who arrives in that carriage with you but those long legs I saw in Sableton."

"And you thought that gave you license to send assassins into my family home to kill her?" James was shaking, every part of him demanding violence, unable to forget the image of Ahnna lying limp in his arms.

His uncle shrugged. "Thought I was doing you a favor."

"By assassinating Aren Kertell's twin sister beneath our roof? Do you have any idea the fallout that would come from her death?"

"What fallout? Ithicana thinks Katarina has murder in her heart, and with the pretty picture we painted, they'd have believed the third time was the charm. But word is that it was you who fucked it all up. Makes me wonder if you are getting cold feet, boy. Makes me wonder if you're turning your back on your mother's blood in favor of the snake charmers to the south."

James's anger burned hotter. "Fuck you, Uncle. I've dedicated my life to making things right between Cardiff and Harendell. To seeing my mother's dream made reality."

"Aye, and there was a time when Eddie took these meetings with me, insisting that his life's work would be to see Siobhan's dream made reality, yet it seems time heals even shattered hearts. Your father appears content to play both sides, promising the same thing to two different kings."

James growled, "He's promised Ithicana nothing but a marriage. And it won't happen. William isn't going to marry her. He can't stand her, and you know Alexandra's views on the matter."

"Then *why* is the princess here? Why is Eddie claiming a marriage is imminent?"

"Because he's concerned that if we send her back, Aren will use her to make an alliance with Katarina. Wed her to the crown prince."

"Marry her to the Beast?" Cormac laughed harshly. "Seems unlikely. Carlo's already been through three brides, so any union via marriage would be short-lived, and Aren has only one sister."

James bristled, hating the very idea of it. "With tensions high with Amarid, it's not a risk my father is willing to take. Keeping Ahnna here means that Ithicana sending her to Amarid isn't an option."

"If Aren is desperate enough to marry his twin to the Beast, then he's weak. Too weak to make a good ally, for he can do naught but levy tolls on his bridge and hurl rocks from Northwatch. If you want your merchants crossing the border into Cardiff without risking their lives, then *send her back*. Or I'll deal with her."

In two strides, James crossed the space between them, his hands slamming into the chair his uncle sat upon, knocking it over backward. Driving his boot heel down on his uncle's chest, James said, "If you or yours step foot in Verwyrd or harm Ahnna Kertell, I will personally cut off your hands for the slight. This is *my* ground, Uncle, and nothing happens without my say. I intend to see my mother's wishes through, but you need not be alive for that to occur. And knowing my uncle Ronan as I do, he would gladly sacrifice a brother for the sake of gaining Harendell's favor."

Though the pressure of James's boot had to hurt, his uncle chuckled. "There are times all I see is the courtier and I fear Edward's blood has claimed you, boy. It pleases me to see my sister's eyes looking back at me from your face, the old blood strong in you. It gives me faith in you, so I will abide by your wishes and leave the princess be. But if this marriage occurs . . ."

"It won't." James stepped back, watching his uncle ease to his feet. "I will handle Ahnna, but while I do, she is under my protection."

His uncle righted his chair, expression considering. "You have your mother's fire, Jamie. But also your father's foolery. Let Siobhan's blood win out."

Not answering, James strode to the door, but as his hand fell on the handle, Cormac said, "Speaking of Ronan and of princesses, how fares your cousin? How is Lestara?"

26
AHNNA

"Has she replied yet?" Ahnna demanded as Hazel walked into the room. It had been over a day since she'd sent a card requesting an audience with the queen, and despite the woman living within the same palace, she'd not responded.

"I'm afraid not, my lady," Hazel said, setting the tray of food on the table next to the window.

"Is it normal for her to take this long to respond?"

Her maid gave a slight grimace. "It is not, my lady. She typically responds immediately, regardless of the answer."

"Shit," Ahnna muttered, then gave Hazel an apologetic wince for cursing as she paced her room, ignoring the food.

"You aren't supposed to exert yourself. The poison might still—"

Ahnna sat down at the table. Not because she was worried about the wraithroot or because she was hungry, but because she was in no mood to argue. Already she was going stir-crazy locked in her room. This was the longest she'd remained in bed in recent memory. At the worst possible time, because years of reading spy reports about the machinations of rulers told her that things were happening. Potentially right down the hallway from where she slept. "I need out of this room."

Hazel sighed, then picked up a card off her tray. "Lady Virginia has invited you to join her and her ladies for tea."

Virginia wasn't who interested her, because she did not strike Ahnna as a woman consumed by politics. But her ladies might feel differently, and Ahnna had gleaned many interesting facts over the years by putting together pieces of gossip. Frowning at the card, she asked, "Hazel, what happens at these gatherings?"

"Cross-stitch and knitting," Hazel answered. "Sometimes flower arranging and poetry readings, and more rarely, singing in accompaniment of the pianoforte. But primarily, they gossip."

Taking the card to the writing desk, Ahnna carefully penned her acceptance, then placed it back on the tray to be returned to Virginia. Attempting to make her voice nonchalant, she asked, "I've not seen His Highness. Is he well?"

"Prince William has gone to the races again." Hazel lifted her head to meet Ahnna's gaze. "Or did you mean James?"

She had, but realizing how that might look, Ahnna said, "Both, I suppose."

"Ah. Well, James has been most preoccupied with the Sky Palace's security after the attack on your person, my lady. Many of the men on duty that night have been reprimanded and docked pay, and some dismissed. The rumor is that he's called in men from his regiment in the Lowlands to serve, though it will be some time until they arrive. You might see changes in your guard when they do."

Ahnna had briefly met the four new guards Bronwyn had selected from Georgie's candidates, all seemingly capable men. Or at least as capable as could be ascertained from her bedchamber. Bronwyn said they were all good fighters and had been willing to spar with her, but said little more. There was still tension sitting between them.

"It may be that Lady Virginia's invitation came at the directive of the queen," Hazel said. "Though I would caution you to show care in what you reveal, my lady. This is Harendell, and in our courts, there is no greater currency than information. Virginia might hold your confidence, but do not expect as much from those in her service or company."

"I understand." Hesitating, she added, "Virginia seemed pleasant enough. And certainly loyal to her family."

"Tremendously loyal, my lady. Most especially to her brothers."

Ahnna did not fail to notice that Hazel had confirmed one of her statements but not the other, which suggested that perhaps the princess's personality was not as genuine as one might hope. Which was perhaps no surprise, given that Virginia was an Ashford, and the Ashfords were supposed to epitomize what it meant to be Harendellian.

Her appetite had not materialized, so though she was typically loath to waste food, Ahnna abandoned the breakfast and eyed one of two dresses that Hazel had secured for her from a modiste in Verwyrd. The cost of the confection of lace and satin had made Ahnna want to vomit when she'd signed for the draw on her accounts. Neither garment was in a color that she favored, but beggars could not be choosers, and having something made custom would have been twice as much.

Hazel went to work on Ahnna's hair, using damp fingers to coax it into loose ringlets hanging halfway down her back. Cosmetics followed, Hazel using pink powder to give color to her cheeks, which remained pale. Then came layers of undergarments, and finally, the dress. Thankfully, a morning dress required no corset, so if it came to a fight, she'd be able to breathe. When Hazel was retrieving a pair of flat silk slippers, Ahnna swiftly secured a thigh sheath beneath the skirt, the blade within it small but sharp.

Her eyes flicked to the clock, which read half past the ninth hour. "Is it rude to be early?"

"Yes," Hazel said, smoothing one of her curls. "Unless what you have to say makes it reasonable that you came before the other ladies. Give her some gossip, my lady."

Ahnna opened the door and stepped outside. She found Taryn standing in the hallway with two of Ahnna's new bodyguards, Louis and Alfred. Her cousin's eyes were bloodshot with a hangover, her color poor, and she gave Ahnna's dress a sad smile.

"Where's Bronwyn?"

"With Jor." Taryn sighed. "He's really not well. His cough is horrible, and Bron is worried. She thinks he should return to Ithicana."

"I'll make arrangements," Ahnna said. "I'll speak to him myself after I know more." She hesitated, then added, "Stay with him, would you?"

Taryn cast suspicious glares at the two guards but then nodded and headed off toward the servant staircase.

"If you'd follow me, my lady." Alfred started up the hallway.

It was still tiring to exert herself, the act of walking the circuitous route around the palace leaving her slightly breathless, just as Bronwyn had warned her. Having been fit and healthy the whole of her life, Ahnna found the weakness irritating.

Another set of guards stood outside the double doors. One of them rapped sharply on the thick oak, which then opened from the interior. "The Lady Ahnna," he said rather unnecessarily to the maid.

The maid bobbed a curtsy, and Ahnna smiled at her, sick of how long it took to do anything in this place with the endless middlemen.

"The Princess Ahnna, my lady," the maid announced as she stepped inside, and Ahnna's eyes went immediately to Virginia. The young woman was seated on a lavender velvet sofa, a saucer and teacup balanced on one knee. Across from her was Lady Elizabeth, daughter of the Duke of Silverthorn, and an absolutely vapid idiot from what Ahnna had gathered at her welcome banquet.

"Ahnna!" Virginia rose, navigating carefully around the furniture, then reaching out for Ahnna, kissing the air next to both her cheeks. "I was horrified to hear of what happened. Jamie gave me barely any of the story, but Georgie was more forthcoming. I hate to think of what might have happened if my brother hadn't been with you."

"I'd be dead, no doubt," Ahnna said. "Both assassins were very skilled."

"Amaridians." Virginia wrinkled her nose. "I swear they are asking for war. This behavior cannot stand. Have you sent word to your brother?"

"Not yet." There had been no need; Lara probably had spies in Verwyrd with instructions to report, and the events were no secret. "I'm fine."

"You're so brave."

Virginia linked arms with her, leading Ahnna to the large windows that overlooked Verwyrd's expansive courtyard, where several men were training with swords. Ahnna immediately recognized James, partly from the copper gleam of his hair but mostly from his size.

"Where is Bronwyn? Hazel was to invite her as well. Did you

know she *sparred* with the candidates for your new guardsmen instead of interviewing them? Beat every last one of them, and I think Georgie despaired finding anyone who suited."

"Bronwyn has had significant training. Unfortunately, she's attending my countryman. He's ill, and she's educated in herblore."

"Shame for the illness and the absence. Bronwyn has a delightfully salty tongue. Veliants are always entertaining. We have several of her cousins and even a few half siblings floating about Harendell. I've heard that her half brother, the Empress of Valcotta's consort, is the most beautiful man in the world. Have you met him?"

"Keris?" Ahnna had only half heard Virginia's question, her attention all on the duel going on below between James and George. Both were stripped down to their shirtsleeves, James's pushed up to his elbows to reveal muscled forearms. He pressed George backward, using his superior height and skill to his advantage. Every step he took was smooth and certain, not an ounce of hesitation. Like he'd been born to fight. The idea rose in her again that propriety was a mask he wore, not at all reflecting the man beneath. The man she'd seen glimpses of. The man who had kissed her like she'd never been kissed in all her life. "Keris is good-looking," she finally answered, her toes curling slightly in her shoes as James disarmed George. "If you enjoy blonds. And salty tongues. He makes Bronwyn seem sweet by comparison."

"You don't?"

"Don't what?" Ahnna asked, distracted by James dragging a forearm across his sweaty brow. The fabric of his shirt strained over his chest, the garment at risk of joining the ruined clothes that he seemed to leave in his wake. Ahnna's heart sped, heat pooling low in her stomach, but she kept her expression schooled to bland interest.

"Prefer blonds?"

Ahnna twitched, turning her head to find Virginia staring at her in that uncanny way she had, as though she saw more than shadows. "Not really, no."

Virginia made a soft humming noise and turned to the window. Below, James was now facing off against two men whom Ahnna didn't recognize, his expression still as grim as one going into the last battle of his life.

"How fortunate that my brother isn't blond."

Ahnna's breath caught, certain that Virginia had noted where her attention lay, but then the princess said, "All three of us favor our father's coloring, though James got lucky with the copper highlights. Not that he cares. Vanity is not one of his faults."

Instinct warned Ahnna that Virginia was prying into her opinions of James. Knowing she couldn't give the princess any clues that her attraction lay with the wrong brother, Ahnna made use of Hazel's suggestion. "Keris saved my brother's life when they rescued Zarrah from Devil's Island. Took an arrow for him and nearly died."

Virginia's eyes widened. "Really? That surprises me, for I had heard that he's quite bookish."

"He is. But Aren said there aren't many people he'd rather have at his back than Keris, and that is a significant endorsement of character."

"Shame he's wed."

"A love for the ages," Ahnna said. "If they'd been unable to rescue Zarrah as they did, I suspect he'd have set the world on fire to win her free. She consumes him to the exclusion of all else."

"Love like that can be dangerous," Virginia replied, causing Ahnna to look sharply at her. But Virginia was already facing Elizabeth. "Lizzie, dearest, would you play something for us? You sing so beautifully."

"Of course, my lady." Elizabeth set down her tea, then went to the pianoforte, her voluminous skirts making soft swishing sounds. Sitting, she began to play competently, then cleared her throat and sang.

Loudly.

Ahnna turned back to the window so that the woman wouldn't see her grimace.

"We applaud effort as much as skill in this house," Virginia murmured. "You've made a tremendous impression on my father, by the way. You were all he talked about at dinner last night." She was quiet for a moment, then said, "He was also kinder to William than he's been in longer than I can remember, despite Will being somewhat drunk. I think my father sees a better future for Harendell with you in it, and that makes him more forgiving that Will doesn't possess the strengths he admires. It made me very happy."

"I'm glad," Ahnna said. "I've not seen William since the night of the banquet."

"Oh, that's probably for the best. Let him come to you, is my advice. Will has had enough pushed upon him in life."

"I understand." Eyes drawn out the window again, Ahnna watched James clasp hands with his opponents, the contest over, and he victorious. He strode to where his coat lay discarded, but then looked up. Through the glass and the distance, their eyes locked. James stopped in his tracks. Ahnna was flooded with the sensation of his hands on her body. His lips on hers, claiming her. Her heart skipped, then whispered, *He's what I want.*

Only for logic and loyalty and good sense to shriek, *And you're a selfish fool for it!*

Twisting away, Ahnna rested her shoulders against the glass. "What advice would you give in approaching the queen?"

"The same." Virginia's tone was flat. "Let my mother come to you."

One of the servants came in and began announcing the names of the ladies who had arrived. The time for private conversation was over, and Ahnna felt she'd learned nothing at all.

An hour later, the wound on her back itched and exhaustion pressed down upon her as she answered the questions the women posed to her about Ithicana, knowing her voice was numb and mechanical. But this had been a waste of her time. None of the conversations she'd been privy to had given her any information helpful to the puzzles before her, and Ahnna half wondered if she'd be better off having slept the day away.

But more than that, she felt stifled and contained. The air in the room was overheated and stank of an awful mix of perfumes. She desperately wanted to be outside. To be near the sea. To hear the waves that had lulled her to sleep every day of her life.

Her heart ached, the deepest sense of loneliness that she'd ever felt crushing down on her, and Ahnna was about to rise, to claim lingering illness from the poison, when the door opened and a beautiful woman entered. Her hair was such a pale blond that it bordered on silver, cheekbones high, lips painted a glossy pink. Her gown was cut in the same style as those of many of the other women present, but the eyes that stared back at her were the same amber as James's. Cardiffian eyes. There was no doubt in Ahnna's mind who the woman was.

Lestara.

"Oh God," Virginia said, ignoring Lestara as she bobbed a curtsy at the group. "Everyone check your shoes. It smells like dog shit."

All the ladies giggled and pretended to check their shoes, but Lestara offered no reaction, only sat on a chair in the corner and began work on a half-finished needlework piece.

Ahnna eyed the woman who'd caused the destruction of Vencia and then asked, "Why is she having tea with us?"

"Lestara was exiled from Maridrina for treason," Virginia answered. "We took on her care as a favor to Keris Veliant. I would have thought you were aware of her."

"I know who she is and why she's in Harendell," Ahnna said. "My question is: Why is she in this room?"

"Ah." Virginia sighed. "A fair question. I, too, thought she was better housed in a cage in the kennels, but Father insists she be treated with the courtesy befitting her rank."

"The mongrel princess," Elizabeth snickered. "Fair warning, you do not want to look too long into those eyes, lest she cast a spell on you. Their women are all witches."

"Bark for us, Lestara," one of the other women said, and Virginia laughed. "Be a good bitch."

The Cardiffian princess did not respond, only continued to stitch a pattern of flowers around the border of her piece. But it was Virginia's behavior that struck Ahnna, because she had not thought the princess in possession of such a mean streak.

"Want a piece of cake, doggy?" another woman said, placing a slice on a plate. Rising, she set it on the floor by Lestara's feet. "Be a good girl and eat it."

Lestara kept stitching, but like sharks scenting blood in the water, all the women were watching, expressions vicious.

"Eat it," the courtier repeated, and when Lestara continued to ignore her, the woman retrieved the plate and smashed the cake into her face. "Eat it!"

The women howled with laughter as Lestara's face was smeared with lemon and meringue, but Ahnna did not laugh. Not because Lestara didn't deserve their disparagement, for she'd caused the deaths of countless innocents in her quest to ruin Keris and put his half brother on the throne, but because she did not care for how much the women enjoyed being the punishers. How they relished Lestara's discomfort as she wiped the dessert from her face and hair, then attempted to salvage her needlework, which was stained yellow.

"You seem to take her crime against Maridrina very personally," Ahnna said, watching as yet another woman took up the pot of tea and poured it on Lestara's head, the dark liquid adding to the stains on the needlework. Lestara left off trying to clean it, staring blankly out the window.

"Hardly," Elizabeth said with a laugh. "What we take personally is that these witches cast spells on our men. Turn them into slavering creatures fixated on lust. She's a witch, and if not for His Grace's order, we'd burn her at the stake."

"Cardiffians do not follow the faith," another woman said. "They sacrifice animals to the stars, smear themselves with blood, and then dance naked beneath skies they claim hold the stories of their ancestors. As though the stars belong to them, such madness!"

"They decorate themselves with bones!"

"Barely human!"

"They run with animals. Eat meat raw!"

Virginia waved a calming hand. "Don't worry, we keep her locked up and always under guard. She'll not slip our watch and slink off into the darkness. We'll keep her as our pet until it's time to put her down."

Aren had warned her. So had Keris. And James. All different words with the same refrain: Harendellians are cruel. But all the warnings in the world hadn't prepared Ahnna for the viciousness of these women.

Lestara's chin quivered, and the sharks in the room all grinned. "Cry for us, doggy," one of them crooned. "We love your tears. We treasure your sobs."

Aren had told her that Keris had deemed sending Lestara to Harendell the worst possible punishment, and Ahnna had questioned the choice. Questioned why he hadn't hanged her or cut off her head, for Lestara had most certainly deserved it. Now Ahnna understood. For the rest of her life, or until she lost her mind and flung herself off the Sky Palace's walls, Lestara would be treated like this. From princess to harem wife to . . . *animal.*

Worse than an animal, for these women treated their lapdogs, which were currently eating the crumbs around Lestara's feet, with more kindness than they did her.

Lestara lifted her face, amber eyes latching on Ahnna's, and she couldn't help but wonder what James thought of this. Whether he resented how they belittled Lestara for the culture and beliefs his mother had held. Whether he considered himself Cardiffian at all.

"She's been out of her kennel long enough," Virginia declared. "Take her back until it's time for her to be walked."

"We put a diamond collar and leash on her," Elizabeth said. "We like to walk her before dinner and make her squat in the corner where the other dogs go." She grinned, but Ahnna gave her a flat stare until the grin fell away, unease filling Elizabeth's eyes.

One of the guards led Lestara away. Ahnna started to rise, disgusted by their behavior, but a servant entered with a silver tray, which he proffered to her. "A letter has come for you, Your Highness."

She immediately recognized Aren's handwriting and personal seal. Unease fluttered in her chest. Plucking it up, she cracked the seal, swiftly reading the contents. All the breath fled from her lungs. "I thank you for your hospitality, Virginia," she managed to say. "But if you would please excuse my early departure."

Without waiting for a response, Ahnna left the room, finding her bodyguards waiting. "My countryman," she said. "I need you to take me to him immediately, please."

"Yes, Your Highness." Without hesitation, they flanked her, seeming to sense her urgency as they took long strides, leading her to the small barracks in a sublevel of the palace.

She heard Jor's coughing before she reached his small room, and through the door, she heard Taryn shout, "You need to go home, you old goat. You're no good to anyone here hacking up a lung!"

Ahnna knocked on the door and Taryn opened it. "He won't go. Because he's an old idiot."

Jor was sitting on a narrow cot, glowering at the steaming cup in his hand, Bronwyn looming over him as though she intended to force it down his throat. For the first time, Ahnna felt herself struck by the age of the man who'd been a near constant in her life. Aren's surrogate father because their actual father had been far too busy and, truth be told, obsessed with their mother to pay them much mind. Jor looked thin and gray, shoulder bones pressing through his nightshirt where once there had been solid muscle. "You need to go back to Eranahl, Jor," she said. "You can travel by riverboat and then book passage, but you're leaving to-morrow."

"I'll be fine. It's just a flux," Jor muttered.

"It's not a flux, it's the cold air here," Bronwyn said. "It's not going to get better unless you return to the hot and humid."

"I ain't leaving." He scowled. "Not with Amaridian assassins at every turn." His dark eyes fixed on her. "You need someone to watch your back."

"I have James's men, hand-selected and vetted by Bronwyn."

"As well as James himself," Bronwyn said. "The man's taken her safety as his own personal mission."

Heat rose to Ahnna's cheeks, but she shoved away her thoughts about *that* and said, "I don't need you to protect me, Jor"—and before the hurt her words might elicit rose in his eyes, she shoved the letter into his hands—"but this little princess surely does."

FOR THE NEXT FEW HOURS, Ahnna celebrated with her companions. Concerns and conflicts were forgotten as they toasted the arrival of her niece, and when she finally left Jor's room, her head was buzzing with happiness. With her guards in tow, she headed to her rooms, the skirts swishing around her ankles not irritating her quite as much as they had. The world not seeming quite as dark.

"Ahnna!"

Edward's voice caught her attention as she reached the top of the stairs, and she turned to see the king of Harendell jogging down the carpeted hallway toward her, a letter in his hand.

"Your brother wrote to me of his good news," Edward said, waving the page. "Congratulations! What a joy for Ithicana."

"Thank you, Your Grace," she said, and when he gave her a dour glare, she amended with, "Eddie."

"Might I add to the good news of the day?" He linked arms with her, and they walked onward. "As it so happened, the dean of Briarcliff Conservatory was in Verwyrd to discuss the needs we will have for the wedding. He would be delighted to accept your cousin into the conservatory as the first Ithicanian student. Was thrilled by the notion, if I'm being honest."

"Even though he hasn't heard Taryn sing?"

Edward laughed. "Well, he was hardly going to say no to the king, now, was he? Of course he trusts my judgment, as I trust yours. It will all go marvelously. It is still your wish that Bronwyn accompanies her?"

"Yes," Ahnna said, because while the thought of having no one she knew to guard her back made her nervous, Bronwyn's obsession with Lestara made her more liability than asset.

"Is she aware of that?"

"Not yet." Neither Taryn nor Bronwyn knew of her plans for them, and even though studying music in Harendell had been Taryn's lifelong dream, Ahnna knew her cousin wouldn't leave her alone without a fight. As for Bronwyn... "Bronwyn and Taryn have become quite close. I am hopeful that will cause her to see the merit of traveling with my cousin."

If not that, guilt and emotional manipulation would have to suffice. Taryn was fragile and needed protection, and Bronwyn knew it.

"It doesn't trouble you to be without your people? I wouldn't fault you for being nervous, given the ordeal you endured." Edward's voice was light, tinged with a level of concern, but she could feel his interest in how she answered, and that made Ahnna cautious.

"It's not ideal," she said. "But if I am to live my life in Harendell, I must develop a trust for Harendellian guardsmen. That won't happen if I cling to my own people. And if we are being truthful, this was always my hope for Taryn. She needs to walk a path with less violence than guarding my back will bring. Bringing peace to her life is worth some risk to me."

"Ithicana's loss is truly our gain," Edward said. "You will make a worthy queen, Ahnna. It's a shame I'll not be alive to see it."

Her cheeks flushed. "I hope that it will not be for many years, Eddie."

He chuckled. "Likewise."

Smiling, Ahnna said, "My guardsman Jor will also be returning to Ithicana, as the weather in Verwyrd has not been kind to his health. They'll all travel together by riverboat once the conservatory is ready to accept Taryn. I'll fund her tuition, of course."

How, Ahnna didn't know, but that was a problem for later.

"Nonsense! Full scholarship on account of her bringing a new nation's worth of musical material into the conservatory. The dean would have it no other way. He is leaving himself in the morning, so perhaps they might join him on his vessel. He has a good many questions for your cousin."

"I'm sure she'd be happy to oblige," Ahnna said as they drew up next to her room. "I truly appreciate your efforts, Eddie."

"It is my pleasure." He patted her hand, then released her arm. "Now I suggest you take an afternoon of rest, young lady." He wagged his finger at her. "Time is required for the effects of wraith-root to subside. And no more wine! It will go straight to your head."

She nodded, feeling flushed with the pleasure of something going right for once. As Edward disappeared down the corridor, her guard Alfred opened the door to the room. "If you would wait here, my lady," he said, stepping inside. Only to immediately step back out again, gesturing inward.

Ahnna's instincts jangled, and she slipped her hand through the hole in the pocket of her dress, closing her fist on the hilt of her knife as she stepped inside.

To find Queen Alexandra of Harendell standing next to the window.

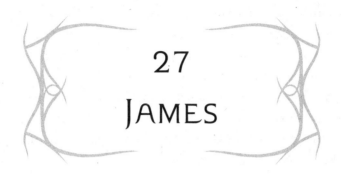

27

JAMES

No part of James wanted this conversation, but it was better for him to check on the welfare of his cousin and report back than for Cormac to send any more of his people into the Sky Palace. Where they might inadvertently run across Ahnna. Because not for a second did he believe that his uncle wouldn't see her dead if given the opportunity. His mother's people took oaths very seriously, but given that James was currently in violation of his own promises, Cormac enjoyed a great deal of flexibility.

The sun was low in the cloudy sky by the time he reached the top of the spiral, his shirt clinging to him with the sweat of his exertions despite the cold wind. A storm was brewing, and James instinctively searched the horizon for any sign of one of Harendell's infamous twisters forming, though they were not common in the river valley. But the clouds bore none of the distinct funnels, so he turned his back on the sky and headed into the palace.

He needed to dress for dinner, for which he was already late, but James decided to take the opportunity presented by everyone of noble blood sitting around a table eating their first course. Nodding to the *very* alert guards at the closed gates leading to the courtyard, he waited for them to open them before saying, "These are to be locked at sundown. No exceptions." Identical orders to those he'd given at the base of the tower.

"Yes, sir," they answered with salutes, and James went inside. The corridors were quiet as he made his way to Lestara's rooms. The two guards posted outside gave no argument, only unlocked the door to allow him entry.

He stepped inside, then immediately turned his back at the sight of Lestara in a nightdress scrubbing a gown in a basin.

She gave a soft snort. "I hardly care, cousin. Your sister just made me piss in the corner of the Sky Palace's courtyard while her ladies watched and laughed. I have no dignity."

Virginia's bias against Cardiff was worse than most, given that Alexandra had been pouring her venom into his sister's ears her entire life, but his jaw tightened when he heard that Virginia was partaking, because this behavior was beneath her. Regardless of the state of his cousin's dignity, James refused to turn until she was dressed. He heard her abandon the gown, then the whisper of fabric as she pulled on a robe.

"Your morals are safe, Jamie."

He turned to find her wrapped in thick velvet and perched on a sofa, her hair damp from washing and face scrubbed clean of its usual cosmetics. Lestara was denied little, dressed in the finest gowns and jewels, yet humiliated at every turn.

For his part, James believed she deserved it. Believed that Keris Veliant had made a fine choice in sending her to Harendell. Children had died because of Lestara's actions. So many that the Maridrinians had buried their dead in mass graves. Pissing in front of laughing ladies was the least of what this woman deserved.

"Why are you here?"

"Your uncle Cormac inquired about your well-being."

Lestara tilted her head. "So playing messenger?"

James didn't answer. He'd been seven or so when his cousin had been born to King Ronan's sixth wife. His fourteenth daughter. But because that particular wife still lived, Lestara had a place of privilege, so James had been in her presence every time he'd been sent to stay with his uncle, and there'd been a time he'd known her well. Then he'd ceased his visits in favor of secret meetings with his uncle Cormac, and Lestara had been sent to join Silas Veliant's harem in exchange for better trade terms for mink fur.

"Oh, I'm fine, Jamie. Just every day wondering if the long drop might be better than the nightmare that prick of a Veliant condemned me to."

"You condemned yourself."

Lestara made a face. "Are you sure it's cattle Harendell raises? Because you bleat like a sheep."

"Has anyone struck you?" he asked, keeping his voice as bland as possible. "Caused you physical harm? Deprived you of the necessities of life?"

"Baa!" Lestara imitated sheep. "Yes, Jamie. The finest food. A diamond collar for when they walk me like a dog."

He inclined his head. "Good evening to you, Your Highness."

Quick as a fox, she scurried in front of him and blocked his path to the door. Her eyes glowed yellow in the lamplight, reminding him that there was power in her. *The sight*, they said. And a fate worth watching.

"Doesn't it bother you how they treat me?"

"No," he said. "You deserve it. You deserve worse, which is likely why your father is content to allow you to languish here."

"Perhaps." Her head tilted, making her look like a wolf. "But the reason your sister and her ladies terrorize me is not dead babies, Jamie. It's because of my blood. The same blood as yours. It's how they'd treat you if not for fear of good king Eddie's wrath."

As if he didn't know that. As if he hadn't dedicated his life to changing that dynamic. But he'd cut his own throat before revealing the stakes to her. "Your tears mean nothing to me, Lestara. They don't mean anything to anyone, so endure your punishment or take the long drop. I care not."

"Perhaps I instead tell them who you really are."

James laughed. "Do it. No one will believe you. None of them would believe that a princess would be sent to serve a scullery maid so that she might spy." He stared her down. "And know that if you cross your father, the long drop will seem the merciful death."

Lestara didn't look away, breathing heavily as her eyes searched his. Then, in an abrupt motion, she scuttled across the room. She picked up a cup he recognized as from Virginia's tea service, the sides foiled with her initials. "This is Ahnna Kertell's teacup. She joined Virginia today, and I stole it."

His blood turned to ice.

Lestara tilted the cup, turning it this way and that. "No matter what I do," she whispered, "it always returns to the same pattern."

Then she slid it across the table toward him, and against his will, Jamie looked down and read the pattern.

Death.

"Tragic," his cousin whispered, but James was already walking out the door.

28
AHNNA

"Your Grace," Ahnna said, catching herself as she started to bow and switching to a smooth curtsy.

Alexandra looked her slowly up and then down, and Ahnna waited for her criticism, but the queen only said, "You look like your mother."

No one was supposed to know what Delia Kertell looked like, but Aren had told her that Petra Anaphora had known their mother well, so this wasn't as great a shock as it might have been. "Yes, Your Grace."

"I was sorry to learn of her death," Alexandra said, taking a seat at the table where a steaming cup of tea sat next to a pot. "Delia was a strong queen. A strong woman."

"But she had a weak heart," Ahnna said. "That was what took her, in the end."

"But not you. You survived a dose of wraithroot that would have killed most men."

It was by no means an admission of guilt, but it was a struggle not to tense as she said, "The Amaridians seemed to want me dead."

Alexandra made a soft noise that was neither agreement nor disagreement, then gestured for Ahnna to sit.

Ahnna obeyed, carefully arranging her skirts as Alexandra poured her a cup of tea. The thought of drinking it made Ahnna profoundly nervous, except she didn't believe that the other woman would be quite so obvious in her poisoning, so she took a small sip.

"I had heard you were like Delia," Alexandra said. "That you were a woman to be reckoned with. The fearsome warrior princess who held command of Southwatch Island and who led Ithicana through much of the war with Maridrina. That you were a woman who picked up the pieces of the failures of men and put everything right."

"I'm nothing like my mother." Ahnna couldn't keep the edge from her voice, because she heard the implication that what happened to Ithicana was Aren's fault. And while she might criticize her twin until she was blue in the face, Ahnna did not take kindly to anyone else speaking ill of him. "As for the rest, I did what I had to do while my brother was absent."

"You're right—you're not like Delia," Alexandra said. "You are quick to react, which is not nothing, for many freeze when faced with adversity. But your mother looked forward, and I've not seen that in you, Ahnna. You fight only the opponent right before you and don't lift your head to see the one shooting the poisoned arrow from afar."

Ahnna didn't answer, only took another sip of her tea, because her mother had been so busy looking forward, she'd not seen the threat standing right in front of her.

"You are a disappointment," Alexandra said.

Ahnna drew in a steadying breath, half because the queen's words confirmed her fear and the other half because her guts were twisting into painful ropes. "I'm sorry for that, Your Grace."

It's the tea. She dosed the tea.

But with what?

"Don't be sorry. Do better."

"Do you want me in Verwyrd?" Ahnna demanded, the rising pain in her stomach making her blunt. "Or do you wish for me to disappear?"

Alexandra rose to her feet, then set a vial on the table. Ahnna's heart skittered with the confirmation that her twisting stomach was not the product of nerves. "Believe me, Ahnna Kertell, if I wanted you to disappear, you'd already be gone."

Ahnna watched the queen of Harendell leave the room. Pain and fear rose in her innards, and as the door shut, she snatched up the vial. Opening it, Ahnna sniffed the contents, recognizing the smell as aloe vera juice right as her innards turned to liquid. "You bitch," she hissed, then bolted toward the privy.

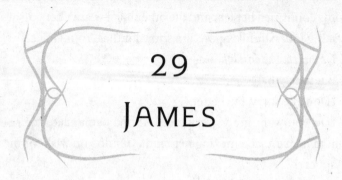

29

JAMES

THE CATHEDRAL BELLS CHIMED IN FULL JOYOUS FORCE AT THE AN-
nouncement of the birth of Ithicana's heir, the sound reaching all
the way to the Sky Palace. Virginia had told him that the baby
princess was named Delia, for the prior queen, and that both the
child and her mother were healthy and strong. His sister was already in the process of arranging a lavish gift to be sent to Ithicana
in congratulations, a king's ransom worth of silver rattles, music
boxes, and toys that any child worth their salt would break within
minutes.

Ahnna, in contrast, was sending Ithicana an aging and ill soldier. James had no doubt Jor would be the more valued gift.

"I want the route leading to the docks cleared," James barked at
the waiting soldiers. "Everyone alert."

Yet James barely noticed the nods and salutes as his men moved
to obey, his eyes all for the carriage circling down the spiral behind
Buck and Brayer. Irritation filled him that Ahnna had chosen not
to remain in the palace, where keeping her safe from both the Am-

aridians and his uncle was possible, though James had known there was no chance that she'd stay in the Sky Palace for long.

His heart beat faster as the mules made their final circuit, for this would be the first time he'd spoken to Ahnna since he'd left her room. The first time he'd stood face-to-face with her since learning that the person who'd tried to have her killed was his own uncle—who might well try again if James didn't find a way to get Ahnna back to Ithicana. How he was going to manage it, James didn't know, only that the anticipation he felt at seeing her face was not making the challenge any easier. His pulse roared as the mules emerged from the spiral's lower gate, the driver stopping near the waiting horse-drawn carriage.

Straightening his uniform, James approached the carriage and opened the door, his stomach tightening at the sight of her.

In a dress.

He frowned, for while there was nothing unusual about the dress Ahnna wore, he did not find that it suited her. She wouldn't be able to move in her usual way in a gown like that. It was too limiting. "I'd heard that you'd caved to propriety but didn't believe it. Yet it seems hell hath indeed frozen over, for that, my lady, is a dress."

"And your dismay at seeing it is understandable," Ahnna replied, "because should we be accosted, you'll have to defend yourself."

"My heart trembles." He held out his hand to her, noting that she'd regained her color, her cheeks flushed pink as her fingers closed around his. Stepping out, she brushed back loose curls that reached her lower back, and he tried and failed to push away the memory of the feel of that hair tangled in his fingers.

Of her limp in his arms because his uncle wanted her dead. The memory caused him to say, "You should sail with them. Go to visit your niece."

Ahnna dropped his hand, eyes narrowed. Instead of responding, she stalked toward the carriage, the effect somewhat impeded by the restrictive cut of her skirts.

Sighing, James turned to help Taryn out. "Congratulations on your acceptance to the conservatory."

"Thank you." Taryn's jaw was tight, feelings on the matter clearly mixed. Indeed, James had heard through the servants' gossip that it had come to shouting between the two women when Ahnna had informed Taryn she'd be joining the conservatory. "Keep my cousin safe. She thinks your men are capable, but that has not been my impression."

"You have my word." He hated how much that felt like a lie as Bronwyn ignored his hand and clambered out, striding toward the waiting carriage without speaking. The Maridrinian princess's expression was a thundercloud—she was obviously no happier about the arrangement than Taryn.

"You going to help me out, too, boy?" Jor asked from inside the carriage.

"Do you need me to?"

Jor snorted. "Not yet, but that day is coming." He climbed out, straightening his tunic. The marks of illness were still heavy upon the man, but he seemed to have renewed vigor, though whether it was because he was going home or what awaited him when he arrived, James could not have said.

"Take care of her, boy. If I have to come back to deal with your failures, you'll learn that age has only made me more creative in my punishments," Jor said as he walked toward the waiting carriage, and instinctively, James said, "Yes, sir."

The old Ithicanian shot him an amused glance, then shut the carriage door behind himself.

Shaking his head to reclaim his wits, James took Maven's reins from the groom and swung up onto the tall black mare. He nodded to Georgie, who took the lead of the column through the gates and into the city.

The civilians were using the news of Ithicana's new heir as an excuse to stop work early and celebrate, the alehouses and cafés all packed with patrons lifting a glass in the name of the princess. While there had been growing resentment over the bridge's tolls, it wasn't enough to overwhelm the long-standing goodwill Harendell had for the Bridge Kingdom, the people delighting in Ithicana's mystery even as they applauded the nation's business sense.

What would it be like to see them lift a glass to Cardiff? he couldn't help but wonder, having spent his entire life watching his people sneer at the mention of his mother's homeland. Unlike Amarid, which, despite their endless squabbles, was regarded with some level of respect, Harendellians saw Cardiffians as barely more than animals. The only reason he was treated differently was because his father was king. And because James was careful never to do anything that reminded the people that he wasn't entirely one of them.

Old biases are hard to break, his father always said. *People believe these things because they were taught to them by their parents and their parents before them. If they are not given reason to question those beliefs, they never will.*

That *reason* had been his mother's dream, shared with his father during their ill-fated love affair, and now James's singular goal. To look north for trade rather than south, to create secure routes back and forth across the border, the ease of commerce and rise in profit gradually destroying the false beliefs and biases that plagued relations between the two nations. Once merchants gained confidence that their caravans were not at risk, they'd flock north, drawn by the allure of keeping their entire profit rather than Ithicana pocketing half.

That the treaty his uncle and father were so close to signing would harm the Bridge Kingdom's coffers, there was no doubt, but the chance to unite Harendell and Cardiff was worth more to James. It would not happen in one fell swoop, but once his father repealed the laws forbidding astromancy and allowing civilians to be persecuted for its practice, it would be a significant beginning. A beginning that would allow him to look up to the stars and know that he'd done right by his mother.

If not by Ahnna.

Ithicana will be fine, he told himself. *It isn't as though trade will cease. The Bridge Kingdom has always been self-sufficient.*

And yet . . . His eyes flicked sideways to the carriage next to him, Ahnna's face frowning as she quarreled with her companions, it sounding as though they were all still arguing against leaving her alone. For which he could hardly blame them. Why did she refuse to go home? Was it because Aren had tasked her with funneling more Harendellian trade through the bridge to line his coffers and she feared failing him? Or, as his father believed, that she knew she'd be used to tempt Amarid into a profitable alliance by marriage to Prince Carlo? Some combination? Or was there another reason for the desperation that had risen in her eyes when James had demanded an explanation? Another threat that she hadn't shared with him?

The question circled his thoughts as they made their way to the western quay, commerce pausing as his men directed civilians and merchants to clear the space. Scanning their surroundings, James dismounted and handed off his reins so that he might open the carriage. He said nothing as Ahnna exited, though the feel of her palm burned through his glove long after she'd started toward the water, her guardsman at her side, Taryn and Bronwyn following.

James walked at a respectful distance behind her. Close enough to come to her aid but far enough that her words to her departing companions were nothing but a murmur of noise.

The passenger vessel they walked toward was grand, with its own guards, something hired by wealthy merchants or minor nobles. The dean of the conservatory abandoned the decks to greet Taryn with great enthusiasm, which, though Taryn deserved it, had likely been purchased by James's father.

Standing with his arms at his back, James watched Ahnna say her goodbyes, only for a ruckus in the distance to catch his attention. Squinting against the sun, James looked upriver in time to see a procession cross the bridge into Verwyrd. The men were mostly in uniform, a handful of them carrying Harendell's banner, but one rode a familiar white stallion.

Shit.

"What's Will doing in Verwyrd?" Georgie muttered. "I thought he was going to Whitewood Hall for the hunts. He should be halfway there by now."

"I don't know." And he couldn't leave to find out. Not with Ahnna standing exposed on the quay.

James drummed his fingers against his thigh, anxiety pooling in his gut over the reason for his brother's return. Not only did Will relish the hunts at Whitewood, but everything he was desperate to avoid was at Verwyrd. And everyone.

Ahnna's companions had boarded the vessel, but rather than waiting for them to make way, Ahnna was walking back to the carriage. Saying nothing, he helped her inside, cursing the slowness of the driver as he wove his way back to the tower, the civilians in the streets calling out to Ahnna their well-wishes for her niece.

Maven, nearly always cool as a cup of water, pranced beneath him. She sensed his nerves, and James rested a hand on her neck to soothe her. But his trepidation only increased as they passed through the gates into the stable yard and his eyes latched on Will, who stood laughing with his friends. All three men went silent as the carriage approached, and to James's everlasting shock, William abandoned his cronies to approach the carriage. Opening the door, he held out his hand to a stunned Ahnna. "My lady."

A flash of jealousy rushed through James as she took his brother's hand, allowing him to help her down.

"My most sincere congratulations on the birth of your niece," he said. "When I saw the riverboat, I half feared you'd abandoned us to return to see the princess without a goodbye."

Ahnna's face was smooth, no doubt searching for the slight in his words, but then she said, "Merely seeing off my people."

"Ah. Well, the baby's loss is my gain." Will gave her a smile that James knew had charmed his way up more than a few sets of skirts, though Ahnna mostly appeared suspicious. And no wonder, for this was an exact reversal of how Will had behaved in their last meeting.

"Why are you here, Will?" James asked, handing off his reins. "You should be halfway to Whitewood. Does Father know you're here?"

Because his father had been very clear that there was nothing to be gained from having Will in Ahnna's presence.

"I've decided not to go," Will answered. Taking Ahnna's hand, he said, "I've come to regret the way I treated you, my lady. You had no more choice in this union than I did, yet you've handled yourself with grace despite my ungentlemanly behavior. It is my hope that as we spend more time together, we might find common ground. Friendship, even."

Ahnna stared at her hand in William's, and it was all James could do not to wrench her free, because his brother was spouting utter bullshit. What was motivating this, James didn't know, but he and Will would be having words later, for there was no doubt in his mind that this would end badly for Ahnna.

"I'd like that," she finally responded. "Thank you."

"You honor me." Will lifted her hand to kiss her knuckles. "As a peace offering, I've a gift for you."

At Will's beckoning gesture, one of the grooms approached, leading a tall bay gelding that James instantly recognized as Will's racehorse, specifically the one he'd backed in this week's races. The high-strung creature pranced and snorted, eyeing first its shadow and then a fluttering sparrow, viewing both as significant threats. What was Will thinking?

"This good boy," Will said, taking the animal's lead shank, "has served me well, but he's aged out of the races. He's cut, so I can't put him to stud, but he's too good to waste out in pasture. I thought you might like him."

Beyond, Georgie was in conversation with Will's cronies, and his friend mouthed *lost*. James's jaw tightened on confirmation that this was no gift of the heart, but before he could speak, Ahnna said, "Oh, he's beautiful."

She reached out a hand to the horse. The foolish creature snorted and jerked away, but Ahnna only smiled. "What's his name?"

"Midday Eclipse," Will said. "Everyone calls him Dippy."

Rather than recognizing that Will was giving her something he wished rid of, Ahnna seemed entranced by the gelding. Taking the lead from his brother, she again held out her hand, showing no fear as the horse let out a loud snort.

Digging into his pocket, Will set a cube of sugar on her palm, then rested his hand against the small of Ahnna's back as he instructed her to keep her hand flat.

Dippy—a more apt name, James had never heard—reached out and tentatively plucked up the sugar, crunching happily until the cathedral bells chimed the hour, which set the gelding off. He reared, and Will jerked Ahnna backward to keep her from taking a hoof to the face. She only laughed. "May I ride him?"

"Do you even know how to ride a horse?" James demanded.

"No, I've never had the opportunity."

"Well, if you're going to be the queen of Harendell, you must become an accomplished rider," Will said.

"Will you teach me?" she asked.

His brother went still, betraying what a farce this really was, though Ahnna was so captivated with the horse that James doubted she noticed. Will recovered quickly. "My father once told me that only a fool tries to teach his wife anything. With our friendship being such a delicate thing, I will defer to his guidance and decline that honor." Will's eyes went sly. "My brother is quite an accomplished rider, so perhaps he will stand in for me, as he has in so many other things."

Will's tone was disappointed, but James didn't miss the hint of venom beneath.

"I don't want to impose." Ahnna stroked the gelding's neck and then fed him an apple that one of the grooms gave to her. "One of the grooms could—"

"Nonsense," William interrupted. "You deserve to be taught by the best. No time like the present, and it's a beautiful day."

It was hot, and thunderstorms were brewing in the east, but James bit his tongue as the groom led the horse away.

"I've correspondence to attend to, though I would like to dine with you tonight, if that's agreeable, Lady Ahnna?" Will asked.

But Ahnna was already hurrying after the groom into the stables, missing his words.

Will smiled, then started toward the gate to the spiral. James caught his arm. "What's all this about?"

For a moment, it looked like Will would give him some flippant excuse, but then he said, "This is my lot, Jamie. Father has made it abundantly clear that he intends for me to marry her whether I like it or not, so I will make the best of it. After all, it's what he did with my mother, so how terrible could it be? Surely I won't end up bitter and gray, drinking by noon and deep into my cups by the seventh hour so as to drown out the voice of the woman who has been foisted upon me in the name of good politics."

"So your solution is to give your future wife a half-broke race-horse that is likely to get her killed?"

"Not sure anything can kill that woman, much less that idiot horse," Will said, then he gripped James's shoulders. "I have nothing but total confidence that you'll bring her back to me in one piece."

Will walked away to join his friends, the trio bypassing the mules to begin the long walk up to the Sky Palace.

Georgie approached. "The gelding came last," he said. "Slow off the start and couldn't rally in the homestretch. Will took it badly. Likely because he lost a great deal of money."

"I don't care about the horse," James snapped. "Do they know why he's here?"

"Interestingly, it seems he gave his friends the same explanation as he just gave to you." Georgie watched the trio circle the tower. "Maybe it's the truth. Maybe he plans to make the best of things, for once."

"Maybe," James said, without feeling, because he wasn't convinced.

The clip-clop of hooves caught his attention. Ahnna was leading Dippy out of the stables, the groom offering suggestions. Sighing, James approached. "Saddle Daisy," he said, naming Virginia's placid mare. "This isn't a horse on which one learns to ride."

Nor was that a dress suitable for riding, but that he kept to himself.

"I'll learn to ride my own horse." Ahnna carefully lifted the reins over the tall gelding's head, the animal eyeing her with far too much interest.

"He's only half broke." James took hold of the reins. "The only thing he knows how to do is a mad gallop around the oval with a boy trained to ride since birth clinging to his back. You're going to get hurt."

Ahnna shrugged, the prospect of pain clearly not enough to dissuade her. "He and I will learn together."

"That's not how it's done." No sooner were the words out of his mouth than he regretted them.

Especially when she shot him a grin. "That's how I like to do everything, James."

"You'd like Daisy saddled, then, sir?" the groom asked.

"No," Ahnna said, right as James said, "Yes."

Her smirk turned into a glare. "This is my horse, which means this is the horse I wish to ride."

Further protest would not dissuade her, so he said, "Fine. If you can get on him, I'll teach you how to ride him."

Ahnna didn't answer, only went to Dippy's saddle, taking hold of the stirrup.

"Mount on the left," he said. "Or your weapons will catch."

"I'm not wearing any."

"Yes, you are." He grimaced at the admission he'd been looking at her thighs for long enough to see the outline of a knife, but she made no comment.

Ahnna circled the animal's rear, dodging as the stupid horse tried to kick her.

"I suppose not doing that again is self-explanatory," he said, and was rewarded with a glower.

Catching hold of the left stirrup, she lifted her foot, making excellent use of both her height and her apparent flexibility as she maneuvered her silk slipper into the opening. "You should be wearing boots," he said.

"Well, I'm not," she retorted, trying to keep her skirt from sliding up her thigh, hold the reins, and grip the stirrup. For a heartbeat, he thought the horse might stand for her and that she'd get it on the first try, but then Dippy snorted and sidestepped, rotating away from her.

Ahnna hopped on her right foot, trying to keep up with the animal as he circled James, skirt sliding up her leg to reveal a very bare muscled thigh, but the horse only shuffled faster. With an *oof*, she landed on her ass.

James huffed out an amused breath, hoping that would be the end of it.

"You don't need to look so happy," she growled, ignoring the hand he offered to pull her to her feet.

"You know what would make me happy, my lady?" James said. "For you to learn to ride on a horse with half a brain between its ears. A horse that is well trained. A horse that isn't likely to get you injured or killed. But as is your habit, you seem intent on doing the exact opposite of what makes me happy, even if it spits in the face of good sense."

"Don't flatter yourself. This has nothing to do with you."

"Foolishness for no reason at all, is it?" James huffed out a breath. "Even better."

"Hold him still."

James had already prevented the gelding from bolting twice, but keeping an animal six times his size from moving wasn't in the cards. "He's not trained to stand, Ahnna. He's trained to run."

"You're not helping."

He didn't bother to correct her, only tightened his grip on the racehorse's reins. And gave every groom watching in the hope of another peek of thigh a murderous glare that had all of them scrambling to find work to do. Never mind that he was hoping for the same.

She tried again, this time not bothering with modesty. Which meant James was treated to a view of stockings that ended just past her knees, the skin above bare and perfect and entirely captivating. Then she was on her ass again in the dirt. She tried again. And again and again. If Ahnna was frustrated, she didn't show it.

"My lord," one of the older grooms said to him, keeping his back to Ahnna's efforts. And her bare legs. "Perhaps the mounting block?"

"What's that?" Ahnna asked even as James shook his head at the groom.

"A crutch that you won't have if you fall off alone in the middle of a field."

She seemed to accept that answer, then her gaze turned sly. "You get on him, James. I want to see if it's even possible or if I'm truly wasting my time."

James ground his teeth. He didn't want her to get on the horse, and he strongly suspected that if he showed her how, Ahnna would have no trouble mimicking him. Except if he refused, he also suspected that she'd only find someone else to show her how. The grooms had returned, enjoying that she'd challenged him, and he'd be lying if he said her tactic wasn't effective. "Fine. Move."

Ahnna backed up. James, forgoing the stirrup and moving too quickly for the horse to do much about it, boosted himself into the saddle. Dippy immediately tried to bolt, but James circled the gelding around Ahnna before sliding off the side again.

"Ah," she said. "I see."

And immediately replicated what he'd done, skirts bunched above her knees, white stockings stained with dirt, the shoulder seam of her dress split where the muscle had flexed.

For a moment, Ahnna and the horse both appeared stunned that she'd managed to make it into the saddle. And then the gelding exploded into motion.

James cursed, Dippy dragging him a dozen paces toward the open gate before he got him stopped, only to realize that Ahnna was no longer in the saddle but flat on her back where they'd started.

His heart leapt to his throat, and he abandoned the horse to run to her. But Ahnna was already sitting up. "Are you hurt?"

"I'm fine." Her tone suggested he was an idiot to think otherwise. "I want to try again."

James's eyes latched upon the crimson stain on the back of her now filthy dress, her stitches obviously having broken open. "We're done here."

"I'm fine."

"You're bleeding."

Ahnna gave him a look of disgust, pulling her arm out of his grip. "So? I don't know how things are done in Harendell, but in Ithicana, you keep trying until you can do it."

He leaned close so that the onlookers couldn't hear. "If you want to do things the way they are done in Ithicana, go back to Ithicana."

Not giving her the chance to voice whatever argument he could see rising in her eyes, he rounded on the grooms. "Stable him." He could feel her glare burning between his shoulder blades.

As James turned to tell Ahnna to get into the carriage so that the mules could take her back to the palace, it was to find her already stomping through the gates into the spiral. She was clearly intent on walking up on her own two feet, the guards he'd assigned trailing after her.

Biting back a curse, James broke into a run. "Why are you so goddamned stubborn?"

"Because pissing you off brings me joy."

His cheeks burned. "That's not the reason."

"Character flaw."

"Try again."

She blew out an angry breath. "Because of my grandmother. If you ever have cause to meet her, you'll understand."

This was the second time she'd spoken about her life in Ithicana, and James had not forgotten that the first time ended with him kissing her. Yet his curiosity to know more about her life refused to be denied. "You mentioned she was a healer of some renown."

"Yes. But she's a real bitch, if I'm being honest, which is probably the only thing Lara and I can agree on. Everything had to be perfect. I had to be perfect, no matter how hard I had to work to achieve it. Aren's shadow, my life dedicated to supporting him, which half the time meant doing all the things he was supposed to be doing."

God help him, but James knew what that felt like.

"I never begrudged my brother that," she said. "I'm not complaining. Only explaining why I am the way that I am."

"I understand." He hesitated. "Are you close with your brother?"

"I used to be." Her jaw worked from side to side. "We don't see eye-to-eye on much anymore."

Sensing he shouldn't press the issue, James let silence reign as they circled higher and higher up the spiral, it broken only when Ahnna said, "I met Lestara."

James tensed, his mind immediately leaping in a thousand different directions, all spelling disaster.

"Your sister's ladies are incredibly cruel to her. They treat her like a dog. No . . . *worse*, because those women treat their dogs like children."

"Lestara is a convicted traitor," he responded mechanically. "Her decision to betray Maridrina to Petra Anaphora resulted in many deaths, and she is fortunate that Keris Veliant chose exile over execution."

"That was no mercy." Ahnna sucked in a breath. "Keris knew exactly how she'd be treated. Knew it would be far worse than a quick death because her mistreatment would slowly eat at her mind until she found a way to end it herself. In his own way, he's every bit as ruthless as Silas ever was."

"You don't think she deserves it?" James asked the question despite knowing that he should steer the conversation away from anything to do with Cardiff. Ithicanians were notoriously ruthless, taking no prisoners, and often known for dumping the heads of those who attacked them on beaches as a message for any who might consider doing the same. Mercy was unexpected.

"No, I don't," she said. "I'm a firm believer in clean executions."

A practical sense of mercy. "Virginia and her ladies may have been harsher on Lestara for your benefit, given your ties with Maridrina. They might have thought you'd appreciate them taking her punishment seriously."

Her voice was acidic as she said, "I highly doubt it was for my benefit, given they don't care about what she did. They treat her as they do because she is a princess of Cardiff, not as punishment for her crimes."

Change the subject, prudence screamed from inside his head, but James said, "That troubles you?"

Her head snapped around, hazel eyes locking on his. "Doesn't it trouble *you*?"

James looked at the smooth stone beneath his feet. "Why should it?"

Silence stretched between them, broken only by the howl of the wind in the spiral, and then Ahnna said, "Because you're half Cardiffian."

"I was born in Verwyrd and raised Harendellian."

"But your mother was Cardiffian. Doesn't it bother you that Harendellians treat Cardiffians as if they are less than human? I find astromancy as peculiar as the next person, but it seems a weak reason to burn women at the stake. Amarid is the nation that causes Harendell grief, but Cardiff bears the animosity? How is that warranted?"

It isn't.

He desperately wanted to tell her how much he hated the way Harendell viewed Cardiff. That his greatest wish was to change the nature of the relationship between the two nations that had given him his blood. That he wanted to make Cardiff and Harendell allies in every possible way. Except his dreams came at a cost to Ithicana, and if she were to learn what he was trying to achieve, loyalty to her homeland would cause her to do everything possible to destroy what he was working for. Which meant he couldn't risk it. "My preference is that my people behave with civility, but my desires carry little weight."

Ahnna huffed with disgust. "Does your father know how they treat Lestara? Is he content with it?"

"Nothing goes on in the Sky Palace that he doesn't know about." This conversation needed to end. "He has set rules, and Virginia will follow them."

"But don't their prejudices trouble him?" she demanded. "Obviously, he's not like-minded, or you wouldn't exist. Or did he not know your mother was Cardiffian until later?"

Bloody hell. "He knew." No point lying, given that the truth was well known.

"So is it the case that he doesn't hold the same prejudices as most Harendellians, or was he just willing to overlook your mother's beliefs because he loved her?"

A question James had asked many times, and one to which he didn't have a certain answer. He did not know how much of his father's motivations were a desire to make change for the better and how much of it he was doing because it had been what James's mother had wanted. "According to Alexandra, my mother cast a spell on my father, so perhaps that is the answer."

Ahnna snorted. "I don't believe that nonsense."

As James blinked, he saw the leaves at the bottom of the teacup. Saw *death* written in them.

"Who killed her?"

He twitched, it seeming as though she'd read his thoughts. "Pardon?"

"Your mother. Who killed her? Because everyone seems to believe it was Alexandra, and that makes little sense to me because your father would have executed her for it, no?"

He exhaled slowly, trying to calm his madly racing heart. "He's never been able to prove the identity of the culprit. If he had, they'd be dead."

Lightning flickered in the distance, and Ahnna mercifully ceased interrogating him and moved to the spiral's railing, resting her elbows against it, eyeing the thunderstorm. Most people feared the height, but Ahnna leaned over the railing as though she wouldn't fall but take flight. "I've heard about Harendell's twisters. That they tear through the open plains, destroying everything they touch."

"This storm will bring only rain," he said, watching the clouds. "It's not warm enough for twisters. Or at least, it's unlikely."

"Have you seen them?"

"Many times," he said. "It's said that the Sky Palace was built in mimicry of them."

Ahnna leaned so far over the railing, he almost lunged to grab the back of her dress. "Yes," she said. "The spiral. I see it now."

"If a twister comes, the only place safe from them is underground. They follow you."

"They sound sentient."

His mouth twisted. "Careful. That's what they say in Cardiff. That the storms are demigods that find their way to earth to punish the God worshipers."

"That's interesting, given that in Ithicana, we say the storms protect us from those who'd do us harm. It was a typhoon that spared Eranahl from Silas's fleet."

He was still angry from her line of questioning, and that anger made him say, "We heard it was Lara who slayed Silas in a duel, ending the battle. They say Lara is the savior of Ithicana."

"That's what they say," Ahnna repeated, her tone suggesting his barb had struck true, though he didn't feel any satisfaction in one-upping her.

But before he could say anything to temper the jab, the sound of running feet caught his attention. A sweating soldier rounded the spiral behind them, breathing hard as he panted out, "Major General, sir. We've just received word that a mob has imprisoned a woman in Marickshire under the accusation of astromancy. Her husband is born and bred Harendellian, and he claims that the accusations are false. He's begged aid from the crown, but the mob is already building the pyre."

James grimaced. The small hamlet was at least an hour's gallop away. He'd never make it in time. But he had to try.

Inclining his head to Ahnna, he said, "If you would excuse me, I must attend to this."

"They don't mean to burn her, do they?" she demanded. "Without trial?"

"That is the way of it." The words came out from between his teeth. "Though as her husband is Harendellian, I have an obligation to interfere until certainty of her offense might be obtained. Enjoy the rest of your day, my lady."

Not giving her a chance to answer, James turned on his heel. The moment he was out of sight, the howl of the wind in the spiral drowning out all noise, he broke into a run.

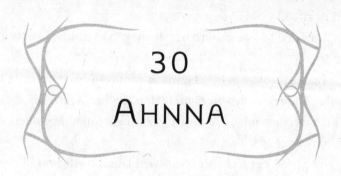

30
AHNNA

NEITHER OF HER GUARDS HAD OFFERED MUCH IN THE WAY OF IN-formation about the situation in Marickshire, beyond that inter-vention required an individual of a certain rank, both men seeming to be of the opinion that no one should intervene at all. So Ahnna immediately went to her rooms and summoned Hazel.

"Hazel," she said the moment the slender woman entered her rooms, "I was with James when his presence was requested to in-tervene on behalf of a woman accused of practicing astromancy. It sounded to me as though the mob intended to burn her without trial."

"A trial is not required," Hazel answered. "Astromancy is illegal, and civilians are encouraged to take action against practitioners."

"An accusation is enough? Do the accusers not need to provide proof before they burn women alive?"

"If someone has been accused, there is proof," Hazel said curtly. "Astromancy is illegal, immoral, and abhorrent in the eyes of the true faith. It is not worth His Highness's time, though he may go to the scene to ensure no further violence results. Oftentimes, the accused's associates will attempt to free them."

She'd thought James's swift reaction had been motivated by the desire to prevent the burning, but Hazel's words cast that into doubt. "Is this a frequent occurrence?"

"Too common by far." Hazel's eyes searched hers with uncharacteristic boldness. "It is the reason the border between Harendell and Cardiff is closed. To prevent Cardiffians from coming into Harendell and forcing our people to take action against them. But they covet our land and gold, so they sneak across and attempt to blend in. I'm sure the clever ones abandon their ungodly practices and survive by blending in, but some insist on holding to their ways. This is the result."

"I see." Every part of Ahnna rebelled against such violent persecution, and her mind instantly leapt to wondering if it would be possible to change the laws if and when she ever became queen. It must have shown on her face, because Hazel's mouth drew into a thin line. "I do not presume to advise you, my lady, but if you were to ask, it would be my recommendation that you refrain from voicing opinions on that particular subject."

Ahnna chewed the insides of her cheeks, then decided this was not a battle she'd fight today. But it was a battle that she intended to fight when the moment to do so was right. "I understand. Would you arrange for a bath to be drawn? I smell of horse."

Seemingly satisfied with her response, Hazel bobbed a curtsy. "Of course, my lady."

NEARLY AN HOUR LATER, THE servants had finished filling the large copper tub with steaming water, and Hazel helped her undress.

"You're bleeding," Hazel said as she examined the small stain on the back of Ahnna's clothes.

"I fell off my new horse." Stepping into the steaming bath, she reached behind her back to touch the injury, and her fingers came away bloody. "Does it need fresh stitches?"

"I don't think so," Hazel answered after scrutinizing the wound. "Only one stitch broke, though you should really take more care, my lady."

"I'm going to try to ride him again tomorrow."

Hazel sighed, but only picked up a file and set to work on Ahnna's nails.

Ahnna was no fool; she knew the horse was not a well-thought gift but rather something convenient. Yet it was a concrete gesture, and that was something. And after her meeting with Alexandra, which had resulted in a night in the privy with vicious stomach cramps and endless questions, *something* was what she needed.

You are a disappointment, Alexandra's voice whispered in her head, and Ahnna fought the urge to sink beneath the surface of the bathwater, the queen's tone hauntingly reminiscent of the tone her own mother had once used.

Hazel finished with her nails, then said, "Would you care to soak while I see about your gown, my lady? I will not be long."

"Yes."

Hazel's footsteps moved away behind the silk screens, the door opening and then shutting, lock turning. Ahnna settled against the back of the tub, though she was careful to keep the wound from being immersed in the water.

Don't be sorry. Do better.

The queen's parting words had been the ones to haunt her the most, because they implied a path forward. A way to become worthy in Alexandra's eyes.

Apparently by becoming more like her mother.

Ahnna scowled, wanting to rebel against the very idea of it, but she forced herself to consider the specific criticisms. Reactionary. Not forward thinking. Blind to distant threats.

Criticisms, yes, but part of Ahnna wondered if Alexandra's words had also been guidance as to how she might succeed in Harendell and gain the queen's support. And the laxative in the tea . . . that had only been a petty way to reinforce Alexandra's very clear statement: The attack on the Sky Palace walls hadn't been ordered by her.

As to what Ahnna should do with all this information, she didn't bloody well know, but the strange meeting had given her hope that her aim of saving Ithicana through marriage to William might actually come to fruition.

At the thought of her homeland, a wave of homesickness passed over her. As much as they'd all needed to leave, for different reasons, having all three of her companions depart had taken a toll on her. As though Jor and Taryn drifting down the river had taken the last piece of Ithicana she had with them, leaving her alone.

"It's fine," she muttered. "You're surrounded by servants who cater to your every need and soldiers protecting your back. You're hardly alone."

Yet it had felt that way as she sat in the empty carriage returning her to the tower, and part of Ahnna had nearly broken in that moment. Had nearly begged the carriage driver to turn around, to catch the boat on which she could flee back home.

And then William had opened the door, offering her an olive branch in the form of a racehorse.

To put so much weight on a horse was foolish, but her heart had latched on to Dippy the moment she'd set eyes on him. Not only an olive branch, but the one thing in this place that could be hers and hers alone.

DANIELLE L. JENSEN

She was going to master riding that horse, no matter what James had to say about it.

James.

He had not been happy discussing his mother or Cardiff today, that much had been obvious. Yet while there might have been clever and roundabout ways of getting the information, in Ahnna's experience, outright asking questions was usually the best way to receive clear answers. Or at least answers as clear as one could get.

Which was to say, not very clear at all.

Cardiff was easily the largest untapped market for Harendell. Except given that Harendellians burned Cardiffian women on the slightest accusation of astromancy, it seemed highly unlikely that the border between the nations would open anytime soon if for no other reason than that Cardiffian merchants would be risking their lives to trade within Harendell.

Though she didn't believe James was as indifferent to the strife between Harendell and Cardiff as he claimed. How could he be when the only reason he wasn't subjected to the same hate was that Edward was his father? More likely, James had learned the hard way about countering his father and his father's laws, so he knew to keep his mouth shut. Which was telling enough. As was the fact that despite having had an affair with a Cardiffian woman and her bearing him a son, Edward had not repealed the laws banning the practice of astromancy in Harendell. Either James's mother had set aside her beliefs for him, or Edward had overlooked them for her, but it obviously hadn't changed his broader outlook in a significant way. And there wasn't a chance that trade would flow with the Harendellians burning Cardiffian women at the stake with full approval of the king's laws.

Which made Ahnna wonder if *that* was how Alexandra had gotten away with killing James's mother. If it had been her at all.

He's never been able to prove the identity of the culprit. If he had, they'd be dead.

Was that the truth? She hadn't expected James to condemn Alexandra, but if it was someone else, why not say so?

"Bloody hell," Ahnna muttered, rubbing her temple. They called the king's seat the Twisted Throne in deference to the storms that plagued the kingdom, but it spoke to the politics of these people. And to the royal family, most of all, for the only thing that seemed to unify them was name and blood, their agendas seemingly quite at odds.

Yet Ahnna's goal remained the same: do whatever it took to push Harendellian trade, and gold, into Aren's coffers.

Which meant staying alive.

At least that challenge was a familiar one. It was also the only thing on which she and James seemed to stand on the same side.

The fire roaring in the hearth next to her disappeared from her vision, replaced with his face, brow furrowed in what seemed like a permanent frown, full bottom lip so reluctant to smile. He was so cursedly rigid and unwilling to bend on *anything*, and yet thinking of him made her toes curl, heat that had nothing to do with the scalding bathwater rising between her legs.

"No," she told herself, even as she traced a finger between her breasts and over her stomach. "Do not think about him."

Yet it was impossible to vanquish the vision of him vaulting onto her horse as though it were nothing, looking down on her as he easily mastered the massive animal. All muscle and broad shoulders, every instinct in her body screaming that beneath the manners and courtesy was a wolf, deadly in an instant if crossed the wrong way.

"Do not think about him, Ahnna," she whispered as her fingers disappeared into the soapy water. "This is folly."

Nor did it make any sense. Good-looking or not, James infuriated her with his endless need to tell her what to do.

Yet every time he offered her his hand, so goddamned proper in his fancy clothes that she wanted to kick him in the shins, the whole world fell away, those amber eyes burning into her soul. Seeing her the way no one else ever did.

"You're going to make a bad situation worse," she whispered, slipping a finger between her legs. "You can't think about him this way."

Especially given that William, despite his rare beauty, made her burn as hot as yesterday's oatmeal.

"You need to learn to feel otherwise," she muttered, trying to fill her mind's eye with images of the crown prince. "You need to be able to at least fake wanting him. You can accomplish none of what you came here to do if you let your mind go down this path. Think about William, Ahnna. William."

But as her fingertip circled her clit, all she could see was James. James soaked to the bone in the cave beneath Northwatch, his hands on her hips as he'd lifted her. James's chest against her back as they'd fought through the storm. James carrying her down the steps after she'd been attacked. James's lips on hers in the maze at Fernleigh House, hands gripping her hard and mouth claiming her in a way no man alive had ever dared. In the way she had always dreamed of.

What would it be like to see him unleashed that way again? For him to set aside the propriety that he wore as a shield and have the man beneath put his hands on her?

Her body crested with shocking intensity that tore a gasp from her lips, and she rode her fingers, imagining that it was him stroking her as wave after wave of pleasure rolled over her, leaving her so spent she collapsed back against the tub, sinking deep in the water.

And inadvertently immersed the wound on her back.

"Fuck!" she yelped, jerking upright as it stung. She rested her chin on her knees as the pain slowly eased. "You deserved that, you idiot."

But there was no more time for admonitions as a knock sounded, a key turned, and Hazel announced, "It's only me, my lady. Your evening gown has arrived from the modiste—the guards weren't going to let it into the Sky Palace, but Prince James returned at that same moment and brought it in."

Cheeks burning at the mention of his name, Ahnna said, "Let me have a look."

Hazel appeared around the silk screens, holding a massive confection of bright-pink silk and white lace. "It was intended for Lady Elizabeth," Hazel said. "Apparently, she refused to pay for it, so the modiste was willing to sell it to me for less than it's worth. Not precisely your color, but . . ."

Don't apologize. Do better, Alexandra's voice said, followed by Bronwyn's saying, *Play the game.*

Ahnna gave Hazel a tight smile. "Does it have matching shoes?"

An hour and a half later, she was teetering down the hallway on a pair of pink silk heels, doing her best not to step on the seemingly endless layers of fabric that surrounded her. It wasn't so much that she couldn't walk in high heels, for she had excellent balance—it was that Elizabeth had small feet.

Her guards took her to a private dining room, and when the doors opened, she was relieved to discover only the three royal siblings were inside. James appeared unmoved by however events in Marickshire had gone, only lifting one eyebrow at the sight of her, his scrutiny making her want to melt into the floor, given what she'd just been doing. William only gave her a dazzling smile, abandoning his seat to escort her to her chair. In heels, she towered over him, and Ahnna instantly regretted not wearing her flat silk slippers, even if they were covered with stains from the stable yard.

"Ahnna," Virginia said, frowning. "I hear the rustle of satin. What are you wearing?"

"A new gown." Ahnna's cheeks burned, and she suspected she looked as foolish as she felt.

"Which dressmaker?" Her bottom lip pressed out. "And why didn't they visit me?"

With every second that passed, wearing the dress felt like a bigger mistake. "Hazel selected it from a modiste in Verwyrd. Something already made, I believe."

"I'm sure it's lovely." Virginia smiled. "James, do describe it for me. You've an eye for detail."

He eyed Ahnna over the rim of his wineglass. "Raspberry cream puff."

Though she hadn't thought it possible, her whole body flamed hotter, his comment made even worse by the fact she'd not long ago been pleasuring herself to visions of him like the idiot she was.

"Ignore him," William said. "Jamie wouldn't know style if it slapped him in the face. His uniform is the only item of color in his wardrobe, and I think if he had his way, he'd change Harendell's colors to black so as to expunge color from his wardrobe entirely."

"I've already petitioned Father for it," James said. "Denied."

The trio laughed, and Ahnna took a sip of her wine, trying to relax. Which was a challenge, given the corset barely allowed her to breathe. What cleavage she had jutted almost to her chin, she was laced so tightly.

"I heard that William gave you a horse," Virginia said. "And that Jamie is teaching you to ride. You're in good hands—he's an excellent rider."

God help her, but Ahnna knew too well what it was like to be in James's hands. "Given I only managed to sit on my horse's back for all of a second before he tossed me in the dirt, I need all the training I can get."

"Oh dear." Virginia motioned to the servants to begin serving dinner. "What horse did you give her, Will?"

"His idiot racehorse," James answered sourly. "The creature has a brain the size of a walnut."

"Oh, really?" Virginia said. "I thought Dippy had another year at the track?"

"You're mistaken," Will said. "Aged out. But he's handsome and tall, so I thought he was a good fit for Ahnna. Fast, too, and I can't imagine that a woman capable of guiding a ship through a storm would want a slow steed." He winked at Ahnna.

"That horse would run straight off a cliff," James said, glowering at his wine. "Daisy would be a better mount to learn on, but Ahnna wouldn't listen to reason."

"You didn't attempt to reason with me," Ahnna said. "Only told me what you thought I should do. I disagreed."

"I don't blame you, Ahnna. Daisy's barely more than a pony," Will said. "And she's the slowest horse in the stables."

"She's not," Virginia protested. "Daisy is the sweetest. But Maven would be the better choice, Jamie. Best-trained horse in the stable, plus she's quick."

"Maven's mine."

Virginia rolled her eyes. "Never learned to share."

"Ahnna will master Dippy, I'm sure of it," William said. "Mark my words, she'll be galloping across the countryside within the week."

"I'm a quick study." Ahnna took another sip of her wine. "Where are the king and queen this evening?"

William yawned. "They left for Whitewood Hall for the hunts."

What?

"It's a three-day journey north of Verwyrd," Virginia said. "I believe they left while you were at the quay. I'd normally travel with them, but Mother wished for me to remain with you."

"I would have traveled with them as well," Ahnna said, still unsure whether this development was good or bad, but understanding very clearly that the timing of their departure had been no accident.

"Given the attempt on your life, it wasn't deemed safe for you to be on the road," Virginia said. "Better for you to remain in the Sky Palace, where it's easy to control who comes and goes."

"Only the most determined assassin would bother with the climb," Will said with a laugh. "And the fittest."

"Assassins are usually fit," James muttered, snatching up his soup spoon and staring at the bowl like it had personally offended him. "If for no other reason than that they need to be able to flee the scene of their crimes."

William waved a hand as though assassins were of no consequence. "The Amaridians have other problems to claim their focus than our dear Ahnna. Skirmishes in the Lowlands is what I've heard."

The Lowlands was a coastal region north of Amarid that had been annexed by Harendell a generation ago. Though cold, the area was productive in the warmer months, and there had long been reports from Ithicana's spies that Queen Katarina desired to reclaim them. It was believed that the reason she'd allowed Silas to rent her navy was to secure his support in the fight to reclaim the Lowlands. Though given the heavy losses Amarid had taken in the siege of Eranahl, the alliance had done more harm than good. "Will you send soldiers to defend the territory?"

William nodded, his mouth full of soup, but once he'd swallowed, he said, "They want a fight, we'll kick them in the teeth, right, Jamie?"

James gave a tight smile, spooning soup into his mouth as though it were his last meal.

"Let's not talk about politics," Virginia said. "It's tedious."

Ahnna didn't agree. "How long do you anticipate the conflict will go on for?"

"Not long. We'll show them what's what, and they'll crawl back south."

James was now attacking a dinner roll as though he desired to murder rather than consume it, and Ahnna suspected that meant he had different views but was declining to share them. Which was worrisome. She was already struggling to get a moment in Edward's presence to discuss trade, and an escalation in the conflict with Amarid would only make his time more precious. Never mind that Harendell might well need many of the resources that they typically exported, namely, steel.

"If it's war with Amarid," William said, "we'll be looking to Ithicana to show itself a true ally by denying them access to Northwatch's market. See how long Katarina can fund her war with no trade east and no trade south."

Amaridian wine was a significant source of bridge tolls, for the Maridrinians and Valcottans alike adored the northern vintages, and the wealthy imported a great deal of it. To lose that? Ahnna could feel the blood draining from her skin. "The southerners would take issue with that, I'm afraid. In our attempt to punish Amarid, we'd risk angering other nations." She gave a tight smile. "Keris Veliant is particularly fond of Amaridian wine."

"How else will Ithicana support us if it comes to war if not in stymying Amaridian trade?" William asked, his eyes burning into hers as he ignored her comment. "As formidable as Northwatch's shipbreakers might be, I don't think you've got the range to hit Amarid."

"We have spies in places that you do not."

William's head tilted. "Are you suggesting that your brother currently withholds intelligence that might aid us?"

"No," she said between her teeth. "I'm suggesting our spies might be deployed to serve your purposes."

He huffed out an amused breath. "Ithicana only has one card to play. I'm sure your brother will see reason and play it, if it comes to war. Remember that we were willing to bleed for you against Maridrina when it benefited us little. If Ithicana isn't willing to do the same, we might have cause to question whether we have an alliance at all. Whether Ithicana is the friend we should be leaning upon."

Ahnna's fingers turned to ice, because William had consumed a great deal of wine and might be revealing things he should not. Things like other alliances. And other markets. "What other friends does Harendell have in the north but Ithicana?"

William was deadly silent, then he burst into laughter. "None, as the case may be. So I shall pray that your brother does not leave us standing alone if war comes to the north. It would be tragic to find ourselves friendless in our time of need."

"This is boring," Virginia declared. "And hardly worth the conversation. Every other year, we teeter toward the same conflict and then back again. The spies have cried wolf about war too many times. I no longer believe it will happen."

James stabbed at a thick slice of roast beef, looking ready to kill the cow it had come from for the second time.

"You don't agree?" Ahnna asked him.

"I'm a soldier, so I hardly find discussions about the potential for war *boring*."

Virginia stuck her tongue out at him, then said, "You should have invited Georgie, then. He would keep me entertained while you bore Ahnna with the same conversation I've heard a hundred times."

"Still fancy Georgie, do you?" Will asked. "I remember when you used to practice signing your name as the Countess of Elgin."

"Depends on my mood." Virginia took a thoughtful sip from her glass, not seeming to be the slightest bit embarrassed. "Elgin is so far north, it's practically in Cardiff. I don't know if I could stand it."

"I'm sure Georgie would keep you warm on those cold northern nights, little sister." William smirked at her. "Since you can't see for yourself, I'll do you the favor of letting you know that in the years since you exited childhood, Georgie has taken to gaping at you like a fish that has found itself on land."

Virginia picked up a dinner roll and threw it at him with surprisingly good aim.

"Cast your aspirations elsewhere," James said. "George is too old for you."

Virginia scowled. "He's the same age as you."

"Which is twelve years your senior."

"Which makes him finally of an age worth noticing," she said. "It's a well-known fact that boys don't become men until the age of thirty."

William shot her a frown.

"Almost there, Will," James said. "On your birthday, I'll teach you how to shave."

Will lifted his glass. "To the last six months of my boyhood. Huzzah!"

"Huzzah!" the other two declared, lifting their glasses, and Ahnna politely sipped at hers, remembering when she and Aren used to bicker like this. Before it had all gone to shit, and jests had turned into jabs intended to hurt rather than amuse. She missed that. Missed him.

Ahnna abruptly realized that all three of them were looking at her expectantly and that a question had been posed. "Pardon?"

"How are unions determined in Ithicana?" Virginia asked. "Your kingdom is such a mystery to us."

"Oh. Well, typically, people wed whomever they wish to spend their lives with. Someone they have fallen in love with."

"Love matches?" Virginia's eyes widened, then narrowed, the wheels in her mind clearly turning as she digested the revelation. "Even the nobility?"

"Yes." Ahnna took another small sip of her wine. "The Fifteen-Year Treaty was the first time in memory that a betrothal was made political. To end the war with Maridrina, of course, but also because my mother wished for Ithicana to cease holding itself apart from the rest of the world. She believed marriages would aid in that."

"It never occurred to her that Silas would take advantage?" William asked. "Because I assure you, no one was surprised that he made a move, only by his methods."

"I think she was so focused on the dream that she lost sight of reality." Ahnna didn't add that Aren had been the same way. Idealistic. "Though perhaps she had the right of it, because thanks to that treaty, Ithicana's bond with Maridrina, and now with Valcotta, is stronger than ever. The southern alliance is held together by blood and"—she nudged Virginia's shoe with her own—"love matches."

Virginia's smile didn't reach her eyes.

"A dream, indeed," William said, his smile bemused. "It is your bad luck to have been sent north where love matches are the domain of novels and plays, reality ruled by the games and power plays of those who rule. Or those who aim to rule."

Apprehension turned her stomach, but Ahnna forced herself to say, "That could change."

Green eyes bored into hers, and for a moment, Ahnna thought he'd lash out at her for daring to suggest their marriage might be more than an alliance of kingdoms, but then William smiled and said, "You're right. It could change. It *should.*"

His burst of furor ought to have pleased her, but the apprehension in her stomach only grew, instincts screaming a warning though she did not see the threat. *You fight only the opponent right before you and don't lift your head to see the one shooting the poisoned arrow from afar.*

"Huzzah," Virginia declared. "To love matches. Let Georgie and I be the first, even if he doesn't know it yet. Now eat faster—I want to play cards."

Cards, as it turned out, were played blindfolded, the cards themselves marked with raised bumps declaring their number and suit.

"When it became clear that my vision would soon be a thing of the past, I had to learn to read another way," Virginia said. "My brothers declared their intention to learn along with me, and one of the first things we did was start playing cards blindfolded to make it fair. Jamie can tell if you're bluffing from the way you breathe, so be mindful."

"Jamie is adept at everything," Will added, and Ahnna sorely wished she wasn't wearing a blindfold because she could not read James's silence.

"It's true," Virginia said. "He masters all of Father's inane hobbies, even taxidermy. Our projects all grace Fairfield House, which is our hunting lodge. While James's wolf appears so alive it might bite your arm off, my deer is lumpy, and Will's bobcat is cross-eyed."

"If I am better, it is only because I make an effort, whereas you two cannot be bothered." A chair scraped back, and Ahnna removed her blindfold to discover James was standing. "Unfortunately, I have some matters requiring my attention tonight, so you will have to find another target for your teasing."

"But it's late," Virginia protested. "And we are having fun."

"Yes, but unlike the three of you, I have duties."

"What duties that you couldn't delegate to someone else?" Virginia demanded. "What is the point of being a *major general* if you do everything yourself?"

"With rank come obligations that can't be delegated."

"Don't neglect your duty to Ahnna," William said. "Riding lessons tomorrow, correct, my lady?"

"I can manage on my own."

"I won't hear of that," William said. "James, you'll make time, yes?"

Making time looked like the last thing James was interested in, but he inclined his head. "Of course. Now if you'll excuse me."

As he turned, Ahnna found herself asking, "What happened to the woman in Marickshire?"

James did not turn around, but Ahnna swore he stiffened slightly before he said, "I crossed paths with a messenger on my way who informed me she was already deceased. They burned her alive."

Then he left without another word.

"Why don't the Cardiffians learn?" Virginia muttered. "It's so frustrating how they endlessly put us in this position."

It was a heartless response, but Ahnna bit down on a retort and instead asked, "What business is there at this hour?"

"Patrols, I assume," William said with a shrug. "James likes riding around in the dark looking for evildoers. Idleness drives him mad. Though in this case, it's because armed Amaridians are rumored to be mucking about the countryside, and there is little he likes better than hunting them. Overachiever, our brother is. Although I suppose he might also have an assignation planned. Who can say."

Ahnna's stomach dropped, but she kept her face blank as she said, "I wasn't aware the Amaridians were still causing trouble." Nor did she think that was what James was attending to, given it was a task that could most certainly be delegated.

Virginia blew out a breath between pursed lips. "If Jamie wanted us to know what he was doing, he'd have told us. His business is his own."

If it had been Amaridians, James would have said so, and jealousy Ahnna had no right to feel bit at her stomach that William's offhand remark might well be the truth. That he might have a relationship with some woman.

Except if that was the case, why had he kissed her that night in the hedge maze? James did not strike her as the sort to be so faithless as to kiss one woman while courting another.

Unlike you, she silently chastised herself. *Apparently, you are precisely that faithless, kissing one brother while betrothed to another. Satisfying yourself with visions of one brother while you pursue marriage with the other.*

Ahnna struggled not to cringe, especially when she realized that William was watching her intently. "His dedication is commendable," she said.

"It most certainly is." William tilted his head slightly as he considered her. "But alas, on that note, I am to bed. I had a long day at the races and will leave you two to your gossip. Good night."

"Good night," Ahnna murmured, her attention turning to Virginia as the prince departed the room.

"More wine?" Virginia asked. "It's early yet."

Ahnna nodded assent. Virginia gestured a hand, and a waiting servant filled both their glasses. "It's a positive sign that William has given you a gift," the princess said. "I know he's not been the kindest to you, but he has a good heart. He's just learned to keep it hidden." She sighed. "It's difficult for him, always having to live up to Jamie, whom our father has always placed on the highest of pedestals because Jamie is good at all the things that our father values. No matter how hard he tried, Will could never please our father, so for years now, he's given up trying at all. Yet in recent days, he's rallied, and I think it's because of your presence. You heard his reaction to the idea of love matches."

The unease Ahnna had felt at William's fervor over the suggestion returned, though she could not articulate to herself why.

"Do you think you could come to love my brother, Ahnna?" Virginia asked. "To build a marriage based on more than just politics? Because in my heart, I think there is nothing William desires more than to be loved. And I believe he deserves love from his wife."

Ahnna felt her throat close up, her heart recoiling because the answer was *no*. She did not see herself ever loving a man like William. What she saw was a future that she'd endure for the sake of Ithicana. But that wasn't the answer Virginia wished to hear. "I have high hopes for a friendship between us," she finally said. "While I hope for more, hope for love, I worry about putting my heart at risk."

"Isn't that the point of love?" Virginia asked. "To risk everything for it, most especially your heart? Like Keris did for Zarrah." The corner of her mouth turned up. "Like your own brother did for his wife?" She narrowed her eyes. "Or must it be my brother's heart that takes all the risk?"

The defensiveness in Virginia's voice was intense, and having been in the woman's shoes, Ahnna understood her position all too well. "I've no intention of hurting your brother, Virginia. But it was your advice to allow him to come to me, your advice not to push, and I took that to heart."

Virginia was silent for a long moment. "You are not fooling me, Ahnna. I know you hold no romantic interest in my brother. My eyes may have failed me, but in their loss, I have gained other instincts. If you were a Harendellian woman, I might think nothing of your lack of interest, as you'd have been raised not to expect sentiment in your marital union. Except what you told me tonight of Ithicana's practices make me wonder why you've so easily come to terms with a loveless future."

"What would you have me do?" Ahnna asked, fully aware she was on the back foot in this argument, the princess more perceptive than she'd realized. "Throw myself at your brother? Wait naked in his bed so as to seduce him? He's not stupid. He will know that after how he has treated me, my behavior is a pretense, and I think it a far better thing for our relationship to have a foundation of honesty rather than deception."

"I could not agree more." Virginia's expression was hard. "I will be frank. You told me that it was your choice to come to Harendell, but I find that suspect. You might have remained in the land of your birth and had everything: power, privilege, and true love. You told me you desired to come to Harendell because you wished to do good things in union with William, but what good things? Harendell's relationship with Ithicana is already strong and prosperous, so what do you aim to accomplish that is worth all that you have quite clearly sacrificed? Why are you here, Ahnna? What are you using William to achieve?"

Shit shit shit! Ahnna silently screamed, because what possible answer could she give that would satisfy the princess?

"My mother gave her word when she signed the Fifteen-Year Treaty with your father," Ahnna finally said. "I committed to the same promise when I met with him to secure aid against Maridrina. When I give my word, I keep it, no matter the cost to me. All that said, I do desire to have a positive union with William. It is my goal to make this marriage work as well as I am able. But I cannot promise an emotion that has not yet been earned by either of us."

Silence stretched, the tension thick enough to cut with the knife strapped to Ahnna's thigh. Then Virginia said, "I believe what you say is true. Yet I do not find that I trust you, Ahnna Kertell."

"Trust is another thing that must be earned." Ahnna rose to her feet. "I should go to bed. Thank you for the lovely evening."

Leaving Virginia to her wine, Ahnna fought the urge to take the painful shoes off and walk barefoot on the thick carpets as she made her way back to her room. The halls were empty of everyone but the guards, the palace quiet. Likely, she now realized, because half of them had left with the king and queen.

Then she heard a yelp of pain. Picking up the pace, Ahnna rounded the corner to find Elizabeth with a riding crop in hand.

And a leashed Lestara on her knees.

"Beg, you little bitch," Elizabeth said, and when the Cardiffian princess refused to move, she lifted her arm to strike her with the crop.

But Ahnna was faster.

Snatching hold of the whip, she jerked it out of Elizabeth's hand. "*Stop.*"

The young woman whirled, eyes filled with outrage. "How dare you!"

"How dare I?" Ahnna used her superior height to loom over the other woman. "How dare you treat another human being like an animal."

"She's from Cardiff!"

"I don't care." Ahnna took a step closer, and a look of apprehension filled Elizabeth's eyes. "If you wish to kill her, I won't stop you, but I will not stand by while you abuse and humiliate her for your own amusement."

"How can you say that, knowing what she did?" Elizabeth retorted. "She's here as punishment. So she deserves punishment."

"But not by you." Ahnna smacked the crop against her own palm with a loud crack, staring the courtier down. "Because you don't care about her crime. You only care about feeling powerful." She lifted Elizabeth's chin with the end of the crop. "But you're not. You will treat her with dignity, or you will answer to me."

Elizabeth took two quick steps back and hissed, "Have it your way, my lady. Though you should have let us have our sport with Lestara. Now when we get bored, we'll turn our sights on the next best thing." Giving Ahnna one last sneer, she stormed down the hallway.

"Thank you."

Ahnna turned to find Lestara on her feet, neither of Ahnna's bodyguards having moved to help her up. There was a livid red mark across her neck and another across her cheek. "Don't thank me. I think Keris should have cut off your head and staked it on the gates of the city you saw burn."

"I wish he had." Lestara lifted her chin, amber eyes boring into Ahnna's. "But men are very good at orchestrating the misery of women. Especially pawns that don't stay in the correct places on their game board."

"You made your own bed. Don't come to me for sympathy."

"I'm not." Unfastening the diamond collar from around her neck, Lestara dropped it on the floor. "But a bit of advice. These women might be kind to your face, but they don't like you. They don't like *anything* that is different from them, because it invalidates how they choose to be. That dress"—she jerked her chin at the gown Ahnna wore—"they planted that just for you, though don't blame your maid for it. Elizabeth arranged it with the modiste. The whole palace has been snickering all night at how stupid you look, though I heard that only James had the balls to tell you."

Ahnna's jaw tightened, now seeing what she'd taken for mockery as honesty. And Elizabeth wouldn't have done it without Virginia's approval, which meant the princess had been in on it.

"It doesn't matter how hard you try. It doesn't matter if you wear their clothes, talk like them, act like them—you'll always be an outsider. Which means you'll always be seen as *less*," Lestara said. "So keep your dignity and don't even try."

"Advice you don't seem to follow, which makes it suspect."

Lestara smoothed her skirts. "I was sold by my father in exchange for better prices on animal pelts. Treated like a broodmare in Silas Veliant's court. Relegated to spinsterhood by the worst king Maridrina has ever had, and then cast into exile for trying to have him removed. Now I live under the eye of yet another king who is content to see me treated like a dog, just as he is content to allow his people to murder my people for their faith. All men do is use me to achieve their ends." Spreading her arms wide, Lestara added, "I have no dignity left to lose."

She took a step toward Ahnna, and her bodyguards moved to push Lestara back. But Ahnna motioned them away, allowing the smaller woman to come close even as she closed her fingers over the tiny knife hidden in her pocket.

"My fate was foretold, and it is not this," Lestara whispered, her amber eyes glowing. "Patience will deliver me."

"The only thing that will deliver you from this is death, Lestara," Ahnna said. "Keris is consort to the empress of Valcotta. Edward will not cross him, for he will not cross *Zarrah*."

At Zarrah's name, hatred bloomed in Lestara's eyes. The seething sort of rage that destroyed sanity and consumed everything in its path, and Ahnna had to curb the urge to draw a weapon and kill this woman. For no good would she ever do.

"I know your past, Ahnna Kertell," Lestara said. "And I have seen your future. Run. Run as far and as fast from Verwyrd as you can, because the only thing here for you is death."

Then she twisted away and, a heartbeat later, was gone from sight.

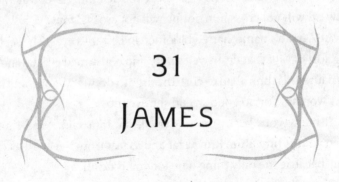

31

JAMES

JAMES RODE THROUGH THE DARKNESS WITH ONLY A SMALL LANtern to illuminate his path, heading toward Thistleford. No one would think anything of him being out, his *relationship* with Elsie well known for the sake of the freedom it gave him to come and go at all hours. Though it had occurred to him after he'd left Ahnna in the company of his siblings that William knew about Elsie. That he might, deep in his cups as he was, tell Ahnna that was likely where James had gone.

Maybe that would be for the best, he silently told himself. *Maybe you should arrange for it.*

Maybe you should rekindle it so you stop thinking about a woman you can never have. Lose yourself in Elsie for a night or two so that you remember your purpose. Remember who you are.

Except Elsie wasn't the woman he wanted, and one night with his ex-lover or a hundred, James knew that at the end of it, he'd still be haunted by hazel eyes, long legs, and the scent of the sea. By stubbornness that vexed him as much as it fascinated him, for he'd met few people in life with the tenacity of Ahnna Kertell. And none who'd captivated him like she did.

Put her out of your head, he instructed himself. *Set your mind to Cardiff. To negotiations. To finding peace so you'll never be too late to prevent a woman from being burned alive again.*

The scent of smoke abruptly filled his nose. Smoke, and burning hair.

Maven snorted, tossing her head, but he didn't need his horse's reaction to know what he was smelling.

Not again.

He dug in his heels, riding at reckless speed down the trails. He crossed the bridge, feeling no comfort that Thistleford stood untouched, laughter coming from the inn, because in the distance, he spotted the glow of flames. Heard the shouts.

Then, through the trees, he saw a wagon aflame, dozens of figures with shovels and pitchforks surrounding it. Tied to what had been the buckboard was a figure, mercifully still.

Maven slid to a stop, the farmers and villagers surrounding the wagon turning, immediately recognizing him.

"A witch, my lord!" one of them said. "She was telling fortunes to the women. We searched their wagon and found signs of astromancy."

The man gestured to the ground where a pile of items that were undeniably Cardiffian lay. Next to a dead man.

"He fought back, but we put him down and then burned the witch," the farmer said proudly. As though James couldn't tell exactly what had happened to the old man, who was punctured through a dozen times, his skull caved in from far more blows by a shovel than had been necessary to kill him. An all-too-common occurrence, for Cardiffians often sneaked across the border in search of an easier life. A life away from the cold. Most were wise enough to keep their beliefs hidden, but some caved to the easy money of telling fortunes to bored farm wives or lovesick school-girls who often turned petty if they didn't like what they heard.

And the king's laws were on their side if they decided to take vengeance.

James had begged his father a thousand times to change the law to demand a fair trial, but he'd always refused. *To take this right away from the people, I have to give them something commensurate in return*, his father always said. *And until Ronan bends, I have nothing to give.*

"Put it out," he snapped, wanting to draw his sword and enact his own brand of vengeance on these murderers. But he couldn't. Couldn't risk lashing out now when negotiations were ongoing and everything stood in the balance. Could only cling to the comfort that when he succeeded in allying Harendell and Cardiff, what these men had done would be a crime, and his blade would be justice. "Bury the bodies."

"Yes, my lord," the man said, more subdued, and James felt the tension rising. Knew that he'd reminded them of his blood, exactly as his father had warned him never to do.

Digging in his heels, James rode back past Thistleford, having no desire to speak to his uncle tonight. But as he crossed the bridge, Maven stumbled, and he heard the clatter of metal. Cursing under his breath, James slid off her side, and then lifted his mare's hoof. As expected, her shoe was missing.

"Not a good night," he said softly, resting his forehead against Maven's sweaty neck for a moment before leading her down the trail.

They hadn't gone more than a dozen paces when her ears perked and James's instincts flared. He tilted his head, listening until he picked up a faintly wheezing breath, then said, "What do you want, Uncle?"

"Your mother's blood runs strong," Cormac said, stepping out. "But you stifle it. Smother it when it screams for vengeance for the murder of your people."

"What would you have me do?" James snapped, because they'd had this conversation so many times before. "Kill them all and then hang for it? Because that's what would happen, Uncle. Is that what you want?"

His uncle snorted in disgust, prowling closer, and James tensed.

"What I want is for every breath you take to be focused on making your father sign the treaty," he growled. "Instead you shadow the Ithicanian woman's footsteps and give her riding lessons." Cormac's head tilted. "Perhaps there is another sort of riding happening in the Sky Palace and that is the cause of your reticence."

"Ahnna is a lady, and you will not speak of her so in my presence."

"A lady." Cormac's laugh was cruel. "I once saw a circus in Amarid. They had a lioness that they'd taught to perform tricks, and she wore a ruffled skirt. A predator capable of killing all who watched, and yet they laughed and laughed. That is Ahnna Kertell. A lioness in a dress."

A metaphor that put into words exactly how James had felt seeing Ahnna in that foolish pink gown, but hearing his uncle say it only made him angrier.

"Set her free, nephew," Cormac said. "Send her home."

"She doesn't want to leave."

"Why? Because of you?"

"Not me," James snapped, unnerved that his uncle suspected his real feelings for Ahnna because it made him wonder who else had seen through to his heart. "I don't know the reason. Only that she's terrified to return to Ithicana. She won't do it by choice."

"That leaves only one solution."

James dropped Maven's reins, the mare dancing sideways as he grabbed the front of his uncle's coat, dragging him close. "My father isn't going to burn bridges with Ithicana until he has what he wants from Cardiff. If you want the betrothal broken, convince Ronan to give my father everything he wants, and he will send Ahnna home on the next ship with smiles and fanfare and empty promises to give to her brother."

"Why must Cardiff bend first?"

James's grip on his uncle's coat tightened. "Because like it or not, Harendell holds the power, Uncle. If Ronan gives my father an offer he can't refuse, the people will support his decision. But if my father breaks the alliance with Ithicana and changes the laws with no bird in hand, they will turn on him. Convince Ronan to bend and let's see this done, because there is nothing that I would like better than to coat my blade with the blood of those who slaughter the elderly in the name of justice. Put the law on my side and I will be vengeance."

Shoving his uncle away, James caught Maven's reins and walked toward Verwyrd, the Sky Palace glowing like a beacon in the night sky.

IT WAS MISERABLY LATE BY the time he passed through the gates. Dismounting, he handed Maven's reins to a yawning groom. "She lost a shoe. Have the blacksmith see to her in the morning."

But instead of beginning the long walk up the spiral, James found himself heading into the stables.

Many of the horses were lying down, but Dippy had his head over his stall door, the gelding giving James a long look as he walked toward him.

"Your behavior was not acceptable," he informed the horse. "You were apparently a shitty racehorse, so unless you wish to find yourself sold off to pull some farmer's cart until you die of exhaustion, you're going to learn to be a good riding horse for her. Am I clear?"

Because if James was going to ruin Ahnna's life, the least he could do was ensure she got a good horse in the bargain.

Dippy snorted and tossed his head. Taking that for a yes, James saddled the horse and led him out into the yard. "The sooner you do this right, the sooner we can both go to sleep."

For the next hour, he worked with the animal, teaching him to stand still. He liked horses, and for all Dippy was as skittish as they came, he was a quick learner. Finally satisfied that the gelding would stand for Ahnna, James restabled him, and then, dawn lurking in the east, he started the long climb to his bed.

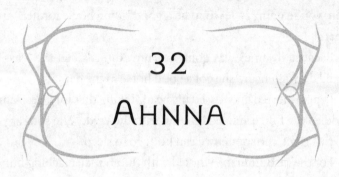

32
AHNNA

LESTARA'S WORDS PREYED ON HER SOUL THE ENTIRE NIGHT, AND when morning came, Ahnna dressed in the silk replica of her Ithicanian clothes that Hazel had made for her, her maid having removed the bloodstains and cunningly repaired the tear. It might not spare her mockery, but at least she'd be comfortable while enduring it.

Two hours after dawn, she was striding down the spiral with her guards in tow, where she found a yawning James sitting on a bale of hay. He eyed her clothing but said nothing, only rose and led her into the stable. His eyes were shadowed as though he'd had little sleep, but he was clean-shaven, and over the smell of horses, she picked out the scent of soap and cedar. He didn't say anything as they walked past the long rows of horses, yet she found herself deeply aware of his presence, and of the scarce few inches between their elbows as they walked. So much so that she passed by her horse's stall without noticing, and James said, "Have you reconsidered your mount?"

"No." Her voice was more indignant than she intended, her cheeks warming.

"God forbid you make a decision that might make my life easy," he muttered, leaning against the stall door. "You need to learn to take care of him. If you're ever caught in a bad spot, a good horse can save your life, but you won't get far if you can't even put on a saddle."

This seemed reasonable and was much the same way she'd been taught to sail. You wouldn't get far if you couldn't lift your own canvas or repair a hole. "All right."

Under James's critical eye, she brushed the horse and picked his hooves clean of a shocking amount of shit, after which he inspected everything like a jeweler inspecting the quality of a gemstone. "Satisfactory," he said, then gave her a long-winded and boring explanation about caring for saddles and bridles. Ahnna focused on every word despite her primary interest being getting on Dippy's back again.

What seemed like an eternity later, they led the horse out into the yard. Putting the reins over Dippy's head, Ahnna bent her knees to vault onto his back, but James shook his head. "Stirrup. You're not a twelve-year-old jockey getting paid for your madness."

"That's how you did it."

Giving her a world-weary sigh, James put his foot into the stirrup and swung into the saddle. Dippy shifted a little, his ears flicking backward as though listening.

"Your turn." James dismounted, holding the reins and stroking the horse's neck, expression bored. Yet he radiated tension.

Likely because he was anticipating another half an hour of her hopping around on one foot, trying to get in the saddle.

Scowling, Ahnna stepped closer and then lifted her foot, fitting her toe into the stirrup. Dippy didn't move. Ahnna held her breath, waiting for him to pull away, and when he didn't, she lifted herself upward, settling in the saddle. The horse didn't move. Neither did she.

"Good boy, Dippy." James patted the horse on the neck.

"What about me?" she demanded. "I got on. Give a little credit where it's due."

Their eyes locked, and James said, "Good girl, Princess."

Ahnna knew he was mocking her, but heat rushed to her face even as it pooled low in her stomach. She had commanded a garrison of soldiers. Ruled in proxy. Fought a war. No one, *no one* ever spoke to her like that, because it would be answered with a fist to the face.

Yet she said nothing, feeling as though the whole world had fallen away, leaving only her and James. And the very forbidden attraction that lurked between them. An attraction they both seemed unable to step away from, despite it having the power to damn them both.

Then a groom coughed, destroying the illusion.

"We're done for the day." James broke eye contact. "Get off."

Ahnna's eyes narrowed. Picking up the reins, she thumped her heels against the horse's sides.

Dippy did a strange vertical leap, and Ahnna found herself rolling off the side to land in the dirt next to his hooves. "Fuck!"

But James was already leading her horse away. "You can try again tomorrow. I have duties to take care of."

No invitation came from Virginia for afternoon tea, which was no shock, given Ahnna's confrontation with Elizabeth. A burned bridge, which was perhaps not the best strategic choice Ahnna had ever made, but she did have to live with herself. Even if it meant one less ally in this family than she'd had before, bringing her to a grand total of *one* individual who seemed to want her in Verwyrd.

Thankfully, that one individual was the king of Harendell.

It made her wonder what Lara would have done in a similar situation. Whether she'd have kept walking or intervened. Whether she'd have put her mission first or her morals. Grudgingly, Ahnna conceded that Lara would have done the same, but then somehow mitigated the damage done.

Pacing her room with a teacup in hand, Ahnna debated the best course of action. Whether she should apologize to Virginia. Explain herself. Justify her decisions.

"Fuck that," she grumbled. Virginia would know damned well why Ahnna had done what she'd done, and if the princess refused to concede that Ahnna was in the right, then no amount of justification on her part would change the other woman's mind.

Taking another sip of tea, Ahnna went to the window, considering what Lara had said about Alexandra. That the queen was the most powerful individual in Harendell, more powerful even than Edward. Ahnna had not seen that. If anything, Edward seemed to run roughshod over Alexandra, showing her an almost shocking lack of consideration, and most certainly blaming her for all the faults he perceived in their shared son. She did what he told her to do, which had been what Aren had suggested was the dynamic.

Which one of them was correct?

In none of the spy reports that Ahnna had read had Alexandra been noted to counter Edward, nor did the spies mention any ambitions on her part beyond the norm. Charity work. Support for the church. Endowments for orphanages. Organizing parties and balls. The facts showed Alexandra as a typical Harendellian lady, but Ahnna refused to disregard the views of Lara and Keris, which suggested the queen was very much a threat.

A threat, it would seem, who had to be working behind the scenes in such a manner that she was never implicated in anything but good works. Which meant she was dangerous. And very, very clever.

Looking at the dregs of her tea, the black leaves floating in the golden liquid, Ahnna ran through her conversation with the queen for the hundredth time, hunting for a clue she'd missed. For understanding of what Alexandra had hoped to achieve with the strange conversation. At no point had she told Ahnna to leave. Indeed, she had indicated her desire for Ahnna to do the exact opposite.

Do better.

"What the fuck did she mean?" Setting the cup aside on the table, Ahnna fought the urge to scream in frustration.

Beyond her own personal safety, did Alexandra even matter? Her concern was the other market that James had alluded to. The *friend of Harendell* that William had mentioned. If there was a competitor to the bridge, she needed to find out *who* in order to mitigate it, because Ithicana would crumble if Harendell didn't use the bridge for trade.

Bronwyn's voice filled her head: *Quit trying to do everything the opposite way of Lara.* But how was spying an option? Her cursed bodyguards were right outside her door. They went *everywhere* with her and would surely take issue with her digging through the king and queen's records. There was no way to sneak out through the window, for the walls of the Sky Palace were absolutely sheer, the windows latched in place, and the endless servants dusting every surface would notice if she left a window cracked.

"How do you find an ally?" She looked down at Verwyrd a thousand feet below. Then she tilted her head, thinking about the nature of Harendell. "How do you find a business partner?"

Her head shot up so fast, her neck cracked. "You follow the money."

Going to the door, she flung it open and said to Alfred, "I need to pay a visit to Verwyrd's lending house."

VERWYRD'S LENDING HOUSE WAS, AFTER the cathedral, the largest building in the city. A solid stone structure that she suspected was built with the same strength as a fortress, for the banks of Harendell had tremendous vaults storing both institutional wealth and the deposits of those who used their services. While Ithicana had no banking system, Ahnna was quite familiar with how Harendell's functioned. The bank representatives conducted a great deal of business at Northwatch, and they often traveled through the bridge. So she knew that not only did the crown maintain much of its reserves in bank vaults, but it also borrowed a tremendous amount of money from them to finance initiatives.

And shipbuilding required a lot of money.

Dressed in a simple gown Hazel had made for her, Ahnna entered the building, which was even more richly appointed than the Sky Palace itself. She was instantly recognized, and a round man dressed in an impeccably tailored morning suit approached, bowing low. "Your Highness. It is our pleasure to have you in our institution, though you need not have made the journey down from the Sky Palace. If you wish to draw upon the account Ithicana created for you, a note with your signature is all that is required."

"I require a loan," she said. "For new dresses."

"Your accounts will surely cover anything you require," the banker said. "Do you wish us to transfer to a specific modiste?"

"My brother has said no more dresses," she lied. "I require a loan."

"Of course." The banker blinked. "And what assets do you wish to use to secure this loan?"

She gave him a small smile. "I'm the future queen of Harendell, sir. So I will secure my loan with Harendell."

He gaped at her. "Harendell?"

Silence stretched, and he seemed to recover his wits. "What amount does your ladyship require?"

Ahnna named an amount that would purchase fifty gowns, keeping her face blank as the color drained from his.

"A significant request," he said. "It will take some time and, of course, a meeting with my colleagues to discuss the risk and rates of interest. We will send word to the Sky Palace when—"

"I'll wait," she said, striding into an office lined with extensive locked cabinets that were surely the records of their customers. "Tea would be lovely."

"Yes, my lady." The banker motioned to a young woman to fetch tea. "This may take some time."

"I've an hour until I meet with the modiste," Ahnna said, sitting in the chair and pulling out a novel from her pocket. "Hopefully that is sufficient time."

"Of course, my lady," the banker said, and Ahnna could see in his eyes that he was already hunting for the words he'd need to turn her down for lack of collateral.

Ahnna waited for the tea to be delivered, then said to her guards, "Wait outside. It's difficult to enjoy my reading while you both are staring at me."

Seeming to deem the windowless room devoid of threat, they

obliged, and Ahnna wedged a chair beneath the handle before going to the cabinets. It had been an age since she'd picked a lock, but with a pair of pins pulled from her hair, Ahnna opened the cabinet embossed with the Ashford crest. In typical Harendellian style, it was well organized, and she swiftly found the document with the transactions done by the crown.

She trailed a finger down, shaking her head at the shocking amount of money Edward borrowed, including the interest paid, funding an incredible range of items. But while she saw the repairs to the *Victoria* listed, no other ships had been commissioned by the crown in the past two years. None of the other recent records gave her any clues to competition for the bridge, and she carefully filed it all back with a muttered curse.

Then her eye fell on the cabinet embossed with the letter *A*. "Ashford," she murmured, picking the lock. Sure enough, there were files for accounts for every member of the royal family. She skimmed over the last several years of Alexandra's account records. The queen received income from multiple properties and an allowance from the crown, and she had also gotten substantial payments from several jewelers in recent years. She funneled a great deal of money to William, but the rest was all endowments and expenditures appropriate for a queen. Virginia spent all her allowance on dresses, jewels, and cosmetics, though she also donated generously to the conservatory. James, as it turned out, was wealthy. Not by virtue of being given more than anyone else, but by what seemed extreme frugalness, the only recent expense of note to a tailor, which was likely to replace his lost wardrobe.

Lastly, she turned to William. Who was, she swiftly determined, almost broke. He spent an incredible amount of money on just about anything one could possibly imagine, all entertainment, except every week for several months, he'd paid a modest amount to someone by the name of C.F. The payments stopped over a year ago. Frowning, she summed the amounts, which added to a significant value, the amount triggering recognition in her.

Flipping back through the pages, she summed the amount Alexandra had deposited in William's accounts.

The amount was the same. And it matched the amount that she'd been paid by the jewelers. If Ahnna had to speculate, the queen had sold off jewelry in order to pay someone William owed money to.

"What did he buy?" She shut the cabinet, her eyes going to the one embossed with C. But before she could open it, the door rattled.

"My lady?" the banker called through. "Your Highness?"

Why was he back already? Fucking Harendellian efficiency!

"Oh dear!" she called, pretending to jiggle the handle. "The lock seems jammed."

Scanning the room to ensure that everything was in order, she leaned against the door and kicked the chair back next to the desk. Jiggling the handle again, she then wrenched the door open with such force it rebounded off the wall and nearly struck the banker as he hurried inside. "It was stuck," she declared. "Do you have everything in order?"

"I have good news," he announced. "We are willing to advance the amount, for indeed, we have determined that Harendell is sufficient collateral."

Ahnna struggled to keep a straight face, knowing that it had more to do with them not wanting to anger the future queen. "Wonderful."

But as she left the lending house with the records for a line of credit she'd never need, her mind was whirling. She'd not found evidence that the crown was pursuing other alliances, but Ahnna now had reason to believe that Queen Alexandra Ashford was up to something she did not wish Edward to know about.

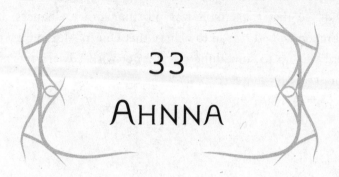

33
AHNNA

THE NEXT MORNING, AHNNA STEPPED OUT OF THE SPIRAL TO FIND James sitting on the same bale of hay as the day prior. "Have you reconsidered your choice of mount, my lady?"

She glared at him, noticing that he looked even more tired than he had yesterday despite having left dinner early again. "There's nothing wrong with my horse."

"He's a fine mount." James climbed to his feet, straightening his dark-blue coat. "For a skilled rider. Which you are not."

"Asshole," she muttered as she bypassed him and headed into the stable. James followed, watching as she repeated what she'd learned yesterday until Dippy was ready. He said nothing as she led her horse out into the stable yard, but when she moved to mount, James said, "Don't kick him once you're in the saddle. He's happy to work, so you need not punish him as though he's avoiding the labor."

"I'm not punishing him."

"Do you like to be kicked?" James asked.

"Of course not," she retorted. "But that's how I've seen most people make their horses go, so I thought that was how it was done."

"Get kicked enough and you grow used to it," James said icily.

They were talking about horses, yet the statement, and his tone, made her flinch. Ahnna covered her reaction by fussing with her stirrup, then said, "So what do I do?"

"Gentle squeeze, though in truth, you need barely think about him walking and he'll go. This is a horse who loves to run."

Sighing, Ahnna climbed on Dippy's back, sitting stiffly in the saddle with the reins clutched in her hands. Sure enough, the faintest squeeze had the horse walking, and she followed James's instructions to steer him around the yard.

Eager for more, she squeezed her legs again, and they broke into a trot. For the first circle around the yard, she bounced like a sack of potatoes, but then she found her rhythm, not unlike keeping her feet on a rocking ship.

Faster.

"Ease off," James called. "That's quite fast enough."

She squeezed her legs, ignoring James's admonition, but instead of a slight increase in speed, the horse flung himself into a gallop, careening around the yard. Terrified that he was going to crash, Ahnna heaved on the reins as hard as she could.

Only to find herself sitting in the dirt, her horse still circling wildly around the yard, reins flapping. As she watched in horror, one of them wrapped around his foreleg, and Dippy stumbled, nearly going down.

James caught hold of the other rein, then untangled him. But the damage was already done, her horse limping.

"How badly is he hurt?" she demanded, scrambling to her feet. "Will he be all right?"

James ignored her, feeling Dippy's foreleg and then shaking his head. "Idiot."

Ahnna flinched, certain that the word was intended for her.

James handed the reins off to a groom, then rounded on her. "I told you no faster!"

Which had been exactly why she'd ignored him. And now her horse was injured as a result. Tears stung her eyes as she watched Dippy limp back to the barn.

"Pulling like that made him feel trapped, which is intolerable for a horse like Dippy. You're lucky he didn't go over backward and land on you. Next time, circle him!"

"You could have told me that part," she retorted, her anger rising. Most of which was for herself. "I wouldn't have done it if I'd known."

"The only way you seem to learn is the hard way, Ahnna. So what is the point of me wasting my breath." James started toward the barn. "No riding until he recovers."

NOT LONG AFTER DIPPY WAS injured, it began to rain.

Not the torrential rain of Ithicana, but a strange wet mist that seemed to sit upon the land like a damp blanket, the view from her window in the Sky Palace nothing but gray clouds and fog. And with her horse recovering, Ahnna was left to pace the near-empty halls of the palace with little company beyond her own footsteps.

Virginia occasionally invited Ahnna to join her and her ladies, but the conversation was stilted, she and Lestara both sitting alone like islands while the others circled around. None of the ladies of the court showed any familiarity with the initials C.F., and Ahnna was reluctant to press lest she draw attention to her spying. Instead, she listened to their gossip, learning a thousand bits of knowledge, though none of it spoke of plans to change the nature of Harendell's trade. None of it spoke of other markets. None of it spoke of growing Harendell's fleet to bypass the bridge. Indeed, very little of it spoke of Ithicana at all.

It made Ahnna start to wonder if she was obsessing over a problem that didn't exist. Whether James had been speaking speculatively when he'd mentioned it on the ship. Whether William had been so deep in his cups that his mention of Harendell *leaning on other friends* had been nothing more than the wine talking. Whether the amounts Alexandra was funneling to C.F. were nothing illicit at all, merely some entertainment that she'd agreed to fund. But her instincts screamed otherwise. Screamed that the threat was real, no matter that no one seemed aware of it.

She was miserable and lonely, but with William gone all day with his friends and James not wanting anything to do with her, there was nothing to do but pace and pace. Like an animal caught in a cage.

Which was why when William suggested one night that they head out for a night in the city in the company of Virginia and Georgie, Ahnna didn't hesitate to agree.

"Whoever built this tower really ought to have thought of a faster way down," Virginia groaned, leaning against the side of the carriage as Buck and Brayer slowly descended from the Sky Palace. "It's so tedious."

"There is a faster way down," William said with a grin. "But you only get to use it once."

Virginia rolled her eyes, then stole the bottle from his hand, drinking straight from the neck. "I truly don't understand why the kings of old decided to build a palace atop it."

"Defense," Georgie said. "Half of the defenses haven't been used in generations, but properly manned, the Sky Palace is impregnable."

Ahnna gave a soft snort. "Everything is pregnable. You need only look at the defense from the inside."

"Agreed, my lady," Georgie said. "Though in truth, only the vaguest accounts describe the Sky Palace ever having to defend itself, so I think we've forgotten how."

Virginia and William laughed, but Ahnna only looked out the window at the foggy sky beyond. "That's more a privilege than you know."

Everyone fell silent.

"Perhaps one day you'll remedy our failings, my lady," Georgie finally said. "It's always good to be prepared for the worst."

"James likely has the answers, so ask him," William said. "Where is my brother, Georgie? He's been even less fun than usual lately, which is to say no fun at all."

"Patrols," Georgie answered a hair too quickly.

"Amaridians?"

Georgie nodded, then added, "That, and it seems civilians have been a bit quick to the torch with those suspected of astromancy lately. Multiple fatalities, many with dubious proof of guilt."

"It is our people's right to defend the faith," Virginia said. "And it discourages the Cardiffians from sneaking across the border."

"I'll not argue that point." Georgie took the bottle from her. "But apparently, some have been burned with no evidence at all, and last I checked, being Cardiffian alone is not a crime."

"Should be." Virginia wrinkled her nose.

"If being Cardiffian was punishable by death, wouldn't James be deserving of murder in the eyes of the law?" Ahnna abruptly asked, not willing to hold her tongue. "Or at least, half of him?"

The tiny carriage fell totally silent.

"My brother is Harendellian." Virginia's voice was deadly soft. "We do not speak of the witch who bore him. He was raised in the true faith, and I will not hear you speak a word against him."

"I didn't speak a word against him," Ahnna countered. "You did."

"Easy now," Georgie said. "We're all friends here."

"I'm not so sure." Virginia's color was high, partially from anger and partially from drink. "Elizabeth told me that you threatened her, Ahnna. That you told her you'd take issue with anyone who mistreated that witch."

"I did," Ahnna said. "And I am pleased that everyone took my words to heart."

"She's a traitor. And she practices astromancy with impunity," Virginia spat. "She deserves to suffer. Deserves to burn, but Father won't let us put her to the torch because she's King Ronan's daughter."

Next to Ahnna, William shifted, and Virginia's eyes shot to him. "Tell her, Will. Make her understand."

To Ahnna's surprise, William only shrugged. "The behavior was beneath you, sister, and I, for one, am glad to see it put to a stop. It saddened me to see you be so cruel."

"You can't be serious?"

"Father took Lestara from Keris Veliant as a favor," William said. "But punishing her is not our responsibility, so I fail to see why you insist on dirtying your hands."

It was a shockingly reasonable view, and not one Ahnna had expected.

"I'll hear no more of this," Virginia hissed. Then she shouted, "Stop the carriage!"

"Ginny," William protested. "Don't *be* like this. We're out for a good time, and you're making it about politics."

"Stop the carriage!"

Georgie banged on the ceiling, and the carriage slowed to a halt. Not waiting for the coachman, Virginia shoved the door open and climbed out, tripping and nearly falling as she started walking up the spiral.

"Go with her, Georgie," William said. "Kiss her before you get to the top, and she'll forget this ever happened."

"I . . ." Georgie looked between Ahnna and William, cursed softly, then clambered out and chased after Virginia.

William closed the door, then called out, "Carry on, then!"

The mules resumed their slow descent of the spiral, Ahnna finding herself alone with William for the first time.

"Don't mind Ginny," he said. "She's a dramatic drunk. And in truth, this might have all been a performance to get Georgie alone."

Ahnna didn't believe that had been Virginia's motivation. It was because the princess doubted Ahnna's intentions, and in truth, she was surprised the princess had left Ahnna alone with William, given her concerns.

"Honestly," William said, "I'm grateful that you held her to task about her treatment of the Cardiffian woman. Whether he said so or not, I'm certain that her behavior is half the reason Jamie has been finding reasons to be absent. I know he's a paragon of stoicism and emotes as much as brick, but my brother does have a feeling or two hidden beneath the surface. And while we try to pretend otherwise, his mother was Cardiffian. I found Ginny's behavior in poor taste, but to say so would have been a bad look. Politics, and all. So thank you."

So James does care. Ahnna gave William a tight smile. "You're welcome."

"I did leave an invitation for him to join us with the servants, but I don't anticipate we'll see him," William said. "Jamie's not one for revels. Are you, Ahnna?"

Once upon a time she had been. "I can be convinced." To add to her words, she took the bottle from his hand and drank.

William laughed, then said, "Have I told you about the new horse I purchased?"

He kept up a steady stream of chatter as they reached the bottom of the spiral, moving into a carriage that already held two of his friends. They were minor lords she hadn't met before, the sort of which he seemed to keep in endless quantities around him. With a few words here and there, Ahnna moved William through his interests, searching for a clue about C.F. while they progressed through Verwyrd to an alehouse he favored.

It was already raucous inside, dozens of minor noblemen and women waiting, clearly having received word that this was where to be tonight, for they let out loud cheers as William entered with her on his arm. "It's always good to slum with the common class from time to time," he said conspiratorially into her ear. "Buy a few rounds and earn their favor."

But Ahnna barely heard him. On the far side of the alehouse, sitting at the bar, was a familiar figure, tall and broad. The patrons instinctively giving him space, though none of them knew his identity. His eyes locked with Ahnna's, and he gave a small jerk of his chin toward the rear of the alehouse.

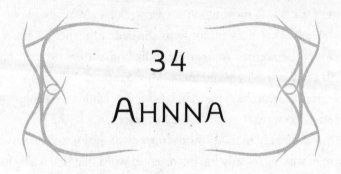

34
AHNNA

"I'LL BE RIGHT BACK," AHNNA MURMURED TO WILLIAM.

Her bodyguard Alfred moved to follow her, but Ahnna said, "I don't need an escort to the privy. I'll be right back."

Not giving him a chance to argue, she hurried through the tables of nobles, brushing elbows with the citizens of Verwyrd. William's voice followed her through the crowd, "A round for everyone on the crown!"

The alehouse erupted into more cheers right as she stepped into a dim corridor that led to a storage room, where Aren leaned against the wall.

"What are you doing here?" Ahnna demanded as she flung her arms around her brother's neck, hugging him tight. Then sudden unease struck her in the chest. "Delia? Lara? Are they well?"

"Right as rain." He wrapped one arm around her, squeezing tight. "Or at least, they were when I left. Nana and Lara might well have killed each other by the time I return."

That she believed. Stepping back, Ahnna asked, "Then why are you here? You shouldn't be away from them so soon."

"You're right, I shouldn't." He hooked his thumbs on his belt, looking down at her. "But I knew that you wouldn't listen to anyone other than me, so here I am."

"Listen about what?" Her hands had turned clammy.

"Leaving. I want you back in Ithicana, Ahnna. It's not safe for you to be here."

"It's safe enough." She crossed her arms. "I'm not leaving."

"Safe enough?" Aren glared at her with incredulity. "Two attempted assassinations while you journeyed to Verwyrd, then another in the Sky Palace itself. You call that safe?"

"Only one of those was an attempt on my life," she muttered. "The other two were intended for James."

"Is that meant to make me feel better?" he demanded. "You were poisoned with wraithroot, Ahnna. You almost died. And I fail to believe that Edward's bastard was the target the other two times. He's of no value."

"Don't call him that," Ahnna snarled. "And believe what you will. It's the truth. Besides, James has taken steps to ensure I'm well protected."

"Has he now?" Aren's voice dripped with sarcasm. "Is that why you're getting drunk with that buffoon William, in the company of the worst rabble of Harendell's nobility? Where is James right now?"

"I'm not drunk." Her hands balled into fists. "And James is on patrols around Verwyrd."

Aren snorted. "Try again. He's with his barmaid mistress in Thistleford. A woman named Elsie."

Her stomach plummeted to the floor, and suddenly it was very hard to breathe. "Pardon?"

Aren shook his head. "For someone who used to manage Southwatch's intelligence, you aren't acting very intelligent. This is what Harendell is like. Rich men have endless mistresses on the side. I'd bet William has fucked half the women in that room out there, and that won't stop if he marries you. Edward kept his goddamned mistress in the same palace as his wife and raised his bastard alongside his other children with no care for what anyone thought. Harendellians aren't just immoral, they're selfish and cruel. I'm shocked you haven't figured that out for yourself by now."

Oh, but she had. Had seen it in droves, but James . . . He wasn't like the rest.

"You being here isn't going to accomplish anything," Aren said. "If some assassin doesn't stab you in the back or poison your cup, you'll only end up shunted off to some estate in the middle of nowhere, visited by your dear husband only long enough for him to make an heir and a spare, who will be taken from you to be raised by wet nurses and governesses and *Alexandra*."

"But—"

"I know what Lara told you, Ahnna. But you are not Alexandra. You'll never hold power here. It's just not in the cards."

When had he lost all his faith in her? When had been the moment that her brother had decided she was no longer the rock at his back?

"Would you listen to me?" she said, trying to curb the breathless panic in her chest. "I'm confident that Harendell is up to something. James mentioned other markets, and William mentioned other friends. I think trade through the bridge is in jeopardy."

"You think I don't know that?" Aren's voice was frosty. "There has been a shift in tone in all the port markets. Rising anger against the tolls we charge, and that godforsaken rumor about Ithicana's mountains of gold has risen again despite the Maridrinians having proven otherwise. Traffic on the bridge is already down by a third, and merchants are defaulting on amounts owed at Northwatch.

Not because they can't pay. But because they don't want to. Harendell is turning on us, Ahnna. They are no longer our friends."

Her breath came in ragged little gasps. How had it escalated so quickly?

"Our spies haven't been able to pinpoint the source of the shift, but I'd bet the bridge it's Edward."

"No," she whispered, because the king was her only ally in Harendell. "Edward wants me here. He likes me. He wants me to marry William. He told me I'll be a good queen."

Aren huffed out a breath. "That could all be true, and this could still be him, Ahnna. How long until he comes knocking at my door saying that more concessions need to be made to regain the support of the people for this marriage? I know you came here believing that you'd open the floodgates of Harendellian gold into Ithicana. Gold that we are desperate for, because Ithicana is hungry and in shambles. Weaker than we've ever been. But my gut tells me this betrothal isn't going to save us. It's going to cost us, one way or another. I refuse to let it cost me your life."

Tears flooded down Ahnna's face, and she found it impossible to speak because she couldn't breathe.

"Go back to the Sky Palace and pack your things," he said. "Get on a riverboat, retrieve Taryn and Bronwyn, and return to Ithicana. I'll put you in command of Southwatch, you can marry whomever you want, and we'll show Edward just how well trying to force Ithicana's hand will work out for him. There is no other market that can compete, and he'll be forced to give up this posturing."

Go back a failure. Remain and be a failure. Hopelessness dragged her down and down, and Ahnna found herself wishing with all her heart that the wraithroot had taken her. "I can't go back."

But apparently, neither could she stay.

Aren gripped her shoulders. "It's not up for negotiation."

"Please." The word croaked out, her throat closed up so tightly that the only explanation she could get out was, "I can't."

Then a naked sword blade appeared from the shadows to press against Aren's throat.

Ahnna tensed, reaching for the knife in her skirts. Only to recognize James's voice as he said, "Remove your hands from the lady."

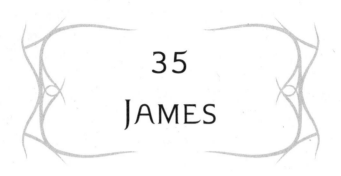

35

JAMES

IT TOOK ALL HIS SELF-CONTROL NOT TO DRAW HIS BLADE ACROSS the man's throat, his rage already hot at William for taking Ahnna into the city, at Alfred for allowing her to wander off alone, and at himself for not being here to prevent this.

The man lowered his hands from Ahnna's shoulders and turned his head, and it was the king of Ithicana who gave James a scowl of irritation as he said, "Good to see you aren't entirely useless."

Fuck.

But king or not, brother or not, Ahnna was crying so hard she could barely breathe, and that was not acceptable. So James did not lower his weapon.

"Why are you here, Your Grace?"

"Not your concern."

James let out a long breath. "The lady's welfare is very much my concern."

"She's fine," Aren retorted. "And you overstep."

"It's you who oversteps." James angled his blade, forcing the other man's chin up. "You are a foreign king on Harendell's soil without permission from the crown, which is grounds enough for me to take action. Made far worse by your choice to threaten a lady of Harendell's court."

"She's my goddamned sister, and I didn't threaten her."

So he said, yet Ahnna's distress was obvious, the reason not something either of them appeared willing to admit.

"While in Harendell, Ahnna is *mine* to protect," James said, voice low and dangerous. "You will not approach her without an appointment and approval from the crown, which you do not have, Your Grace."

Aren's eyes narrowed, but before he could answer, Ahnna said, "Enough. Both of you." Her hand closed on James's arm, moving his blade away from her brother's throat. "It was just a conversation. It was nothing important."

James didn't believe that for a heartbeat.

"Go," he said to Ithicana's king. "Get out of my city and back to Ithicana, or we will have a problem."

"I think we already do," Aren replied, then his eyes flicked to Ahnna. "Get your head on straight."

When she didn't answer, he gave an angry shake of his head, then strode out of the hallway.

James waited for the sound of his boots to disappear into the din, then sheathed his sword and stepped close to Ahnna. "Are you all right?"

The light was dim, but he could see she was pale, eyes swollen from crying. "I'm fine. You shouldn't have done that."

James didn't agree. "He upset you."

"Yes." Her throat moved as she swallowed. "But maybe I deserved it."

"What did he want?"

She only shook her head. Keeping Aren's secrets. Ithicana's secrets. Her own secrets. He could see her regaining control, her breathing steadying as she smoothed her hair and straightened her skirts. Then she asked, "Who is Elsie?"

Shock radiated through him, and without stopping to think, he demanded, "Who told you about Elsie? William?"

"It's common knowledge, apparently."

Which was exactly how he'd intended it to be. For no one to ever question his regular visits to Thistleford because men like him were supposed to have women like Elsie. But faced with Ahnna believing he had a mistress, James found himself feeling sick to his stomach over how that would change things between them.

But not so sick that he lost reason, for the last thing he needed was anyone questioning his absences.

"A woman I used to take up with. Now she's just a friend." James grimaced. "I need to be away from court sometimes. To be around normal folk who have some decency to them."

"You can do what you like," she said. "You aren't betrothed to anyone. I only wondered why you'd never mentioned her."

"Mistresses are not appropriate conversation topics," he said, though the answer in his heart was, *There is no one who will ever measure up to you.*

Ahnna gave a soft laugh, but there was no humor in her eyes. "When did it end? Before or after?"

He needed no clarification of what she meant. "Does it matter?"

"Yes." She stepped closer, looking up at him. "Because it tells me what sort of man you are."

Lie, logic screamed at him. But James said, "It ran its course before I left for Northwatch."

And from the moment Ahnna had knocked him off the deck of the *Defiant*, his heart had known no one but her. Part of him wondered if it ever would.

Ahnna's shoulders sagged. "I'm sorry. It's not my business. You should do as you like. It's better if you do."

For reasons James couldn't articulate, her words were a punch to the stomach, and he uttered the first thing he could think of to keep her from pulling away. "Your horse is sound, so you can ride him again. It will make the tedium of the Sky Palace more bearable."

Rather than erasing the misery from her face, the news only seemed to deepen the shadows in her eyes.

"And here I thought the tedium was part of your plan," she said. "To use boredom to drive me to beg Aren to bring me back to Ithicana so your brother won't have to marry the wild Ithicanian woman who wears all the wrong things, says all the wrong things, does all the wrong things."

"Ahnna—"

"Don't." She lifted her chin. "A stolen kiss in a garden doesn't change the very real fact that you'd rather have better trade terms than have me. What exactly am I worth, James? A five percent reduction in tolls? Ten? Or will something as simple as better seats at Northwatch's auction yards be all it takes? Articulate my value. Since you are so very Harendellian, that should be no challenge to you."

Her voice was harsh with bitterness, and James hated that she'd been made to feel this way. That he'd made her feel this way. Like an animal at auction to be poked and prodded and then stamped with a price. It didn't matter if his motivations to send her away were good—his methods had harmed her, and James hated himself for that. But the truth was worse. "Ahnna—"

"You don't want me here," she interrupted. "You've made that abundantly clear, because your every action demonstrates a belief that I'll soon be gone. Now if you'd excuse me, William will be wondering where I am." Then she strode back into the common room, leaving him standing alone.

Prudence demanded that he let Aren Kertell's presence go. That he give the king at least the opportunity to leave Verwyrd before escalating the situation.

But James was too angry for prudence.

Going back into the common room of the alehouse, he watched Ahnna sit next to William, only her red eyes betraying the distress she felt. Approaching Alfred, he said, "You don't let her out of your sight, understood? If she goes to the privy, you follow and stand right outside the door."

"Yes, sir," the guardsman said, cheeks coloring in shame at having let her wander the first time.

Catching Georgie's eye where he stood against the bar, James gave his friend a tight nod and left the building.

"Please tell me that was not the king of Ithicana who just stormed out," his friend said once he joined James outside.

James didn't answer, and Georgie winced. "What is he doing here?"

"That's a good question," James replied. "And I intend to find out."

Approaching a pair of prostitutes loitering on the corner, he said, "You see a big man in the company of a handful of others?"

"Yes, Your Highness," one of them answered, giving James a slow smile. "Went that way."

He tossed her a coin, then started toward the quay.

"What precisely is the plan here?" Georgie asked. "Because you look like you're going to pick a fight, and if it's a fight with the king of Ithicana and a group of his warriors, we might need more men."

"I have you."

His friend gave a soft laugh. "I'm flattered, Jamie, but I'm not sure that my prowess with a blade will be sufficient. The Ithicanians fight to kill."

"So do I."

Georgie cursed softly, then caught at James's arm. "What did he do that pissed you off?" When James didn't answer, Georgie said, "Is this something to do with Ahnna? She looked upset when she emerged. What happened? What was said?"

"She wouldn't say," James finally answered. "But it looked to me as though he threatened her."

"Why?" Georgie demanded. "What possible reason could he have to threaten his own sister?"

"That's what we're going to find out."

"Shit." Georgie gave a sharp shake of his head. "James, I know you're fond of Ahnna, but you cannot pick a fight with the king of Ithicana over a few tears. They are our allies, and if they want to bar us from the bridge because you decided to take justice into your own hands, it will not go well for you. Hell, he might decide to kill us and toss both of us into the river, no one the wiser!"

"That's a risk we'll take for the sake of answers."

"I don't want to take this risk." Georgie stepped in front of him, pushing James to a stop. "Speak to your father on the matter and see what he says about Ithicana's king free-ranging around Harendell. Find out if this is an altercation he wishes to pick, because if it is, you'll have his backing with whatever comes from it."

"Aren will be long gone by then."

"Good!" Georgie's grip on his shoulders tightened. "Ask yourself the real reason why you're pursuing this. Is it because of a quarrel between siblings or an unnegotiated royal visit, or is it because you're pissed off Ahnna is out with William?"

All of the above.

"You shouldn't have allowed her to leave the Sky Palace without a more significant guard," James said, struggling to keep his anger in check. "William is careless and drunk and doesn't consider the risks. You shouldn't have left her alone."

"I didn't have a choice," Georgie snapped. "Virginia got into a row with Ahnna and got out of the carriage. Would you have preferred I'd allowed your sister, who'd had far too much to drink, to stumble blindly up the spiral by herself?"

"I'd have preferred none of this had occurred," James snapped. "Now is not the time for carousing in the city, George. You know that."

"And I protested. Vigorously. But William was bent and determined, and as much as I might wish otherwise, I do not get to give orders to the crown fucking prince." Georgie gave a sharp shake of his head. "Where were you?"

James had been in Thistleford, meeting with Cormac.

"Elsie didn't get it out of your system?" Georgie huffed out a breath. "Maybe instead of picking a fight, you get on Maven and head back to Thistleford, Jamie. Because don't think for a heartbeat that I haven't noticed how you look at Ahnna. Or how you lose your head over anything to do with her."

James's anger vanished, hands turning to ice.

Georgie gave a soft laugh that was devoid of humor. "We've been friends all our lives, and you think I didn't notice that you were taken with her? I could tell from the moment that I saw you standing barefoot on that pier, staring at her like she was a candle in the darkest night, Jamie. You're falling for the woman who is betrothed to your brother."

"I'm not . . ." James trailed off. "It's nothing."

"Nothing? That's what you call losing sleep so that you can turn that fool of a racehorse into a proper saddle horse for her? That's what you call locking the Sky Palace up like a prison so no one can get in or out? What you call dragging our best men in the Lowlands back to Verwyrd to play bodyguard? What you call picking a fight with the king of another nation over? Nothing?"

James grimaced because there was no good answer in the face of Georgie's accusations. "I'll get over it."

"The only way that's going to happen is if she's out of sight," Georgie said. "Get your father to send you back to the Lowlands. Work off this frustration fighting the Amaridians. I'll stay and do what needs to be done until you've gotten her out of your system."

If only that were possible. In more ways than one.

Yet though he couldn't take Georgie's advice, his friend's words had done their duty in dousing his anger, reason making its way back into his head.

"Go get some sleep," Georgie said, giving him a gentle shove. "I'll keep an eye on Ahnna and William tonight."

Giving a tight nod, James turned and started back toward the Sky Palace.

36
AHNNA

Turning on her heel, Ahnna opened the door and headed back into the common room, sitting down next to William. Out of the corner of her eye, she saw James circle the common room and leave out the front door, Georgie on his heels.

"There you are," William said. "Another round on the crown! And a toast to Ithicana!"

Everyone in the common room shouted, "Huzzah!" and lifted their glasses, but all Ahnna heard was Aren, his voice urgent as he said, *Harendell is turning on us, Ahnna. They are no longer our friends.*

The core of her heart didn't want to believe this was the case. Wanted to believe that all of Edward's kind words and promises were the truth. That the king of Harendell thought she was worthy, even if no one else did. But the pragmatic part of her knew that Aren wouldn't have left Lara so soon after Delia's birth if he wasn't certain that the treaty was souring.

"William," she said, waiting until he turned his head to look at

her, eyes glazed with wine. "Are you familiar with someone with
the initials C.F.?"

He frowned. "What an odd question."

"Humor me."

"C.F." He made a soft humming sound, considering the initials,
then shrugged. "Nothing comes to mind. Ask me again when I'm
sober."

Ahnna wouldn't bother, because it was clear to her that William had no idea that his mother was moving money through
his accounts. And in truth, the answer might well not be worth
Ahnna's time. After what Aren had said, it was probably some
mistress William had gotten with child, Alexandra making the
payments to keep the mother silent and content with being ignored.

*You are not Alexandra. You'll never hold power here. It's just not in the
cards.* Her stomach tightened as Aren's voice filled her head. *This
betrothal isn't going to save us. It's going to cost us, one way or another.*

His words carved out her heart, the sense of worthlessness that
had plagued Ahnna all her life rising to fill the space. Was refusing
to leave a selfish choice? A decision made by the desperate desire
for atonement that burned in her soul? Was she a fool for digging
in her heels? Because Ahnna didn't think it was that simple.

Next to her, William was jabbering on. About his racehorses.
His bulls. His hunting trophies. His skill with cards. He didn't even
notice her silence, which was just as well because her mind was
consumed with the dilemma she faced.

Leaving would mean Ithicana was breaking the terms of the
Fifteen-Year Treaty. Breaking an alliance that ensured peace and
prosperity between Ithicana and Harendell. Even if Edward's
words to her were lies and he didn't want her here, he would have
to act to save face if she left in the night. All it would take was a few

months' embargo on Northwatch as punishment for the violation of the treaty, and Ithicana would be plunged into a true famine. To avoid an embargo, Aren would be forced to make concessions that would result in the same.

Whereas what were the costs of her staying? What were the risks beyond the obvious jeopardy to her own life? Try as she might, Ahnna came up blank as to how her presence in Verwyrd would cost Ithicana, and if Aren had known concrete reasons why she shouldn't remain, he'd have said. He'd been driven here out of fear for her life, and while it warmed her heart that he cared so much for her well-being, Ahnna wouldn't allow him to put her life over the lives of their people.

If she remained, she could keep searching for information that could aid Ithicana. Details about competition against the bridge or plans that negatively affected her homeland. Even if the Harendellians had no intention of giving her any influence, knowledge was power, and she could learn more in Verwyrd than anywhere else.

Leaving would be a mistake, and one Ahnna refused to make, no matter how much it cost her personally.

They stayed late into the night, Ahnna listening to William's endless conversation, pretending to be interested in everything he had to say. As the carriage delivered them into the Sky Palace's stable yard, William's overindulgence finally caught up with him. Leaving his friends to stand next to him while he vomited several bottles of wine onto the dirt, Ahnna made her way into the stables.

Walking down the dimly lit row of stalls, she smiled as Dippy stuck his head over the door and whickered softly at her. "I'm sorry," she said. "I don't have any apples."

She stroked his head, then kissed his nose, wishing for all the world that she could climb on his back and ride off into the night.

"Good evening, my lady," one of the stable boys said, passing by her as he checked the horses. "Will you be back riding soon?"

"I hope so," she said. "Though I don't wish to push him, given he's only just regained his soundness."

The boy gave Dippy a pat. "Oh, he was right as rain within a few hours of his stumble, my lady. Been going nicely for days now. Taking to his training quite well."

Days.

More confirmation that James wanted nothing to do with her, yet the revelation still hurt. And then the stable boy's words registered. "Training?"

"Yes, my lady. His Highness has been working with him for hours every day, even in the rain. Bent and determined on turning Dippy here into a proper saddle horse for you, and did a fine job of it." The stable boy hesitated, then added, "Pardon my asking, my lady, but do you have horses in Ithicana?"

"No," she whispered, seeing the faint sweat marks on Dippy's back that had not yet dried. Marks from a saddle, meaning James had come here after she'd walked away from him in the alehouse. "Ithicanians have no use for horses."

Which meant James hadn't been trying to find ways to make her leave. He'd been planning for her to stay.

A familiar voice filled her ears. "Enjoy your evening, my lady?"

Ahnna turned to find Georgie walking down the aisle. He jerked his chin at the stable boy, who swiftly disappeared, leaving her alone with the lord.

She'd seen Georgie in the alehouse leaving with James, so she suspected he was well aware of Aren's presence in Verwyrd. "I've had better nights. But also worse nights."

He rested his elbows on Dippy's stall door, watching the horse munching on hay. "Your brother has departed by way of river-boat."

She made a noncommittal noise.

"Why was he here? It's more than a little untoward for the king of a foreign country to be roaming Harendell's lands."

"It's nothing new," she grumbled. "He's been here dozens of times, though he always favored Maridrina. Aren struggles to sit still. No need to make more out of it than that."

"He seems a man of action," Georgie said. "Though to leave his wife and newborn daughter so soon after her birth suggests a more pressing concern than . . . itchy feet. A concern that you clearly shared, given you were distressed."

"I appreciate your interest, but it was Ithicanian business."

"I know," Georgie said. "Because I had him followed. Verwyrd's underbelly is full of individuals with a talent for listening in the shadows and who will relay what they hear for a bit of silver."

Ahnna's jaw tightened, but she had no grounds to get angry at him for spying on her brother, given that Aren had no right to be in Verwyrd. "And what did your spies learn?"

"That Katarina has made overtures to Ithicana."

She silently cursed Aren for keeping that from her, even though she knew James had interrupted the conversation before he'd really had the chance. "Ithicana has an existing trade relationship with Amarid. It's not new for her to ask for revisions to terms."

"Overtures of alliance." Georgie brushed a bit of hay off his sleeve, the gesture at odds with the anger that seethed off him. "I don't recall an existing agreement of the sort between Amarid and Harendell. Especially given that Amarid's navy laid siege to Era-nahl alongside the Maridrinians. Though I suppose you forgave

the Maridrinians swiftly enough, so why not their northern bed-
fellows?"

Ahnna's hands turned to ice, because if Aren truly believed
Ithicana was at risk from Harendell, he might have such a conversation with Katarina. Except it felt entirely wrong: She knew he
disliked the queen on a personal level, and the idea of trusting
Amarid felt like madness. "He said nothing of the sort to me, if
that is your question."

"Then why was he here, Ahnna?"

"Concern for my safety. He heard about the incident with the
wraithroot."

It was no lie, but George's face hardened. "Don't give me half-
truths, woman. He was here to take you home. Here to steal you
away in the night, which, if he truly cares for your life, was a prudent act if his intent is to side with Amarid against Harendell."

Ahnna blinked, stunned by the accusation. "He has no such intention. Anyone who has led you to believe that is the case is a
goddamned liar."

"The words come from the lips of the king of fucking Ithicana,"
George snarled. "He said, *We can't hope to stand against the Harendellians without Amarid's aid.*"

Ahnna's heart lurched, for though the statement had surely
been taken out of context, it was damning. She cursed her brother
for speaking without care, though she bore part of that blame, for
it had been she who'd put him in the sort of mood that would have
caused him to be reckless in his words.

"James was convinced the Amaridians acted alone in their attack, but I always had my doubts," George said. "It was too carefully orchestrated for them to have been working alone."

"Ithicana had nothing to do with those attacks," Ahnna
snapped. "Our people died in that attack. I nearly died saving

James's life. Nearly died again when they pursued us with their ships, and then nearly died a third time when they attacked me in the Sky Palace. This accusation makes no sense!"

"Nearly died, and yet here you are." He looked her up and down. "And I cannot help but think that you've taken a page out of Lara Veliant's book, Ahnna Kertell. A fox in the henhouse, and James is too goddamned smitten to see the threat you pose."

Bile burned its way up her throat. "No! Please, George. I don't know what conversation my brother has had with Katarina, but I swear I'm here in good faith. I'm here to honor the treaty and marry William and ensure peace and prosperity between Harendell and Amarid. On my life and honor, that is why I came here."

"Here to marry William, yet you flirt shamelessly with his brother," George retorted. "What is your goal, Ahnna? To tear the Ashfords apart from the inside? I heard the way you undermined James in the carriage. How you painted Virginia as the villain for holding Lestara accountable for her crimes. I see your angle now."

"You are mistaken." Ahnna shook her head, not knowing how to reverse a situation that had spun so far out of control, with yet another person wildly misconstruing her intentions. "The last thing I wish to do is cause conflict between them." Her hands balled into fists, for it seemed the only way clear of this was the truth. "Aren was here because the tone toward Ithicana has soured. Your merchants aren't paying their bills at Northwatch. He wanted to know what had happened to cause the change and was worried it was something I'd said or done. But the truth is that I don't know why it's happening. And James . . ." Tears burned in her eyes. "The only excuse for that is my foolish heart. Nothing has come of it, and nothing will."

"I don't believe you."

He took a step back, and Ahnna's first instinct was to act with violence. To silence him and get rid of his body because if he took this accusation to any of the royal family . . .

But she couldn't.

He was James's friend, and his only crime was loyalty to his kingdom. "What do I have to do to prove that I have only good intentions in Harendell? Tell me what I must do, and I'll do it. Because on my honor, my brother has no desire for conflict with Harendell, only a desire to protect his people. He will not act against you, I swear it."

"I cannot keep silent on this."

Kill him, her instincts shrieked, but instead, Ahnna fell to her knees. "Please, George. I've never begged anything of anyone in my life, but I beg you to believe that these pieces do not fit together to form the picture you fear. But if you take them to Edward and he retaliates, it will be catastrophic. So many innocents will die, and all because your shadows heard words out of context. Take steps to investigate further if you must, but please don't escalate this without compelling proof."

He took another step back, and Ahnna started to go for the knife beneath her skirts but stilled as he said, "I'll not say anything while my emotions run high, Ahnna. But my resources are many, and I already have spies watching your brother as he travels south. I will learn the certain truth, and if it is damning, do not think that I won't bring it to the king. His children are beloved to him, and he will not take kindly to your behavior."

Ahnna gave a tight nod.

He leveled a finger at her. "If you try to leave, Ahnna, I'll know your words were lies. So do us all a favor and make like a good Harendellian lady and sit still." His expression hardened. "And stay the fuck away from James."

37

AHNNA

TRUE TO HIS WORD, GEORGE HAD HER WATCHED DAY AND night. Her bodyguards were his men, but Ahnna also felt the increased scrutiny of the servants, and even Hazel seemed different. Watchful. Which was perhaps no shock, given the familiarity that George had always had with the maid.

Ahnna was desperate to warn Aren of the threat, but she did not dare try to write him a message, even in code. Didn't dare seek out any of the Ithicanian spies in Verwyrd. The slightest misstep on her part had the power to bring down calamity on Ithicana, and for days, Ahnna abided by George's will and sat still, rarely leaving her rooms, though her mind never ceased racing.

Of James, she saw nothing, and every time he came into her thoughts, Ahnna would bite her cheeks. Dig her nails deep into her palms. But all her self-punishment achieved was raw flesh and an even sorer heart, because there was no denying to herself that the wrong prince had left a mark on her soul that would never be erased.

William alone seemed blissfully unaware of the tension in the

Sky Palace. Though she had no real interest in his occupations, Ahnna accepted every one of his invitations, dressing like a Harendellian lady and sitting in near silence while he filled her ears with chatter, all while she waited for the knife to fall. For George to reveal his false truth about Ithicana's schemes and for Harendell to turn on them.

But the knife never fell.

So, knowing that Aren might well be digging himself a hole that would be his grave, Ahnna contrived a scheme to warn him. "Hazel, would you deliver this to Her Highness?"

The maid took the card, but then hesitated. "Is this prudent, my lady? It is my understanding that you two had cross words."

"For which I hope to make amends."

Silence stretched, then she said, "Yes, my lady."

Hazel departed, and Ahnna paced back and forth across the room, her nerves making her palms sweat. When her maid finally returned, Ahnna nearly leapt out of her skin.

Hazel handed her the card, and opening it, Ahnna read:

I accept your apology. If we invite the jewelers to visit, they have time to prepare. Better to catch them out and take them for all they are worth. Dress for riding and be ready to leave the palace in an hour.

Virginia

P.S. Georgie and James will attend us. The former because I wish to cater to his taste and the latter because he will be honest if Georgie's taste is tacky.

Hazel was watching her, so Ahnna gave her a smile. "I will make amends."

Her maid sighed, then said, "Be wary, my lady. The Princess Virginia is not known to be forgiving, so this note causes me suspicion."

"I am always wary, Hazel."

But so far, her plan to warn her brother was working.

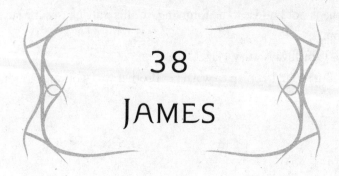

38

JAMES

"You are a princess of Harendell," James said to his sister flatly. "The jewelers will come to you."

Virginia glared at him as though he were the stupidest creature to ever stand in her presence. "When I invite them, they choose what items they bring to show me."

"I've no doubt they bring their highest-quality items."

Her scowl deepened. "They come prepared."

James set aside the report he was reading. "I should certainly hope so."

"Why are you so stupid?" She tossed her long curls over her shoulder. "They know they have to be generous to me, so they bring jewels they don't mind parting with at a bargain and hold back the choice items to show individuals with gold but no power. If I catch them unawares, they must show me everything in their cases, and I can extort them as I see fit."

James cast his eyes skyward. "You are the pinnacle example of our people, Ginny. Harendellian to the core."

To his surprise, his sister turned away from him and walked to the window, drawn by the light. "Ahnna wishes to purchase new jewelry. She requested my advice."

He tensed.

"You have not spoken, but I can feel the argument radiating out of you, Jamie," she said. "I am bored of being locked up in the Sky Palace, with most of the court either trailing after Mother and Father or returned to their homes. And with you and yours patrolling the lands around Verwyrd day and night to root out any Amaridians with ill intent, I daresay that the journey to Abertford is safer than it's ever been. You and Georgie will ride with us, of course, and I'll not argue against whatever escort you might care to drag along."

James knew that he should argue, and that if he forced the issue, Virginia would likely bend to his wishes. But it had been over a week since he'd argued with Ahnna, and he'd not seen her once. It was partly by design, for true to his word, Georgie had taken control of her security, but it was also because she was quite clearly avoiding him. A behavior he should encourage. Yet James found himself saying, "When do you wish to go?"

"Now," Virginia said with a smile. "Else one of the servants will warn the jewelers, and they'll hide the items I am likely to want. I told Ahnna to be ready in an hour, which gives you"—she walked to the ticking clock and opened its face, fingers brushing over the arms—"ten minutes to ready yourself. I shall meet you in the courtyard."

She left the room, cane thudding softly against the carpet, and James gave a soft curse. Leaping to his feet, he donned the coat he'd tossed on one of the sofas, then straightened his cravat in the mirror on the wall. Glaring at his reflection, James abandoned his father's study and strode through the Sky Palace corridors, flinging open the door to his room. "Uniform," he said to Thomas, who showed no sign of being startled, only went to the wardrobe and retrieved the necessary items as James flung off the clothes he was wearing. Donning his uniform, he retrieved his sword and an extra set of knives, glanced at the mirror and then the clock. "Goddamn it," he snarled, ignoring Thomas's affronted stare, then bolted out the door.

Moving as swiftly as he could without raising alarm, James stepped out into the courtyard just as the palace clocks began to ring the hour. Georgie was helping Virginia into the carriage, but at its head, stroking the nose of one of the mules, was Ahnna.

She wore a dark-blue riding outfit: a belted coat with divided skirts, as well as polished riding boots. Sunlight glinted off her long hair, which hung in loose curls down her back, a hat that matched the clothes perched atop her head. Her skin had lost much of its suntan during her time in Harendell, the flush of her cheeks more noticeable as she glanced his way, then back to the mule, feeding it a lump of sugar from her pocket. If one ignored her height, she was the image of a Harendellian lady, though the longer he stared at her, the more weapons he noticed hidden about her person. Still Ahnna, albeit dressed in a costume. James bit down on a smile.

"You needn't trouble yourself with this venture, Jamie," Georgie said, and from his friend's flat tone, James's scrutiny of Ahnna's attire had not gone unnoticed. "You've more pressing matters to attend to."

"No, he doesn't!" Virginia shouted from inside the carriage. "Get in, Jamie. Already, we are at risk of those greedy jewel setters having learned of my visit. We need to move faster! Ahnna, hurry, or all they'll show us is settings in last year's styles."

James approached, holding out his hand to Ahnna. "My lady."

She gave him the slightest of nods, gloved hand taking his as she climbed inside, though she immediately drew it away as she sat next to Georgie. James bit down his jealousy and sat next to his sister, who immediately started shouting at the coachman to make haste. An impossibility, for Buck and Brayer moved at only one speed.

"Is there something particular you are looking for?" Virginia asked, then waved her hand. "Do not answer that. One should never shop for jewelry with something in mind, only with a mind for something, because beautiful jewelry demands a certain dress, not the other way around. Wait and see what sings to you."

"I think that wise advice, Virginia." Ahnna turned her gaze out the window while Virginia kept up her chatter, for she never enjoyed silence. Georgie obliged her, but James could feel his friend's displeasure at his presence, and he kept his eyes on his boots, regretting agreeing to Virginia's demands.

He'd thought that he could keep his wits about Ahnna. Keep the feelings that he had no business feeling in check for the space of an afternoon's ride, except even with the heavy scent of his sister's perfume, James could smell the scent of salt and the sea, his senses telling him a storm was in the sky though he knew it was only the woman seated across from him.

Choosing to be around her was a mistake, and as he muttered answers to his sister's questions, James vowed to find an excuse to abandon this excursion when they reached the bottom of the spiral. To fabricate some duty that he needed to attend to. Georgie would back him up, of that James had no doubt.

His friend had said little about what had transpired after they'd parted ways on the streets of Verwyrd, only that Ahnna had remained with William for the balance of the revels, returning with him without incident, though apparently his brother had indulged to the extreme. Georgie's spies had watched Aren Kertell board a riverboat, on which he'd traveled with apparently no incident back to the coast, where he'd booked passage on a merchant vessel to Northwatch. The spies indicated that Ithicana's king blended into the masses with ease, adopting a Harendellian accent and the pretense of being a minor merchantman. A skill that spoke to many such ventures, which simultaneously irritated and intrigued James.

They reached the bottom of the spiral and exited the carriage. James opened his mouth to say that his presence was needed in the garrison and that he'd follow along later, but instead of an excuse coming out, he said to Ahnna, "Do you need help mounting, my lady?"

"I'll manage, thank you." She took Dippy's reins from a groom, mounting the tall gelding with ease. James held his breath to see how the horse would react to her in the saddle, but Dippy stood steady, ears flicked back as he listened to Ahnna speaking softly to him.

"I can handle this," Georgie said under his breath. "Make an excuse, Jamie. You shouldn't be around her."

There was an edge of anger in his friend's voice, and though James knew he should listen, knew that Georgie spoke wisdom, he said, "Better not to risk it. If anything goes wrong, I need to be here."

"It's already going wrong," Georgie snapped, but he gave up arguing to help Virginia onto Daisy.

James took Maven's reins and mounted, then called out orders to the soldiers who would accompany them, the gates in the wall surrounding the spiral opening and their party trotting out into the city.

It was hard not to hold his breath as he waited to see how Ahnna's horse acquitted himself, because a couple of weeks of training did not a quiet saddle horse make. But Dippy trotted calmly down the road, his ears flicking occasionally to distractions but his attention primarily on his rider.

And his rider acquitted herself just as well.

Some people took naturally to the saddle, and while her first lessons had spoken more to tenacity than talent, James was rapidly revising his opinions. Ahnna was a natural, moving in response to the horse with the same instinctive grace she'd used while captaining the ship through the storm. James was struck with the memory of how she'd talked to the ship as though it were alive, listening to it, feeling it, and though he was too far to hear her words, he could see her lips moving as she spoke to her horse.

Admiration grew in his chest as he watched her ride, hips shifting to urge the racehorse into a canter as they crossed the bridge on the road west to Abertford. Though it was the gelding's nature to want to be at the front, Dippy seemed to sense his rider's calm as she looked around at the trees, his pace sedate as he followed the soldiers leading the group. Ahnna's hair trailed out behind her, beams of light illuminating all the colors in it as she rode beneath the canopy of trees above the road, and she nodded politely at the travelers who had moved to the side to allow the group to pass.

Not a princess, but a queen in the making, and James's chest tightened with the knowledge that Harendell would be blessed to be led by a woman like Ahnna Kertell. A woman who could both stand in defense of her people and empathize with them. Who was both fierce and kind in equal measure.

Then something struck him hard in the ankle.

Startled, James looked sideways to see Georgie riding next to him, his friend clearly having kicked him.

"Would you mind Daisy?" Georgie said pointedly. "I need to speak with the soldiers up front about vigilance."

The jab struck true. Irritation flooded James and turned his cheeks hot with the desire to snap a retort, but he bit down on it because Georgie was in the right.

This had been a mistake.

He shouldn't have come.

But he also couldn't very well turn around without raising questions, so instead James dropped back alongside his sister. Her horse was trained to follow the other horses, but otherwise, Ginny needed no assistance, for she was comfortable in the saddle.

"Georgie is in a mood," his sister said. "Do you know why?"

"I hadn't noticed," James lied. "Do you wish me to inquire?"

Ginny snorted softly. "Hardly. I already asked him myself, and he said nothing is amiss. That he's merely concerned to have me out because of the violence that has occurred around Verwyrd of late. Two statements in direct objection to each other, which surely means he's lying about both."

"The violence is a fact, Ginny."

"Obviously, but his concern about it is a lie. There is something else that has him in a twist, and he doesn't want to admit it." She frowned. "I changed my mind. Go ask him and report back to me immediately."

James bloody well already knew what Georgie was in a twist about, but he said, "I'll ask while you're with the jewelers."

They rode in silence for a time, then Ginny said, "I was surprised she requested to meet with the jewelers."

"Why is that?"

"Because I believe she is something of a pauper princess. Which is madness, given that Ithicana possesses mountains of gold. Do you think her brother doesn't like her? I heard she is on sour terms with Lara, which I was at first hesitant to believe. Now I think that must certainly be the case. Do you think he sent her to us without a copper to rub between her fingers because his wife told him to?"

James's mouth opened, but before he could answer, Ginny added, "Promise me that you'll always put me before whatever woman Father decides you should wed. I couldn't bear being set aside by you, Jamie. Or William. But especially you."

"I have no plans to wed," he said. Then, because his sister had hit on a suspicion he himself had once had, he asked, "What has Ahnna done that causes you to believe she's without means?"

"Well, for a start, she has not worn jewelry since she arrived."

"Perhaps that's not something that is done in Ithicana."

Ginny ignored him. "She came with one trunk. One. And since arriving, she's only purchased gowns that the modiste was getting rid of at a steep discount, including that travesty of a pink dress that Elizabeth paid the modiste to make as a lark. The majority of what Ahnna wears has been made by Hazel."

"Hazel is a talented seamstress."

Ginny made a face. "She's a *laundress*, Jamie. Not even intended as a lady's maid, but we all know what befell poor Agnes on the *Defiant*. It was only luck that Mother lent Hazel to Georgie to do his laundry on the *Victoria*, and she's only kept her position because Ahnna seemed not to know the difference between a laundress and a maid."

"Don't be a snob."

"I'm not!" she huffed. "But all that could, of course, be blamed on her being Ithicanian, except she went to the lending house to secure a loan and tried to use Harendell as collateral."

"Harendell?" He shook his head. "That can't be right. And how do you know that anyway? The bankers keep confidence like no other."

"But blather on without care for their own servants in the room. My maids heard that it was quite an upset among the lenders as they debated whether a nation could be used as collateral, and they decided that it could not, but a future queen's goodwill certainly could. Either way, what need has she of such a large loan if her brother is rich as sin *unless* he's cut her off?"

"You know I have no patience for gossip," he said, even as he took in his sister's words. Yet another secret that Ahnna was holding close to her heart?

"It is not gossip, it is a puzzle. A puzzle I wish to solve, which is why I agreed to this venture," Ginny said. "Bankers keep confidence, but jewelers do not, so I will learn how she pays for her purchases."

"To what end?"

"If she has no influence in Ithicana, then she is not the asset Father believes she is, and he ought to know that. Perhaps he might consider negotiating for something of more value."

His sister had latched on to something that might actually have weight with their father as far as breaking off the betrothal, but all James felt was anger that his sister was attempting to undermine Ahnna. "This is an about-face, Virginia. I heard that Elizabeth and Ahnna had words regarding Lestara. If this is about that, you're being petty."

"It's not about that nor anything else she's said or done," Ginny snapped. "It's about discovering whether she's being deceitful. I once hoped her to be the greatest of assets and worthy of William's love, but now I wonder if she's only using Harendell to elevate her own fallen position. I wonder if she has been lying all this time."

"I feel as though I'm speaking to your mother, not to you."

Ginny's face twisted. "Perhaps Mother had the right of it not to want Ahnna. But if you must know, she's not said a word to me about Ahnna since she arrived, so all that I have said is spoken from my own heart out of a desire to protect our brother. But by all means, please do take the side of the woman you barely know over your own sister."

"I didn't—" James broke off, because Ginny had already heeled Daisy for more speed, the mare moving through the group until Georgie noticed and fell in alongside, head bending close to Virginia's.

If Ahnna noticed the tension, she didn't show it, her posture relaxed and her focus alternating between her horse and her surroundings. Ginny's mood could change with the weather, but instinct told James that this ran deeper than a spat, and his skin prickled with the sense that there had been a shift in the Sky Palace against Ahnna's presence. A shift that echoed some of the rising complaints about Ithicana that he suspected were fueled by Cormac and his agents. All of which fed into James's goals, and yet every part of him wanted to defend her. To argue that she deserved to be queen and would make a good one at that.

If anyone was deceitful, it was him, and not for the first time, James wondered how his sister would react when the day came that their father and King Ronan came to terms and she learned his true feelings on Cardiff. Neither his sister nor his brother knew anything, not even of the weeks at a time that he'd spent with his uncles in his youth, the excuse always being that he was learning survival skills in the north.

Lies upon lies, and he'd held it all together until Ahnna Kertell had strode into his life.

James risked a glance at her again, just in time to watch her entire body tense and her hand reach into the pocket where a knife was hidden.

39
AHNNA

WHAT PRECISELY WARNED HER, AHNNA COULDN'T HAVE SAID. Some sixth sense gained from a lifetime of people trying to kill her, animals trying to kill her, and storms trying to kill her, perhaps. But there was no mistaking the crawl of sensation across her skin warning that malevolent eyes were watching her.

Experience kept her from revealing her awareness by overtly searching their surroundings, but she slowly slipped her hand into her skirt pocket, the hole Hazel had sewn into it allowing her to close her fingers over the hilt of the six-inch blade strapped to her thigh.

Beneath her, Dippy gave a small buck, and Ahnna took a deep breath to relax herself lest the gelding give her away.

Then James was alongside her.

"There's someone following us," she said softly. "In the trees, left side of the road."

"I haven't seen anyone." He stretched, expression bored, though Ahnna knew it was an act.

"Trust me."

"I do." He patted Maven on the neck. "But one curious individual isn't going to attack this many soldiers. The greater risk is a well-placed arrow."

Which was why he was riding alongside her, Ahnna realized. So they'd have to get through him to hit her.

"Georgie!" he called, and the other man turned his head. Ahnna didn't miss the sour expression on his face, but it fell away as James added, "I think a pint is in order when we arrive. Fortitude for an unpleasant task."

A code, she had no doubt, especially as Georgie moved his horse closer to Virginia's small mount, even as she cast her brother a glare over her shoulder.

"How much farther?" Ahnna asked, tightening her grip on Dippy's reins, then forcing herself to relax again. "And what sort of place is it?"

"Half an hour." James glanced into the trees, face still unmoved. "The town is fortified and also has a garrison. A lot of wealth in Abertford."

"Should we race?"

"The road isn't good for it. Winding and muddy."

Her lips parted to ask if they should go back, but the crawling sensation between her shoulder blades warned her that it would be a mistake. The only thing to do was to press onward and keep their eyes open.

They kept their pace down the road, the silence between them heavy, and every time they rounded a bend and crossed paths with a traveler, Ahnna tensed. She felt exposed and poorly equipped to fight in the dress with only her knives, when what she wanted was a sword and clothing that would allow her to disappear into the woods if she had to.

"Thank you," she finally said, lest the tension be the thing that put her in a grave. "For training my horse."

"Unnecessary, in hindsight," James said, and Ahnna's heart sank with certainty that he would reference her inevitable departure, but then he added, "I think you would have sorted him on your own if given the time."

"Saved me bruising my ass again."

The corner of his mouth turned up, though his eyes were on the trees. "Then I'll consider it time well spent."

A flicker of motion caught her eye. A horse, she thought, moving through the forest but far enough away that it was swiftly obscured by brush. "Who do you think it is?"

"Any number of possibilities," he muttered. "Let's hope it's only a spy."

Silence reigned once more, and Ahnna felt no small amount of relief when the walls of the town appeared ahead, the guards manning the gate drawing to attention as they recognized the royal banner at the head of the party.

"Stay with Virginia and Georgie," James said as they passed through the gates, then fell back to speak to one of the guards.

Ahnna did as he asked, staying close to the princess as Georgie rode deeper into the town, the wide street having trees planted equidistant down the center, branches shading them as they rode beneath. The buildings to either side were three stories tall and made from stone, wrought-iron railings framing the front steps, all of it exuding wealth. He stopped in front of a large building. The stone above the door was carved with the name *Partridge & Co.*, which was familiar to Ahnna from her survey of accounts at the bank, for this was the jeweler that had paid Alexandra, presumably for the sale of something.

Perhaps she might kill two birds with one stone in this venture.

Stable boys appeared from around the building, taking the horses even as a man in a gray morning suit appeared on the steps. "Your Highness," he said, bowing low. "This is an unexpected surprise. We would have been happy to have brought you a selection of our best—"

"I know, Lionel, but I feel you give better advice with less time to prepare," Virginia interrupted.

The man, Lionel, gave a soft sigh as though already defeated, then bowed to Georgie. "My lord Cavendish, it is a pleasure." Then his gaze settled on Ahnna, widening in surprise. "It is an honor, Your Highness. It has been many years since we've served the needs of the Ithicanian royal family. It was always a delight, for requests came by messenger, and it was always very cloak-and-dagger."

"No longer any need for that." Ahnna dismounted. "I'm of a mind to purchase a gift for Ithicana's queen. Maridrinian rubies, if you have them." She could feel the sharp look that Georgie cast her way, but she did not allow herself to react.

"Of course, of course." He gestured for them to follow him inside, and Ahnna's eyes skimmed over the heavy bars on the windows, alert guards with sharp blades standing to both sides of the large foyer.

"We have several pieces with stones from Maridrina in the gallery," Lionel said, gesturing down the hallway.

"Let's visit the vaults instead," Virginia said. "This is for a queen, Lionel. Not just any queen, but also the woman who is half sister to the queen of Maridrina, as well as sister to the prince consort of Valcotta. Harendell must put its best foot forward, yes?"

The man paled. "Yes, of course. This way, my ladies."

Ahnna glanced behind her, but James had not yet joined them, so she followed the jeweler down a wide set of stairs into a subterranean level. The walls were thick stone, Valcottan glass lamps burning every pace or so, and the carpet beneath her feet was so thick that her boots made almost no sound. They approached a heavy steel door flanked by two guards, who stepped aside, allowing Lionel to fiddle with some sort of mechanism, his motions obscured.

But not the loud *clunk* of a heavy lock disengaging.

They stepped inside, and Ahnna's heart stuttered at the long cabinets marked with labels indicating gemstone type and region, as well as the gold bars stacked floor-to-ceiling at the far end of the room. The irony that this was what Harendellians believed could be found in Ithicana was not lost on her.

A glass case ran down the center of the room with completed pieces. Tiaras and necklaces and rings, all incredible craftsmanship and bearing gems of such size that each must cost a king's ransom.

Lionel gestured to the table sitting before the bullion, heavy oak and surrounded by upholstered chairs. Ahnna and Virginia sat, Georgie standing behind Virginia's chair, expression impassive.

"As chance would have it, we have many pieces with Maridrinian rubies," Lionel said. "A year or two past, Her Most Royal Majesty, Queen Alexandra, brought to us a selection of rubies that she desired to sell, for red is not her favored color."

Ahnna blinked, surprised that the man was making no effort to hide the transaction, which she had to assume meant that Alexandra had not asked for discretion. Though it was not the reason for her being here, a flood of disappointment filled her—it seemed that her one piece of leverage might not be leverage at all. Or at least, not this part of it. C.F. remained a mystery.

"Nor mine," Virginia said, accepting a glass of sparkling wine that had been brought by a servant. "I've always believed red to be a masculine color."

"Lara favors many pursuits that others might deem masculine," Ahnna answered, feeling an idiot for saying so. But Virginia smiled and nodded, so she added, "And of course, she's a Veliant. Rubies are their stone."

"Blood-red ones, I'm sure." Virginia sipped at her wine. "Show us what you have, then, Lionel."

The jeweler unlocked a case, then brought a pair of earrings made of rubies and diamonds that would reach down to the wearer's shoulders. Before Ahnna could pick them up, Virginia gestured to be handed them, her fingers running over the gems, eyes fixed beyond Ahnna's shoulder. "No," she declared. "These are jewels a man buys his mistress. Put them away and bring something else."

Next came a delicate tiara of gold and ruby, formed to look like flowers.

"No," Virginia said sourly after running her fingertips over it. "Lionel, truly. Think of Lara's reputation and choose something fitting."

The man hesitated, then went back not to the case but to one of the cabinets. Unlocking it, he removed a velvet-wrapped object, then brought it back to the table. "Intended to be shown to the Veliant harem," he said. "But then . . ."

Ahnna's breath caught as he unwrapped the velvet, revealing a choker of close-set rubies nearly an inch thick. Virginia ran her fingers over it and then said, "Georgie, what exact hue are they?"

"Crimson," he answered. "As fresh blood."

"Perfect."

"If I may, my lady?" Lionel asked. At Ahnna's nod, he fastened the choker around her throat. Retrieving a mirror, he held it up, and her stomach clenched, for it looked for all the world as though her throat had just been slit.

"I can tell from the silence that it's perfect," Virginia said. "She'll take it, of course."

"How much is it?" Ahnna fumbled with the clasp, wanting the choker off, though it took Lionel's nimble fingers to unfasten the catch. Setting it on the velvet, he went to a side table and wrote down a number, folded the paper, then handed it to her.

Ahnna glanced at the amount and almost gagged. "Perhaps something—"

"This is the one, Ahnna," Virginia interrupted. "Of course, if you find yourself short, I could lend you the coin."

This was a *fucking test.*

Anger filled Ahnna's chest, but she smiled. "No need. My accounts will cover it."

The choker would drain the account Aren had set up for her entirely, but that was of no matter. He could sell the piece and recoup the cost, and the real value was in the message it sent. A message, *a warning*, that she trusted no one but Lara to understand. Smiling at Lionel, Ahnna said, "I trust you can arrange for it to be sent to Northwatch?" When he nodded, she added, "If you could do me one small favor, and be sure to include a bottle of Maridrinian wine with it. It absolutely must be Maridrinian."

"That's no small favor," Virginia said. "No one of quality will have anything of the sort. Their vintages are awful."

"I know," Ahnna said, signing a piece of paper that Lionel's clerk handed her. "But Lara is very familiar with that particular taste."

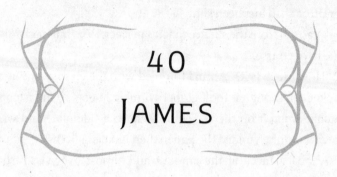

40

JAMES

"THREE OF YOU WITH ME," JAMES SAID TO HIS MEN, HAVING warned the city guards that someone had followed the party. "The rest of you on watch outside the jeweler's. Tell Lord Cavendish that he is not to allow either woman to leave the town until I return."

"Yes, sir."

Nodding once at those who would remain, James urged Maven into a trot and left through the city gates, his soldiers following.

The air was thick and cloying, and James gave the darkening skies a wary glance before focusing his attention on the forest around them. The weather was turning, and potential assassins aside, it would be wise to remain in Abertford until the storm had passed, even if it meant staying overnight.

They spread out, moving through the trees, searching for motion. For signs of anyone in the woods who shouldn't be.

Then he saw a horse through the brush, brown hide almost perfectly camouflaged. "There," he said softly, and his soldiers gave nods as they caught sight of the animal. The young man in the saddle was watching the road, but James marked his red hair. The long knife sheathed at his belt. The fletching of the arrows in the quiver at his back. James had fought these bastards for most of his life, and goddamned if he didn't know them when he saw them.

Amaridian.

"Try to catch him alive," James told his soldiers in a low voice. "I'd like to question him."

The men signaled understanding, spreading out as they approached the Amaridian from behind. The soft earth muffled the horses' steps, but all the birds and creatures that lived in the trees had fallen silent.

Watching.

They prowled closer, and James carefully unsheathed a knife, not wanting to risk killing the man with a sword.

Closer.

Crack!

At the sound of a branch cracking beneath a horse's hoof, the Amaridian jerked around, eyes widening in panic as he saw how close they were. He dug in his heels, but James was already moving.

Maven leapt into speed, weaving through the trees in pursuit of the man, who was riding as though his life depended on it. Which, in fairness, it did.

"I don't think so," James hissed, leaning over his mare's neck to avoid being taken off by a branch.

His soldiers rode with equal speed, keeping low, one lifting the bow he carried.

"Shoot the horse!" James shouted, and arrows flew in quick succession, all hitting trees instead of the animal galloping ahead.

They reached the road, but instead of heading down it, the Amaridian plunged into the brush on the far side. Wisely understanding that his survival depended on his cover.

But James and his men had faster mounts.

Out of his periphery, he saw one of his soldiers press ahead, and then abruptly, the man was flying through the air and his mount going down.

"Trap!" James shouted, pulling Maven up.

But it was too late.

Amaridians exploded from where they lay hidden beneath brush, weapons in hand. Arrows flew, striking his other two men, one narrowly missing James's face.

Too many to fight. Too many by far.

"The queen wants a word with you, bastard," one of them said, lifting a long sword as he strode toward James.

Boom!

James's eyes flicked to the sky, to the midnight clouds now blocking out the sun. And whirling his mare around, he galloped toward the storm.

41

Ahnna

Needing to escape the oppressive confines of the vault after the exchange, Ahnna left the building, her guards and several soldiers trailing at her heels.

"Where is His Highness?" she asked, not seeing James anywhere in sight, unease filling her.

"He took a company to search for whoever was following us, my lady," one of the men answered. "They just rode out."

Overhead, clouds had gathered, and a gust of wind sent Ahnna's hair blowing out behind her. She could feel a charge in the air. From the coming storm, yes, but also something else. "How big a company?"

"Three men, Your Highness. Enough to run any spies off."

Her jaw tightened, knowing he hadn't taken more because he'd wanted them to stay with her and Virginia.

Taking Dippy's reins from one of the stable boys, Ahnna mounted her horse, ignoring the protests of the soldiers as she rode down the street to the gate. The wind continued to rise, whipping her hair and tearing at her skirts, and the citizens were all scowling at the sky and drawing indoors anything that might be blown away.

As she reached the gates, one of the soldiers standing guard said, "You should head indoors, my lady. This storm will bring heavy rain and worse, mark my words."

She could smell the rain. Smell the charge of lightning and violence the way she did in a typhoon, except somehow different. Somehow worse.

"How long ago did he ride out?" she asked, resting a hand against Dippy's neck. Her horse was pawing at the ground, sensing the storm and Ahnna's unease, and she knew it made him want to run.

"Not long, my lady." The man squinted down the road. "They'll come back to escape the storm. Winds won't be too bad here, but over the crest on the Ranges, it could be a much different story."

Ahnna could have told him that, for she'd seen the blackness of the sky to the east.

"Lady Ahnna!"

She turned her head to see Georgie striding up the road, displeasure written across his face.

"You should send men after them," she said to the gate guard. "They've been gone too long."

"With respect, my lady, it's not been more than half a turn of the glass. Those are experienced men."

Ahnna barely heard his words, her eyes on the riderless horse galloping down the road toward them.

A very dead soldier dangling from one stirrup.

Ahnna dug in her heels, and Dippy exploded down the road at a gallop, shouts of protest following in her wake. But she didn't care. Not as she passed the incoming horse and saw two arrows jutting out of the soldier's chest.

They'd come under attack. James had come under attack.

Lying flat to Dippy's neck, she let the gelding have his head so that she could retrieve one of her knives. It wouldn't do much in a battle, but it was better than riding into a fight empty-handed.

Within moments, she saw where the conflict had crossed the road, dirt and brush torn apart, and she followed the trail, her chest clenching as she reached a small clearing and saw still forms on the ground.

"James!" she shouted, leaping off Dippy's back and running to the first figure. A soldier. As was the other. James was nowhere in sight. But the ground was torn up with hoofprints heading east, swiftly joined by more.

East into the storm.

Snatching up the dead soldier's bow and quiver, she vaulted onto Dippy's back and took off after them.

They were probably only minutes ahead of her, but so much could happen in that time. All it took was a well-placed arrow between the shoulders, and it was over.

But Ahnna had never been very good at conceding defeat.

The terrain sloped upward through the trees, the ground rough, and Ahnna let Dippy choose his footing. Ahead, she saw a soldier standing next to a lamed horse, the man cursing. Red hair and the distinctive knife in his hand told her he was Amaridian, and nocking an arrow, Ahnna took aim and let it fly.

It sank into his neck, but she was past him before his body hit the ground.

Higher and higher she climbed, and then her horse exploded over the crest of the hill, and before her was wide-open terrain.

The Ranges.

Black clouds obscured the sky, but in the distance, she could see a dozen mounted figures in pursuit of a single familiar form.

Rage overtook her fear, and leaning over her horse's neck, Ahnna growled, "Catch them."

As though he knew her will, Dippy's stride lengthened, and he flew.

Boom!

The rolling thunder of the storm drowned out the sound of his hooves as he tore after the other horses, every part of him wanting to catch them. To pass them, and Ahnna knew that the horse beneath her would win any race she ever set him to.

Wind whipped her hair and tore at her skirts, but Ahnna ignored the storm, eyes all for the men who were trying to shoot James in the back.

Dippy drew closer, faster than any of the Amaridian mounts by far, and drawing an arrow from the quiver, Ahnna let go of the reins and sat up straight. She'd spent her life shooting from a tossing ship deck. Fighting wind and rain and worse, and with a good bow, Ahnna never missed.

Waiting for the storm to take a breath, she let the arrow loose.

It soared through the air and struck the man at the rear in his spine, what cry of pain he might have made muffled by the storm. He rolled off the back of his mount, landing in a way that ensured his death even if the arrow hadn't.

Ahnna pressed onward, Dippy gaining on the group with every stride.

But Maven was flagging. The mare was bleeding from the haunches, and the Amaridians were gaining ground.

Ahnna shot another one. Then another.

Dippy leapt over their bodies without losing his stride.

Taking aim at a large man, Ahnna let loose right as his horse stumbled. It made him shift sideways, and the arrow hit him in the arm.

He roared in pain and looked backward right in time for her last arrow to take him in the face.

But his fellows had heard.

Heads snapped around, and two of them broke off the chase to wheel their horses to meet her.

James chose that moment to look over his shoulder. Horror filled his expression, and then he was wheeling Maven around, sword in hand.

What he did next, Ahnna didn't know, because her focus shifted to the man galloping toward her with a sword in hand.

Her small blade wouldn't do well against the long, slender sword, especially given he held the blade like he knew how to use it.

Which meant she couldn't let him get close.

Flipping her knife so that she held it by the tip, Ahnna drew in a deep breath and threw. It flipped end over end, striking the man in the shoulder. He dropped his sword and flew past her, but her eyes were on the second man. Drawing her skirts up so they were out of her way, Ahnna rode straight at him, veering to the left at the last minute.

He tried to adjust his swing, but she was already throwing herself at him.

Ahnna caught him around the waist, shoulders screaming even as her momentum ripped them both off the back of the horse.

They hit the ground and rolled. Their tumble stopped with her on top, and Ahnna smashed her forehead into his nose. As he screamed, she regained her feet, and then brought her boot heel down hard on his throat, and the screaming stopped.

She was shaking.

No . . . The *ground* was shaking.

Ahnna lifted her head to see James riding toward her, mouth

opened as he screamed something at her, but she couldn't hear it over the thunder.

Then she understood. Not thunder. A massive herd of cattle racing directly toward them.

Dippy had circled around and was galloping alongside Maven. James caught his reins, hauling him to stop next to her. "Get on!"

She didn't need to be told twice.

Dippy was running as her ass hit the saddle, and she knew that fear was driving him now. Because all around them were cattle.

"Give him his head," James shouted above the deafening thunder of hooves and storm. "Run with them!"

Boom!

There was no other choice but to run with the stampede. The Amaridians were doing the same, all interest in trying to kill her and James forgotten as they fought for their own lives.

Ahnna looked over her shoulder, her heart clenching as she watched the circling clouds take on a funnel shape. Like waterspouts she'd seen on the sea, except bigger. So much bigger.

And then it touched the earth.

With violence she'd never seen before, the twister tore up the ground, rock and dirt flying out from around it. But rather than veering out of its path, the herd raced onward, the twister gaining with every passing second.

Terror filled her, because she could not get out of the flow of cattle. James fought the same battle as they tried to break free, but the terrified animals pressed too close.

The wind was deafening, bits of debris cutting into her face, but there was far worse to come.

"Ahnna!"

James's voice barely reached her over the wind and cries of the terrified animals, but she saw where he was pointing. An abandoned stone house, the roof long since collapsed. The cattle parted around it, but she kept her horse heading straight, Maven nearly colliding with them as James reined her alongside.

"Get off!" he screamed. "Into the cellar!"

"The horses!"

"Leave them!"

But she couldn't. She wouldn't.

Seeing her hesitation, James reached up and hauled her off the side. She fought him, unwilling to abandon her horse to the monster raging toward them, but James slapped both mounts on the haunches, and they rejoined the stampede.

Ahnna stared after them, but James hauled on her hand, dragging her in among the rotting timbers. "Help me!" he shouted. "We need to get in the cellar!"

Fear took over, and Ahnna ripped up a piece of wood, eyes fixed on the salvation that was the hole in the ground even as the twister raced closer. The timbers were wedged in collapsed rock, and Ahnna screamed as she dragged them out of the way, James doing the same. Trying to make enough space to fit down.

There was only one beam left.

"Lift!" James shouted, and Ahnna heaved with all her strength, wood splintering and snapping, moving a few inches to make just enough space as bits of rock and wood and God knew what lashed against her skin.

The twister was here.

James shoved her into the opening. Ahnna fell, landing hard in the rubble, instinct making her roll out of the way as he dropped next to her. Blackness and noise surrounded her, it feeling as though she stood in a void until James's arms folded around her. Pushed her against the wall, his body shielding hers as the twister roared over them, debris whipping around the cellar. Ahnna's ears popped, the pressure unbearable as she pressed her face into James's chest, clinging to him lest the storm try to tear him away.

And then it was over.

As quickly as it had come, the twister drifted away, leaving behind nothing but their ragged breathing and darkness.

Ahnna didn't let go of him, lingering terror that he'd be ripped from her grasp still filling her veins. Each inhalation brought the scent of soap and cedar, her ears now filled with the rapid hammer of his heart.

"Are you all right?"

James's voice cut the blackness, his solid chest pulling away from her, though his fingers remained tightly gripped on her arms.

"I'm fine." She coughed on the dust. "The horses . . ."

"Likely fine themselves. They do better without riders. I think we disrupt their instincts." He let go of her, the absence of his hands making her feel alone in the blackness. "Maven will head back to Verwyrd, and Dippy will follow her. With any luck, the storm took care of the Amaridians."

"Is the twister gone? Will another come?" She hated not understanding the nature of these storms.

"Gone, yes. But it's not unusual for there to be more than one." She heard him climb to his feet. "I'll have a look."

As he stumbled through the cellar, Ahnna got to her feet and followed him, feeling blood trickling down her face from a small wound at her temple, though it didn't feel deep. She bumped into James, nothing visible in the darkness.

"There is debris over the opening," he said. "If I lift you, can you try to clear it?"

"Yes." Squinting up, she could make out a few bits of light fighting their way through the timbers.

"I'll . . . I'll need to put my hands on you."

Cloaked by blackness, Ahnna allowed herself a smile. "We've been in this position before in the cave under Northwatch, James. You didn't hesitate to put your hands on me."

"I didn't know who you were."

"Shouldn't knowing me make touching me easier?"

He huffed out a breath, the warmth of it brushing her cheek. "And therein lies the problem."

She blinked, certain she'd misheard, but James was already on one knee before her. "On my shoulders. Keep your hands up so I don't knock your head on the ceiling."

Circling behind him, Ahnna rested her hands on his broad shoulders, then lifted her leg over one. His hand gripped her thigh, and a jolt of heat ran through her.

Idiot, she quietly admonished herself. *You're trapped, and all you can think about is the man you're trapped with.*

She lifted her other leg into place, teeth catching her bottom lip as he tightened his grip on her thighs.

"Put an arm up."

She lifted her right hand in the air as he slowly rose to his feet, her weight not troubling him in the slightest. Her fingertips hit the debris. "I can feel the opening."

"Can you move what's blocking it?"

Glad she was wearing gloves, Ahnna dug at the debris, closing her eyes as bits of dirt and rock fell down. "Sorry."

"It's fine."

She managed to clear away enough of the debris that light streamed through, allowing her to see the beam stretched across the opening. Shoving at it accomplished nothing, so she said, "Brace. I'm going to try to lift this."

Hooking her legs under his arms, she dug her toes into his back even as she felt his fingers tighten above her knees. Grunting with effort, Ahnna heaved with all her strength, body shuddering. But the beam wouldn't move. Muttering profanity, she caught hold of it and pulled herself up, balancing her shins on James's shoulders.

Though it must have hurt, all he said was, "Can you see?"

Pressing her face to the opening between the beam and the stone frame that had once held the cellar door, Ahnna peered up and immediately snarled, "Bloody fucking hell."

"What do you see?" James asked, for once not commenting on her language.

"One of the walls collapsed, so there are blocks of stone holding the beam down. I don't think we're going to be able to lift it."

"I have my sword. Can we saw through it?"

"Maybe. Turn so I can look at a different angle."

As James turned, her blood chilled. "We can't cut it," she said. "We can't even move it because it's all that's holding the other wall up. We'll bury the opening entirely."

"Can you squeeze through?"

"I am not that small," she muttered. "Shit."

"We'll just have to wait for them to come find us," James said. "Climb down."

Ahnna slid down his back, holding on to him for longer than was necessary to regain her balance. James was staring up at their predicament. He was covered in dust and dirt, and she fought the urge to brush the bits out of his hair. "It may take some time, given the magnitude of the storm, but they know we are out here. They'll come find us."

"What if they don't?"

"Ahnna, you're a princess. No matter the chaos, they'll—" He stopped speaking as his gaze fixed on her. "You're hurt."

"It's nothing."

But James was having none of her excuses. Pulling her into a beam of light, he extracted a starched white handkerchief and dabbed at the cut, cleaning away the blood. "Not that deep," he said softly.

"I told you so."

That should have been the end of it. The moment when he stepped back, confident that she had suffered only minor damage, propriety again becoming his utmost concern. But James didn't move.

And neither did she.

"You are unlike any lady I've ever met, Ahnna Kertell," he said, smoothing back her hair, the sensation achingly familiar, though she didn't know why. "Wild and irreverent and brave."

"Because I'm not a lady." Her heart was hammering, blood roaring through her veins. "Though I'm trying to change. Truly, I am."

"For you to become something other than who you are would be the greatest tragedy." James's throat moved as he swallowed. "And yet no one has been more complicit in trying to make you change than me."

"Why?" She asked the question that had been making her heart bleed because she'd been so convinced that he thought everything about her was wrong.

"Because if you become the perfect woman for my brother, you will cease to be the perfect woman for me." His amber eyes seemed to burn as the sunlight caught them, searing into her soul as much as did his words. "And then perhaps I can be free of this compulsive need to be in your presence every waking moment and might again sleep without you haunting my dreams every night."

Logic and duty and the inevitable *fucking consequences* should have demanded that she back away from this. Shut it down before it became a larger problem than it was. Yet the only thought in Ahnna's head was that for the first time in what seemed like forever, someone wanted her as she was, and the one who wanted her was the man she desired more than life itself.

She caught hold of the front of his coat, pulling him closer even as a thousand warnings screamed *Do not do this.* "Then I don't want to change."

It was as though her words cut the last fibers of his self-control, for in the next moment, his lips were on hers, kissing her like he'd starved for weeks and now sat before a feast. Hard enough to bruise, but instead of snapping sense into her head, the bite of pain opened a well of desire within her that had no bottom.

Ahnna slipped her arms around his neck, burying her fingers in his hair so that she could pull him closer. So that every inch of her was pressed against his body, her curves against hard muscle. He groaned, then thrust his tongue into her mouth, the feel of him making her back arch. Making her claw at the buttons of their coats, the need to feel his skin against her own like the need for breath when one is dangerously far beneath the surface.

He obliged, removing his hands from her ass long enough to tear off the garment and cast it aside, his shirt following. The beams of light filtered through the opening above, illuminating his naked torso, the sight of him nearly bringing Ahnna to her knees. Every inch of him was hard muscle, a tattoo she hadn't realized he bore inked across one shoulder, and a long pale scar running the length of his ribs. Deprived of the civility of clothing, he seemed large, her body petite by comparison as he dragged her against him, his mouth claiming hers again.

She ran her fingers over his skin, exploring every hard curve, the heat of him sinking into her fingers. A whimper stole from her lips as he moved from her mouth to her jaw, biting at her throat. The lobe of her ear. Each press of teeth sent a jolt of need surging up from her core.

"I want to see you," he growled between kisses, his hands unfastening her belt. "I want to suck your perfect breasts until you're wet for me and then fuck you until my name is the only word you remember."

"It already is," she gasped, every part of her relishing the departure of the mask he always wore, the man beneath having finally cast it aside. This was who he really was, and *oh God*, did she want him.

James caught hold of her blouse and drew it over her head. A snarl of annoyance passed his lips as his eyes fixed on the silk camisole beneath, and with one jerk, he tore it down the front, baring her breasts. Her nipples peaked as the cool air hit them, the ruined garment slipping down her arms to fall at her feet.

"So goddamned beautiful," he whispered, sliding his palm up her torso, his fingers closing around her throat to gently lean her back, the sunlight illuminating her breasts. She was at his mercy, yet instead of fear, her body thrummed with feral power.

"Kiss me," she said. "Now."

His body shook with dark laughter, then he wrapped an arm around her and lifted. She instinctively wrapped her legs around his waist even as his hand abandoned her throat for her hair. Pulled its length so that her spine bowed backward to expose her breasts to his mouth.

A gasp of pleasure tore from her lips as he sucked her left nipple into his mouth, and Ahnna rocked her hips against him, the buckle of his belt rubbing her clit in a way that turned her body to liquid fire. In a way that made her want to rip his belt off and unleash the thick cock she could feel beneath it. To sink herself down upon it inch by merciless inch, because that was the only way her desire would be sated.

He moved to her other breast, his teeth scraping over her nipple. The jolt of pleasure made her sob. Made her plead, because pressure was building in her core, and she needed release. Needed him.

"Not yet, Princess," he whispered, lowering her slightly so that it was his cock she pressed against, his grip on her implacable as he worked her against him, his breath growing ragged. "I want you wet and ready."

"I am," she gasped, her body shuddering as he bit at her nipple. "Oh God, I need you!"

"Show me."

Dropping to his knees, he lowered her to the ground. Pulled off one of her boots and then the other before his fingers caught hold of the waist of her skirt, tugging it slowly downward, her undergarments with them. Tossing them aside, he gripped her behind each knee, his hands like fire against her skin as he kissed the bruises on them, then parted her legs.

The beam of sunlight had grown brighter as the clouds had cleared, and it fell across her body, exposing her in a way she'd never been exposed before. Yet instead of feeling self-conscious, Ahnna parted her thighs wider, eyes on James's face as he looked down at her.

"So fucking perfect," he whispered, trailing his finger down her belly, then parting her sex with a gentle stroke that made her back arch. "Every part of you is perfect, Ahnna."

The way he said her name made Ahnna shiver, but then his finger slipped inside of her, and her eyes rolled back in her head at the pleasure of it.

"Not wet enough," he murmured, sliding a second finger into her and stroking her core. "Ahnna, look at me."

His eyes were shadowed, but she met them as he added a third finger, working her body in slow strokes that drove her to madness.

"For once, Princess, I want you to do what I tell you," he said. "I want you to listen. Will you listen?"

His thumb rubbed over her clit, and Ahnna gasped out, "Yes."

"I want you to come for me." He bent over her, kissing her once. "I want to watch you come with my fingers in you."

She nodded, incapable of words as his thumb rubbed in slow circles around her clit, her body rising to climax on his words alone. Sitting back, he toyed with her, eyes drinking her in as he unbuckled his belt with his free hand, pulling free his cock. It was as big as the rest of him, and he ran his hand over it as he fucked her with his fingers. "I want you in me," she pleaded.

He shook his head, expression dark and merciless as he stroked her faster. Ahnna writhed beneath him, her body strung taut as she stood at the very edge of release.

Then her climax crested.

She sobbed his name as pleasure rolled over her, her body clenching around his fingers. Wave after wave, until she collapsed backward, her body feeling boneless and spent.

Until her eyes met his.

James gripped her knees, the fingers of his right hand glistening in the sunlight as he lowered his head, tongue sliding into her. Tasting her. Lifting his face, he murmured, "Good girl, Princess," then sucked her clit into his mouth.

It should have been too much, her body already spent. Maybe it was too much, yet that somehow was exactly what she wanted. Ahnna buried her fingers in his hair, holding him against her as he consumed her, barely feeling the rocks and debris digging into her back. "I want you in me," she begged. "Please, James."

He growled against her, rearing up, shoulders illuminated by the sun. "You want this?"

"Yes," she gasped, reaching for him. Needing the feel of him against her. "I want this."

Taking hold of his cock, he pressed it against her, and Ahnna moaned as he eased inside her, the feel of him making her shake.

She wrapped her legs around him as he leaned over her, pulling him deeper, his groan turning her body liquid as he pulled back and thrust again, harder this time. Then again and again, the tide of a second climax rising in her body. "Harder," she whispered, desperate to have all of him. "Make me yours."

James froze, and Ahnna realized in an instant that her words had been a mistake. Had snapped him back to the harsh reality of what they were to each other.

And what they were not.

He pulled out of her. Back from her. And the expression on his face as he said, "But you're not mine. And never will be," shattered Ahnna's heart.

"James . . ." She reached a hand for him, but he jerked away. Picked up a rock and threw it against the cellar wall as he screamed, "Fuck!"

Ahnna sat up, pulling her knees to her chest as she watched him pace back and forth across the small space, trousers pulled up but his still-hard cock straining against the fabric.

"I've lost my mind," he muttered. "Lost my fucking mind to have done this."

"It's fine," she said, despite knowing that it was very much not fine. "No one—"

"It's not fine," he shouted. "It was a mistake!"

Ahnna flinched, squeezing her legs tighter to her chest, his words a knife to her heart because she knew they were true.

"I can't make mistakes, Ahnna." He was still pacing, for all the world like a wolf caged against its will. "I'm the king's half-

Cardiffian bastard who is reviled by the queen. It is only my father's goodwill and that of my siblings that keep me from being
treated like Lestara. I cannot make mistakes. I cannot be anything
less than perfect, or I will lose everything."

She knew how that felt, knew the need to hold oneself to a
higher standard than everyone else lest everything fall to pieces,
and it explained so much about him. Explained his rigid self-
control and his need to follow the rules, to do everything by the
book.

Her lips parted, but before she could speak, James said, "You
asked me before if it bothered me, how my sister and the others
treat Lestara." He stopped pacing, pressing his hands to his face
for a heartbeat and then dropping them to look at her. "I lied to
you when I answered. I hate it. Not how they treat her, specifically, for Lestara earned her lot, but how Harendellians treat people from Cardiff. How Harendell's laws allow civilians to murder
Cardiffians without consequence just because of their beliefs."
His voice shook. "Do you know how many times I've seen innocent Cardiffians burned alive and had to stand there and do
nothing?"

She bit her lip, because knowing the laws allowed such things
and seeing it with one's own eyes were very different things.

James wasn't finished, though, emotion having overwhelmed
his usual taciturnity. "And I don't understand why. Have never
been able to understand it." He began pacing again. "My father
used to send me to Cardiff for weeks at a time when I was a boy to
spend time with my uncles. To learn their ways out of respect for
my mother, and there's not a goddamned thing about astromancy
that anyone in Harendell has reason to fear. Stories in the stars?
Fortune-telling? Potions that are nothing more than herbs and
muttered words? It's nothing to fear, yet I've had to keep those vis-

its a secret all my life lest anyone question my belief in the true faith."

James spent time in Cardiff? Not only knew his mother's family, but had lived with them for weeks at a time? Had learned about *astromancy*? A thousand questions rose to her lips, but she bit down on them lest her voice silence his. Lest she lose this one chance to learn more about the enigma that was James.

"I couldn't live with doing nothing, so I . . . I've been working to change the laws. To at least give people a fair trial in a court to spare them vigilante justice for a crime they may not have committed. But for me to have any hope of making Harendell safe for Cardiffians, I need to keep my position in my father's court. And in my brother's."

She'd thought the worst he risked was a slap on the wrist. Maybe being sent back to the Lowlands to fight. Had been so certain that the stakes were high only for her. How incredibly wrong she'd been, and her selfishness made her feel sick. "I'm sorry."

James stopped in his tracks, eyes snapping to her. Then he was on his knees before her, pulling Ahnna into his lap. "Don't," he said. "Don't be sorry. You have no reason to be. This is . . . this is my fault. I took advantage of you."

Her face was buried in his throat, and she laughed only because the alternative was to cry. "James, I'm six feet of solid muscle and have been killing grown men in battle since before my first kiss. No one takes advantage of me. And if you are worried that I was a maid, you can go ahead and banish that thought. I'm fine."

Silence stretched, the only sound the steady thud of his heart, until James said, "Then why are you crying, Ahnna?"

Ahnna twitched, only then realizing that tears were running down her cheeks, her breath catching with little hiccups, her heart aching worse than any wound she'd ever suffered. "Because I don't want to marry William. I don't want to be queen of Harendell. I . . ." She trailed off, not willing to admit that what she really wanted was to ride away from all of it with him at her side. To make a life away from politics and obligations where no one would pull them apart. No one would judge them. And part of her wanted to break down entirely because she finally understood why her brother had wanted to run away with Lara. Why he'd been willing to abandon everything for her.

Finally understood the price he and Lara had paid to remain in Ithicana and do their duty.

"What is the reason you won't return to Ithicana?" James asked, catching hold of her chin and lifting her face so that she was forced to look at him. "The real reason."

She drew in a deep breath, then asked, "Can I trust you?"

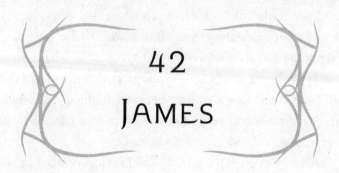

42

JAMES

He should have said no.

Because it would have been better not to know.

Instead, James said, "I swear it."

Sitting upright in his lap, Ahnna drew in a ragged breath. "Ithicana's coffers are empty."

He didn't answer, because he'd already gathered as much, and while Virginia hadn't gotten the story entirely right, his sister had been goddamned close.

"I know that other nations believe Ithicana is rich beyond sin," she said. "But that's never been even close to the truth. The truth is that to live off the land in the middle of the Tempest Seas requires ceaseless toil. Day in and day out, my people go to war against land and storm to bring home enough to feed their families, so for as long as living memory, the crown has used the bridge's revenue to buy food and supplies from other nations, all of which is dispensed to the people in exchange for years of service. Everyone serves, in some capacity, and in exchange, they are given what they need to live a life worth living."

The weight of her words sank down upon him, but James said nothing.

"When the Maridrinians invaded, they either took what they found back to Vencia or destroyed it," Ahnna continued. "Homes reduced to rubble, vegetable plots sowed with salt, and fishing boats put to the torch. And that doesn't begin to touch upon the harm done to the people. So many were hurt in ways one can never recover from, and they no longer have the means to toil day after day. So the bridge must provide."

He didn't want to hear this, but James forced himself to listen.

"Aren has drained the coffers dry," she said softly. "Sold off nearly everything of value, including all of Lara's jewelry except what she was wearing and what she sent with me. Sarhina is in no position to help, because Maridrina's situation is even worse, and Zarrah is struggling to support them, for many Valcottans refuse to let old animosities go. But Harendell . . . Harendell is rich and strong and our oldest ally. The only nation capable of moving enough trade through the bridge to keep our people alive while they rebuild."

It hurt to breathe.

James had known his and Ahnna's goals were at odds, that Ithicana needed Harendell's gold. What he hadn't known was that her people risked starvation if they didn't get it.

"Yet despite how badly Ithicana needs me here, Aren came to Verwyrd to try to make me come home when he heard about the wraithroot. That's what we were arguing about."

James winced, realizing how badly he'd misread the king's intentions. How badly everyone had misread Aren Kertell's sentiment toward his sister.

She wiped her face with her sleeve. "But I can't go back. Not without your father demanding concessions from Aren that he can't afford to make. So not only must I remain, but I must encourage Harendell to export *more*. To pay *more*. Because if I don't, I'll have failed my people again."

"Again?" he made himself ask, needing to know the whole truth even though what he'd already heard made him feel sick to his stomach.

Ahnna was crying harder now, her sobs so fierce that she shook against him, instinct demanding that he pull her closer even though he had no right to touch her.

"The success of Silas's attack was my fault," she choked out. "I'm the one to blame."

"No—" James started to argue, but Ahnna cut him off.

"Yes. I suspected Lara from the beginning," she said between sobs. "She wasn't anything like other Maridrinian noblewomen. She was head-to-toe muscle, her knuckles had scars from fighting, and she walked like a predator. Every instinct in me told me that she was dangerous, but I allowed myself to be convinced otherwise. After I almost got her killed, Aren would barely speak to me. I was so worried I'd turned him against me that I held my tongue and gave her my support when I should have stood my ground. My duty was to my people, and if I'd only trusted my instincts and dug deeper, we might have stopped the invasion. Instead, I only thought of myself."

She was on the verge of hyperventilating, cheeks ghastly pale in the sunlight.

"When the end of the calm season is looming, Aren always sends me an invitation to Midwatch. We always celebrate it together. But he didn't send for me. I was so upset that the night of the celebration, I got blindingly drunk. So drunk I passed out on the floor of my room at Southwatch. I have no idea how long the alarm bells sounded before they woke me, still so drunk I could barely stand." She reached up to touch the scar on her face. "I found out later that in my drunkenness, I'd told my garrison not to bother with guard duty. That we were married to Maridrina, so we needed to get fully in bed with them. And they listened."

Shit.

"The attack came from inside the bridge itself, so none of Southwatch's defenses would have saved us," she continued. "But if there'd been guards on duty, we wouldn't have been caught unaware. If I hadn't ordered all those casks of wine opened, my soldiers would have been sober enough to fight. Maybe, just maybe, if I hadn't been only thinking of my hurt feelings, we would have held Southwatch and had a chance against Maridrina. I should have been the one to save my kingdom. Instead, I was the one who damned it."

"The Maridrinians struck from multiple locations, with information you had no way to know they had," he said, hating that she blamed herself for something that was not her fault. Harendell's spies in Maridrina had learned a great deal about the plans after the fact. Ithicana had no chance. "Even if you'd posted double your usual guards, you might not have been able to stop them."

Ahnna had stopped crying, her hazel eyes staring blindly into the dark corner of the cellar. "Everyone believes I hate Lara. That I blame her. But the truth is, when I look at her, all I see is my failure. And the hate I feel is for myself."

He could see the truth in her eyes, the grief of guilt, and it cut out his heart because she was not to blame.

"Hate Silas," he said. "And Katarina, for aiding him. It's not fair for you to carry the blame for the actions of so many people."

"I neither need nor want absolution." She leaned into him, her skin cold against his chest. "Only for you to understand why I can't be the one to break the treaty by going back to Ithicana."

"I understand." Understood all too well.

"It might all be for nothing, anyway," she said. "Your people are accusing Ithicana of extorting unfair tolls while my brother sits on a throne of gold, and those rumors can't be countered without admitting just how weak we are and how badly we need Harendell's wealth. Aren thinks I'm making it worse. Maybe I am."

"Those are old rumors that predate your arrival," James muttered, though he'd noticed they were once again on the rise. An edge of unjust bitterness toward Ithicana that he'd attributed to his uncle and his agents trying to push merchants to look elsewhere for trade. "You didn't cause them."

Picking up his coat, he draped it over her icy body, knowing he should dress but unwilling to pull away from her right after she'd unveiled her broken heart.

The broken heart you're about to grind your heel down upon, his conscience whispered. There was no arguing with it, for if his plan came to fruition, all the trade that Ithicana so desperately needed would go north to Cardiff. It was because of *him* that she'd fail in her goal, and that truth settled into his soul like poison. But if he backed away from his ambitions and the treaty between his father and uncle was never signed, how many more Cardiffians would burn as a result?

James didn't know what he was going to do. Did not see a path through that didn't cause harm.

What he did know was that in being intimate with Ahnna, he'd made everything a hundred times worse. That in listening to her confess, he'd ensured that the moment she understood he was her enemy, knowing she'd let him have her would be like poison to her soul. He couldn't undo what had been done, but it could not happen again. It needed to end now.

"We need to get dressed," he said quietly. "They'll be searching for us."

Ahnna didn't answer, but she mechanically reached for her clothing. James averted his gaze, though in truth, fifty years from now, he'd still close his eyes and see the naked lines and curves of her body. Still hear the whisper of her breath and feel her hands on his skin. It might end now.

But she'd haunt his dreams forever.

Tucking in his shirt and buckling his belt, James eyed the setting sun, knowing it would get colder as night fell.

"I'll light a fire," he said, picking up pieces of fallen wood. "It will help them find us. There's a flint in my coat pocket."

Again, Ahnna didn't answer, and when he turned around, it was to find her dressed but staring at the camisole he'd torn off her like an animal. More flickers of what he'd done filled his mind, and James cursed himself for treating her as he had. For allowing his baser instincts to take control.

Then she abruptly knelt before the wood, shoving the silk beneath it and extracting his flint and her knife. "Stinks when it burns," she said, "but it lights more easily than damp wood."

With far more proficiency than he would have shown, Ahnna lit the fire, nurturing it to a steady glow. She moved to hand him his coat, but he shook his head. "Keep it. I'm used to the cold."

They sat next to the small blaze as night fell, the air growing cooler. The wolves that hunted the Ranges howled, his ears picking up the noise of them passing, lured by what he had no doubt was a large number of dead cattle.

Then Ahnna said, "I know this can't happen again, but—" She drew in a breath. "—but I don't want to lose you because we let it happen once."

Being near her would be akin to an addict sitting next to a full opium pipe, and James knew it. The smart choice would be for him to leave Verwyrd until the treaty was signed and the truth came out. But as Ahnna's icy fingers locked on his, James said, "I'm not going anywhere."

43

AHNNA

SHE MUST HAVE DOZED OFF, BECAUSE AHNNA WOKE WITH HER head resting on James's shoulder.

"Did you hear something?" she asked, fear filling her that the Amaridians had found them. "I swore I heard something."

"There are wolves out there." James let go of her hand, rising to his feet. "More than a few cattle will have been lost to the stampede or the storm, and they're gorging on the meat."

She didn't have time to think about the carnage because she heard it again. "There!"

"James!" a voice cried out. Then another shouted, "Ahnna!"

"It's William and Georgie."

Ahnna had only a heartbeat to grieve the end of a moment her heart had half wished would last forever before James shouted, "We're here! Will! Georgie!"

"I hear them!"

Boots thudded against the ground, then Georgie's face was above them, peering down. His eyes skipped from her face to

James's, and Ahnna could feel Georgie's displeasure that they were together. Yet all he said was, "Thank God we found you! Are you hurt?"

"We're fine," Ahnna said. "Have you found the horses?"

"Maven came galloping into Verwyrd with your gelding on her heels," William said from over Georgie's shoulder. "We knew from her injury that something had gone wrong. We sent out a search party and crossed paths with Georgie, who told us about the ambush."

"My men?" James asked, and Georgie shook his head. "Dead. And it's a small miracle you aren't as well. Both of you." His tone was frosty.

William didn't seem to notice Georgie's displeasure, for all he said was, "All that's left of the Amaridians is meat, though it's impossible to tell whether that's because of you, the herd, or the storm. Some of the herd was lost, and it looks like a battlefield out here with the wolves feasting. You'll see when we get you out, James. Bloody massacre. Not fit for a lady's eyes, though, so you might wish to close yours, Ahnna."

"I'm sure she can handle it," Georgie muttered. Then he shouted at his men, "Come help with this beam!"

"The last wall is ready to fall," she warned, half wishing that it would fall on Georgie and solve that particular problem. "Take care."

"Don't concern yourself," he said. "We will manage."

James kicked dirt over the fire to smother it while the men outside worked to secure the wall, then clear the debris. It wasn't long until the opening revealed the starry sky and James was lifting her, Georgie pulling her out of the cellar and then helping James.

"My God, Ahnna," William said, gripping her arms. "I

thought I lost you and Jamie both, whether to the Amaridians or to the storm. We've been looking among the dead cattle for hours."

The concern in his voice seemed genuine, but hers was wooden as she said, "I'm fine. We were caught in the storm, but James had the wherewithal to seek cover in the cellar. If not for how the old house collapsed, we'd have walked back to Verwyrd."

"What happened that brought you onto the Ranges?" William demanded.

"I was outnumbered," James answered. "I hoped to lose them in the storm."

"Not. You." The words came from between William's teeth. "*Her.*"

"I knew something had happened," Ahnna replied, understanding how her reaction had looked, especially to Georgie, who was glaring at her. "I was already on horseback, and my horse is fast. I meant to catch them and even the odds."

"Not that fast," William snapped. "Else he'd still be on the tracks. It's only luck the Amaridians didn't ambush you."

"He's right," James said. "You shouldn't have taken the risk. But if you hadn't, I'd be dead, so you have my gratitude for your actions even as I pray you'll never have cause to undertake something similar in the future."

"She won't." William leveled a finger at her. "Because you will not leave Verwyrd again, am I understood?"

Ahnna stiffened, every part of her rebelling at such a restriction on her freedom, but then William gave his head a shake. "You are too precious to risk, Ahnna. Promise me you'll not endanger yourself again."

Her anger deflated, but she still choked on the words. "I promise."

"Good." He went to his horse, mounting and then holding out a hand. "Come along, then."

"Georgie and I will hang back," James said as she mounted. "See if we can get a better idea of the losses we took."

William gave his brother a measured look, then shrugged. "Don't get eaten by wolves."

He heeled his horse into a trot, soldiers forming up around them as they headed toward Verwyrd.

Don't look back, Ahnna told herself. *You cannot look back.*

But her heart said otherwise, and she glanced over her shoulder.

There was only darkness.

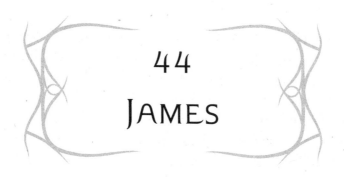

44

JAMES

"YOU ALL RIGHT?" GEORGIE ASKED AS THEY WATCHED THE GROUP disappear into the darkness.

"Fine." One of the greater lies he'd ever told, because James was most certainly not *fine*.

"You two were trapped alone together for a long time," Georgie said softly. "Anything I should know?"

"No."

"I don't believe you."

James slowly turned to face him. "We've been friends a long time, George. But there are still lines, and you've stepped across this one."

Though they stood in total darkness, the only light to be seen held by the soldiers waiting well out of earshot, James could feel George's scrutiny. Then his friend said, "Why are the Amaridians trying so hard to kill you?"

James stiffened.

"Four times, James. Four times, Katarina has tried and failed to have you killed. Why? Because it's not because of Carlo's missing *fucking testicle.*"

Ahnna was far from the only one he was lying to. Georgie had been his closest friend almost his entire life, yet the other man knew nothing about his weeks-long stays in Cardiff. Nothing about James's mother's royal blood. Nothing about how James had spent his entire adult life as the liaison between his father and his uncle, trying to mend a conflict of ideology that was core to Harendellian belief.

Decades of lies.

He was so goddamned tired of it, so he said, "I can't tell you."

Georgie blew out an angry breath. "Fine. Keep your secrets, but I'm through keeping mine. The night the Ithicanians were in Verwyrd, I had them followed."

Though he could feel the rift widening between them, James had no interest in hearing Georgie berate him further about Ahnna, so he interrupted. "Later, Georgie. What you have to say can keep. I need to speak to my father."

"I don't disagree," Georgie said. "I'll escort you. It will give us time to talk about—"

"I'll ride to Whitewood Hall alone. Give me your horse."

"Jamie, the Amaridians are trying to kill you in earnest," Georgie snapped. "This is no time for you to be galloping about the countryside."

"Perhaps not, but I'll ride faster alone." Not waiting for an answer, James strode to where the guards held the reins of George's horse. Taking them, he said to his friend, "One day I'll be able to tell you everything, Georgie. And I hope you'll forgive me for keeping it from you." Then he swung onto the horse's back.

"Damn it, Jamie!" George shouted. "There's something I need to tell you about Ahnna!"

But James wasn't interested in his friend's admonitions that he needed to keep his distance from Ahnna, so before Georgie could say more, he dug in his heels and galloped north.

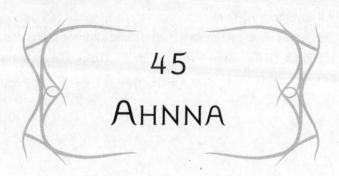

45
AHNNA

EXHAUSTION TOOK AHNNA IMMEDIATELY TO BED, THOUGH IT was not her body that was spent but her mind.

And her heart.

What had she done?

Aren was right to fear that she was making things worse, because what else could be said about what she'd done with James?

The wrong prince.

The wrong brother.

Yet in the moment, no part of it had felt wrong. Though she willed herself to sleep, it was impossible when her mind was filled with the feel of his lips on hers, his tongue in her mouth. His hands on her body, and the weight of him as he'd driven himself into her. The remembered sensation turned her skin hot and body liquid, because though it should never have begun, it had ended too soon.

Seeing the faint glow of dawn around the curtains, Ahnna rolled facedown on the pillow, hunting for a solution to her predicament. Racking her brain for a path forward that didn't have consequences she didn't wish to pay. Her warning to Ithicana would be on its way, and she knew Lara would see it for what it was. Would understand that whatever conversation Aren was having with Katarina of Amarid was no secret, and Ithicana would prepare accordingly.

But what terrified Ahnna most was that she didn't know what Ithicana was preparing for. Aren had said that he believed Harendell was turning on them. She'd thought that had meant from the standpoint of business and trade, a severing of ties. But what if it was something worse?

War?

The word echoed through her thoughts, except it made no sense. Why would Harendell declare war on them? What could possibly drive Edward to take such an action?

It felt as though a box of wooden puzzle pieces had been dumped before her, but one piece was missing to make them all fit together.

The Harendellians were master schemers, and she was deeply out of her depth. Her skill was in combat. In leading soldiers. In controlling a battlefield. Not trying to understand the plots and ambitions of dozens of nobles who seemed to be working for and against one another interchangeably, all trying to achieve different goals.

But what Ahnna did know was that if she believed Ithicana was in danger of attack, she'd be doing everything in her power to solidify defenses and to ensure that Ithicana's soldiers had what they needed to fight. That the people had everything they needed to live through a northern blockade, given that Maridrina and Valcotta were in no position to help.

And God help her, it made too much sense that her brother was turning to Amarid, despite all that Katarina had done, to do just that.

The door clicked, and Hazel entered. Out of the corner of her eye, Ahnna watched the maid walk to the window and open the drapes, light streaming in. She turned to the bed and said, "You've been summoned, my lady."

"By whom?"

"I don't know." Hazel walked to the wardrobe. "Only that you are to come to the throne room immediately."

DRESSED IN A SIMPLE BLUE gown with her hair woven into a tight braid, Ahnna walked through the halls of the Sky Palace until she reached the throne room. She'd never had reason to go inside before, but she regretted not exploring it as her eyes landed on the soldiers standing to either side of the entrance.

The doors were opened, and she stepped inside, instantly blinded by the beam of dawn sunlight streaming in through the windows at the far end.

Thud.

Twitching, Ahnna glanced at the closed oak doors behind her, but her attention snapped forward again as Edward said, "I understand you had an encounter with one of Harendell's storms."

She dropped into a curtsy. "Your Grace! I wasn't aware you'd returned to Verwyrd."

"Ahnna . . ." His tone was chiding. "What have I said about titles?"

A laugh tore from her lips, wild and slightly panicked, and she bit down on it. "Apologies . . . Eddie, what are you doing in Verwyrd?"

Boots thudded against marble, and he approached, face hidden in shadow as he was backlit by so much brightness. "To see you, as the case may be."

He caught hold of her elbow and tugged her back the way he'd come. "Tonight is the night, Ahnna. I've just dispatched invitations to everyone within riding distance to attend a banquet where I intend to declare my intentions. Make things official, as they say. I wanted to tell you myself before the big event; I aim to make you queen, Ahnna. A queen who will go down in Harendell's history books, mark my words."

Her chest hitched, but Edward led her onto the dais, where a monstrous throne of spiraling metal sat.

The Twisted Throne.

"It holds more meaning than it did this time yesterday, doesn't it?" Edward asked. "Now that you've met the storms. They have a habit of changing things. Setting one off in a different direction than intended. Tonight will be a similar such storm. Now, sit."

Ahnna sucked in a breath, twisting to look at him. "I can't sit on this throne. Only the king can sit on this throne."

"I'm the king and I give you permission."

She didn't move. "Your Grace . . ."

Edward sighed. "It's just the two of us here, Ahnna."

"Eddie, it's not right for me to sit on Harendell's throne."

"There has never been anything more right." He gestured to the silvered metal, light glinting off the twists and spirals. "I want to see you on it."

Ahnna clenched her teeth, her instincts screaming, but she didn't dare disobey. Moving in front of the throne, she adjusted her skirts and sat. Cold seeped through the silk and into her flesh, the throne hard and unyielding. Every part of her wanted to leap to her feet, but then Edward retrieved a crown and approached, setting it on her head.

Alexandra's crown.

The crown of the queen of Harendell.

Tension sang through her body, partially because if anyone saw her wearing the queen's crown, it would be a disaster. But mostly because it felt as though if she wore it in truth, every goddamned struggle she faced would cease to exist, for the power of Harendell's throne would be hers to wield. "Eddie, I . . ."

But the look on his face froze her tongue, and Ahnna fell silent.

"You remind me so much of her," he finally said. "Seeing you on this throne makes me think of what might have been if the stars had been in our favor."

Ahnna frowned, unease filling her because she was nothing like Alexandra. But then she understood. "You mean Siobhan? James's mother."

"Yes." His response sounded strained, as though hearing her name caused him physical pain. "Your commitment to Ithicana reminds me of her. The willingness to do whatever it takes for the sake of your people."

She held her breath, no part of her understanding what was going on here.

"Siobhan was the love of my life," he said gently. "There was nothing I wouldn't have done for her, no lengths I wouldn't have gone to. I think, Ahnna, you've seen love like that more than once. Seen the consequences of a man loving a woman so much he forsakes all else."

Ahnna swallowed hard, but then gave a tight nod, for she knew the toll of that sort of love all too well.

"There were times I wondered if higher powers took Siobhan from me as punishment for making her first in my heart. If God believed taking her away from me would correct my course. Would make me walk a different path." His head tilted. "If that was the case, he erred, for her death only ensured that I'd dedicate my life to achieving everything that mattered to her."

Ahnna's breath was coming rapidly, too rapidly, because she had no idea what was happening. Why he was telling her this. "Do you know who killed her?"

He gave a slow nod. "And I intend to destroy her and everything she holds dear."

Did he mean Alexandra? Someone else? "Who?"

"An individual who feared Siobhan's dream and stood to lose a great deal if it were achieved." Reaching out, Edward removed the crown and set it back on its cushion. Then he took her hand and pulled Ahnna to her feet. "She was right to."

He had to mean Alexandra. He had to.

A thousand questions rolled through Ahnna's head, not the least of which being what this confession meant for her and Ithicana. Yet the question she found herself asking was not for herself but for James. "If you loved Siobhan so much, why haven't you changed the laws allowing the persecution of astromancy? Why do you allow her people to be burned?"

"Because changing a deep-seated belief in Harendellian people is no simple task, and if I'd tried to force it, there'd have been a revolution against the crown." He hesitated, then added, "The people had to want the change."

"What would make them want to change?" she demanded.

He smiled. "The perfect storm."

It was no answer, but the look in his eyes made her skin crawl because it spoke to layers of designs that he had yet to reveal. "Eddie, I don't understand your intentions. Please speak plainly."

"All will become clear when the time is right." He clasped both sides of her face with his hands. "Tonight we will change the trajectory of Harendell's future, Ahnna. It will be a moment that will go down in the history books."

Letting go of her, Edward started toward the entrance of the throne room, but Ahnna called after him, "Does the queen know your plans?"

He looked over his shoulder and gave her a sad smile. "The queen is already dead."

Shock radiated through Ahnna's core, but before she could ask him what had happened to Alexandra, Edward exited the room.

Alexandra was dead?

Except how was that possible? The whole palace would be in a frenzy.

A sudden certainty struck her. "Oh God," she whispered. "He plans to kill her. Intends to have his revenge for Siobhan."

Ahnna stared at the closed doors, sickness rising in her stomach because she suspected having justice was only part of what Edward intended to achieve tonight. She needed to get answers, because every instinct in her soul screamed that clouds were circling, a storm brewing.

And not just over Harendell.

Ahnna broke into a fast stride across the throne room, only for her toe to strike something, sending it rolling across the marble floor. Frowning, she bent down and picked it up.

It was a bird skull, a small hole drilled in the top of it.

Cardiff.

Ahnna stared at the tiny skull in her palm, unease pooling in her stomach because Cardiffians wore skulls as part of their ceremonial garb. Someone from Cardiff had been in this throne room, and it had been for something important enough to risk wearing the symbols of astromancy.

Changing a deep-seated belief in Harendellian people is no simple task. Edward's voice filled her head.

What would make them want to change?

The perfect storm.

All the pieces fell into place. Edward was, after all this time, making peace with Cardiff.

The revelation came with a stab of pain to her heart because James knew. James goddamned knew what his father was planning, and despite knowing, he'd . . . he'd . . .

The agony of it almost made her vomit, but Ahnna shoved aside the emotion and broke into a run. She needed to get a warning to Aren. Needed him to know that the rug was about to be pulled out from underneath him, because there was no doubt in her mind what sort of perfect storm would make the Harendellians let go of their right to persecute astromancy.

Edward intended for trade to flow north.

But just before she reached the doors, they opened, revealing Georgie and a dozen guards.

"You can make this easy or you can make it difficult, Ahnna," he said. "Either way, you're going back to your rooms."

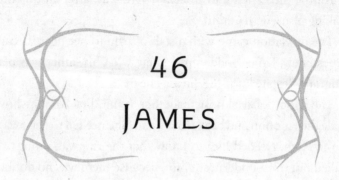

46

JAMES

I T TOOK THE REST OF THE NIGHT TO CROSS THE RANGES, BUT NOW
James was moving at speed up the highway to Whitewood Hall,
his thoughts no clearer than they'd been when he'd set out because none of the pieces quite fit together.

The Amaridians were trying to kill him—that could not be
denied—and James was certain now that it was because Katarina
knew he was at the center of negotiations between Cardiff and
Harendell. United, the two nations would be a force far greater
than Amarid, so it made sense that Katarina would desire to destroy or delay the negotiations from coming to fruition.

And yet the hardhanded tactic was out of character for Amarid's
queen, especially given that it was ill considered.

Assassinating him wouldn't be grounds for an end of the negotiations. If anything, it would only drive his father and uncle together in the united purpose of revenge against Amarid, and
Katarina had to know that. Which meant her motivations had to
be more complicated.

James rubbed at his temple, his head pounding, yet he forced himself to turn his mind to the reason he was galloping in pursuit of his father.

His goal had never ever been to destroy Harendell's relationship with Ithicana, but James had been so focused on setting things right with Cardiff, on stopping the burnings, that he'd been blind to the ramifications of cutting the bridge usage by half or more.

Willfully blind, if he was being honest. Because it had been easy to put Cardiff ahead of Ithicana until he'd met *her*. Ahnna had forced him to see the faces behind the nation he'd callously disregarded, and shame burned in his chest that he'd been so narrow-sighted in his ambitions.

Ahnna's confession of the dire straits of Ithicana made him feel compelled to take a step back. To find a moderate strategy that would see the borders with Cardiff opened without stripping Ithicana of the trade they needed to survive. To find a path forward without consequence.

Except he suspected no such path existed.

A small amount of revenue wouldn't be enough to compel Harendellian merchants to set aside old biases and hatred: It had to be wealth that they couldn't dream of achieving any other way. If the border was opened with no taxes, they'd all take their business north and forsake Ithicana's expensive bridge without a second thought. There was no possibility of a small drip when the floodgate was opened. That had been the crux of his plan all along, and he'd paid little mind to Ithicana.

Until her.

James closed his eyes, his mind filling with Ahnna's face. So wildly fierce and dangerous, yet possessed of a heart made vulnerable by her commitment to her people. Never in his life had a woman consumed him like she did, made him feel the way she did. Yet not only was there no future between them, but Ahnna would hate him when she learned that his life's work had the potential to achieve what Silas's violence had failed to accomplish: the destruction of the Bridge Kingdom.

Beneath him, Georgie's horse snorted, and James's eyes snapped up to see a caravan on the road ahead, royal banners flapping in the wind. Relief flooded him, because by some stroke of fortune, his father was already returning to Verwyrd.

Digging in his heels, he urged the exhausted horse for speed, the soldiers parting ranks as he was recognized, the royal carriage drawing to a halt. Dismounting next to it, he handed off his reins and opened the door. "Father—"

He broke off, because his father wasn't in the carriage, only Alexandra. She set the knitting needles she held down on her lap. "James. This is a surprise."

"Your Grace." He inclined his head. "Apologies for the intrusion. I have urgent need to speak with the king."

"Edward has ridden ahead to Verwyrd," she said. To his shock, she added, "Travel with me, James. It has been an age since we talked, you and I."

His skin crawled with trepidation, because no good ever came from conversations with Alexandra. Yet there was no declining the request of the queen, so he climbed inside. The carriage rocked from side to side as it began moving again.

"Tell me of this urgent need you have of Edward," she said, picking up her knitting, the needles making little clicking noises as she worked. "You look as though you've been dragged through a pasture by your own horse, so I expect it is nothing good."

"Caught in a storm on the Ranges," he said. "A significant number of cattle were lost."

"You didn't gallop through the night to tell Edward about dead cows," Alexandra said, eyes not moving from her work. "Try again."

James didn't answer.

The trouble with lying to Alexandra was that she always knew more than she reasonably should, and the consequences of being caught in a lie by her were unfailingly painful. "It's for my father's ears, Your Grace."

She made a soft humming noise, then began another row of stitches, fingers moving swiftly. "I don't suppose this has anything to do with Ahnna Kertell?"

The muscles in his jaw clenched, because of course she knew. Alexandra always knew.

"She's why Edward returned to Verwyrd," Alexandra said. "We have come to believe that there is a great deal of conflict between the Kertell twins, and that perhaps Ahnna does not have the influence over Aren that we had hoped."

"Does this information come via Virginia?" James asked flatly.

"It comes from many places. The Ithicanians are not as secretive as they once were, and our spies posing as merchants have learned of the bad blood between Ahnna and Lara, which has caused a rift between Ahnna and her brother. He sides with his wife in all things, and it has caused tremendous conflict. The rumors sway two directions: The first being that Aren sent Ahnna to us to get rid of her and the second that Ahnna abandoned Ithicana because she could not stand to watch her brother simper to the Maridrinian woman who nearly destroyed Ithicana. Edward seems inclined to believe the latter, for he is convinced that Ahnna is the people's princess."

"She is the people's princess," James hedged. "But the conflict between her and Aren has been overstated. Likewise the extent of her animosity toward Lara."

Alexandra tilted her head. "She told you this?"

"Yes." To give more detail felt like he'd be betraying Ahnna's confidence.

"Interesting." Alexandra pursed her lips. "And yet it is in direct conflict with every other source, including her own cousin Taryn, and Lara's sister Bronwyn. *Hate*, I believe, is the word most often used to describe Ahnna's sentiment toward her sister-in-law. Ahnna holds Lara entirely to blame for the hurt inflicted upon Ithicana."

"That they believe so doesn't make it the truth."

"That Ahnna told you otherwise doesn't make it the truth." Alexandra gave him a small smile. "That's the game, isn't it, James? To puzzle through reams of gossip and speculation, all of which seems in direct contradiction, to find the truth. And once one has it, to know what to do with it."

"I know that Ahnna harbors no ill will toward her brother," he countered. "Nor he to her."

"He did not even grace her with a goodbye when she departed Northwatch," Alexandra said, starting yet another row of stitches. "Sent her with a laughable escort, put gross restrictions on her spending, and has sent no communication beyond an announcement of his daughter's birth. Would you treat Virginia so, Jamie?" Not giving him a chance to answer, she added, "Unless it is an act, it seems that Aren wants nothing to do with his sister. If it is not an act, I worry of what greater plans might be afoot."

Why would Aren pretend to quarrel with his sister? James silently wondered even as he asked aloud, "What does my father intend to do?"

"He is quite taken with Ahnna, so he's furious at how he perceives Aren has treated her. He was fit to be tied when he rode out, if I am being honest. Cursing and carrying on." Alexandra sighed. "And you know how Edward reacts when he's angry. Digs in his heels. All the worse when he's in his cups. He did not share his precise plans before he went galloping out the gates of Whitewood Hall, but I anticipate we'll discover them when we arrive in Verwyrd."

Trepidation filled James's chest, because if his father's ambivalence toward Aren had turned to dislike, there would be no chance that he'd risk the negotiations with Cardiff to protect Aren's interests. Yet all he said was, "I've never known you to be content with waiting for information, Your Grace. What do you predict he will do?"

"I expect that we'll see a wedding very soon. Edward is the most powerful man in the known world, James, and he will have his way."

It hurt to breathe, because his mind kept trying to forget that it was William whom Ahnna would marry. "You are content with that? For William to marry Ahnna even if she brings no power over Ithicana's ruler?"

Alexandra did not answer. And experience had taught James not to press.

Silence stretched. For minutes. Then an hour, James's stomach twisting into tighter and tighter knots with each passing mile they drew closer to Verwyrd.

As the carriage rolled into the gate town, wheels rattling over cobbles, Alexandra's hands finally stilled. "I know you and I have not been friends, Jamie. That for all we share the name of Ashford, we are not family. But I don't think you have any doubt in your heart that everything I do is for the benefit of William and Virginia."

"Of that I have no doubt." His mouth was dry, his voice hoarse.

"William needs a strong woman as his queen," she said. "And while Ahnna is not the sort of woman I would choose for him, I do think she is the key to the bridge. She's far more valuable than anyone gives her credit for."

"How so?"

Alexandra gave a small shrug, leaning against the window, eyes fixed on the Sky Palace. "That, James, is a question you need to pose to your father."

47

AHNNA

AHNNA PACED THE CONFINES OF HER ROOMS, HANDS BALLED into fists as she revisited everything that had happened, her imagination running wild over what Edward intended to do tonight.

And what price Ithicana would pay.

All this time, she'd seen the king as her only true ally in this nation. The one who wanted her presence the most, who wanted her to marry William, who wanted her to be queen of Harendell one day. She'd been taken in by his charm and kindness, and with all that she'd heard about Alexandra, it had been easy to see the queen as the one she needed to fear. Too swiftly forgetting that Edward had ruled Harendell for longer than she'd been alive, which meant his skill at politics and manipulation were rivaled by no one.

But worst of all, even now knowing that she was but a pawn on his game board, was that she still had no idea how Edward intended to play her.

Every part of that performance in the throne room indicated that he still intended to make her queen, but that meant nothing at all if he also intended to rip up the Fifteen-Year Treaty and begin trading north. She'd be trapped as William's bride, as powerless as Aren had predicted she'd be, and likely used against her brother as leverage. Rather than an asset, she'd be the most extreme form of liability. Yet if she ran now, she'd only give Edward yet more leverage to use in his intent to turn his back on the alliance with Ithicana.

Had he always intended to turn on Aren? Or had George revealed his belief that Aren was negotiating with Katarina, and this was a reaction against what he perceived as a betrayal?

George had refused to answer any of her questions as she'd been escorted back to her rooms. Refused to say anything at all other than to inform her she'd be confined until the king ordered otherwise. Which likely meant confined until whenever Edward's plans for announcing trade with Cardiff came to fruition and Ahnna could do no more damage. George had made no comment on her speculations, seemingly unmoved by the idea that Edward would open the border with Cardiff. When she'd tried to push the issue, he'd shut the door in her face. Whether it was because he already knew, didn't care, or didn't believe her, Ahnna didn't know. But she'd been trapped alone ever since.

There was no way to escape. The walls were stone, the door solid oak, and the drop outside her window a thousand-foot plunge to the city below.

And the only warning Aren would have that all of this was coming was the cryptic message she'd sent with that cursed necklace. If it made it to Ithicana at all.

Why did I stay?

There were layers of logical reasons, but Ahnna forced herself to set aside those justifications for the selfish motivation beneath all of them.

James.

She'd been trying not to think of his involvement. Trying not to allow her heart to drown in the depths of painful certainty that all this time, he'd been conspiring against Ithicana. That he'd . . .

"*Stop,*" she ordered herself. "Your hurt feelings are not the pressing concern."

But all the admonitions in the world couldn't silence her grief, because she'd trusted James in a way she hadn't trusted anyone in so very long. Perhaps ever. To be rejected was a familiar pain, but to learn that her trust had been misplaced hurt the worst of all.

The door that led to what had once been Taryn's rooms abruptly opened, and Hazel stepped inside carrying a tray of food. "My lady?"

In long strides, Ahnna crossed the distance to her. "Hazel, what is going on?"

"There is to be a ball tonight," her maid told her, setting the tray on the table. "Announcements went out late this morning, and the whole palace is in turmoil to prepare, as are the nobles who were invited."

"A ball with what purpose?"

"No one knows," Hazel said. "Only that anyone who could make the journey in time was ordered to be here. The queen has only just returned."

Not dead, then. But there was no doubt in Ahnna's mind that part of Edward's plans for tonight involved exposing the woman who'd murdered the love of his life.

Hazel drew in a deep breath. "I should say, though it pains me to do so, that you are not to be in attendance tonight, my lady. There are guards outside your door to ensure it."

"Pardon?" Ahnna stared at the younger woman. "That can't be correct. The king was very clear that tonight was critical for me and . . ." She trailed off, because no pawn's presence was critical. Edward hardly needed her in attendance to make his announcements and likely much preferred her absence, given Ahnna wouldn't remain silent as he betrayed his alliance with Ithicana.

"Lord George told me himself that the king had ordered you confined until tomorrow," Hazel said. "I am only allowed to bring you food and to ensure you are well."

Turning to the window, Ahnna took quick stock of her situation, which felt as though it grew worse by the heartbeat. Hopeless. Yet if Edward felt it necessary to keep her away tonight, that meant he believed she could disrupt his plans. And she goddamned intended to do just that.

Yet to succeed meant allying herself with the one person in Harendell that she'd been certain was her enemy. Allying herself with a known murderess. "Am I forbidden from sending messages?"

Hazel frowned. "I suspect it depends on who the message is for, my lady."

"I wish to speak with the queen."

"How very convenient, given that I also desire to speak with you."

Alexandra's voice cut the air as she appeared from the other room. Dressed in a simple gown as though she'd come directly from the road, her eyes were weary. "Georgie brought to me your fears that Edward aims to replace Ithicana with Cardiff. For once, you are better informed than I am, Ahnna Kertell. So tell me, what do you know of my husband's ungodly plans?"

Ahnna ran her tongue over her lips, suddenly frozen, because all this time, she'd been so sure that Alexandra was not to be trusted. Lara had warned her against the queen, as had Keris, yet despite all that, Alexandra might be the only one who could stop the plans Edward had in motion. "Cardiff is the least of it, Your Grace. I believe the king intends to have you executed. For murder."

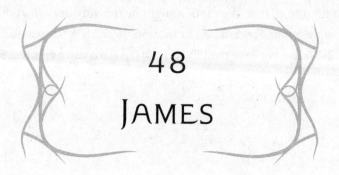

48

JAMES

The climb to the Sky Palace had taken an eternity in the mule-drawn wagon, but Alexandra would not give him leave until they reached the top. "Go discover the answers to your questions," she said, eyes taking in the rush of servants and soldiers in the courtyard. "I will go find answers to my own."

James did not need to be told twice. In his periphery, he saw Georgie appear, but he wasn't interested in conversation with his friend, so he crossed the courtyard in quick strides and headed into the palace. The servants directed him to find his father in his study.

"What is going on?" he demanded even as his father said, "Where the bloody hell have you been? George sent riders in search of you."

"I crossed paths with Alexandra on the highway, and she insisted I travel with her back to Verwyrd."

"She's here, then?"

"Just returned."

Irritation flickered across his father's face, but he made no comment.

James sat in the chair across from him. "She told me that—"

His father held up a hand. "Never mind Alexandra for now. Her time for meddling is drawing to a close." Pouring a glass of wine from the decanter on the table, his father pushed it toward him. "Drink and listen, because, my boy, we've done it. After all these years, we've finally achieved your mother's dream."

James didn't take a sip. He downed the full glass, then filled it again and downed another before he was able to say, "What do you mean?"

"I was not hunting at Whitewood Hall," his father said. "I was meeting in person with Ronan."

Reaching into his coat, his father withdrew a rolled document, handing it over. "An alliance between Harendell and Cardiff, the first of its kind."

"He agreed?" James unrolled the paper, eyes skipping over the words to the familiar signature of his uncle Ronan, scarcely able to believe it was done. That the endless back-and-forth between his father and his uncle was over, and the real work could finally begin. "How? You . . ."

"I believe Ronan finally accepted that if he wanted this, he needed to bend. It's signed and done, and when I announce the alliance tonight, I will also change the law allowing persecution of those who practice astromancy. If any Harendellian kills a Cardiffian for reasons of their faith, it will be murder. And they will hang."

If James hadn't been already sitting, this would have brought him to his knees. No more burnings. No more senseless killings. And anyone who made the mistake of breaking the law would find themselves on the sharp end of his blade.

"And the border?" he asked. "It's now open? Merchants can trade north?"

His father grinned and nodded. "Ronan and I agreed that the best choice would be to create a market at the border, policed together by our soldiers until merchants grow confident enough to travel beyond. No taxes. Free trade. But first, we will march together to make war against Amarid. We will raze that entire godforsaken kingdom to the ground. Ronan and I have both sworn it will be so."

All James's elation drained away as his father's words registered. "You aim to start a war?"

"To finish it." His father's eyes were bright. Too bright, making him seem almost manic. "Ronan is marshaling his forces, and within weeks, we will be marching. And you, my boy, you made this possible. You will be Amarid's damnation."

That had never been James's goal. Had never been what he'd wanted.

Like a slap to the face, James understood why Amarid had taken such risks, first at Northwatch and then in the gulf. Not to stop trade.

To stop an invasion.

"Why?" he demanded. "Why are we going to war against Amarid? Is this about the Lowlands?"

"It is about vengeance." His father drank deeply from his glass, then set it down. "I've kept this from you all these long years, and I hope you will forgive it of me, my son. But I couldn't risk you taking vengeance into your own hands and getting yourself killed. For to bring the Amaridian bitch down, we must bring down her kingdom."

James swallowed hard. "Katarina."

His father gave a slow nod. "She discovered Siobhan's plans. Who she was. And Katarina murdered her for it."

James drew in a steadying breath, this revelation not striking his heart as much as the truth of his father's ambition. "This was always your goal, then? Vengeance? Do you even care about mending the relationship between Cardiff and Harendell?"

"Of course I care," his father said, even as he looked away. "It was Siobhan's dream. I'll see it through. We'll see it through, but vengeance for her murder must come first. Ronan agrees."

It was like seeing his father for the first time, and James did not like what he saw. Not a revolutionary seeking social change for the better, but a bitter old man hunting for revenge for the death of the love of his life. How many people who had nothing to do with his mother's murder would die to appease his father? How many families would be destroyed? How many children orphaned? "What of Ahnna?" he asked, voice toneless. "What is her role in this?"

"Ronan and I came to terms on the matter of betrothals," his father said.

"You can't still mean to wed William to her when this"—James gestured to the signed pages—"kicks Ithicana in the teeth. Let her go, Father."

"I'm not sending Ahnna anywhere," his father replied. "She's worth far too much, and Katarina knows it. I'm not letting her have Ahnna."

A knock sounded on the door, and his father said, "Come."

A servant stepped inside. "The guests have begun to arrive, Your Grace."

His father nodded. "I'll be along shortly." When the man departed, he rose. "James, I know you feel a step behind, but trust my intentions. I will let no harm come to Ahnna Kertell, which is why I've ordered her kept to her rooms. Now go put on something appropriate. We're going to change the world tonight."

His father rose, circling the table to clasp James's shoulder, fingers tightening in a way that told James any argument he gave would be poorly received. "All will be as it should be, and I think you'll be pleased with the results. But I need to go now. Alexandra will be upset that I've gone behind her back, and I need to ensure that eyes are on her before she causes trouble."

"Does she suspect?"

Edward laughed. "Are you mad? Of course not." Letting go of James's shoulder, he said, "Only you know the truth. Because of all my children, you have always served me best. Your mother's dying words were that your fate would be revenge on her murderer. And there is no doubt in my mind that you will be the damnation of Amarid."

Then his father was gone.

James sat, feeling the weight of his new moniker drag him down.

Amarid's damnation.

Ithicana's damnation.

But above all else, the damnation of the woman with whom he'd fallen in love.

49

AHNNA

THE QUEEN'S EYEBROW ROSE. "IS HE NOW? AND JUST WHOM HAVE I murdered?"

"Siobhan."

"That is an old rumor propagated by the Amaridians," she responded coolly. "Edward knows it is *not* true."

"Then he's either been lying, or his opinions have changed." In quick, terse terms, Ahnna explained to Alexandra everything that Edward had said in the throne room, the queen's lip curling with disgust as she listened.

"I knew he hadn't let it go," Alexandra said between her teeth. "Knew in my heart that he still conspired with those ungodly menaces to the north. He would destroy our relationship with Ithicana, a God-fearing kingdom, all because of the hex that witch put upon his soul. And to what end? What is Cardiff compared to the bridge and its access to Maridrina and Valcotta? He would have us trade our steel for sealskin when we might trade it for rubies. Fool!"

"Can he be stopped?" Ahnna demanded.

Alexandra bit at her thumb as she paced the room. "Not easily."

"So what do we do?"

"I suspect Edward means to reveal a deal with Cardiff tonight, which is why he does not want you there. Which means that you *must* be there."

"What will that accomplish?"

"There will be outrage over what he has done, of that you can be sure. Your presence will remind the people of Ithicana. Of the old and secure alliance with a God-fearing nation. They'll see an opportunity to undo Edward's idiocy with a union between you and William. A king only has power if the people will it, Ahnna. Edward will not have the support of the people tonight, and you must capitalize on it."

It wasn't much of a plan, and seeming to understand that, Alexandra gripped Ahnna's hands. "You are betrothed to marry William. No matter what Edward achieves, you will one day be queen and have the power to undo all that he has done. No matter the hurt in your heart over his deceptions, cling to the truth that Edward will not live forever."

"How do we get her to the ball, Your Grace?" Hazel asked. "There are guards on the door. They might allow us to come and go, but if they see Lady Ahnna, they will surely interfere."

"Georgie will be our ally in this, I think, for not only are his family's lands near to Cardiff's border, but they are also good and God-fearing people. Most of all, Edward's actions will put Virginia at risk, and Georgie would die before seeing harm come to my daughter. That he came to me with your speculations speaks volumes of his feelings about the situation. It is no small thing to go against the orders of one's king," Alexandra said. "Hazel, get what you need, and we'll move to my rooms to prepare. I'll go speak to

Georgie. Be ready to leave when I return." Her eyes locked on Ahnna's. "This is your moment, Ahnna. Your moment to live up to your mother's aspirations for you to forever unify Harendell with the Bridge Kingdom. Do not disappoint."

She turned and strode into the other room, the door clicking as she exited into the hallway beyond.

Ahnna had no idea how this would work, but she didn't intend to face it wearing a dressing gown. Striding to the wardrobe, she wrenched it open, staring at the gowns hanging within. "I hate all of these."

Silence stretched, then the maid said, "There's another option. Wait but a moment." Hazel disappeared into the other room, then returned with a box. "Lady Bronwyn brought the dress with her, and I've kept it hidden because with what I'd learned about your relationship with your queen, I thought you might have thrown it away. Which would have been a tragedy."

For the first time in a long time, Ahnna didn't tense at the mention of Lara. Didn't feel emotion rising in her veins. As though in finally confessing the truth to James, she'd expunged that poison from her soul. "What dress?"

"Better to show you."

Hazel opened the box, then handed Ahnna a piece of paper.

> Ahnna,
> Not all armor is made of steel.
>
>   Lara

She reread the note twice, looking for a code or hidden message, but there was nothing beyond the obvious. Setting aside the note, she nodded to Hazel, who reached into the trunk and lifted out a gown unlike anything Ahnna had ever seen. Setting it on the bed, Hazel retrieved a smaller box and handed it to her.

Inside glittered gold and emeralds and black diamonds. A crown Ahnna recognized as her mother's—a gift from Valcotta decades past—along with matching earrings. But nestled among them was the necklace her father had given her mother. The necklace that Aren had given Lara. And that Lara, for a second time, was trying to give to her. There was another note in the box, and it said, *Once, when I was lost, this helped me find my way. May it do the same for you.*

Hazel had been right to hide this from her, because if Ahnna had seen it when she'd first arrived, she would have shipped it back on the next riverboat. But so much had changed. "It's perfect."

Alexandra reappeared. "Georgie will distract his men. Put on a hooded cloak. All of this is for nothing if Edward realizes what we are up to."

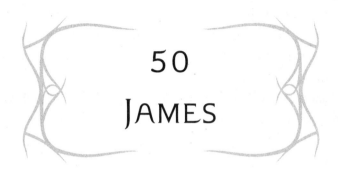

50

JAMES

HE HAD TO TELL AHNNA THE TRUTH.

Needed to tell her about the agreement with Cardiff before she married William so that she could make a decision of whether to wed into the family that had stabbed her in the back or return to Ithicana. His father might be willing to trick her into nuptials, but he'd not force her to say them. At least, James didn't think he'd stoop to that level.

Rounding the corridor, he reached the door to Ahnna's room, which had two of Georgie's soldiers before it. "I need to speak to her."

"His Grace's orders are that the princess remain in her room, sir," one of them answered.

James's jaw tightened with anger at the reminder that Ahnna had been effectively locked in a cage. "I'm only here to speak to her."

Elbowing one of the men aside, he knocked. "Ahnna?"

No one answered, so he knocked harder. "Ahnna?"

Still no answer. Both guards were frowning, and after extracting a key, one of them unlocked the door and opened it.

The room was empty, and on the far side, the door to the bedroom that had once belonged to Taryn was open wide.

Ahnna was gone.

"She was here," one of the guards said. "Hazel brought her a tray of food..." He trailed off as he saw the untouched meal on the table.

Which meant Ahnna had either convinced the maid to let her out the other door, or forced Hazel to help her. But where had she gone?

And what did she intend to do?

"I'll handle this," he muttered. "You two check the battlements to see if she went up for air. She does not care to be confined."

James twisted on his heel, heading in the direction of the ballroom, the music from the orchestra and the laughter of guests already filling the air.

The Sky Palace ballroom was full to the brim with nobility, everyone within riding distance having dropped everything to be here for the mysterious announcement. Men and women dressed in their finest swirled around the room. Others stood with glasses of sparkling wine in their hands, plucking delicacies from the trays held by liveried servants. The conservatory's orchestra was playing enthusiastically, dance cards rapidly filling, but James ignored all the coy smiles sent in his direction as he searched for any sign of Ahnna. She wasn't here either.

"I see you dressed for the occasion," George said, appearing at James's elbow. "My God, man, you stink like horse."

"I've been busy," he said. "Where is William? Off somewhere getting drunk?"

Georgie shrugged, then took a glass of wine from a passing servant and drained it. "I saw him this morning, and he looked pleased as punch but very sober. Do you know what this is all about?"

"This is all my father's doing."

His friend was silent for a long moment, then he said, "The gossip over this surprise event, which obviously wasn't orchestrated by Alexandra, has rumors flying. You would not believe the speculations I've heard."

James only grunted a response, every part of him praying that Ahnna had taken her forced confinement as a reason to run. That she was already out of the Sky Palace. That she'd taken Dippy and run as far and fast from Harendell as she could. Somewhere she would be free from people trying to use her to their benefit.

"I asked Ginny if she knew what was going on, but even she is entirely in the dark. Seems the same for you, Jamie, if I'm being honest. If I were a betting man, which I am, I'd wager that Will is the only one in the know, which is a first for him."

James hardly heard Georgie's words, but his thoughts were interrupted by the herald bellowing, "Her Most Royal Majesty, Queen Alexandra of Harendell."

James turned his head to watch Alexandra enter. She was dressed in an elaborate gown with enough jewels to buy a kingdom, but her hair was pulled into a simple twist, speaking to the speed with which she'd gotten ready. She gave James a half smile as she passed, heading to where his father was arguing with Ginny. Their conversation broke off as the queen reached them.

Nearby, Elizabeth said rather loudly, "Are simple hairstyles to be the new fashion, then?"

Speculation over the queen's hair broke out among the ladies, and George said softly, "You don't suppose that your father didn't plan for Alexandra to be here tonight, do you?"

James supposed exactly that, and the fact that Alexandra had the wherewithal to return to Verwyrd just in time made him wonder what else she knew.

Murmurs filled the air, then the herald bellowed, "Her Most Royal Highness, Princess Ahnna of Ithicana, beloved sister to His Royal Majesty, King Aren of Ithicana, the Master of the Bridge."

At the herald's words, his father's gaze snapped to the end of the ballroom, dismay written across his face. James slowly turned, rendered speechless by the sight of her. As was, judging from the silence in the ballroom, everyone else.

Ahnna wore a gown made of leather such a dark green that it was nearly black. It was high-necked, the garment encircling her throat like a choker, her shoulders and arms entirely bare. The thin leather clung to her torso until it reached her hips, where it spread out in a full skirt, the tips of black boots peeking out with each of her long strides. Her hair was woven into a severe coronet of braids, on which she wore a crown. Not a tiara, but an actual crown of gold, emeralds, and black diamonds, earrings of the same reaching almost to her naked shoulders. Her eyes were rimmed with black, cheekbones shaded in a way that made them look sharp enough to cut as she walked past James, not giving him a sideways glance.

Only carried on toward his father, allowing James full view of her back. While the front of her gown spit in the face of fashion, which favored a tremendous amount of visible cleavage, Ahnna's back was entirely naked, the dress plunging down until just above her curved ass, the fabric twisted in such a way that the skirt flowing to her feet looked like a midnight river. A chain of jewels set in an asymmetrical pattern hung down her spine, swaying as she walked.

"Ithicana shows her true colors," Georgie murmured, but

James was already following Ahnna, drawn to her like iron to a lodestone. Ahead of him, she dropped into a perfect curtsy.

"Your Majesties," she said.

His father had regained his composure and swiftly reached to take her hand, giving her a wide smile that made James want to scream, because it was so entirely false. "Ahnna, you are the most beautiful woman in the room."

Instead of commenting on the fact that she was not supposed to be here by virtue of having been locked in her room, all Ahnna said was, "Thank you, Your Grace."

Alexandra stepped forward to kiss both of Ahnna's cheeks. "You are perfection. Ithicana incarnate."

His father's jaw tightened, understanding as readily as James did that Alexandra was the reason Ahnna was in attendance.

"Thank you, Your Grace," Ahnna said. "You are kind to say so."

"Music!" Alexandra called to the orchestra. "I want to see my guests dancing."

They lifted their instruments, the nobility obediently moving onto the floor in pairs.

"You might have taken the time for a bath, Jamie," his father said, looking him up and down. "And dressed for the occasion. This is a night for celebration, yet you look as though you have been to war. Why don't you remedy that."

"I'm fine as is, thank you." James suspected his father knew exactly what he intended to do.

"It wasn't a suggestion."

"Edward, let him be," Alexandra said, examining a ring on her finger. "There's not a person here who isn't aware that our Jamie is more soldier than prince, so they'll be forgiving of the clothing." She gave James a smile he couldn't read. "And amused by the smell."

An unlikely ally, and James knew that Alexandra was only siding with him because his father was the target of her ire tonight. Judging from the tenseness of his father's jaw, he knew it, too. He hadn't wanted her in Verwyrd for this moment, and yet here Alexandra was.

Here *Ahnna* was.

Taking the opportunity, James rounded on Ahnna, who was more fiercely exquisite than he'd ever seen her, and held out his hand. "A dance, my lady?"

She stared at him for a heartbeat, face fixed in the way of someone hiding their emotions, but then she inclined her head. "I would love to."

A jolt surged through him as she took his hand, allowing him to lead her out to where the dancers were gathering, the first strings of a waltz beginning to play. Turning toward her, James rested his hand on her back, no part of him not reacting to the feel of her bare skin beneath his palm. Ahnna rested her other hand on his shoulder, her gaze on his chest. Which was just as well, because with guilt threatening to drown him, he couldn't meet her eye.

As the other dancers began to move, he led her into the steps, guiding her around and around the dance floor. Part of him wanted to extend the moment, but he forced himself to say, "I shouldn't . . . we shouldn't have done what we did."

Ahnna didn't answer, her eyes fixed on the buttons of his coat. "Why? Because I'm to marry your brother? Or because you're a lying prick who has been planning to stab me in the back the entire time you've known me?"

She knew.

The world seemed to tilt on its axis. James had thought that admitting the truth to her would be the hardest thing he'd ever have to do, but having her discover another way was proving to be far, *far* worse. "Both."

Her lip quivered. "Not going to defend your actions?"

"I cannot," he answered. "Any claim I had to honor is gone. There is no defense."

"I should hate you," Ahnna whispered. "But I know you were driven to defend your mother's people. That you wanted to end the persecution. The burnings. That your motivations were good, if not your goddamned consideration of the consequences. Or perhaps you considered them and just decided you didn't care about Ithicanian suffering. We are not people, just greedy monsters in masks who sit upon thrones of gold."

She was not far off the mark. "There may be a happy medium, Ahnna. Something that achieves both ends. That makes all three nations happy."

"I highly doubt that," Ahnna hissed, "as it is clear to me that Harendell thinks only of itself."

"You don't need to marry my brother," he said. "You can leave now. It is against my father's own laws to make you wed anyone you do not accept. Leave, Ahnna. Go back to Ithicana. Go back to your family and be happy."

Her lip curled. "As though my happiness matters. You only wish for me to leave because you know that your father will not live forever. Because you know that if I am William's queen, I'll have the power to undo all of this. All it will take is one nasty tax on trade into Cardiff, and you know exactly what your greedy countrymen will choose to do, don't you, James?"

"You are not that cruel," he said. "You'll not invite that kind of horror back on innocent people."

"You don't know me half as well as you think," she replied. "To defend my people, there is *nothing* I won't do."

A commotion at the rear of the ballroom stole away his ability to respond, the orchestra quieting and the dancers falling still as all eyes fixed on the panting and filthy messenger now speaking to his father. There were grim nods, then his father said loudly, "Dire news, my friends. Word has come that Amarid has crossed the border into the Lowlands in numbers not seen in a generation, their first bid in an attempt to reclaim the land. Our garrisons have called for aid. Long have we danced with war, my friends, but today, war has come to Harendell."

A dozen women screamed, at least two swooning into their companions' arms, but more stood with their shoulders squared and jaws tight as they waited, sensing there was more to come. Next to him, Ahnna seethed tension.

"But we do not face it alone," his father continued. "For we have a formidable ally at our side—one capable of not only helping us drive the Amaridians off our lands but of helping us enact justice for a crime that is long overdue."

James drew in a deep breath.

"Twenty-six years ago," his father said, moving to stand on the dais so that all might hear, "the mother of my firstborn son was murdered in cold blood. There has been much speculation over the years as to who murdered her, blame cast"—he glanced at Alexandra, whose expression was unreadable—"but I reveal to you today that Siobhan was poisoned by the assassins of Queen Katarina of Amarid."

There were a few surprised gasps, but James knew that most were waiting for the real shoe to drop. An explanation for why they were discussing the death of a woman they'd all presumed to be a commoner when Harendell stood on the brink of war.

"Why, I'm sure you are all wondering, did Katarina condescend to murdering a Cardiffian maidservant?" his father said. "The answer is that Siobhan was no commoner, no maidservant. She was sister to King Ronan Crehan of Cardiff."

More gasps erupted, dozens of eyes going to James, but he kept his expression still even though one set of those eyes belonged to Ahnna. Yet another piece of information he'd kept from her.

Yet another lie.

"Yet that still might seem paltry motivation, for Amarid has no quarrel with Cardiff, and to assassinate a foreign princess in the confines of the Sky Palace invites severe retaliation. Only the greatest of motivations would be worth such a risk. What, you are all wondering, did Katarina know that all of you did not?" He waited, scanning the room until the tension reached a fever pitch, then said, "The answer to that question is that Siobhan and I were working together to create a true and lasting alliance between Harendell and Cardiff. A friendship that would see our trade flow north instead of south, that would see Harendellians reap the profits from the sales of their goods rather than bleed money in tolls and taxes."

God, but his father was the consummate politician, giving these people information that was sure to spark outrage but then chasing it with that which ruled their hearts: profit. For there wasn't a man or woman in this room who wouldn't turn a blind eye to just about anything, including astromancy, if doing so made them richer. Yet for all this had been his *fucking plan,* James felt no elation at watching it unfold, because the ends were not his dream.

They were his nightmare.

"This alliance was Siobhan's dream," his father continued, "a dream that turned to a nightmare when Katarina discovered it, the Amaridian bitch slipping poison into the cup of the greatest woman I've had the privilege of knowing in order to destroy an alliance that would make Amarid quake at the knees."

Beyond, Alexandra's mouth twisted, but his father only pressed onward.

"For a time, Katarina succeeded, her foul propaganda mongers slandering Alexandra as the culprit in order to sow dissent with the Cardiffians. But the truth always comes out, my friends, and King Ronan is as eager for revenge against Katarina and Amarid as I am. Which is why he and I have signed a treaty of alliance, his army moving to join ours as we speak. Amarid will bleed for its actions, but none more so than the woman on the throne!"

Such was the power of his oration that the ballroom exploded into cheers and demands for revenge for the murder of a woman that, until moments ago, they'd only ever disparaged. His father's expression was one of vicious delight, but all James felt was hollow. Because he did not believe that this was what his mother had wanted. For her name and legacy to be that of violence, when all she'd ever wanted was peace.

Ahnna was silent, but her skin was blanched.

His father held up a hand, calling for silence. "And none of this would have been possible without the tireless efforts of James, my firstborn and the son that I shared with Siobhan. It is because of James that this alliance has been achieved, and I ask that all of you lift your glasses in his name. Huzzah!"

51
AHNNA

THROUGH ALL OF EDWARD'S SPEECH, AHNNA CLUNG TO HER COM-posure. But as the masses of nobles lifted glasses and voices to shout "Huzzah," her control fractured, because she sensed that Edward's alliance with Cardiff was but the tip of what would be revealed tonight.

You will be queen, she chanted to herself. *No matter what he does, you will one day be able to undo it.*

Part of her wanted to flee. The other to lash out in violence. Yet all she did was stand frozen as Edward again held up his hand for silence.

What more could he possibly have to say?

"James is not the only son of my blood whose efforts will yield great dividends for Harendell," Edward said. "Which, as you all suspect, is why we have gathered here tonight."

Chin up, Ahnna screamed at herself. *As queen, you will have the power to remedy this. You need only bide your time.*

"I am so pleased to announce that this morning, my son William took a bride," Edward said.

What?

Ahnna's blood turned to ice even as Alexandra gasped out, "Edward, what have you done?"

He ignored her and said, "Allow me to formally announce the union of hearts that forms the final piece of our alliance with Cardiff. Please welcome Harendell's heir and his new bride, Princess Lestara of Cardiff."

Only willpower kept Ahnna on her feet, her knees shaking violently beneath the leather of her skirts as everything fell apart.

You failed Ithicana.

Again.

William entered the ballroom with Lestara on his arm, the Cardiffian princess no longer dressed in the garments of her captors but in a gown of watered silk trimmed in fur and a headdress from which dangled charms and bird skulls.

Bird skulls just like the one she'd found in the throne room.

William ignored Ahnna as he walked past, but Lestara turned her head, mouth silently moving with the words, *I'm sorry.*

A knife to the chest would have been better.

They stepped onto the dais, William's face a self-satisfied smirk and Lestara's unreadable, but it was not at them everyone was staring.

It was at Ahnna.

Every eye in the room was on her, every goddamned one, not an ounce of sympathy or guilt in the lot of them. Only the predatory gleam of those who smelled weakness like sharks smelled blood in the water, all of them waiting to see if she would flee or fight back.

The very same question Ahnna asked herself.

Edward's expression was faintly irritated, as though he'd hoped his people would merely forget about her. As though she were dirt easily swept beneath a rug.

Ahnna refused to be so easily dismissed. "I did not realize Harendell was so faithless," she said. "Nor that its king's word was worth no more than that of Silas Veliant, for I am coming to discover that you are two of a kind. Ithicana has long been a true and faithful ally of Harendell, our alliance allowing safe and profitable trade for both our peoples."

There were murmurs of agreement from the masses of nobles, and Ahnna's heart quickened with the certainty that Alexandra was right. That the people would side with Ithicana and force Edward to end this agreement with Cardiff. So she added, "You signed a treaty with my mother, and reaffirmed those terms with me."

Edward's gaze was frosty as he answered. "Circumstances have greatly changed in the years since that treaty was signed, and Ithicana is no longer the power it once was, courtesy of your brother's ill-considered choices. Harendell seeks alliances that are mutually beneficial, not those that will bleed its people of their hard-earned profits and offer nothing in return." Edward drew in a deep breath. "I hold you in the highest of esteem, Ahnna, but your worth is not commensurate with my son's, whereas Lestara's most certainly is."

She wanted to scream that Lestara was a faithless traitor who'd caused the death of thousands. But the Cardiffian princess wasn't the villain here. Wasn't the one who'd lied to her face time and again, pretending to be her friend while he conspired behind her back.

Yet all around her, the nobles were nodding as though the king spoke sense, and Ahnna knew that she would not win this battle of words. Squaring her shoulders, Ahnna said, "It is your right to make this decision, Your Grace. But do not think for a moment that you won't pay for it."

Lifting her skirt hem with one hand, Ahnna turned and strode from the ballroom.

The second she was clear of the doors, her stoicism crumbled, her breath coming in too-fast gasps as she headed to her room, every part of her wanting to run.

"Ahnna!"

His voice was a punch to the gut, and her control snapped. Snatching her skirts up higher, Ahnna broke into a sprint.

"Ahnna, wait!"

She reached the grand staircase, taking the steps two at a time, then she was racing down the corridor. Her room was no haven, yet she ran for it anyway, needing to be away from everyone.

Needing to be away from him.

Then hands caught her around the waist. James lifted her off her feet and pressed her against the wall. She shoved him away, nearly falling as her heel caught on the gown.

"Ahnna, I didn't know."

"Liar!" she screamed, then pulled her arm back and punched him in the face. Pain blossomed across her knuckles, but though she might well have cracked his cheekbone, James barely swayed on his feet.

"Would you listen to me?"

"You listen to me!" Her hands remained in fists, blood dripping off the knuckles of her right hand. "I trusted you with everything, and you used that information against me by telling your father Ithicana was weak. You knew how important this was, not just for Ithicana but for *me*. You *knew*, and still you—" She broke off, unable to say it. "You watched me make a fool of myself trying to be everything William wanted while you *fuckers* secretly conspired to wed him to Lestara!"

"I didn't know about his plans to wed Will to Lestara," he replied. "I was as much in the dark on that as you."

"You think I'm such a fool to believe that you didn't know there were plans for William to marry your *cousin*?" She pressed her hands to her face. "Of course you think that. I believed every other bloody word that came out of your mouth."

"Ahnna, I didn't want this." James caught hold of her wrists, pulling her hands from her face. "This wasn't what I was trying to accomplish. My father . . . He's more obsessed with avenging my mother than I knew. He doesn't care about trade or any of the things I fought for, only for destroying Amarid, and he's giving my uncle everything he wants in order to achieve it."

She jerked her wrists out of his grip. "Maybe that's so," she hissed. "But it doesn't change that you made me yours with lies on your lips. If you come near me again, if any of you come near me again, I'll kill you all. I swear it."

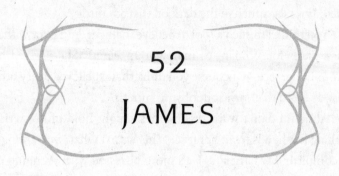

52
JAMES

STUMBLING OVER HER SKIRTS INTO HER ROOM, AHNNA SLAMMED the door in his face.

James stood staring at the wood of the door, stomach twisted with nausea, feeling like the whole world had spun out of his control.

"Sir? Is the lady in her rooms?"

He turned to see the guards he'd dispatched to the ramparts approaching at a trot. "She is," he answered, seeing them taking in his rapidly swelling eye. "Keep guard, but don't disturb her."

"Yes, sir."

James started walking down the corridor, his stride increasing along with his anger, because he and his father would have words. Not just words about his choice to marry William to goddamned *Lestara* but also how he'd humiliated Ahnna in front of everyone.

But before he reached the ballroom, a servant intercepted him. "King Edward is in the study, my lord," the man said. "He wishes to see you."

Through the open doors, James could see William dancing with Lestara, seemingly entranced by her. A thousand little pieces fell into place, and he felt blind not to have seen it, and he silently cursed Keris Veliant for delivering to Harendell the final piece needed to secure an alliance with Cardiff: a bride.

Switching course, James stormed through the Sky Palace, slamming the doors to the study open so hard they rebounded off the wall. "What the fuck are you thinking?"

"Have a drink, Jamie," his father said, shoving a glass into his hand. "And calm yourself down. I've already had to listen to Alexandra scream in my face for marrying her son off behind her back, and I'm in no mood for more of the same. Especially since today has given you everything you wanted."

"What part of this did I want, Father?" James snarled. "The part where you use what was supposed to be an alliance of peace to pursue a war? The part where you marry William to my murderous cousin? The part where you humiliated the finest woman I've ever met, and very likely shattered the relationship with Ithicana beyond repair? Do tell, which part of that did I ever ask for?"

His father sighed, then reached out to raise the glass in James's hand to his mouth. "Have a drink and I'll explain."

James only glared at him. "Give me a good reason why you want Lestara, who once sacrificed all of Vencia in pursuit of Maridrina's throne, to be Harendell's queen, and I'll drink your stupid drink."

"I can't," his father said. "Because I don't. Lestara will never be queen, James. Nor will your brother ever be Harendell's king."

Shock radiated through to his core, and despite himself, James took a long mouthful of the bright-purple drink.

"Because once the dust is settled and the people have come to terms with the alliance with Cardiff, I will name you, my firstborn son, as my lawful heir."

The blood drained from James's face. "You can't," he said. "I was born out of wedlock. Unless you plan to change that law as well."

"Oh, I married your mother, my boy," his father said, motioning for him to sit. "I was married to her when I was dragged into the cathedral to appease an old agreement with Alexandra's family, but those vows were lies, everything that came out of it for the sake of politics. It's William and Ginny who are bastards, not you. I'll get your sister married off to Georgie before I reveal that, though, so don't fret about her."

James's tongue was frozen, speech having abandoned him.

"Keris sending us Lestara was only a happy coincidence, as she made short work of seducing your brother, which kept him away from Ahnna. Because the princess of Ithicana?" His father leveled a finger at him. "She's for you. Ahnna will be your queen, Jamie. You two will create an alliance among Harendell, Cardiff, and Ithicana that will eclipse the southern alliance, and the peace that you have long desired will be yours."

James stared into the drink in his hand, then downed it, the liquor burning his throat.

"It's meant to be," his father said. "Even if I hadn't heard of your moment in the maze at Fernleigh, I knew as soon as I set eyes on the both of you that you were taken with each other. She's a remarkable woman, Jamie. Far too good for your brother. While you'll have your hands full earning her forgiveness for this little bit of deception, once Ahnna understands the long game, she'll come around."

James highly doubted that. "You humiliated her."

"I know." Edward sighed. "She wasn't supposed to be there. Her bodyguards were supposed to keep her in her room, and I expect we have Alexandra to thank for slipping her past them. I took no pleasure in shaming her, but in truth, Aren is the target of my ire. He treated Ahnna horribly."

"Alexandra told me the information you received, Father. I don't think it's accurate. Ahnna holds no ill will toward Aren or Lara—"

"If that is the case, it is because she is a good and forgiving woman, not because they deserve it," his father interrupted. "Aren Kertell is the worst king Ithicana has ever seen. An idiot of the first order, making decisions with his cock because all he can see is the pretty face and large breasts that Silas so cleverly sent to be his bride. Every decision he has made since Lara arrived has harmed his people. Thousands dead, Jamie. *Thousands*, because of the choices Aren made, whereas Ahnna has been a stalwart defender of Ithicana since she was a child. She led them through that invasion, kept Ithicana alive, and do not for a heartbeat think that the Ithicanian people don't have a favored Kertell sibling, and it is *not* their king."

James's skin prickled. "What do you intend?"

His father's smile was vicious. "To give Ithicana a ruler they deserve."

"A coup?" He couldn't believe what he was hearing. "You plan to overthrow Aren Kertell? Father, Ahnna will never support that."

"She will if we do it right. We'll offer the Ithicanian people an opportunity in Harendell under the patronage of their princess. Bring them here and show them just how good life can be under the right rule, and build Ahnna an army of supporters. Think of dear Taryn, living and thriving in our conservatory, full well knowing that the opportunity came to her via her cousin. Ahnna already has a lifetime's worth of goodwill; we'll merely take it to the next level, and then the Ithicanians will do the hard work for us and depose their king."

"And through her, you'll then control the bridge."

"Have primary access to the bridge," his father amended, giving him a pointed look. "I've no desire to annex Ithicana, nor interest in the war that would require. Not everything has to be achieved through force, Jamie. Sometimes one must just back the right horse."

"She won't agree to this plan."

"You'll convince her. We will create a triumvirate of power in the north that no one can stand against. Valcotta and Maridrina might gripe, but I believe Sarhina and Zarrah are the sort of rulers who will see that Ahnna as queen of Ithicana is best for the people. They can take Aren and his murderous wife under their wing as royals in exile, and everyone will be content."

James highly doubted that. His lips parted to argue, but his father swiftly said, "Aren has negotiated an alliance with Katarina. He's promised Ahnna to the Beast of Amarid. Our spies heard Carlo bragging about how he'd relish bedding an Ithicanian princess. Only a handful of individuals know this information, and I'd like to keep it that way to protect Ahnna and her people from anger that only her brother deserves."

It was a struggle to breathe. "You can't be serious?"

Rising to his feet, his father opened a locked box and withdrew reports, tossing them on the table. "Unless Aren has betrothed his infant daughter to a grown man, there is only one other princess of Ithicana alive that Carlo could be talking about."

James's eyes skipped over the reports, which all mentioned variations of the same. That Katarina's agents had traveled to Northwatch to meet with Aren. That an alliance had been agreed upon. That the agreement included a princess bride.

"I can only assume that either his spies learned of our conversations with Cardiff, or Katarina informed him. Either way, his retaliatory actions are the last idiot move I'll accept from that man because I will allow no more harm to come to Ahnna," his father said. "We'll shatter Amarid, remove Katarina's head, and then remove Aren from power. After that, it will be profit and peace."

James let out a slow breath, shaking his head at the audacity of this scheme even as he saw the logic of it. "What does William know?"

His father made a face. "Very little. Your sister even less. William is dancing around with his madwoman of a bride under the deluded belief that they'll sit on the throne together. That he'll be the one named in the history books for uniting Cardiff and Harendell."

"Is Ronan aware his daughter will never be queen?"

"Yes. He no more wants Lestara and William on the throne than I do. He wants you to inherit, my boy. What he is unaware of is my intention for you to wed Ahnna, and in truth, that should come from you when the time is right. He holds you in such high esteem that when you approach him with your desire to take Ahnna as your wife, he'll concede with smiles."

"And Alexandra?"

His father's smile was cold. "She will have to come to terms with the knowledge that she is not queen. And never will be."

Except Alexandra wasn't the sort of woman who would lie down without a fight.

Rising to his feet, his father retrieved a bottle from the sideboard and set it on the table. Then he moved to rest his hand on James's back. "I know it is a great deal to take in, Jamie. I know that you are angry about my methods, about my deception, and about the embarrassment that Ahnna has endured. But I hope that you will come to see that everything I've done is for you. And to see you have the opportunity to wed for love makes all the heartache worthwhile."

He squeezed James's shoulder, then left the room.

Outside the window, brilliant lights burst bright over Verwyrd, the noise of the revels filling his ears.

James didn't move for a long time, and when he finally did, it was to drink straight from the bottle. His father might believe that Ahnna would easily forgive, but James suffered no such delusion. Because after tonight, whatever love Ahnna might have had for him had been burned to ash.

53

AHNNA

SLAMMING THE DOOR, AHNNA LOCKED IT BEHIND HER AND pushed a chair under the handle to keep it from turning.

Crossing the room, she fell to her knees in a pool of leather skirts, sobs tearing her body apart because she'd failed again. Failed to protect the kingdom she loved above all else. And though she wanted to scream and blame Edward, the fault was her own for not rooting out the truth.

Instead, she'd been outmaneuvered, and she'd spilled her heart to the enemy.

And she had no idea what to do about it. No idea how she could make this right because no part of her felt like she could go back to Ithicana with the news that not only had she failed to gain the increase in trade they needed, but the one nation that had been stalwart for decades had now turned their back on Ithicana entirely.

"You have to go back," she whispered between sobs. "You need to explain what has happened so they can react accordingly."

She wouldn't be punished, Ahnna knew that. Instead, she'd be shuffled off into a corner where she'd be out of sight. Unable to cause any more problems. A name that faded from conversation until, over time, she was nearly forgotten.

Visions of her future filled her mind, tears rolling down her face as her imagination subjected her to a taste of what it would be like. To watch her country decay and crumble, her people abandoning their islands for chances at new lives in other kingdoms. To watch her home cease to exist and know that she was to blame.

How much time passed, she couldn't have said, her miserable reverie broken only by the sound of an explosion.

Lifting her head, Ahnna watched the sparkle of fireworks drifting past her window, the palace putting on a show to celebrate its prince's union. A show of strength as the nation headed to war with a new ally at its back and the old left in the dust.

Climbing to her feet, Ahnna watched the explosions of light over Verwyrd, not moving until the smoke had cleared and her mind was certain.

She'd leave tonight.

Going to her closet, Ahnna took out her Ithicanian garb, neatly pressed. Unfastening the gown, she put it on the bed, then dressed, making a bundle for a spare set of clothing, along with the crown and earrings, which she'd return to Lara. Her mother's necklace she kept on for safekeeping.

Shoving knives into her boots, she buckled on her sword, then sat to wait until it was late enough that she could move through the palace without having to face endless nobles who'd laugh at her misfortune.

Music played on and on, shrieks of laughter reaching her even through the thick walls as the Harendellians celebrated. Gradually, the noise began to quiet, the nobility slowly shepherded down the spiral to the city, where they'd find their beds in their fancy homes along the riverbank.

Only when there was utter silence did Ahnna go to the door. Moving the chair, she unlatched it and then pulled it open, an argument for her bodyguards to let her pass already rising to her lips.

But there was no one in the hallway.

"Why would there be?" Ahnna muttered. The Harendellians had only been pretending that her well-being mattered, and they need pretend no longer. Hefting her bundle over her shoulder, Ahnna started down the hallway on silent feet.

The air felt charged, but Ahnna ignored the goosebumps rising on her arms as she headed toward the servant staircase. She didn't make it far before stopping in her tracks.

Alexandra was walking toward her. "I've been waiting for you, Ahnna," the queen said. "I suspected you'd leave after he humiliated you. That you'd wait for it to quiet, then slip out in the night."

"Are you here to stop me?"

The queen gave a bemused laugh and said, "Hardly. You've played your role to perfection, my dear. I had worried you wouldn't rally, but tonight? Tonight you were magnificent. Every bit the Ithicanian we were promised. Twice the woman that blond bitch will ever be."

Ahnna's skin was crawling, her instincts screaming danger, but Alexandra was unarmed, so she held her ground as the queen drew in front of her. She gripped Ahnna's shoulders. "I hope that you won't take this personally, Ahnna, for this really has nothing to do with you. I merely needed someone to take the blame."

"Pardon, Your—"

Alexandra jerked one of Ahnna's knives from its sheath.

Ahnna reflexively stepped away and pulled another knife. But the queen didn't move to attack. "I highly suggest you run, my dear," Alexandra said. "You might well escape with your life."

Before Ahnna could answer, Alexandra lifted the knife she'd stolen and stabbed it down.

Through her own left hand.

Barely able to comprehend what was happening, Ahnna watched in horror as the queen slid the knife free of her flesh and then, without hesitation, shoved it through her own cheek.

"Stop!" Ahnna reached for her. "What are you doing?"

Alexandra only stepped back, took a deep breath, and plunged the knife just below her belly button.

And then she screamed.

Shrill and desperate, she howled, "Help me!"

"Oh God," Ahnna breathed, catching Alexandra as she fell into her arms. Alexandra's hands locked around her neck, pulling Ahnna's ear to her mouth. Then the queen of Harendell whispered, "Run."

More screams split the night. Shrill and piercing, they echoed through Verwyrd. "Assassin! Assassin!" And then, worst of all, "The king is dead!"

Guards exploded around the corner, and at their head was James. He slid to a stop, eyes widening, and Ahnna knew exactly how it looked. Because it was exactly as Alexandra had planned.

"Help me," the queen sobbed, trying to push out of Ahnna's arms. "Help me, Jamie."

"I didn't do this," Ahnna said, allowing Alexandra to crawl away. "She did it to herself. James, you know I didn't do this."

A soldier appeared around the corner. "The king is dead, my lord! Murdered in his bed by assassins unknown . . ." His voice trailed off as his eyes landed on Ahnna.

"Edward!" Alexandra howled. "Oh God, she killed him!"

"It's not true," Ahnna protested, even as she saw how damning her position appeared. "On my life, I have not done any of this!"

James drew his sword. "You killed my father."

"I didn't." She lifted her hands. They were covered with blood. "James—"

"Don't," he whispered.

If you come near me again, if any of you come near me again, I'll kill you all. I swear it. Her last words to him filled Ahnna's head, and she knew James was hearing them again, too.

Scrambling to her feet, Ahnna took several rapid steps back. "I didn't do this. You know me. You know I wouldn't do this."

But she could see in his eyes that James was past reason, so deep in grief and anger that there was nothing else. The queen of Harendell was framing her. And Alexandra had picked her moment well.

Run.

Spinning around, Ahnna broke into a sprint, her boots pounding on the thick carpet. But not as loudly as James's as he pursued, shouting orders to secure the palace and lower the gates.

The gates that were the only way out of this palace in the sky. Which meant she needed to get to them before those taking the orders.

Adrenaline burned through Ahnna's veins as she rounded the curved hallway, elbowing past those who'd spilled into the corridor.

"Stop her!" James shouted, but everyone saw Alexandra's blood on her clothes and recoiled in fear. The door to a servant staircase appeared ahead, and Ahnna wrenched it open. Only for a hand to close on her tunic, ripping her backward.

She fell into James hard enough that he stumbled. Ahnna let

herself fall, her weight pulling her clothing free of his grip. Rolling, she lunged to her feet, feeling his fingers catch at her sleeve.

But she had already thrown herself down the stairs, leaping all eight of them to hit the landing. She nearly fell, catching her balance against the wall, her left wrist jamming hard.

Ahnna ignored the pain and jumped down the next eight.

The door at the bottom was closed, and with James on her heels, she didn't try to open it, only cut right down the narrow passage until she reached another door. Ripping it open, she exploded into the kitchen, crashing into screaming servants.

Ahnna shoved them out of her way, knocking crates over to block the route behind her as she wove through the chaos toward the exit.

Only for two guards to appear, blocking her path.

She didn't want to hurt them. Didn't want to make this worse, but neither did she want to die. And Ahnna did not think James would allow her to plead her innocence if he caught her.

So instead, she picked up speed.

The soldiers lifted their blades, grim determination on their faces, but at the last minute, Ahnna dived.

She slid along the polished floor. Her momentum sent her between them, but the sound of blades striking stone made her jerk her legs beneath her. Scrambling on all fours, she got her footing even as James shoved the men out of the way, gaining ground on her.

There would be no outrunning him.

Ahnna's heart roared, her eyes burning because, despite his betrayal, she didn't want to hurt him. Wasn't sure that she could, even if it meant her own life.

Think.

There was an exit to the courtyard ahead, but soldiers appeared, blocking her path. She skidded to a stop. Pulling her sword free, Ahnna turned to face James. He was stalking toward her, weapon raised. One of his eyes was swollen shut from where she'd hit him earlier.

Which meant his depth perception would be off.

"Why?" he demanded. "Why my father? Why not me? I'm the one you're angry with. I'm the one who lied to you. He had *your* interests at heart! He was trying to protect you from your fucking brother!"

"I didn't kill him!"

Her words only seemed to enrage him more, and James attacked. Their swords clashed, his blows making her arm shake. She met each of his strikes, staying on the defense even as she looked for a way through. "James, I don't want to hurt you!"

"You already have," he screamed. "Why didn't you kill me instead?"

He would not see reason, that much was clear. He was lost in grief, and Alexandra had masterminded this situation too well. Which meant Ahnna's only option was to escape.

Ahnna stepped close, but as James moved to strike, she swayed backward just enough that his sword tip sliced through the front of her tunic. Having thought her in range, he overcommitted and stumbled as the force of his swing pulled him sideways.

Ahnna could have killed him right then. Instead, she threw herself into a roll, coming up to her feet and running.

Flinging open the doors to the drawing room, she slammed them shut and turned the latch. A second later, the wood rattled as it was struck. The oak was strong, but the lock wouldn't hold.

Dropping her blade, Ahnna pushed a sideboard in front of the door, and then a sofa and a toppled bookcase, the books falling every which way across the floor. Racing to the floor-to-ceiling window, she stared out into the black night, clouds having rolled in to obscure the stars.

The door rattled, shouts emanating from beyond. She had minutes before James broke through, no more.

Picking up a chair, she heaved it through the glass, a gale-force wind immediately blasting inside. Ahnna yanked down the billowing curtain, tearing the fabric into lengths, which she tied together. Her hands shook, eyes skipping to the door with every impact of James's shoulder, the furniture she'd put in front of it shuddering.

Tying the makeshift rope to the legs of a heavy wooden table, Ahnna climbed onto the windowsill.

Below, endless darkness loomed. To fall would be like falling from the heavens themselves.

"So don't fall," she growled to herself, taking a steadying breath before turning and leaning back, praying the fabric would hold.

It did.

Leaning near horizontal, she edged, hand over hand, down the tower, the texture of the stone painfully familiar. She wasn't certain how far down the first ring of the spiral was, and it wasn't lost on her that if her rope wasn't long enough to reach it, she was a dead woman.

One way or another.

Wind buffeted her body, trying to knock her loose from her perch, but it wasn't loud enough to muffle the explosion of wood above her. Nor the shouts of triumph.

Faster, she told herself. But instead, Ahnna looked up.

To see the outline of a familiar figure leaning out the window, hands grasping hold of her makeshift rope.

Then James was lifting her.

Ahnna lost her footing on the wall, a yelp tearing from her lips as she slid down the curtain. The railing of the topmost ring of the spiral flashed past her, and then she caught her grip on the fabric.

Swinging wildly, she desperately climbed, hearing the fabric above her starting to tear.

Hand over hand, she edged higher, seeing the spiral railing that would be her salvation. Twisting her leg around the curtain, Ahnna reached, fingers brushing steel—

And then she was falling.

Ahnna screamed, her nails scraping against the rock as she plummeted, terror filling her veins.

Only for her hands to catch on the railing the next level down.

Her momentum nearly ripped her arms from their sockets, but she held on, adrenaline pumping through her veins.

Twin tears squeezed from her eyes, but Ahnna ignored the pain in her body and in her heart as she hooked a leg over the railing, easing over to the other side. On her knees with solid rock beneath her feet, she tried to calm her racing heart.

There was no time for more, because above, the noise of running feet entering the spiral filled her ears.

Moving as quietly as she could, Ahnna ran down the spiral, each footstep sending a knife blade of pain through her shoulders, but it was the words that kept repeating in her thoughts that hurt the most. *Why is this happening?*

Words that only silenced as she picked out the noise of men running *up* the spiral toward her.

Shit.

Hand resting on the hilt of her sword, she kept going. When the soldiers coming to aid those in the palace appeared, the torches they carried illuminating her face, she gasped, "Assassins! The king is dead!"

Eyes widened in horror. Most raced past her, though one stopped. "Are you injured, Princess?"

"I'm fine. Go!"

As he carried on, she increased her pace, running like the wind as she spiraled down and down, hearing the shouts of, "She's alive!" and "She's the assassin! Catch her!" when the two groups met.

Faster.

A cramp formed in her side, but Ahnna pushed for more speed. Running round and round, the spiral seemingly ceaseless.

Then she reached the bottom.

"Shut the gate!" she screamed at those who were on guard. "The king has been murdered! There is an assassin in the Sky Palace!"

Horror marched across their faces, but the men had no reason not to trust her, so they complied and the gates clanged shut.

Ahnna was already sprinting to the stable.

The horses were stirring restlessly in their stalls, sensing the madness in the air, but Ahnna paid them no mind as she moved to Dippy's stall. Easing inside, she clipped the lead hanging on the door to his halter, and then looped it around to form reins because there was no time to find his tack.

"Steady," she murmured, leading him out of his stall. Only to hear James's shout, "Which way did she go?"

Ahnna's heart leapt into her throat. Moving next to her horse, she bit down on the pain and vaulted onto his bare back. Pressing her heels to his sides, she edged him into a trot, then dug in her heels as figures appeared at the stable entrance.

Her horse raced between them, shouts ringing after her. She clung to his mane, attempting to guide him toward the gate to the city.

But it was closed.

No.

She tried to haul on the lead rope to stop Dippy, but without a bit in his mouth, her horse was off to the races. He galloped straight at the closed gate, which stood as tall as she did.

It's too high.

But he didn't slow.

It's too fucking high!

She shrieked the last, but Dippy didn't care. Gathering himself, the gelding jumped.

Only her grip on his mane kept her from falling off as they soared upward and over, her ass lifting off his back as they descended on the far side. As he landed, she slipped sideways, nearly falling off.

Ahnna clung to his mane, barely managing to heave herself back in place as Dippy galloped into the city.

The civilians were out in the streets, having heard the alarm bells ringing in the palace, and astonished eyes gaped at her. If it had been Ithicana, every civilian trained to react to danger, she would have been stopped with an arrow through the chest. But the Harendellians only stood frozen.

She didn't think the soldiers on the bridge gates would be so helpless, so Ahnna heeled Dippy down to the quay. Hooves clattered in pursuit, and she risked a backward glance to see James bareback on Maven, chasing her through the streets.

She didn't have to urge her horse to go faster. Sensing that he was being raced, Dippy careened wildly through the streets, hooves skidding on cobbles.

They exploded through the market that ringed the quay, only for the gelding to skid to a stop just at the end of the stone, snorting at the raging black water.

"Go!" she shouted at him. "Jump! I know you can swim!"

But he was having none of it. Remembering what James had taught her about horses, she dismounted. Ripping off her tunic, she placed it over the horse's head. She knew he'd probably never trust her again, but she still led him over the edge.

Water closed over her head, infinitely colder than she'd expected. Breaking the surface, Ahnna held tight to the lead rope as she and Dippy were hurled downstream. A backward look showing Maven standing at the edge of the quay.

"You can't run from this, Ahnna!" James screamed, his fury cutting her like a knife. "There is nowhere you can go that I won't find you!"

Pulling hard on Dippy's lead rope, Ahnna swam in the direction of the opposite bank, her horse snorting in fear as he followed.

She couldn't see the bank in the darkness, and cold dug into her with each passing second. Then her foot hit rocks. In a few more strokes, the water was only waist-deep. She and the horse stumbled up the bank in the blackness.

Dippy let out terrified snorts with every panted breath, and afraid he'd stiffen in the cold, she led him onward. She was frozen to the bone, dressed in only trousers and a camisole, but Ahnna gritted her teeth and carried on until she reached the road.

Putting the looped lead rope back over his head, she climbed on her horse and urged him to a trot. Once his shivering ceased, she risked asking him for more speed, for she had no doubt that James had already crossed the bridge in pursuit.

And that if he caught her, she'd die on the edge of his sword.

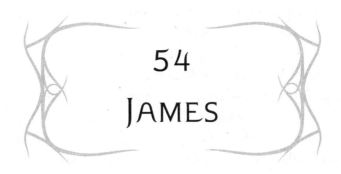

54
JAMES

WEARY TO THE BONE AND HIS HEART CARVED FROM HIS CHEST, James entered the Sky Palace and walked through the corridors to where Will and Lestara waited under heavy guard.

My father is dead.

The soldiers parted to allow him into the sitting room, where his brother wept, his face buried in Lestara's lap, her hand stroking his hair. "James has returned," she said softly. "My love, we will have answers."

Will slowly lifted his head, eyes swollen and face wet with tears. "Is she dead?"

"No." James swallowed hard, his mouth parched. "She swam her horse across the river. We found the trail where she climbed the far bank, but her horse is fast. I have men with dogs in pursuit, and eventually we'll catch her."

"And then she'll hang!" William screamed the words, then pressed his hands to his face. "No, it needs to be worse. Hung, then drawn and quartered. I'll send her head to her brother on a spike so that he knows his is next. Ithicana will bleed. They'll burn for what that bitch did to Father. And to Mo—" William broke into sobs. "Oh God, Mother's face!"

"The physician is still with the queen," Lestara said. "As are Virginia and George. It's difficult for the queen to speak because"— she swallowed hard—"because of the injuries to her face, but she was able to implicate Ahnna."

James said nothing, guilt drowning him because he should have seen the threat that Ahnna had posed. He knew better than anyone how deadly she was, but more than that, he knew how much this alliance had meant to her. What losing it had meant, and instead of being on his guard, he'd been drowning his sorrows with his father's liquor.

My father is dead.

"I saw him, Jamie. I saw Father." Will could barely get the words out. "So many stab wounds they were beyond counting."

"A crime of passion," Lestara whispered. "The tea leaves spoke true."

My father is dead.

James wanted to fall to his knees. Wanted to press his forehead to the carpet and weep, because it should be him who was dead. Him who Ahnna had stabbed so many times, the wounds merged into one.

But he couldn't weep.

Not with Will bereft and the palace in chaos. And the king dead.

His father, who had always seemed so indomitable and immortal, now still and cold.

He's with her now, James quietly told himself. *He's with your mother, which is all he wanted in life. Now he'll have it in death.*

It was a hollow comfort. "Will," he said quietly, knowing that many of his father's plans had died with him. "You are king now, and though it is painful, you must turn your mind to Harendell. Amarid has crossed the border. We must join with Cardiff's army and deal with that threat before anything else."

"He's right, my love," Lestara said, pulling Will upright again, her skirts soaked with his tears. "You must be strong."

Will wiped at his face, finding some composure as he nodded. "Yes. I . . . I am king of Harendell. I cannot weep. Amarid—"

"Can wait," a garbled voice said.

James turned, shock filling him as Alexandra entered the room, supported on either side by Georgie and Ginny, his sister's eyes swollen from crying. George had dried blood in his hair and a faint crimson spray across his throat that was partially smeared, as though he'd tried to wash in a hurry. James felt sick thinking of what his friend had witnessed as the physicians had stitched Alexandra back together.

"Ahnna Kertell murdered your father," Alexandra said, her mouth struggling to form the words beneath the thick bandages. "But that is not the extent of Ithicana's crimes. George, tell Jamie what you told Ginny and me."

Georgie exhaled a steadying breath. "King Aren formed an alliance with Queen Katarina. From his own lips, my spies heard him the night he was here in Verwyrd." He sighed. "I should have told you immediately after I discovered the information, but Ahnna told me to hold my tongue. Yet given the Amaridians had made another attempt on your life, I felt I could keep the secret no longer. I informed the king of what I'd learned, but he said that he already knew of Aren's duplicity and that Ahnna was as much a victim of her brother as Harendell. He also told me to hold my tongue, but *God*, I wish I had not listened."

"The spies in Katarina's court informed him," James said softly.

"Tonight, he told me everything, including his intention to fund a coup in Ithicana to overthrow Aren and put Ahnna on the throne in his place. He believed her wholly innocent of Aren's conspiracies with Katarina."

"Do you still think her innocent?" Alexandra asked, tears of pain leaking from her eyes. "Because I think Aren knew of Edward's plans for an alliance with Cardiff and sent Ahnna here with the goal of undoing those plans. When she realized she'd failed, she became the beast we know all Ithicanians to be." Gesturing to her face, Alexandra whispered, "I had gone to her to apologize for the embarrassment she'd suffered, and this is what Ahnna did, Jamie. That I still live is only because you arrived in time to stop her, else you'd be burying me alongside your father. She's a vicious, murderous creature, and I have no doubt she scurries back to hide beneath her brother's wing."

Alexandra drew in a ragged breath, a soft sob of pain escaping her lips. "But there can be no hiding. Not for her. Ithicana must hand her over to be executed, or pay the price."

"They are all masked monsters," William hissed, eyes fixed on James, green orbs seeming to glow with the ferocity of his anger. "I must lead Harendell, brother. But you I set to another task. A task that is just as important, if not more so."

James squared his shoulders, shoving down grief and guilt until all that was left was the cold need for vengeance.

"I command you to hunt down Ahnna Kertell," his brother ordered. "And when you find her, which I know you will, I want you to drag her back to Verwyrd in chains."

55
AHNNA

AHNNA CREPT THROUGH THE DARK ALLEYS OF SABLETON, HEADing toward the glowing port.

She'd lost track of the number of days since she'd fled Verwyrd. The number of days since Edward had been assassinated. The number of days since Alexandra had framed her for the deed and James had chased her into the night. All she knew was that every one of them had been spent on the run, chased by men on horseback and their dogs, she and Dippy pushed to their limits to stay ahead of them.

Exhaustion weighed upon her like a shroud, her body aching from new injuries and old, but Ahnna pushed her personal suffering aside as she hid next to a wall, waiting for a pair of soldiers to pass.

They were everywhere.

With the speed of boats on the river, James had been able to beat her to the coast, and every man who could be spared was hunting her. Yet it was the civilians who'd kept her from making an escape.

Edward had been a much-beloved king, and the fury over his assassination that had exploded across Harendell was unlike anything Ahnna had ever seen. Militias patrolled the streets of even the smallest hamlet, the beaches up and down the coast guarded day and night. Vessels even patrolled the water, because she'd heard more than one person claim that she had the capacity to swim back to Ithicana, if given the opportunity. Worse still were the things they promised to do to her if they managed to catch her.

The soldiers moved out of earshot, and Ahnna continued her progress down to the water. It was a long shot, but she was hopeful that in the bustle of ships that were still, despite the impending war, doing busy trade with Amarid, she might be able to sneak onto a vessel destined for the other nation. From there, she'd be able to catch a ship to Northwatch, or steal something she could sail herself.

Because there was no traffic between Harendell and Ithicana.

All trade had been halted, and when Ahnna thought too hard about how much that would be costing her people, it brought tears to her eyes.

She darted between two buildings, moving closer to the noise of the port, which was loud even though it was the dead of night. Trade never stopped. Work never stopped—not here.

Many of the civilians wanted a blockade on Northwatch. More still felt retaliation was in order, but with Amarid having invaded the precious Lowlands, that was where Harendell's armies would surely focus.

Revenge on the Ithicanians can wait, she'd heard men and women say. *They are going nowhere.*

Or worse, *Once Amarid is defeated, Ithicana will be a prison of its own making, and we can starve them to death.*

Which meant that the true horror was yet to come.

All beneath William's rule. Which meant all beneath Alexandra's rule.

It had been sour medicine to swallow to understand that she'd been nothing more than a scapegoat that allowed Alexandra to rid herself of Edward with no consequences. Ahnna had been perfectly set up to be the obvious villain with such mastery that she finally understood the true depths of Lara's warning. Of Keris's warning. Yet even if she'd heeded them, Ahnna wondered if it would have made a difference. For the queen hadn't been the only one with schemes in play.

Ahnna had been in a tangled web of plots with more than a few nooses closing around her throat. She saw that clearly now, as one so often did when looking back. It felt much like the hindsight she'd experienced after the invasion, and the emotional toll of it happening again dragged her down and down.

She moved through another series of alleys, ignoring the squeaks of rats and the mutters of those who slept in the shadows, then paused next to a large stone structure. From inside emanated the rushing noise of overheated air in bellows and the clang of hammers. One of Harendell's many foundries, but Ahnna kept moving past it, only to draw up short at the sight of another patrol.

Waiting, her mind again went back to Alexandra. It was no struggle to understand why the queen had wanted to be rid of Edward. He'd been a poor husband to her, his heart with James's dead mother. To learn of the conspiracies he'd been executing behind her back must have been a knife to her heart. Edward's choice to marry William to Siobhan's niece had probably been the final straw that had driven her to murder. Still, there were parts of her strategy that troubled Ahnna, not the least of which was that an alliance with Cardiff had to be the last thing that Alexandra wanted, which meant she'd be sure to put a stop to all of Edward's plans for trade flowing north. Yet in using Ahnna as her scapegoat, she'd also destroyed Harendell's capacity to trade south, and the cost to the people that would come as a result would be astronomical. It would not be long until the people turned on William, demanding he offer a solution, and it struck Ahnna as strange that a woman as clever as Alexandra would not have considered this element.

The soldiers had passed, so Ahnna crept onward. She glanced backward at a particularly loud bang and saw the name *Cartwright* on a large sign above the door. She scowled, remembering the name on the endless crates of weapons that the Harendellians had shipped through the bridge. Weapons that Silas used in his scheme to take the bridge.

Cartwright. She drew up short. *Cartwright Foundries.*

C.F.

"Oh God," she whispered.

Then a shout echoed up the street: "It's her!"

Panic rolled through Ahnna as soldiers raced toward her, and she broke into a run. A dead sprint through the alleys she'd just crept through, the soldiers racing in hot pursuit.

Jumping, she caught hold of the bottom of a balcony and hauled herself up, still-injured shoulders screaming. Ahnna ignored the pain and clambered onto the roof.

Below her, the soldiers raced past, and Ahnna caught her breath before pressing on, keeping to the rooftops as she moved to the edge of Sableton.

Cartwright Foundries. C.F. That's who Alexandra had been paying through William's accounts, and the timing couldn't have been a coincidence.

Reaching the edge of the city, Ahnna made her way through

the darkened woods and pastures, heading to where she'd left Dippy loosely tethered in case she managed to find a ship. Her horse nickered softly as she approached, and she swiftly put on his stolen tack, mounting as the glow of dawn began to light the sky.

Aren had approved the trade of weapons through the bridge before the invasion as part of his agreement with Silas. They were supposed to be shipped dull, but instead it was discovered they were razor-sharp, used to great effect against Raina and her men who'd been escorting Keris's entourage of soldiers in disguise. It had always been assumed that Katarina or Silas had made that arrangement, paid off the right inspectors, but now Ahnna suspected differently.

It was Alexandra.

Alexandra, who'd received rubies as a *gift* from Maridrina. Alexandra, who'd exchanged those rubies for silver with the jeweler, and then used that silver to pay Cartwright to violate the terms of trade, ensuring Silas's soldiers had the weapons they needed to invade.

What is Cardiff compared to the bridge and its access to Maridrina and Valcotta? He would have us trade our steel for sealskin when we might trade it for rubies.

Sickness roiled through Ahnna's stomach, the pieces of the puzzle finally coming together, and the picture they revealed terrified her. Because if Alexandra had been allied with Silas in a plot to take the bridge, that meant she was allied with Katarina. Every instinct in her stomach told her the two women had not let their aspirations go, and that whatever overtures Amarid had made to Aren had been with a mind of feeding Harendell's spies and manipulating Edward.

Which meant the war for the Lowlands was nothing more than a distraction while the two queens made plans to achieve their real goal.

Ahnna reined Dippy through the trees, then drew him to a halt when she reached the road. James was on the coast hunting her, but his life was in as much danger as her own. Alexandra hated him, and that she allowed him to still live had to mean he had a role to play in her schemes.

I need to warn him.

Her eyes burned as her mind filled with a vision of his face, marred with the hurt of betrayal. Sickness rose in her stomach at the fate he faced, because her heart still refused to let him go. Refused to forget every moment that had passed between them, and Ahnna knew that no matter how many years went by, she'd never feel like that about a man again.

Because she'd never allow herself to do so.

Love had made her blind, and the consequences of her refusal to see James as a threat were proving catastrophic. Love had allowed her to be turned into a pawn in a years-long gambit to take that which was most precious to Ithicana.

The bridge.

Wheeling Dippy around, Ahnna headed west toward the towering mountains, on the other side of which was Amarid. Alexandra had been right when she'd said that Ahnna was not her mother. Her mother had dreamed of peace, but Ahnna knew only the nightmare of war. Lived it and breathed it, and there was no one who knew how to defend Ithicana better than she did.

Alexandra knew it. Was prepared for it.

What she wasn't ready for was Ahnna bringing the fight to the gates of the Sky Palace itself.

Read on for an exclusive,
never-before-seen bonus chapter from
Bronwyn's point of view . . .

BRONWYN

"THAT WAS INCREDIBLE!" BRONWYN SWUNG THE DOOR OF THE shared room in the dormitory shut, then caught hold of Taryn's hands. "You had everyone in the audience transfixed."

"It was nothing." Taryn's cheeks turned pink. "They were only being kind."

"It was a standing ovation, my love." Bronwyn twirled her in a circle. "The Harendellians don't do that for *anyone*, but they did it for you."

And it had been glorious. Taryn on the stage in the theater with the conservatory's orchestra in the pit beneath, the audience filled with minor aristocracy and students and townsfolk, all eager to hear Ithicana's voice for the first time. Taryn sang the same lament she'd used to calm cows and her cousin alike, and it had been as though the audience was captivated by magic. Bronwyn had found herself moved to tears, which was saying something, because the Magpie had beat her capacity to cry nearly clear out of her.

Humming, she moved one hand to Taryn's waist and began to slowly guide her around the small room in a waltz. Each rotation brought them closer together until the tips of their breasts brushed, and Bronwyn could take the anticipation no longer.

Stopping, she curved her hand into Taryn's dark hair and then bent to kiss her. A gentle brush of the lips, and then she whispered, "I love you, you know. Love your face, love your voice, love your *heart*."

Taryn smiled. "And I did not know what it meant to live until I met you."

"Are you happy?" There had been long days when Bronwyn questioned whether it was possible for Taryn to feel the emotion. Whether there was a place, a circumstance, a love that could drive away the pall that her father's soldiers draped over her during her imprisonment.

"Yes." Taryn's gray eyes flooded, but her tears were tears of joy. "I dreamed of this place, Bron. Wanted it so very badly, and it has been everything I imagined. So full of peace." Her lips brushed Bronwyn's. "But it is you who makes me happy."

"Let me make you happier still," she breathed, pushing Taryn back toward the bed they shared. "Take off your dress."

Taryn's smile darkened with sultry promise, and she unfastened the laces at her throat and allowed the thin wool garment to slip down her lean body, revealing that she wore nothing beneath.

Bronwyn allowed her eyes to drift over her lover's body, lingering on the large oval scars that dominated Taryn's side, courtesy of a vicious shark bite. She murmured, "You own my heart, Taryn. To look at you is the purest form of happiness I'll ever know."

"I'd like to test that theory."

Taryn's clever fingers made short work of Bronwyn's clothes, leaving them in a heap next to the bed, though habit had her slide a knife beneath the pillow before she slid between Taryn's thighs, kissing her way down her lover's torso, no part of her ever wanting their time here together to end.

Thump thump thump!

Bronwyn twitched at the heavy impact of a fist against the door, and meeting Taryn's gaze, she drew the dagger from beneath the pillows. "Who is it?"

"Open up in the name of the crown!" a male voice bellowed.

"What the fuck is going on?" Taryn demanded, then reached down to retrieve her discarded dress.

Bronwyn had no notion, but her skin broke out in goose-bumps, every instinct screaming danger. "Just let me get decent!" she called back, finding her own clothes.

"Open the door now, or we enter by force!"

Her heart was throbbing, and a light sweat formed on her fore-head as her eyes flicked to the open window. Faint scuffs of feet reached her ears, and Bronwyn knew that the window would be no escape. Or, at least, not without bloodshed.

Forgoing footwear, she slipped her knife up her sleeve with the pommel hidden by her hand, then mouthed at Taryn, *Stay back.*

Her lover instead drew her sword from its sheath.

"You can't hurt anyone," Bronwyn hissed at her. "Put that away."

Taryn shook her head, naked fear visible on her face, and Bron-wyn knew this was dragging her back to the moment Maridrina had attacked Ithicana. To the moment her father's soldiers had ex-ploded into the barracks on Midwatch and killed most of Taryn's comrades.

This was going to go badly.

Grinding her teeth, Bronwyn lifted the latch and—

—barely managed to leap out of the way as a soldier's heavy boot sent the door flying inward.

Soldiers poured into the room with weapons in hand. Her first instinct was to attack, but seeing James was with them, Bronwyn instead raced across the room to stand between the men and Taryn, her blade like fire where it pressed against her wrist. "James, what the *fuck* is going on?"

He ignored her, eyes scanning the room. "She's not here. Search the campus. Move quickly."

Bronwyn grabbed Taryn's sword arm, holding it steady as she demanded, "Who isn't here?"

James finally looked at her. "Arrest these two."

She let go of Taryn's arm, preparing to draw her blade. "For what? Of what crime have we been accused?"

"Conspiring against the crown. Espionage." His tone was flat, but his amber eyes burned with anger. "And as accomplices to murder."

Dread pooled in Bronwyn's stomach, and it took all of the Magpie's training to keep her face and voice even as she asked, "The murder of whom?"

James huffed out a breath, but behind the anger, there was no mistaking the weight of grief that radiated from him. Names spooled across her thoughts, but even before he answered, Bronwyn *knew*.

"King Edward." His voice sounded like it was dragged across gravel. "He was stabbed to death in his sleep by Ahnna Kertell."

Taryn drew in a sharp breath, and in her periphery, Bronwyn saw her lover sway on her feet as shock took hold.

"Tell me where Ahnna is and this will go easier for you," James said. "You are known accomplices, and the king *will* have justice, one way or another."

Breathe, Bronwyn instructed herself even as she took in the numbers of soldiers, calculating the odds of escape. Which were not good. "James, until the moment you came through that door, we were entirely unaware of the king's death. I assure you—"

"Ahnna didn't do it!" Taryn burst out. "It was someone else! She's being framed!"

James's expression hardened, eyes growing dark and unyielding. His voice was acidic as he said, "After she stabbed my father to death, she turned on the queen. Stabbed her multiple times and cut up her face. That Alexandra yet lives is *only* because my men and I came upon her in the middle of the act with knife in hand."

Ahnna, what have you done? Bronwyn forced the thought from her head and focused on extracting as much information from James as she could. "Ahnna would not turn to violence without cause. What happened? What drove her to this?"

James seethed with barely contained violence, his amber eyes burning like suns. She tensed, certain that he'd rather attack than answer, but instead he said, "Revenge for my father marrying William to Lestara as part of a trade agreement with Cardiff."

Oh God. Bronwyn felt all the blood drain from her face as the pieces fell into place. Ahnna had hung her entire heart upon the idea that her union with Harendell would save Ithicana. That it would bring her homeland out of the ashes to make it strong again. To have that dream torn away from her . . .

"Where is Ahnna, Bronwyn?" The threat in James's voice brought goosebumps to her skin. "It is not a matter of if but *when* I will find her, and your cooperation will impact your own fate."

Blistering rage exploded through her veins that he'd dare to think she'd turn on a friend to save her own skin, but Bronwyn kept her face impassive. The same could not be said for Taryn, who ever and always wore her heart on her sleeve.

"Fuck you, James!" Taryn snarled. "Ahnna didn't do this. I know she didn't!"

His fingers flexed on the hilt of his sword. "Are you calling me a liar?"

"We're saying that we aren't involved." Bronwyn lifted a calming hand—the one where she wasn't palming a knife. "Taryn and I have been at the conservatory since the day you watched us board the riverboat with the dead. Every day, witnesses have seen us here and we have no knowledge of what happened in Verwyrd. We have not seen Ahnna since the day we left, and I've no doubt that Harendell's spymasters have read all our correspondence. I will withhold judgment on what occurred in Verwyrd until I have all the facts, but suffice it to say, we are not complicit in the king's murder or the attack on Queen Alexandra. You have no grounds to arrest either of us."

"The king feels otherwise." James moved closer, the fury radiating from him so fierce that Bronwyn swore she felt the heat of it. "Where is Ahnna?"

"I don't know." The words came out from beneath her teeth, and Bronwyn allowed the blade in her sleeve to slide lower into her palm. Because she knew how this would go. They'd be arrested and brought to Verwyrd, then the Harendellians would put them to question, innocence be damned. If it had been anyone else murdered, she might hope they'd be reasonable, but it was Edward who Ahnna had killed. Alexandra who she'd attacked. With witnesses. The Harendellians would be out for blood, consequences be damned. If there was to be any chance at survival, they needed to escape.

Now.

"Arrest them," James ordered his men, then glanced over his shoulders. "Put them both in irons."

And that was when Bronwyn *moved*.

Her blade dropped into her hand, and she slashed at James, the tip slicing through the front of his coat. He recoiled, but Bronwyn skirted past him and moved on the soldier holding the irons.

Her fist connected with his temple, and he staggered backward. The irons dropped from his hand, and Bronwyn caught them. Swinging them hard, she wrapped them around the outstretched arm of another man and yanked.

He cursed as he fell toward her, Bronwyn's elbow catching him in the forehead. He dropped like a stone even as she whirled, foot striking out to catch the third soldier. Her heel smashed into his nose, and he fell through the doorway into the others.

She lunged and slammed the door shut. The latch fell into place but her instinct screamed warning, and Bronwyn ducked.

The first soldier's sword slammed into the wood right above her head, splinters flying.

He tried to pull it free, but Bronwyn slammed into him and pinned his hand to the doorframe with her knife.

Ignoring his shriek, she ripped his sword loose and lifted it, finally ready to engage with James.

Only to find him behind Taryn, his sword blade pressed against her throat.

"Put the weapon down, Bronwyn," he said softly. "And get on your knees."

Her arm trembled, an equal mix of terror and fury raging through her body. "Let her go."

James pressed the blade harder, and a droplet of Taryn's blood dripped down it. But her lover only hissed, "Don't surrender, Bron. Go. Run."

As if there was any chance of that.

"She is the king of Ithicana's cousin. If you murder her in cold blood, there will be consequences for you."

His amber eyes showed a myriad of emotions, none of which

was fear. "Not murder, Your Highness. War. A war declared by Ithicana when Aren Kertell allied with Amarid. A war *fucking* declared by Ahnna when she murdered my father in his bed. But it will be Harendell that ends it."

An alliance with Amarid? Her mouth turned sour, because it seemed a thousand things had happened in the weeks when she and Taryn had been living and loving, politics a distant concern. Yet the world had marched on without her, and now she found herself on the back foot. Ignorant and unprepared, and her eyes stung. Not out of fear but because goddamned Serin filled her mind's eye, lash raised high as he screamed that she could never let her guard down.

"Knees," James repeated. "I will kill her, Bronwyn. I will cut her fucking throat without thought or care, because it was you and yours who started this war. Ithicana hurt my family, and I will have blood. It's only a matter of whose."

It was no false threat. This was a man who'd spent his adult life at war. Who'd killed enemies beyond number and felt no regret for it. But more than that, this was a man who was in the throes of grief over the death of his father, and every choice he made would be fueled by that pain. There would be no mercy.

Bronwyn dropped to her knees.

"No!" Taryn shrieked. "Get up, Bron! Fight!"

Every part of her wanted to. Except Bronwyn knew that it wasn't a fight she could win, whereas if she survived this moment, it would mean another day of life to find a way to escape. *Be like Lara,* she told herself. *Be the cockroach that always survives.*

She shoved the sword across the floor, and in an instant, the other soldiers slammed her down against the cold stone. Cold steel wrapped around her wrists and ankles, but her attention was all for Taryn's screams of fury.

"Let her go!" Taryn howled. "She hasn't done anything!"

James forced her to the ground next to Bronwyn, and she met her lover's eyes through the tangle of hair that covered her face. "Be calm," she pleaded. "Taryn, be calm. It will be all right. We'll be together."

I will get us out of this.

But Taryn only fought against the Harendellians restraining her. "Bronwyn is not Ithicanian! She's the sister of Queen Sarhina of Maridrina! Sister to Prince Consort Keris of Valcotta! If you take her prisoner, you will answer to *them*, you self-righteous sack of Harendellian shit!"

Bronwyn's eyes burned because Taryn was trying to protect her, but they needed to be together. They were stronger together. "Taryn," she whispered. "It's all right."

James reached down and hauled on Taryn's chained wrists, easily lifting her to her feet with one hand. "I'm aware of who she is," he replied, tone frosty. "Which is why she'll be deported rather than incarcerated."

No.

Bronwyn twisted onto her side in time to see relief fill Taryn's face, and she wanted to scream and scream because in trying to save Bronwyn, she was damning herself. "I'm a spy," she shouted at James. "I'm a spy for Lara. I confess!"

James only gave her a wry glare, then his attention went to the soldiers. "Have her brought to the harbor and returned to Northwatch *alive*. But she is to be kept in chains and watched by two men at all times. This woman is more dangerous than you can possibly comprehend."

"I think we comprehend it just fine, sir," the soldier whose palm she'd stabbed growled, clutching his bleeding hand to his stomach, his eyes promising that while she might make it to Northwatch alive, she would not be unscathed.

James ignored his comment and said to the other soldiers who had appeared, "Have the Ithicanian taken back to Verwyrd for questioning. Make sure she arrives in one piece."

"Yes, sir." They took hold of Taryn's arms, dragging her away.

"No!" Bronwyn screamed, twisting and pulling against the irons. "Let her go!"

Because Taryn would not survive imprisonment again. Would not survive the harsh hands of the enemy upon her again. Not after what the Maridrinians did. Not without Bronwyn to protect her. "Let her go!"

The Harendellians only ignored her, so she howled, "I'll come for you, Taryn! Do not give up. Promise you won't give up!"

But Taryn was dragged from sight.

She turned her eyes on James. "If you hurt her, I'll fucking kill you. I'll kill you in the worst way imaginable. Make you feel a kind of pain that will have the Magpie smiling from his grave."

He reached down and hauled her bodily to her feet. Shoving her back against the wall, he closed a hand over her throat and gently squeezed. "I invite you to try to surpass the pain I currently feel, Your Highness, but some things are worse than knives and hot pokers."

"Please," she whispered, trying another tactic. "I can't explain why Ahnna did what she did or tell you where she is, and neither can Taryn. She's innocent. Please, James."

"Please." The corner of his mouth turned up, but his eyes were frigid. His fingers tightened slightly, and he leaned down. His breath was warm against her ear as he said, "Let me tell you a secret, Your Highness: my father *adored* Ahnna. Everything he did was to protect her. From Carlo. From William. From her own brother. He believed she'd be the greatest queen Harendell had ever known, but rather than trusting him at his word, Ahnna stabbed him *forty-seven* times."

Oh God, Ahnna.

"So fuck your *please*, Princess." James straightened so their eyes were locked. "We'll use Taryn to try to bait her back. Do what we must to her to get Ahnna to surrender to spare her cousin's life. But in case that doesn't work, in case there is enough humanity in her to motivate surrender, you will be our backup plan. You will travel to Ithicana and act as messenger. Tell Aren Kertell to bring us his sister in chains, or what Silas did to Ithicana will seem like child's play."

Bronwyn's skin turned to ice. "I see now why the Amaridians hate you," she whispered. "You bastard."

James's fingers again tightened on her throat, and he murmured, "We all hate what we fear, Princess, and I think it's past time Ithicana understood why Amarid hates me most of all."

ACKNOWLEDGMENTS

As always, I have nothing but the utmost gratitude to my family for their endless support of both me and my novels. Thank you for forgiving the late nights and unforgiving schedule of this past year, as well as for being the greatest joy in my life.

Emily and Team Del Rey US and Team Michael Joseph, you have all been so enthusiastic and tenacious in seeing these beautiful editions to shelves—thank you for always being amazing. To Jessica at Audible, we've been working in this world together for so many years, but your passion for the Bridge Kingdom world has never wavered. Tamar, I could not ask for a better agent—thank you for everything that you do. Celsie, so much appreciation for you keeping me on schedule! Amy, you were the first and most vocal champion of James and Ahnna—thank you for always being there for me!

Last, but not least, thank you to my readers! As we enter the final chapter of the Bridge Kingdom world with Ahnna's story, I want to express how much I appreciate every single person who has read or listened to this series. The heights you lifted these books to changed my life, and I am so grateful to have such an incredible readership.

DANIELLE L. JENSEN is the *New York Times* bestselling author of *A Fate Inked in Blood*, as well as the *USA Today* bestselling author of the Bridge Kingdom, Dark Shores, and Malediction series. Her novels are published internationally in twenty-one languages. She lives in Calgary, Alberta, with her family and guinea pigs.

danielleljensen.com
TikTok: @daniellelynnjensen
Facebook: facebook.com/authordanielleljensen/
Instagram: @danielleljensen

ABOUT THE TYPE

This book was set in Albertina, a typeface created by Dutch calligrapher and designer Chris Brand (1921–98). Brand's original drawings, based on calligraphic principles, were modified considerably to conform to the technological limitations of typesetting in the early 1960s. The development of digital technology later allowed Frank E. Blokland (b. 1959) of the Dutch Type Library to restore the typeface to its creator's original intentions.